Love H
2018

About the Author

Trevor worked in the film business. Starting at Beaconsfield Studios as a clapper loader then at Pinewood and Shepperton studios, MGM, Disney, Warner Brothers and on and on. At some point he found the making of TV commercials was more profitable and much less stressful than feature films so he switched and ended up with his own commercials company where he was Director Cameraman. A combination of age and falling off a ladder provoked his retirement which led to his returning to his education studying creative writing at Ewert College, Summertown Oxford. The course was named 'Starting the Novel', which he did and this is number ten.

Dedication

For the Lawrence family who have been such a help to me. Tony on his computer. Sarah, my daughter, keeping his nose to the keyboard, and Rosie, as my number one reader.

SOLDIER OF FORTUNE

BY

TREVOR WRENN

Copyright © Trevor Wrenn (2018)

The right of Trevor Wrenn to be identified as author of this work has been asserted by him in accordance with section 77 and 78 of the Copyright, Designs and Patents Act 1988.

All rights reserved. No part of this publication may be reproduced, stored in a retrieval system, or transmitted in any form or by any means, electronic, mechanical, photocopying, recording, or otherwise, without the prior permission of the publishers.

Any person who commits any unauthorised act in relation to this publication may be liable to criminal prosecution and civil claims for damages.

ISBN-13: 978-1548625481
ISBN-10: 1548625485

PROLOGUE

The Duchess of Richmond's Ball, in the Opera of Bruxelles, set for the evening of the fourteenth, was to be the most brilliant of the season. All the officers of the Seventh Coalition were invited excepting those junior officers already patrolling the intended battlefield at the village of Waterloo.

The Lord Wellesley, recently ennobled as the Duke of Wellington towards the end of the Peninsular War, sat at a high placed table surrounded by a dense mass of scarlet and gold clad senior officers and aides de camp, paying some attention to the beautiful women who came to be presented by husband's or fiancé's. He wondered, as each woman came forward, which of them would be widows by the next evening and how they seemed to show so little interest in the battle to come.

The dance floor seethed with a blaze of officers, polished and shining, each escorting a wonderfully dressed woman in every colour of the rainbow although virginal white was very popular. The dance was the waltz, a fairly new import from Vienna via Paris and the merry music drove the young men and women into a spinning frenzy of excitement for war, death and destruction is a very overwhelming sexual emotion.

In odd dark corners, individuals or small groups maintained a deeper decorum as if some, with the experience of what war really meant, mostly veterans of the Peninsular Wars, talked quietly, if they talked at all since a few mostly stared at the over excited dancers, wondering if they would be coming to the victory ball. In other corners, uniformed men played cards. Loo mostly. A simple game that one could leave at a moments notice which might be useful but one where the debts of the night might never get paid to the winners; for none knew who the winners might be this time and there were those, especially amongst the beautiful women, who planned, in their subconsciously treasonous minds for, at least, a desire for pleasure, to dance again here the following night, whoever won the battle.

At one of the card tables in a candlelit side room, a school of four red clad officers and one, oddly, wearing a dark green hussars uniform. In front of this man was a substantial pile of golden guineas and white paper five-pound notes that had accumulated; for he was a skilful player on whom Lady Luck had smiled this momentous night.

Through the music and the murmur of voices; through the turbulent heaving masses of celebrating men and women, came hurrying servants carrying a seemingly endless succession of bottles of champagne and trays of fresh glasses and behind them came a small, insignificant, but totally sober, dark green clad, very young cavalry trooper, whose rank was Korporal and whose name was Tully. He swerved around sparkling groups of the most brilliantly dressed men and women, wove his way between the tall, booted, sabre carrying, gold frogged and epauletted officer's and their gorgeously apparelled ladies. A dark figure, one might even be tempted to say a messenger of doom for he wore the leather satchel of a messenger, and after a moments hesitation to peer through the swirling people, he hurried into one of the side rooms devoted to the playing of cards and swiftly found our contained, very sober, long fair haired officer in the dark green of the Hessians in the Prussian Army that even now faced Napoleon at Quatre- Bras and a little further on the village named, Vigny.

As the hand ended and gold guineas were swept into a neat piles, the messenger whispered words from lancer to officer together with the folded order paper and with a distant, polite smile the officer rose to his full height, scooped up his gold coins and stack of paper and picking up his tall, black fur shako from under his chair, he stepped back a pace, apologized, bowed and turned sharply away.

The dance seemed to be reaching a high frenzy as the green clad officer presented himself before the Duke. He bowed into the rowdy silence that seemed to form about the famous man and said the words that only the Duke could hear. Lord Wellesley, Duke of Wellington instantly stood and the Grand Ball was silenced, over, finished.

He announced in a strong voice. 'It is time Gentlemen. Napoleon awaits us. For the final time I trust.'

He strode away into a distant fanfare of trumpets sounding the alarm in the square outside, surrounded by a red cloud of officers but William Saxthorpe, a slim man of something over medium height, high cheek boned with a blaze of golden hair worn long; a Horse Major of the Hessian Cavalry, a mercenary and soldier of fortune, turned briefly to the tall, fair haired Colonel of the Household Brigade, who still stood quietly, to say. 'A merry day before us Lawrence. It seems that the Orangemen have held the French at the cross roads of Quatre Bras but are very short of munitions. My Germans too have received something of a thrashing at Ligny but are retiring in good order.'

'Part of Blutcher's plan, no doubt?' The middle aged officer said as he pulled on his tall bearskin shako and buckled it tight under his chin.

'I believe so brother. He has had defence's constructed all the way back for some eight kilometres.'

'Eight what?'

'Five miles Lawrence. The Prussians plan for every eventuality, even defeat.'

'Well, little brother. Your joining the Hessians came as a surprise to me, an annoying surprise,' and he did indeed look annoyed.

'Half pay and find your own way home from Spain came as a surprise to me also. The Hessians offered me double wages and a ship to Bremen for me and my horses,' the young man smiled a charming smile.

'You always did take the easy path brother.' The senior officer finished adjusting his uniform and turned his full attention to the younger man.

The hussar said quietly. 'Today will not be so easy Lawrence. Think twice or maybe three times before you and your Household heroes charge the French guns.'

The brilliantly uniformed British officer, his silver breast plate reflecting a hundred candles, smiled and hugged the smaller man to him. 'Go with God, Will.' For a long moment he stared with love into his brother's eyes. Turning, he strode away, heels crashing on the polished marble of the floor, spurs jingling.

Courage and honour embodied, thought Will as he watched his elder brother go.

CHAPTER ONE

Lady Alice Forfar, her so fair, almost silver hair blazing in the dawn light reached up on tip toe to kiss the bravely dressed but rather small English cavalry officer about to mount his charger in the turmoil of an army getting ready to march. Her kiss was somewhat perfunctory for although newly married Alice had already formed a somewhat low opinion of her husband compared with some of the other great soldiers at the Ball. Colonel, the Lord Forfar, had purchased his rank for a considerable sum and was about to take part in his first battle so that, although highly ranked, he had not been a party to any of the battle decisions made by the Duke and his coterie of very experienced officers.

A waste of a large sum, Alice had thought, her pretty face a picture of exasperation as she watched her husband and his Aide de Camp brother the Right Honourable Anthony Forfar trot away, with much jingling of accoutrements, across the crowded square to join up with the mass of cavalry assembling there. She turned, her wide silver and gold dress spinning out around her, to the younger, dark-red haired woman by her side. 'This is so stupid Jane, they leave before the party has finished, surely it is just like men to want to go off and play without...'

'What? Without consulting you sister? The woman's voice cool, '...perhaps they should have invited Napoleon and his officers to the Ball.' The somewhat plain, dark-blue silk dressed young woman shrugged and turned away to return to their hotel.

Cavalry Horse Major Will Saxthorpe, on his strongest horse, 'Hector', crested the small hill on the right flank of the advancing Grande Armée and followed by Korporal Tully, the signal trumpeters and his squadron of Hessian lancers rode forward a little way through the tall, standing crop of rye to survey the battle spread out, like some great sunlit panorama, before him. The weather was good, but the ground was still soaked after the night's heavy rainfall so that lighter horses could make easier running than the heavy horses favoured by the French cavalry.

So he was the first of Blutcher's cavalry to make it to here. The Prince General's orders had been quite specific. The French heavy cavalry was a fearsome monster of nearly fourteen thousand horsemen all on heavy horses, the riders wearing breastplates and steel helmets. The lightly armed Hessians with their lances and sabres, were forbidden to attack them frontally; for that way lay annihilation. But the Prussian General, with his own savage smile, had left open the possibility of cutting in behind the great charge; that would happen at some time very soon.

Will could see the huge columns of French infantry marching straight at farmhouse buildings of Hougoumont and that large formations of cavalry were indeed assembling behind the concentrated lines of the French artillery and soon there would be a substantial number of them ready to pour out upon the English on their tree topped hill in front of the village of Waterloo.

Major Saxethorpe turned in his saddle to glimpse, behind the stands of trees in the far distance, the advancing regiments of Prussian infantry, each seeming laid out like sets of toy soldiers marching off to war.

'Tully...' he called out to his Korporal of Horse, '...get them ready, it will be soon, very soon...'

There was, Will thought, an exact moment when light cavalry, ridden with some great gusto, even through such a high tough crop, could inflict a heavy blow on armoured cavalry as they retired in disarray from a charge. He had seen it many times when the wounded and exhausted would mill about still shouting from the excitement of the charge but essentially leaderless for a some minutes until what remained of the officer's in the vanguard returned to reorganize their men and that was when Will hoped to strike through the French rear for there was a good chance that the Frenchmen would not recognize the green and grey clad Hessian mercenaries as the enemy. Not, that is, until the charge started and the first lances found their targets, when sabres started to slash and blood started to flow.

A deep rumble, as if of a huge approaching storm, came, as a cannonade started with two hundred and fifty guns firing in salvoes. There was the maelstrom of action as each gun reloaded and the gunners could see that a good deal of damage had been inflicted on the light defences manned by the redcoat infantry of the British. Another great salvo was sent on its way and then ten thousand heavy cavalry galloped out from behind the cover of the guns. The thunder of forty thousand hooves pounding the ground as the cavalry surged up the gentle slope towards the first much battered line of red infantry crouched in the British squares on the skyline.

The first kneeling line of the infantry fired their muskets in a volley at the solid surging wall of approaching horsemen and before the first rank of horses had crumpled the second line of musket men had risen, aimed and fired in a howling storm of sound, smoke and death. More than half the horses fell, for the infantry have no love of large savage horses and it was there that they aimed. The third line of musket men rose from cover, aimed, fired. The remains of the first rank of cavalry was now within lance distance of the first line of kneeling infantry who, now with bayonets fixed, braced themselves to withstand the remains of the charge.

On his low hill, Will thought that now would be the time and with a simple hand signal and a shout to his trumpeter, his one hundred lancers trotted, shoulder to shoulder, down the gentle slope that would bring them to the rear of the French charge. Firstly the tall rye then a meadow, pleasant with daisies and buttercups passed swiftly, crushed under the thundering hooves of the German cavalry's advance. Suddenly the disarrayed rear echelons of the French charging cavalry were there before them. Remounts, tents for the wounded, lines of replacement lances plunged into the soft earth, a group of officer's of high rank and the standards and eagles of the Legion.

Will's scream of 'Charge!' was roared out by all his men and the long line of horses galloping abreast poured in amongst the unprepared French. The battered, over excited remains of the French cavalry was just returning to reform when the line of lancers struck.

Will aimed for and hit a senior, much medalled officer who was standing high in his stirrups, the better to survey the battlefield ahead, seemingly unaware of the danger from his flank. The sharp lance blade went through the man's body just behind the gleaming breastplate and came out the other side in a huge spurt of blood, the lance snapped and then Will was past the falling man and drawing his sabre, crouching low, his head close to 'Hector's' blowing mane he spurred the horse for the Legion's standards, guarded by a dozen, tall Guardsmen but before they could raise and aim their muskets he was in amongst them slashing, spinning his horse so that he could strike and strike again, in a whirling corona of blood droplets, at the standard bearers and their guards. In a mad moment of blood lust Will felt the wood of the flagpole strike his leg, the broken shaft gouging at his calf muscle and he grabbed at the brilliantly coloured flag with its many embroidered battle honours with the metal of the eagle above and then driving in his spurs he was through the back area and galloping for the rising land just beyond. After two hundred metres he reined in amongst the mass of his over excited men and spun the foamed and blood spattered 'Hector' around to survey his company. More than three quarters gathered, seventy five at the very least in a maelstrom of spinning, surging horses, the blaze of their blood rimmed sabre's waving high in the air, a flinging down of broken lances as they whirled around him and his captured Standard, blood stained horses and men gasping for breath in their excitement.

'Reform!' Will shouted and heard his order repeated, trumpets resounding down the line. A manoeuvre rehearsed so very many times was carried out well. He looked back to see the last remnants of the great charge now limping back in disarray and knew that now was the moment.

Waving his sabre above his head he screamed at his men, 'You've done it once! Let's go home! Turning, sabre pointing the way, he shouted, 'Charge!'

Later, such was his excitement and his blood lust, that Will was unable to remember the second charge clearly. The field was clear but very soft and churned up for the horses and every man was battle mad but their training had taught them not to linger where infantrymen, with fixed bayonets, could hook them from their saddles. A mad, galloping plunge, shoulder to shoulder, was best and that was what Will remembered. The thundering of hooves, standing high in his stirrups, sabre in one hand, fluttering standard in the other, its steel bladed shaft pointing forward and suddenly they were amongst the French again, some still mounted on horseback, some still armed, some totally confused and in a few seconds they were through the melee of men and horses and Will still had the broken, blood stained, Legion standard clutched in his left hand and a gore covered sabre in the other.

Will had lost twenty two of his lancers in the two mad charges but the others were, mostly, apart from the odd slash wound, in very sound condition, although grossly over excited. Shouting firmly he retired them up hill to the safety of the advancing Prussian infantry so that after a two kilometre canter he came upon Marshal Blutcher and his staff.

Will cantered up to the group of smiling Staff officers and coming to the grim faced steel helmeted Prussian Marshal he spun his horse and handed the General the broken, blood stained standard of the French Heavy Cavalry.

'A gift sir, from the French, for you!' half shouted, so happy was he.

The old soldier took the Eagle Standard with his famous tight smile as he said. 'Some compensation for yesterday's loss then. Thank you Major, a good morning's work indeed.'

CHAPTER TWO

Alice had pushed the straps off the bare pale skin of her shoulders and dropped her gown to the floor where, even as it landed in a sibilantly hissing brilliant silver silken puddle, she carried on her complaints in a harsh bitter voice. 'No servants! My so called husband is indeed a stupid, penny pinching kind of man when we cannot even afford to take a chamber maid with us.'

Her mother, Lady Walden, who had come at the invitation of her son in law, did not quite come to the man's defence. 'Forfar has little experience of travel outside of England; I think he imagined that house servants could be hired by the day as hairdressers can be.' She sat back, holding a half empty champagne bottle, and poured herself another glass of the sparkling wine.

Lady Jane, reddish hair somewhat wind blown, stared from the open window of their sitting room across the huge square to where companies of red clad soldiers were forming into columns obeying distant shouted orders, the crash of thousands of studded boots hitting the cobble stones of the square filled the air, with distant trumpets sounding from afar. She didn't bother to listen to her sister Alice's complaints since they were almost continuous, one following upon the other. The thought of a great battle worried her for she could see that the fine uniforms, the horses, the swords and guns were just dressing for a very serious business indeed.

The newspaper, 'The London Times,' had run a number of long articles about the battle's of the Peninsular War and Napoleon's stupid attempt to march the huge distance to Moscow losing most of his Grande Armée in his retreat. To come here just to dance before such a huge battle was, in Jane's opinion, the very height of stupidity. It never seemed to cross either of the Forfar's minds what would happen if Napoleon won the battle and Alice just wanted to know what she should wear if that happened. It was just as well that Alice was so beautiful, thought Jane, since, if she was not, she would be taken for a dunce.

Through the drifting smoke of the cannon fire the half shattered remains of a great elm tree still sheltered the Duke and his Staff as they surveyed the result of the first French charge. The first 'squares' had been only half broken but the advancing French had no infantry to hand to take advantage and the Reserve soldiers had quickly filled in the many empty spaces so that the line was held. The great man issued his orders calmly, succinctly, to maintain his plan to hold this shallow ridge with its deeply concealed lane, now full of replacement soldiers and the wounded. He had been a bit puzzled by the confusion in the French rear, which was clearly revealed from his high viewpoint. To the rear of the massed Artillery charging horses had been seen and he wondered how his light cavalry had got so far ahead.

Amongst the hurly burly of the officers, aides de camp and mounted messengers swirling around him he was an island of calm. A little later the mob split for a moment to allow a green uniformed, black shako wearing cavalryman to come cantering through and the Duke instantly recognized the messenger from last night's great Ball as an aide de camp from his Peninsular campaign.

'Major Saxthorpe?'

The blood stained and somewhat battered soldier brought his horse shoulder to shoulder with the great general. 'I bring a message from Marshal Blutcher, sir, who is, even now within a mile of your left flank. He says that his infantry is fully battle ready and when he has positioned his artillery, say, in about an hour, he should be able to give you flanking fire when the French charge again.'

The Duke looked at the somewhat sweating and bloody faced officer and knew now that he had been in the maelstrom of action earlier. 'You charged the French rear Saxethorpe?'

'It seemed to be a good idea your Grace, lost very few men and captured the Standard and eagles of the 25th Cuirassiers.'

The moment was broken by the appearance of the tall, Household Brigade Colonel mounted on a very big grey who swirled in his own cloud of dust to a standstill in front of the group of officers. 'Damn young fool, don't think I didn't see you showing off as usual....' Colonel Saxethorpe acted angry but his pride was manifest.

'Tell Papa will you then brother?' The young Major shouted back.

'Damned fine thing that you made it out of there, charging around in the middle of the French Army.'

'Marshal Blutcher's idea actually, perhaps you'd better take it up with him, Oops!!' A loose cannon ball swished through the air only a few feet in front of them, and rolled, a nearly spent force, until it hit a gun carriage behind them, shattering the wheels. 'Dangerous spot your Grace, you could get done for here.'

'Thank the Marshal for me Saxthorpe. Tell him my left flank was feeling a little uncomfortable until you came up. I heard about Ligny though.'

'It was a hard run thing at Ligny but the Prussians fought like... like Prussians, I suppose, and he pulled his army back in good order.'

Wellington looked at the young officer and wished he had fifty such so he said. 'Later, this evening, probably, after the next charge we will counter Nappy's attack I trust and then a united thrust between us may well set him on his way home.'

The green clad hussar and the red and silver magnificence of the Household Colonel, a grey horse and a black circled each other briefly when the Colonel shouted out. 'God speed brother and victory!' He watched as the Hussar drove his light black horse back through the lines with a farewell wave of his right hand.

The open landau that the Times correspondent had hired had two empty seats and he had found quite quickly that some of the wives wished to see their hero husband's exploits at first hand. Offered at a price the seats would have been fought over save that Lady Jane Walden had made the acquaintance of that same newspaperman two days earlier. When Jane had suggested to her sister the outing to see a real battle in progress she was swiftly set in her place.

'There is a street here in Bruxelles that is famous for Haute Mode and it is to there that Mother and I shall be repairing. If you wish to see the men making fools of themselves then so be it.'

It was but a quite short drive, perhaps an hour, and then the open carriage climbed to the top of a low knoll close to the trees of the forest Soignes that surrounded the city. Below and almost to the horizon a vast panorama scattered with villages, each with its manor and church spire but now wreathed in the cordite stench and smoke of the big guns that fired without relief. Below the landau, in something of an ancient sunken lane a long column of wounded men, limped, hobbled and bled their way from the vortex of the battle. Jane stood in the carriage by the side of the battle-hardened journalist and stared out with justifiable horror at the scene of human degradation that she could see just below her. Borrowing the man's telescope for a few moments, the better to see the centre of the battle, she was swiftly rewarded by seeing an advancing line of cavalry take the full force of a cannonade from a line of French light, horse drawn guns. A great hole was cut in the British lines; bodies of men and horses chopped into the smallest pieces and sent spraying into the air... Jane, pale faced, handed the 'glass' back to the man saying. 'It seems that our side is being roughly treated sir.'

The man swung his telescope back and forth before saying. 'The battle sways back and forth Ma'm; a charge here, another there; squares formed, muskets discharged in a great volley, another charge; men and officers tumbled by storms of a veritable hail of shot...'

Jane thought, this man thinks only of the columns that he composes in the newspaper and the way he will write it but down below us many men are dying. She could hear now, between the concussions of the heavy guns, the thin, wind driven screams of dying and wounded men. Men far from home and their loved ones; the lament of those who would never return.

The day ground on, swirling smoke from the hundreds of guns filled the air, trumpets blared, drums, their steady heart beat making the soldiers march to victory or to death. Cavalry charged the advancing columns of shot exhausted men, sometimes succeeding, sometimes meeting a harrowing volley of musket shot. Horses plunged in their death agonies onto fixed bayonets or fell to grapeshot and canister volleys but then, it seemed, the weight of the advancing sea of red uniforms meeting and joining with the green-grey Prussian masses meant that only one last push, one last great charge would be enough; and it was.

Blutcher ordered his Light Cavalry to sweep up the remnants of Napoleon's Grande Armée and Major Will Saxethorpe turned his rearmed and rested lancers to the task and full of the blood lust they stormed down the hill and gave chase with many a brave halloo...

The drummer boy was running, as best he could, with his big battle drum banging against his knees. He looked back and saw, through the smoke of battle, a long extended line of galloping horses, lances lowered, red pennants blowing in the wind, green-grey uniforms and hearing the lancers high pitched screams he threw away his precious drum sticks.

Will's shouts of 'Charge! Kill!' had numbed his voice but still his sabre had flashed in the early evening light, droplets of claret red running down the blade's edge until the wind of his passage blew a shower of the reddest rain in his face. The running Guardsmen, heavy boots slowing them. First to go the shako, next the heavy black coat. Musket and ammunition belt dropped, abandoned to break on the ground, accoutrements flying after and then, the slash of the battle sabre.

The little figure running, trying to run with the weight of the big battle drum banging on his young thighs, a sort of agonized limping run. His precious drum-sticks had already gone, thrown through the air of battle. The thunder of hooves bore down on him getting closer, too close, so he stopped and turned back, to see his fate coming close and Will saw the drummer boy pulling at the buckles and straps that wrapped his fate so firmly with the drum then... The boy looked up, even as the heavy drum fell, rumbling, to the ground, and smiled shyly, tilting his head almost as if to welcome the final slashing cut to his neck.

Will, quite suddenly, felt that his killing days were over, that he could never kill a little drummer boy. 'Hector' felt his rider's knees, his bit and bridle, pulling him up; stopping his mad charge; the raised, blood dripping sword falling slowly down to Will's side.

The boy shrugged and smiled almost apologetically, before turning to continue his run towards the forest trees.

'Halt! Will gasped out, almost his last battlefield command. 'Halt!' he screamed out. 'Trumpeter! Sound the recall, the Reform!' The air rang with the brazen blare of the signal trumpets even as Will watched the boy run, fast now, without his load, into the trees and saw the glitter and shine of musket barrels levelled at extreme range from the thicket. Napoleon's Grand Guard. The remnants reforming in the woods; a volley and he and his brave men would have been gone. The smoke of battle swirled around him as his horse curvetted again and again but his eyes never left the sight of the smiling boy disappearing into the trees and the sick feeling in his stomach eased.

CHAPTER THREE

'We have won a great victory Milady!' The journalist shouted in triumph as he turned from pointing down at the great tangled mass of men, horses and guns that lay now below the small village the English had been defending all day. 'See how the Frenchie's run!'

Jane could indeed see how the French line had broken and was now running back pursued by a horde of figures on horseback; how the stragglers were cut down and she felt a terrible sadness that this war had been fought for the comforts of people like her. Many of her countrymen had died or been crippled so that her class could carry on living; living high.

The carnage. There was no other word for it. Mountains of the dead, men and their horses sealed together in blood and lead and in the front rank of the fallen; a headless great grey horse and its rider who had met the French cannon head on. But the cannon were made of iron, gunpowder and shot and the attackers of flesh, and the iron won the moment but not the day.

An exhausted green clad Hussar, leading his foam covered horse and the remains of his column of cavalrymen through the smoke of the battle field, stopped to survey the great mountain of the dead; for it was his brother who had led the last charge. His brother who had jumped, carved his way through the first two ranks of guns and then had found that there was a third and last.

The hussar loosed his horse and picked his way through the tendrils of smoke and over the tangled mass of the slaughtered artillerymen and up to the dead man. He knelt, his face streaming with a seemingly endless river of tears, then leaned forward and closed his brother's eyes with trembling fingers. He straightened the dead man's fine bear fur shako then took the great blood dripping sabre from his hand choking out as he did so. 'It's back home for you brother. Papa would like it if you rested by him...' his voice cracked, so unhappy was he.

The Korporal, who had ridden at Will's shoulder for all these many days, pulled at his master by the arm saying as he did so. 'You have orders still to carry out sor....' he saw the tears running unchecked down his officer's face and continued, '...we will carry your friend.'

'He's my brother.' The young officer's voice choked with emotion.

The lancer looked very sad for his officer then said. 'I will put your brother in the baggage cart sir, and later...'

In a tear-choked voice Will Saxethorpe replied. 'Thank you Tully, treat him gently, for he must have fought well this day.'

Jane stepped down from the carriage into the wildly cheering mob of British families and their supporters, on the Grande Boulevard de Bruxelles, but her face was pale as she thought; but you, none of you were there, you did not see and do not know the true cost of this to England and France and she pulled her lace shawl over her head and fled into the Hotel Bristol.

It was as the three women, two chatting merrily, one silent and pale, were dressing for dinner; Alice and her mother in their just purchased latest fashion dresses and Jane in last night's dark blue gown when there was a hesitant knock at the door.

Just before the dawn, the ship packed quay at Ostend was almost as it had ever been, dark, wet; a place of silent comings and goings. The remains of the huge British and German armies had marched away on the road to Paris and the end of the Emperor Napoleon. This was now a place for lesser beings, the detritus of a great army, the paid off, the wounded, the sick, the dead.

A recently arrived cross channel packet boat rocked gently alongside its quay on the rising tide. Gangplanks were being thrown down as the hushed, soldier crowded jetty stirred at the thought of going home.

First carried aboard was a fine, lead lined coffin, with a mahogany domed top, a crucifix projecting upwards then a long line of lesser pine boxes each to be stowed without reverence in the damp darkness of the ships hold.

Secondly, the horses were walked aboard. The padded stalls on deck were swiftly filled, a boy rushing from horse to horse with water buckets and oat bags.

Forward the wounded were limping or being carried on board and next came the paid off infantrymen to crowd onto the lower decks. Then the officers, quiet now, some still a little brandy drunk but all sobered by the terrors that they had seen, had experienced, but some now accompanying, guarding, a group of ladies, all wearing black.

Almost the last to board, just as the mooring lines were being cast off, was a green clad hussar of the Hessian Cavalry. He limped slightly from a late bayonet thrust, which he had half turned away with his sabre before cutting down at the fusilier. He shook the hands of his Sergeant and of Korporal Tully and pulled them to him in a hug of remembrance for he would not be going back to Prussia. He was finished; decorated, promoted and then paid off. He'd smiled, for this was the way of the great armies of Europe. There would always be another Army to join if you were a true mercenary, until you led one charge too many; then, if you were lucky, it would be the hold of a cross Channel ferry for you.

Will walked, somewhat unsteadily on the rocking deck, to the horses in their padded stalls and quickly found 'Trojan' and 'Hector,' wide, white eyed in the darkness. The horses had come back from Spain like this but still did not like it any more than did their master. Will grasped 'Trojan's' head and whispered into the horse's twitching ear that everything would be over soon. The rocking, the swaying, the pitching back and forth would end and then he and 'Hector' would get a double ration of oats to see them home to England.

England. Will hadn't been home for nearly seven years. Leaving, at his big brothers shoulder, for the Peninsula as an aide de camp to Lord Wellesley and now he would come home alone. The big, lead, sealed coffin in the hold offered no companionship with his dead brother lying so quiet. A great pity, for his brother had been life itself. Lieutenant at twenty then Captain, and Major at twenty eight in the finest Regiment in the land. The King's bodyguard, the Household Brigade, until one day the Duke had promoted him to Colonel so that he could stand at the shoulder of the finest soldier in England and Spain and there he had stood through battle after battle and Will still didn't understand why he had found his brother in the mangled vanguard of a great charge, a battle winning charge. He should still be alive by Wellington's side but instead he was nailed into a lead coffin in this floating graveyard.

Fate had intervened and now his other elder brother, the Right Reverend John of Ely in Saxthorpe was now both Bishop and Baron. Will had never liked his middle brother. A vain, sanctimonious man. Short, fat and vicious. Will had never understood how a man who preached the word of God so vociferously could believe in so little of it but now, none of that mattered. Get Lawrence home to be with his Papa and Mama in their tomb and then? Will had no idea what he was supposed to do. He had no money save his 'card stake' and the value of his possessions that stood currently at four horses, two rifled horse pistols, two sabres, two epee, two muskets both rifled out, two carbines each bored out for the new cartridges. He had, in the baggage, his brother's possessions but of these he took no account. He had thrown them into an ammunition cart that they'd found abandoned on the battlefield, and he assumed that some money must be amongst them but he did not look. Before the lid of the coffin had been nailed down Will had placed his brother's still blood stained sabre in his right hand and the 'If I should fall' letter in his brother's left. The letter that most officer's wrote and, Will supposed, the more erudite of the Army wrote as well. A farewell to family and life he supposed and as it had been in Lance's breast pocket, shot through with blood and lead, he thought that it might be addressed to him, Brother John or their sister Anne but he thought it too sad to open as yet. First things first, get his brother home; the home in England that he had loved so much.

There was much pulling of ropes, the hauling up of sails and plenty of shouting and then the little ship pitched into the first of the Channel waves and Will suspected that not eating or sleeping for two days and a night might prove something of a blessing since to vomit one needed something in one's stomach.

On the quarterdeck of the ship a cluster of red clad and black cloaked officer's gathered at the rail around the black dressed figures of a small knot of women, one of whose brilliant fair hair seemed to blaze in the half light. Will, barely noticed her nor her military companions for they seemed to be of the type that had barely made it from the Bruxelles party to Waterloo. Ennobled young men, fearful for their lives, their purses and their women.

Jane wondered at the performance of her beautiful sister who smiled, joked and flirted with the black cloaked, red-jacketed officers that surrounded her. Jane stood off at the rail and watched the final passenger board after an emotional farewell on the dock. She'd noticed this one group in particular, mostly she supposed, because they were not of the British Army. Dark grey-green seemed to be the colour of their uniforms in this half-light. The men hugged each other, shook hands, clapped each others backs and then two turned away leaving one man alone on the dock. The are happy because they live, Jane thought, they have survived to fight again unlike my poor brother in law and his brother. Jane, remembering the appalling slaughter that she had witnessed on the battlefield, wondered if, in fact, she had seen her sister's husband and his brother die. Not that it made the slightest difference to her sister who had wasted not a minute before hastening back to the dress shop to purchase something suitable in black lace for the journey home. Only the wait for the men to be coffined, which had annoyed Alice greatly, and the fact that the Duke did not see the necessity for a triumphant Victory Ball.

Will went back to his horses and noted the assiduous way that the stable boy went from frightened horse to horse, reassuring, stroking, whispering to each in turn.

The boy seemed to feel his eyes on him and turned to smile reassuringly and even as he turned away Will remembered another boy, a drummer boy alive instead of dead and food for the crows. He instinctively knew that the horses would be well looked after so he decided to go below, perhaps for an hour or two's rest from the now howling wind that came from the north west into which they must 'tack' in order to make progress.

The main saloon cabin was crowded and every seat taken with the exception of one chair, rocking as the boat pitched and rolled, that stood at an empty space by one of the card tables. Will moved forward and acknowledging the other players with a small bow, asked their permission to join the game or at least to take the seat.

A large, bluff man, overdressed in the style of the just past century, satin embroidered waistcoat, high stock, long blue silk coat and white powdered wig sat at the head of the bolted down table and smiled a somewhat disagreeable smile at the green clad hussar. 'Welcome sir, if you have the stake for this table?'

'And what would that be sir?' Will could see a pile of gold sovereigns in front of each of the players.

'A guinea to the pool sir. Only cash I'm afraid...'

'And the game sir?'

'Now that you join us we could change to 'loo,' it's everyone's favourite I think,' he chuckled heartily but was a little disconcerted by the blank look that this foreign officer gave him.

Will pulled back the chair and seated himself but found that he must brace against the pitching and rolling of the north Channel seas. He reached into his inner, much lined and very deep pocket and pulled loose a fat purse which he dropped onto the table.

The other four players smiled in agreement at the sound of gold coins hitting the table with a dull clunk and proceeded to stack their guineas in front of them but the motion of a sharp wave knocked down the neat piles and sent the men hurrying to flatten the stacks onto the rough wooden surface. The fat man produced a pack of playing cards from an inner pocket and Will's first thought was that a rather bad card sharp was in the game so, leaning forward he took the pack from the man's unwilling hand and fanned out the cards across the table.

'A pity,' Will said, almost instantly, '...a fine looking deck but two cards are missing. One is the ace of spades and the other the 'Pam' or jack of spades. A new deck is required sir if we are to play 'unlimited loo' which I assume is your intention...'

The fat man looked most discomfited and embarrassed and his explanations and apologies filled the first quarter hour but with a new deck and the deal passing on each hand a straight game quickly developed.

As the sea grew choppier and the little ship pitched and rolled, the number of players varied from time to time as a man would be overcome and need to 'take the air.' The smell of vomit would fill the air for a moment or two only mitigated by the sharp draught of wind from forward that, on occasion, would sweep clean the cabin of the nauseous smell. One of the last players to be replaced was the 'card sharp' who ran out of both money and the contents of his large stomach at almost the same time.

It became obvious that the hussar was a very careful player always paying attention and never betting where he might have prayed for Lady Luck to attend him. In consequence by the end of the first six gale tossed hours he was already somewhat ahead and when the cry of 'Land ho' came after twelve hours he had nearly all the ready cash in the game.

'I must attend my horses gentlemen,' he said, as he rose to his feet and despite their protests, left the table.

On deck, the gusting fresh air revived him somewhat and the melancholy that had attended his every move for the last two days and nights returned with some vengeance. His brother dead for so little reason and he wondered if he had not been in part to blame. His charge of the French had been observed by the Staff through their telescopes and his brother knew that his sibling was now something of a hero. Hero, Will thought. A large decoration, something or other Military Medal of Honour of Prussia 1st Class and an Iron Cross, that was the kind of hero he was but maybe his beloved brother had thought that seven years of standing by such a famous General was too long and maybe...? Conjecture counted for nothing, Will thought, his beloved brother was dead.

Will turned as he caught a movement out of the corner of his eye as coming up the other companion steps on the windward side came one of the black clad women that he'd seen before. As she noticed him he bowed slightly then turned to observe the approaching coastline, leaving her to stare after him, her brownish red hair, whipped into a streaming tracery by the sharp gusts of wind, seeming to glow warmly even in the cold morning light.

An officer in green, she thought, foreign then, his jacket somewhat ripped, the silver epaulettes, some torn loose, some shredded into silver threads blowing in the sharp wind. So a veteran of the battle most probably. Lady Jane Walden thought him rather handsome, his golden hair windblown, his short cloak pulled loose, his black astrakhan fur shako tucked tight under his arm; but he has eyes only for England.

White cliffs towered above crouching little towns far off to starboard; so they had made land fall south of Dover, not sailed straight up the Thames as was planned but Will supposed that wind this strong and tides could play havoc with the best plans and the like on a sailing packet boat such as this

The quarter-deck was somewhat crowded, what with all the officers and the party of ladies returning from Bruxelles. Jane took a place by the stern rail so as not to hear her sister's constant complaints. The cabin they had been allocated was not big enough; there was no entertainment for the passengers; the wine was poor in quality, the food worse and so on. Jane thought that her sister was heartless to a fault since the remains, and that was the right word Jane thought, had been stowed in the hold. All she thought of apart from her own comforts was the possibility that a new husband might be found amongst the crowd of officers on board but to Jane, who suspected that these smartly dressed, unwounded and untried men might just be the rearguard of the Army; lowly supply officers and the like.

Dismissing everyone from her thoughts she observed that the ship seemed far to the south of England and would have to beat to starboard to make port somewhere on the south coast. Her talk with the bo'sun and steersman had kept her informed of progress and she was depressed at the thought that they would have to travel so much further than just from the docks in London to Saffron Walden.

Looking forward she caught a glimpse of the green uniformed officer who seemed to be inspecting his horses and once again wondered why a foreign officer would be coming to England.

Will went down the long line of animals to where his two war horses; 'Hector' and 'Trojan', who, sniffing the land breeze, had begun to whicker and whinny at the thought of steady, dry land beneath their hooves.

The little stable boy came around saying. 'They are all in good heart and keen to get ashore sor.'

As indeed am I, Will thought, even though the mal de mere had never afflicted him as it did others. He just felt monstrously fatigued, exhausted and knew that he must sleep soon.

Some two hours later, as the ship closed with the land, sails fluttering as they lost the north easterly wind in the lee of the land, Will leant in close to the stable boy to ask. 'Where are we to land, boy?'

'See the white cliffs sor, back over there. We were blown a long way to the south west of the Thames; that's Dover over there sor. We'll likely moor up in Rye or Hastings; wait for the wind to turn...' he paused for a moment then continued. 'On your horse,' he turned to look at 'Hector', '...it would be easier to ride to Lunnon than to wait for the tides and winds to change. You have some fine horses sir. I should ride if I were you, we might wait here for a week otherwise.'

Will looked at the boy, probably the same age as the drummer boy, perhaps eleven or twelve years of age, and thought him both polite and intelligent. 'If I disembark here what chance have I to remove the lead coffin in the hold and hire a wagon to put it on?'

The boy, whippet thin, with staring, deep set eyes, a face seeming carved from red raw wood with rough cut ragged dark hair, surveyed the hussar. He had heard from the crew about this man's card playing exploits so, thinking that he might have some ready money, he said, 'I know of a carrier in Rye sir. Hiring a wagon shouldn't ordinarily be much of a problem but with the cargo this ship carries...' he left the line unfinished for he knew now that he was talking to one of those thus encumbered.

'I live...' the man looked a little uncertain, '...I am going to Norfolk which is some way to the north,' Will said distractedly.

The boy had no idea how far Norfolk was, save that it was to the north of Town or Lunnon as he had heard it called but he thought it no difficulty; the driver would return the cart easily enough. 'When we have unloaded this sad cargo,' the boy said, for almost the entire hold was full of coffins, '...I shall, if you wish, take you to Mr Rushton's yard.' Then the boy was called away to help haul on the sheets of the foresail as the boat crept towards a narrow inlet with the town just beyond.

A good lad that, Will thought, but the mooring and the melee of horses and men leaving the ship drove all other thought from him for the lead coffin was at the very bottom of the hold and was the last to be hauled up and over onto the quay.

Some hours had passed and Will felt the lack of a servant as never before. The life of an officer in a fine regiment had always provided him with a good man to fetch and carry but now he stood alone for the first time in nearly seven years.

Will watched the sad cortege that had followed the black clad women and their companions from the ship. They had two flag draped coffins with them and Will thought of the tragedy that gripped that family. A husband? A son? Brother's like him? Three black dressed women, two coffins, tragedy indeed. The group was led by a beautiful, middle aged, bewigged woman. A silvery haired young woman had smiled sadly at him as she was helped down the gangplank, the smile that women save for men that they think might help them one day or perhaps she thought him an acquaintance surrounded as she was by so many officers, and the third and last, who was hooded against the wind peered out, her face shadowed, her reddish hair caught again and again by the sharp wind, the tendrils flicking around her somewhat plain face. Will wondered vaguely who they were, for they had a good deal of fine baggage with them.

'A battered old coach like this?' Alice's voice rose in complaint, '...we are to be forced to travel in.'

'There is no other Alice,' Jane said quietly. 'It's this coach and a wagon for the... your husband and his...and Anthony...'

'Yes, yes...' Alice's voice wearily resigned even though she had seemed to sleep well enough on the boat.

'It will add only a day or so to the journey but it is better than waiting for the wind to turn.' Jane explained more to her mother than her sister.

Alice snarled out. 'Well, don't just stand there Jane. Let us be gone.'

When the quay became quieter Will finally led 'Trojan' and 'Hector' down the wide gangway followed by the stable boy leading the two pack horses then Will turned and asked him. 'The carrier you spoke of boy?'

The boy looked worried now that the quay was emptying and he realized that all the wagons for hire, in the little town, were probably already booked up and away. 'I did not think sor. So many coffins, so many dead, and you the last to come ashore.'

'Your Mr Rushton?'

'I saw him earlier and he thought that with all the...'

'So there is no cart for me to hire?'

'He did say that he had an old farm cart that could be purchased sir,' the boy stood shivering before the harsh faced officer, '...that would save on having to return a hired one and you would have had to put a good sum down to ensure you returned it...'

Will collapsed down to sit on his brother's coffin and thought or tried to think of all the possibilities that could and probably would befall him on his journey north but the sheer fatigue that drained him stopped any sensible thought. 'Could you...?' He paused for a moment, '...what's your name?'

'Tom, sor.'

'Tom, could you... could...' his mind had gone blank but Will had to think, had to decide. 'Could you run to Mr Rushton and...'

'If I take your pack horses sir; I could bring the cart back here and it would also test the strength of the axles and the wheels. Mr Rushton would likely come to fix the costs but I think you would be well off with your own cart.'

He thinks he is me or acts for me, Will thought in his muddled state, a boy, just a boy. 'Yes Tom, run off and fetch your Mr Rushton and his cart; I will stay to guard...' his voice faded away as his eyes clicked shut and he swayed as if he was still aboard.

'I'll fetch a friend from the ship sor, if you like. It'll cost you at least a shilling but he's a good steady lad, is Jim.'

William stared at the boy trying to understand him then realizing the sense of what the boy said. 'Fetch Jim please...' he dug into his inner pocket, '...here's a couple of shillings and another half crown for you Tom. See to it, but keep my brother safe...' Will Saxethorpe looked down at the great coffin.

'I'll bring a canvas for you to sleep under sir for it will likely rain soon. I'll fetch Jim and go get Mr Rushton.'

The rest became a kind of dream for Will. There was a black coach with four greys passing through the smoke, the gun smoke, two coffins on a small cart, a face peering down at him from the coach... a bloodstained letter... a silver haired beautiful woman with a sneering smile on her face, weapons broken, standards fluttering in the wind, cannon firing, smoke ripping through the air and horses galloping, plunging, falling and over it all a dead brother lying somehow next to him, comforting but sad. He woke. His hands grasping for his pistols as young hands tugged at him.

'Wake up sor, it's me, Tom!'

Will came around slowly, feeling the soft, summer English rain, so dreamed of in the heat of Spain, coursing its way slowly down his face and neck helping to waken him. He sat up and stared at young Tom and another boy, wrapped in an old canvas, who was perched on top of the coffin. 'Who's that?'

'That be Jim sor. I paid him half, a shilling, from the money you gave me and he's kept watch this past four hours.'

Will stared at the boy before him and then back to the gnome like figure squatting on the coffin and slowly nodded. He needed to piss, to wash, to eat. God, but he felt hungry and come to that thirsty but first, it seemed, he had to deal with Mr Rushton.

The bargain was swiftly struck. Six pounds for the plain unpainted old cart, two for new spare axles if needed and another three for the old harness that he was trying to get rid of but Tom assured him that the money was about right and Will had no way of knowing the rights and wrongs of such a bargain.

In another hour, the ship's boom, with much creaking and groaning, had lifted the lead coffin up onto the cart with everyone watching to see if it would break and before long the boys had loaded the rest of Will's baggage and the chests and boxes that had belonged to his brother. From the ship's chandler, on the quay, a pound had purchased a new large canvas, a great deal of rope and an oil-skin treated cover for the load. Tom coaxed the two pack-horses into the old harness and traces, backed them between the shafts and standing there they looked like they meant to do what they were trained for. They were young war horses so they had been trained to pull guns, limbers and ammunition wagons but the heavy cart loaded with baggage and a lead lined coffin would be a hard pull on the hills to come.

Tom and Jim, Will thought. I need servants for this journey so why not ask them, for it would save time. 'Tom?' he asked.

'Sor?' the boy turned from where he had been adjusting the girths of one of the horses.

'Tom, are you free from the ship or must you stay aboard, you and Jim?'

The boy, thin rain trickling down from his soaked hair, down across his face and neck, that looked so like tears, replied, 'We are only asked when there are a deal of horses and the like sor. So no, we have not a return passage so far,' he looked excited as though he had been able to anticipate this man's desire for a servant.

Will felt sick with fatigue but knew that he couldn't drive all these horses and the cart to Norfolk on his own. Well, not in his present state, 'Would you like to be my drivers up to Norfolk and perhaps beyond?'

Jim asked, a worried expression now on his underfed face. 'Beyond sor? Where's beyond?'

'Answer my question Tom, will you serve me or not for I cannot drive so far alone.'

'We must talk of pay sor.'

'We must eat Tom, me, you and Jim; and I must take a piss before I burst.'

At the doorway of a waterside inn, they took turns to eat and to watch the loaded cart. Tom fed and watered the horses again and they seemed content enough although 'Trojan' and 'Hector' looked eagerly up at the green of the grass beyond the town.

'I agree sor,' Tom had said, '...and Jim would like to be my friend. He's not the sharpest card in the pack but he is very steady.'

'I will pay you... How much will I pay you Tom?'

Tom looked at him and thought that he must be very tired indeed so he said. 'When you are rested sor, we will talk more of pay but for now I think that you must mount up in the cart and sleep. Jim and I'll get the cart out of the town for there are hooligans and ruffians in here who are taking too much of an interest, sor.'

'You'll drive the cart you say; what about my riding horses?'

'They'll follow along nicely sor. We must need be away from here or else.'

CHAPTER FOUR

Four hours later, Will woke slowly from where he lay bundled up in the horse's bulging hay nets, the stillness and silence of the cart waking him as the constant creaking movement had not. He felt, apart from the sore patches caused by the shaking rubbing of the cart, like a new man. He pushed his head above the edge of the cart and stared about him. Under a tall hedge, a few yards away, a campfire was starting to burn well. The two boys appeared to be cooking something on a stick thrust into the flames. Rabbit, Will thought, the smell very appetizing. He rose up, checked his inner pocket for his card stake, jumped down and strode to the two boys.

'Tom, Jim, where are we at?'

The older boy stood and half smiled as he looked at his new master thinking that he looked like a scarecrow with hay sticking out all over his once smart uniform. He paused for a moment before speaking, for the experience of the last few hours was beyond him in many ways. 'I asked a shop keeper, seems we are hard by a place named Cripps Corner sor; it's a village nearby the road to somewhere called Royal Tunbridge Wells.'

Will squatted down to stare hungrily at the roasting rabbit. 'And how far have we come Tom?'

'Don't rightly know sor; about three hour or so from Rye. The land is flat alright around here although we did have to hitch the riding horses up to give us a bit of a pull in one dippy place but there were gyppo's and returned sojers all about and we didn't feel too safe so we kept going until we saw a good place to pull off the road.'

It was late. Darkness was sweeping in from the east and the red sky to the west meant that the boys had done well for a long time and alone at that. No trouble, that was a good thing, for Will knew a great deal about trouble. Riding in an army was one thing but a man and two boys alone on the road was another. He had his pistols with him but would he have the opportunity to use them?

'You've done very well Tom; and you Jim, so here...' he searched in his pockets for a coin or two.

'I still have some coins from the half crown you gave me sor,' Tim spoke firmly.

Will found his purse deep down safe in his uniform's inner pocket and rummaged out two half sovereigns which he gave to the boys.

'Sor! This is too much.' Tom gasped out, while Jim stared down at the small gold coin just looking astounded since he'd never seen one before.

'If you are to be my...' Will couldn't bring himself to call them servant's but didn't know why, '...'companions' you will need some spending cash and the wages I agreed are not due until the first; I believe you insisted on that.'

'That be the proper way sor; paid on the first day of each month.'

'You are a proper man of business Tom and...' a thought struck him, '...what if I were to promise you the cart when I have finished with it.'

'This cart sor?' The suddenly frowning boy looked astounded. 'You must not jest with me sor.'

Will felt somewhat chastised as if the boy thought him a joker. 'I do not jest with you Tom. When we part you will have the cart.' The thought had come unbidden to Will and like most things unbidden it was not thought through with great care.

The boy though thought swiftly for a moment before saying, 'And what will I do for horses to pull my cart sor?'

Will's admiration for the lad increased when he realized what he had talked himself into, so he replied, frowning a little. 'When I get home the pack horses will not be necessary to me so let's say that they will be yours as well and the harness,' Will smiled, when he saw the delight on Tom's face remembering taking the horses from a half destroyed French ammunition limber somewhere on the battlefield. Jim stood by and nodded with satisfaction at his friend's luck.

Jane had just finished thinking that the black coach, that they had hired, was going too fast when, with a sharp 'crack!' followed by a deep splintering and tearing sound the passenger cabin descended sharply to the ground throwing the three women into a pile in one corner.

By the time that Alice and her mother had finished bitterly complaining Jane was more than tired; she was exhausted. She had the driver take one of the horses and go back to fetch another carriage or the like. After two hours he'd returned with a spare axle and someone to fit it so it was late before they had arrived at a small, impoverished Inn where the accommodation was, even by Jane's less that exorbitant taste, very poor.

After an uncomfortable night in the cart Will stretched with first light of dawn and thought that they might make an early start. The boys, Jim had snared two more fine rabbits and with some bread that Tom had purchased in the nearby village, they all made a fine country breakfast for Will was used to living off the land.

In the cold grey light of the coming day, after two hours of driving along the ridge road, they saw a sign for the town of Tunbridge close by a milestone that put Rye fifteen miles behind them.

Tom shouted out to his mounted master. 'Why don't you ride on sor, I need keep the pace slow, for this cart creeks madly with the weight of its load.'

Will looked at what he was beginning to think of as his cart and the two boys so proud to be in charge and thought why not. Perhaps he could find an Inn and wash up and change from his tattered, bloodied uniform, which was beginning to smell unwholesome. 'Very well Tom, but stay on this road...' After Tom had loaded up 'Hector' with Will's campaign box, and riding 'Trojan,' Will trotted away, glad to find the chance to give his horse's something of a run.

Tunbridge had been easy to find on the Post Road and was a pleasant Market town with two good Inns and Will quickly chose the Blue Flag as the more amenable looking of the two.

A room rented for the remains of the day and the night to follow. A good wash and scrub down under the pump in the yard and he felt almost presentable. He wondered about the uniform and thought to himself that clothes had not been high on his list of necessities so that apart from evening dress he had no other clothes save yet another 'foreign uniform' and his Horse Guards equipment so he sallied forth to find a haberdasher or outfitter and on the next street corner found just such a shop.

Cord britches, such as farmer' wear, would do. A woollen shirt, a cotton the same, and a light jacket with a waistcoat and a heavier almost winter weight coat for riding at night and all rounded off with under garments. The tailor recommended a saddler's where boots of all kinds could be purchased but Will found none to fit.

Later, when the cart meandered into the little town the boys found a well dressed, by their standards, well fed man sitting in late afternoon sun in front of the Blue Flag coaching Inn. Will strode out into the street feeling distinctly odd in his baggy farmer's clothing but nevertheless happy to be wearing clean clothes again. 'Tom!' he called out, '...over here. I have stables engaged and a room for the night. So tonight we will sleep well and tomorrow we can start our journey refreshed.'

'Very good sor.' Tom turned the equipage into the yard of the Inn.

Later, after the horses had been stabled and the boys fed a good filling meal the three of them strolled around the town.

Will was fascinated by Tom's apparent ability to think ahead and learn a great deal from every experience so he led the two boys into a shop that appeared to sell everything to see if he couldn't buy them some small reward for their efforts on his behalf.

Tom swiftly found, ignoring the bolts of cloth, the lace and the countless reels of ribbons, a glass case full of pocket-knives, pen knives and the jack knife so popular with seamen. He and Jim stared in fascination and wondered at their cost.

'You like them Tom?' Will asked, amused.

'Them jack knives would come in handy sor.' Tom answered, '...and,' he looked worried before continuing, 'Jim wants to go back to the ship sor, says his Da expects him at home at Portsmouth in the autumn.'

Will thought that unfortunate but the boys would know that he was going a good way north and that they might be long time gone; so if Tom stayed? 'But you'll stay Tom?'

'Of course sor! I promised din I,' he looked scandalized that his word might be considered broken.

'Well, boys, sorry to hear that you are to leave us Jim but I intend to buy you a gift anyway.' Turning to the counter where a young man was waiting somewhat impatiently he asked, 'I'll have two of the best jack knives please.'

Across the store, two black clad women sat in the women's corner, one with the most brilliant silver hair and the other, plainer, with dark reddish hair, sorting through the ribbons and bows displayed. At the sound of the men's voices from the other room the younger woman moved enough to hear something of them. A farmer and his boys except that the farmer sounded more gentleman than yokel she thought. Like most of life, their talk was of the mundane, the ordinary, something about knives. Looking at the reels of multi coloured ribbons in a disinterested way she mused, if only their hired coach had not broken an axle they would be well on their way home by now. Jane had seen a bookshop further down the street and thought that a visit there might well be rewarding, at the very least as a remedy against the boredom of the journey.

She excused herself from her sister's company, thinking how was it possible to regard the selection of gew gaws, ribbons and buckles as in any way important, the very opposite surely. Reading, music, learning; this was something to stave off the dullness of her life, of her existence. She brushed past the farm men still at the counter now trying the quality of their purchases; for an instant, a glimpse, a flash of fair hair, the turn of a profile made Jane frown at the partial, perhaps, recognition and then she was in the mild sunshine of the street.

A leather bound book; the frontispiece saying Miss Jane Austen, a new author noted for the oddity of being a female and a writer. Good, Jane thought and decided to buy it even though or perhaps because of the coincidence of names. To be able to write, how wonderful and to earn a living perhaps; wonderful indeed and she hoped that the novel would be as good as the best of the men who wrote those endless three volume novels so enjoyed by the women of her class.

The next morning, Tom, with Will sitting on the seat next to him, had the cart rolling steadily towards London Bridge, which lay some fifty miles ahead.

Will now really regretted the wind that had blown them so far to the south but the advantage of purchasing the cart almost outweighed that. Progress was slow but steady, in the manner of large armies on the move, Will thought. You kept going for hour after hour until you arrived where you would camp for the night and he thanked Heaven that the weather remained clement. The same journey in the rain would be dire indeed.

It was nearly dark and the horses were very tired when they came near to Seven Oaks and Will had no time to be choosy about this Inn or that tavern so he had Tom drive straight into the yard of the King's Arms.

Will set Tom to negotiating the costs for the night. A secure stable for the cart and a loose box for the horses, oats and hay, clean straw for the floors. Two shillings for the watchman, another five for the stable. It was just as they were finishing up that a big, black painted coach, drawn by four matched greys rumbled into the yard accompanied by another cart laden with boxes and followed by five uniformed horsemen.

Will watched as the coach stopped by the door of the Inn and liveried footmen opened the doors for the passengers. One man helped a black dressed woman from the coach and on the other side two more, somewhat slimmer, younger women descended and Will caught sight of a silver flash of hair tumbling from the black hood of one of them

Will could only think that something had delayed the women and their entourage but decided that it was none of his business. Before the large party could interrupt him Will persuaded the Innkeeper to show him to the rooms that he had rented.

Most of the mourners from Belgium, that had crossed the Channel with him, had dispersed, like seeds blown in the wind leaving only the slower behind and this was as far as his thoughts went as he caught a glimpse of himself in a simple wall mirror in the bedchamber. A country yokel stared back at him so he smiled at the joke he seemed to be.

He undressed, washed very thoroughly, shaved and combed his hair into the long flowing style that he liked. His vanity was admitted by him so he knew that he couldn't go down into the tavern dressed like a farmer. He unlocked his travelling campaign case and was pleased to see that his army servant had packed everything with great care. He would have fresh underclothes, a new shirt and a well-washed but neatly pressed uniform to wear and with his best boots on he would once again cut a fine figure of a military man. Will thought himself stupid and suspected that in the next part of his life he would have little time for fancy clothes and fancier attitudes but for now, his military presence would have to do. He dressed carefully; the final touch was the Iron Cross at his throat and the Star of Prussia on his breast then to transfer all his money, a still considerable amount, into his deep inside pocket and he wished that they had played for more paper notes rather than heavy gold sovereigns that weighed him down.

A knock at the door and there was Tom looking tired and dirty, 'Horses all be abed sir and the watchman is watching your... coffin, sor.' He frowned as he looked around the small sitting room, his face a little puzzled.

Will hastened to reassure his companion. 'Tom. I'm sorry, but you slipped my mind; being in the Army you see; you think about your soldiers only as soldiers not as ordinary people. Anyways there is a small bed in the bedchamber and I'd like you to stay up here. I'll have food, small beer and some warm water for you to wash in, sent up. I want you to bolt this door when the servants have been...' Will tried hard to think but the fatigue of battle and death still lay upon him, 'I will knock three times very quickly for you to let me in; alright.'

And a very tired Tom nodded.

It was all quickly arranged with the Innkeeper and Will finally sat down before a decent looking chicken pie and a bottle of claret. He realized that it would not be long before sleep claimed him though. Every so often his eyes clanked shut and he had to force them open again and concentrate so that he could eat but just as he started two black clothed women swirled down the stairs and across the tavern. The rattling clamour in the crowded, heavy beamed room fell silent as the women made their way through the crowd of pipe smoking men to the Innkeeper working at his barrels. The very beautiful, fair-haired woman was the leader and the second woman kept her close company.

Jane thought, what a strange place to find oneself in but it must be very normal for most people. The village Inn in Saffron Walden must be just like this and had been for three or four hundred years she supposed. Where the servants, the gardeners would go to for amusement although for Jane it seemed just very smelly and now noisy again as everyone started to talk, puff at their pipes and stare at the two newcomers. They talked of the great battle, the dead and wounded coming home with the thousands of dismissed soldiers. Alice didn't seem to notice anyone she just concentrated on the Innkeeper, demanding bigger and better bedchambers although Jane had the feeling that they were already in the best. The Innkeeper kept gesturing towards a man sprawled in one of the better chairs by the unlit fireplace and when Jane looked to where he pointed she thought, for a moment, that she recognized the dark green uniformed Hussar officer and then thought how stupid that was, for in the last two weeks she must have seen five hundred officer's in uniform's of every hue. This one was all but asleep and he looked somewhat childlike half curled up in front of his unfinished dinner his fair hair falling across his face. Probably drunk Jane thought. She saw her sister Alice go over to him and after saying something to him several times was surprised when she leant over and shook him by the shoulder. Jane was even more surprised than Alice when the young man leapt to his feet his right hand half drawing his sword.

'Sir! I merely touched your shoulder to awake you,' Alice remonstrated.

The young officer looked very embarrassed as he apologized profusely. 'I was half asleep and I... you took me by surprise; I was...'

'Well, you frightened me sir,' a shudder ran through her, but Alice didn't look frightened.

Jane thought that she had seen Alice play the frightened young woman too many times to be impressed and wondered what she was about.

'I would like you to change rooms with me and my party,' a seductive smile hovered around Alice's near perfect lips.

The very tired man shook his head as if not understanding.

'You will not change rooms then?' Alice now looked aggressive, angry.

The Innkeeper, a thin, small man, tried to explain. 'You have the largest suite of rooms sir and this lady and her companions have to manage in somewhat smaller accommodation.'

The tired man's head turned to look again at the beautiful, fair-haired woman and he seemed to become more alert.

Alice has that effect on men, Jane thought.

Alice said sharply, 'I will recompense you sir. Just tell me how much money you would need to leave the rooms?'

Alice was now playing the proud widow, her Baron, Knight of the Realm, Colonel of the Irish guards, husband and his brother now secure in the cart not wandering around after other women and gambling at the tables, Jane half smiled knowing that she would not have the nerve, the audacious cheek, to attempt to throw this somewhat handsome young man from his rooms.

'You have other rooms for me Innkeeper?' he asked a little wearily.

'I believe Milady wishes to exchange rooms; hers are somewhat crowded what with there being three ladies...'

Will remembered the black clad ladies from the boat and wondered who they were but managed to feel affronted at her rudeness. 'Are we to be introduced or is this just a commercial exchange?'

Alice stared at him with some contempt but as she had no idea what his rank was just that he was much decorated, she said coldly, 'Lady Alice Forfar... and you are?'

'Saxethorpe, Major, Hessian Army, at your service ma'm,' but his bow was the very shortest he could manage, barely a nod of the head. 'So I will remove my servant, my baggage and myself from the rooms I have paid for and move to?' His eyebrows rose in question.

'My sister and I,' a tiny nod was sent in Jane's direction, 'are in very, no, not very small but nevertheless too small rooms at the back of this...' she looked around the tavern with some contempt, her red lips curled.

Jane thought, Alice looked very pretty when she was angry or annoyed but having to deal with this man obviously upset her, used as she was to just ordering servants to do her bidding. The ship being blown off course; and then an axle breaking on the somewhat overloaded hired coach, last nights sad little inn, the necessary delays had all contributed to Alice's and Jane's fatigue and now; poor Alice, first her new husband and his brother get shot off their horse's almost before the battle started and now nowhere comfortable to sleep.

The Major half snarled, his tone bitter. 'It would be my pleasure Lady Alice...' he turned towards Jane but no one offered an introduction, so he shrugged, raised his eyebrows and added, '...to exchange rooms with you Milady; and you don't have to consider some kind of payment; knowing you is payment enough.' The smooth words were roughened by his cynical and ironic tone and then by him turning away and striding up the stairs with a distinct limp.

'He's very rude,' Alice said frowning, '...at least I think he is.'

Jane thought to herself, clean, well dressed and more than somewhat good looking, handsome and almost a gentleman even if foreign. She wondered if he had been in the great battle and thought that with the slight limp, that he'd displayed, he might well have been amongst the wounded. Seeing him, hearing this man talk with his sudden anger she could see him on the battlefield; see him high in his stirrups sabre raised high to slash down; disgusting but somehow, oddly thrilling. A killer then, probably, but most certainly a real man.

CHAPTER FIVE

Morning came and Will decided that he would never sleep in the same small room with Tom again. The boy had washed but still smelt more of horses than horses did which Will supposed was quite natural considering his profession.

Will washed, throwing the cold water provided over his face and hair. He considered shaving but could not bring himself to do so for what would the purpose be? He could not be bothered to think of the women from the previous night he just wanted to get on the road but was seriously discomfited to discover that they had overslept and it was past ten of the morning. He and Tom breakfasted together in the empty, beer smelling tavern in silence, with Tom glancing at his Master wondering at the deep emotion that the man seemed to be showing. When Will said, 'Eat enough for your dinner Tom, for we'll not stop until...'

Tom looked up at him seriously, then said. 'We have four horses to feed and water sor, a heavy wagon to pull and we cannot go so fast as you might alone.'

The boy is right, the stone-faced Will thought. I keep forgetting the cart and its load. I just think of myself alone, my wants, my needs. He thought again of the military years that had slipped past taking his youth with it. This is just like an Army on the move. A route must be planned. Food and water arranged and him with no soldiers to help him. All these years and what had he learned? Not as much as his driver it would seem. 'You're right Tom, stupid of me. We will go at a steady pace. I shall ask the best way to...'

The boy brightened up, almost smiling, to tell Will. 'I asked the Innkeeper how to get to London and he said take the Post road outside and follow it north until we fetch up in Greenwich; that be twenty five mile he says; course we has to pay at the tolls.' Tom looked at his master and wondered if he had said or done too much but then he carried on. 'Twenty five mile will be more than enough for the cart horses sor. We'll have to find a place for the horses in this place, Greenwich. I gather that it be important, that there is a palace there and all kind of public buildings and there'll likely be an Inn for us.' Tom stopped wondering if his master planned to say anything.

'Good Tom. Well done indeed...' Will paused to think then asked, '...but what do we do then?' *If he is so far ahead I might as well ask.*

The boy nodded, pleased now. 'Get a ferry to take us across the big river, the Thames. Landlord says there's a regular trade across and they be used to taking horses and the like. Or we could go into London and cross the river by London Bridge.'

'Is the ferry better?' Will asked.

'It's much shorter sor. He showed me some old map and I saw where Norfolk lies; due north of where we are now I think, but some good way on.'

Will sat back and thought to himself that Tom was turning into a life saver. He did nearly all the work, no that wasn't true, he did all the work and most of the thinking. 'Right Tom, very well done. We shall do as you say, Greenwich will be our next sleeping place.'

Twenty five miles behind a pair of overloaded pack horses was a very slow process and since they didn't start until just before twelve it was twenty minutes past three when they came upon the black coach again.

It was tilted sharply over and the driver and the two footmen were trying to fit a new wheel with much hammering and a great deal of black axle grease. The three ladies were seated on the ground off to one side looking rather beautiful but with discontented faces at their food and drink free picnic.

Will and Tom, on their cart, came slowly up to them. The unshaven Will had resumed his farmer's clothes so that the ladies did not notice him and he wondered if there was the slightest point in getting down save that the men seemed to be having a great deal of trouble setting up the new wheel. Will leant over to his driver to ask. 'Do you know anything about wheels Tom?'

'I dus know that that one is not the right size for that there axle,' he looked somewhat amused by the men's struggle with the almost fitting wheel.

'So, no matter what they do?'

'It will never fit unless the axle hole be cut a little bigger....'

'And we cannot help them?'

'Only a coach maker or perhaps a blacksmith would have the tools...' Tom sounded both certain and very amused, '...the wood is too hard to cut without big, very sharp chisels. My Da worked in a carriage shop and they had extra special tools for that kind of work and you can see that the wheel is too small; It's been taken from another smaller carriage I think.'

The cart with the two coffins is where the wheel has come from; thought Will, these women are happy to abandon their dead in some farmer's field without ceremony or guard.

Lady Jane Walden surveyed the heavily laden canvas covered farm cart, which she half remembered from seeing it in the stable of the coaching Inn back in Tunbridge but for a moment she didn't recognize the straw hatted farmer as the young officer of the previous night. But then recognition came. The realization that the smartly turned out officer and this... this yokel were the same man was an odd one. First she wished to know why he wore such outlandish clothing then whether he had some way of helping them. After a moment, Jane climbed gracefully to her feet, and tried to brush down her black lace dress, now somewhat tattered and torn, with many catches on the fine work, as well as grubby from the five days of travel. She walked, she hoped gracefully, over to the cart. He discusses our predicament, she thought. We seem always to be troubled when he sees us and we... She had arrived at the cart and she looked up at the young man and asked, 'Can you help us?'

He stood and took off the broad straw hat that he wore and she was once again struck by the long fair hair, his strong features, the broad brow, the sloping eyes, the cynical turn of his features when she realized that he recognized her.

'Afternoon Milady, you always seem to be troubled do you not?'

She frowned. 'Can you help us?'

He looked down at her and then carefully replaced his hat,

'You have the wrong size wheel, my driver here tells me.'

'The cart is in that field,' the girl gestured over her shoulder, '...they took a wheel off that hoping to get us to the next town.'

Will looked over at the three men now surveying the mess they were in. 'Where have your outriders gone to?'

'Oh, they were only interested in Alice. You met her last night.'

'Did I? Is that her over there?' He sounded only faintly interested.

'That is Lady Alice Forfar,' Jane said or rather announced.

'And you are?' He said casually.

'Is this how people are introduced here in Sussex?' She asked, acerbically.

'I wouldn't know since I do not come from around here,' he dropped himself back onto the hard wooden seat, '...where I come from a Lady addresses a gentleman as 'sir' and if I ask her for her name then she would usually give it.'

Jane frowned at being corrected then, pink faced, said, 'My name is Lady Jane Walden...sir.'

Will looked at this troubled young woman who may well have lost a loved one at Waterloo and then he said almost without volition, 'Lady Jane. It is good to be introduced to you, no matter under what circumstances, so what I will do is get on one of my horse's and see if by riding ahead I can find some form of transport or possibly a blacksmith who might come.'

And that's what he did. He had Tom saddle up 'Trojan' and then he was away. During his ride he was confused by his reaction to the somewhat plain young woman and her predicament. She wasn't pretty so why would he want to help her, but she was polite and seemed intelligent.

Jane had, after a few moments, walked back to her family and sat herself down.

'What were you doing talking to that farmer, Jane?' The middle aged woman asked in a tired tone of voice.

'He kindly goes ahead to see if he can find an alternative to this coach for us.' He may be a battlefield hero but he does also seem kind and helpful, she thought, the memory of the man's golden hair stirring her, half annoying her.

Alice lifted her head from where she had been studying the lace work on her dirty dress to say harshly. 'And did you tell the yokel to hurry?'

'I asked him if he could help us, that's all.'

'We could have gone ourselves if we had taken that old farm cart.' Alice snarled.

'They are resting and watering their horses...'

'No matter, it's too late now. We just have to wait I suppose.'

Alice must learn a little patience, Jane thought, not that she had ever had the smallest shred.

Gone for nearly two hours Will came back leading a large, well set up coach and four and another wagon with a blacksmith and two new, spare wheels.

Will rode up to Tom, who'd unhitched the horses and fed them and who were now contentedly munching the long roadside grass, 'Tom, we're too late to make Greenwich now so I've taken a room in a coaching Inn not so far down from the top of the hill.'

'Very well sor. I'll just get everything ship shape and then we can set off.' Tom jumped down and went to the horses.

In the turmoil of blacksmiths, wheels taken down for fitting, a swirling mass of men, horses; Will pulled the saddle and a large wicker basket off his horse's sweating back, for the late afternoon was warm, then he looked over to the three ladies who sat, in their sad black, as if at a picnic except that the food and drink was long gone. Will picked up the hamper from the ground and carried it over to them.

Lady Jane climbed to her feet and then stood there, looking down, giving due deference to her mother and sister.

'Thank you for getting help for us,' the older lady glancing up spoke casually to him staring meantime at the hamper.

'He was very slow, was he not; almost two hours for Heaven's sake...' Alice just glanced, unrecognizing, at the unshaven farmer.

They do not recognize me or are very impolite so Will just said. 'My name is Saxethorpe and you are...? Unless the other lady would care to introduce us?'

Lady Jane, embarrassed and pink faced said. 'This is my mother, Lady Walden of... Lady Walden, and this lady you have already met, Lady Forfar, it was her husband who fell at... and his brother. They were together.'

'A somewhat sad family outing then?' The straw hatted man said.

The two women stared at up at the rudely mannered farmer who now laid the hamper down before them. 'I brought food and drink but if you...'

'Thank you sir,' Lady Jane said quietly, her head down a little as she looked at him.

Will looked back at this somewhat plain young woman briefly, grateful that at least one of them was polite for the other two women just looked at the hamper as if they had never seen anything more interesting.

His tone sarcastic, Will asked. 'Would you like me to open it ladies?'

'If you would, my good man...' Lady Alice rejoined.

'Well, I wouldn't actually, since I am not your good man and currently you owe me four guineas for accommodation, food and drink,' Will smiled at the group who looked back at him astonished, '...and I trust that you have some way of recompensing the blacksmith and his men to say nothing of the hire of the new coach.'

Lady Jane, now red faced with embarrassment gasped out. 'Sir, we are most grateful for your help. My mother will, of course, pay you for the money that you have laid out.'

'I don't want your few coins but common civility would be welcome. In a smart uniform I am respected but in the garb of a farmer you all treat me like dirt; not a happy prospect for the country if the wealthy act so boorishly. Good day to you and I trust you will survive the remainder of your journey.' He bowed shortly and strode away to lead his horse to the cart where Tom was finishing harnessing the cart horses.

CHAPTER SIX

The dark figure of Lady Jane stood alone by the roadside and watched him go with some regret wishing that her sister was not such a bore but she was surprised at her mother's indifference to the helpful man.

'Why did you not thank Major Saxethorpe Mama?'

'Who?' her mother answered with her mouth rather full.

'The Major, the man who was just here,' Jane snapped back.

'Oh yes, sorry my dear but I feel so very fatigued.'

'You always told me that feeling tired or bored was no excuse for rudeness.'

'Don't worry about him. He's only a Major in some foreign army or other...' Lady Alice had torn a leg from the chicken in the hamper and was well into eating it.

They've lived their lives with servants all around them and there's always been some man to pay for them, Jane thought. They are something left over from the past, something that will be gone soon I trust.

The Major's cart lurched forward and an untied down corner of the covering canvas blew back for a moment so that was when Jane realized that the load was the same as the load that their cart carried. A coffin. A dead comrade? Perhaps the Major had a father in the Army or perhaps a brother? He too is pulled down by grief. Jane looked at her sister and thought her very unaffected by her husband's and his brother's deaths. Alice had been very animated in Brussels especially at the last great Ball but had displayed no emotion except annoyance on hearing of the death of her new husband and now she sat on a rug munching a chicken leg provided by the much slighted young man, uncaring.

In the early evening sunlight, the Post Road, dappled with the broken light that came through the trees that met overhead clip clopped slowly under the hooves of the horses. Slowly Will's anger faded away and he wondered why these pampered women showed so little civility to him and to everyone else that they met. We were only there to feed and clothe them it seemed. To house them in luxury and surround them with servants and he, to his annoyance had fallen into that role; the provider; the servant.

Tom, noticing that his master was now in a mood said. 'They must be very rich, those women...' he waited for Will to answer but he appeared not to have heard him or was ignoring him and Tom didn't know which was the worse of the two things so he added, 'They treat their servants real bad sor; did you see the way that they were so rude to the blacksmith who had kindly come all this way to help them.'

Will raised one eyebrow and thought on what Tom was saying. Was he complaining about him or was it general conversation he was after as if an officer like him would... Yes, he thought, frowning, why should he not talk to Tom? He was very knowledgeable about some things; horses, coaches, the prices of things and services, for Will knew that he had paid too much at the first Inn that they'd been in and resolved to let Tom do all the paying in future. He turned on the driver's seat and eased the numbness that his arse was feeling but then observing the determination on Tom's face asked, 'Sorry Tom, I was far away in my anger at those stupid women. I didn't hear what you had to say.'

Tom turned and smiled up his officer, a brilliant and happy smile, which reminded Will, once again, of the running drummer boy. 'I was saying that they spoke very rough to the men helping them. The mean one with the fair hair was the worst; they shouldn't treat their servants so cruel or if the Revolution were to come here; she would be the first to the guillotine.'

Will swept his straw hat off his head and stared in amazement at the small unlettered boy with the reins and whip in hand. He speaks of the French Revolution that had so changed France and most of Europe, ending with Napoleon. He knows something of the effect so he asked, in French, 'What know you of the French and France Tom?'

The reply came in a rough patois, 'I've been on the packet boat since I was nine sor; spent a lot of time in France and talked to the matelot's on the quays.'

Will sat back amazed then asked. 'How old are you Tom?'

'Thirteen sor, at least that's what my Mam said before...'

Will took another look at the boy seeing the confident way he handled the horses; how he steered the clumsy farm cart, the whip flicking gently down the lead horse's flanks to keep him straight and began to think that he'd made a very good bargain and that Tom was a very special young man. Thirteen, a good manager, trustworthy and able to converse in two languages; a bargain indeed at twenty pounds a year and a cart.

'Tom?'

The boy glanced up at him and smiled again, suddenly, brilliantly.

God! Will thought, that smile. 'When we get to... to Saxethorpe; and you are free with your cart and horses?'

'You think it will take a year, surely not sor?'

'No. Two weeks without more diversions and broken wheels.'

'And then I can go to be a carrier.'

'Surely you'll sell the cart and horses?'

'Sell the horses! Never Sor!' Tom looked surely horrified.

'What if you continued to be my...' Will was about to say 'servant' and then thought that Tom might be offended so he said, '..my 'companion' at an increased salary?'

'Salary sor?' Tom said in a somewhat distracted way, for the crest of the hill was in sight, '...what's 'salary,' it sounds like something that you can eat.'

Will smiled at the boy. 'You're thinking of the word celery or 'salad' which is lettuce, radishes, tomatoes and the like. A 'salary' is how much I would pay you for a year of...' Will couldn't think of another word so continued, '...of service to me.'

The boy glanced at him again and realized that he had a chance to bargain with this generous man and then wondered what he wanted that the young officer could give him that he hadn't already so he said. 'I'm happy enough sor. The horses, a place to live, warmth in the winter, food, yes, that I need. Not too sure about living in some strange country place after Dover and Calais but I'm happy enough.'

'I was going to give you more money Tom.'

'Well sor, money is only of use to buy something and you've promised me everything I've ever wanted.'

I give him horses and an old cart and he is happy with that, amazing Will thought.

'Tell you what sor?'

'Tell me Tom?'

'You could teach me. I can read a bit and write bout the same but you could...'

Will suddenly thought of this hungry little boy starved of all the good things of life. Reading, writing, music, intelligent conversation and quite suddenly he could see that he and Tom might be able to learn many things from each other. Tom could teach him the more arcane things about horses, how to drive a farm cart for example and he could teach the boy. What? Then he realized that in this world, learning the civilities, the ways of gentlemen and all that pertained could be better used than a few extra pounds. 'All right Tom, it's a bargain. I'll teach you of the world, manners and the like.... even dancing perhaps, and you can teach me of horses and what boys think; be my companion Tom and we will get on fine.'

The horses topped the rise and spread before them across the deep sun filled valley, some ten miles ahead, lay the blackened smudge of the coal smoke stained City of London.

The first coaching Inn at Sevenoaks was a fine place indeed and Will decided to send in a somewhat tired Tom to strike the bargain with the Innkeeper and Stable master. In half an hour all was settled, for the Inn was half empty. A safe lockable stable for the cart and good, dry, straw filled looseboxes for the horses.

Tom, at Will's insistence, showed him how to properly take off the heavy collars and harness from the cart horses and rub them down with brush and curry comb. Give harness and saddles a good coating of dubbin and with all the animals fed, watered and comfortable the two 'companions' finally went to their room.

Will insisted that the maid bring up another small bed for Tom since his smell was as pervasive as ever and also as large a quantity of hot water as she could arrange for as he wished to bathe and he had the thought that Tom could bathe after him.

A somewhat riotous hour later, for Tom had never actually submerged his naked body in water before, except by accident, with Will explaining loudly that this was what gentlemen did after a hard days riding or in Tom's case driving. Tom acquiesced after listening to the explanation and said he'd heard of it but hadn't believed it was necessary.

Arriving later in the new coach, the Lady's Walden had found comfortable rooms. Although Lady Jane was unaware of the presence in the next room of Will Saxethorpe, was a small bedchamber that Jane was grateful to have on her own. Her mother and sister were sharing the much larger suite of rooms across the hall way but Jane was grateful to get away from the constant complaining of her sister and mother. The endless discussion about which Brussels lace would go with which materiel. The blue with the white, the pink with the green...endless and pointless Jane thought and she felt bored to distraction.

The noises from the next room were, she thought, to be expected from a low class place like this Inn. Possibly animals were being slaughtered or most likely strangled and she was grateful when the noises ceased. She had decided that, tradition or not, wearing a black dress for the sake of her sister's husband and his brother was not to be countenanced any longer, for the cheap Belgian lace dress bought on the morning after the battle was disintegrating about her and was also filthy.

At her toilette, Jane wondered again about the foreign officer who was sometimes apparently a farmer, who had been so kind to them and whom they had treated so badly but supposed that the officer farmer was now far ahead of them on the road but in her day dreams, as the coach had rolled along the seemingly endless green lanes the hero character had lost his farmer's coat and turned up in a dark green hussars uniform and Jane had smiled at her silly girlish dream

Will had finally persuaded a newly cleaned Tom to come with him to a haberdashers and outfitters that he had spied in the main street of the prosperous little town and now they walked back to the Inn with several cardboard boxes.

Will decided that since they were now so smartly dressed that they should eat their evening meal in the main saloon of the tavern. Another chicken or rabbit pie sounded a little boring but he was as hungry as a fox and managed to persuade Tom that no one would laugh at him, while secretly thinking that they probably would for Tom had selected and was wearing a black velveteen suit with a white, wide collared shirt and his own rather large and dirty boots but he was hungry too and they set off downstairs into the crowded main room where they attracted little attention.

What did attract attention was the appearance of the three ladies in what looked like full ball gowns. The older Lady Walden in green, Lady Alice in a brilliant gold and Lady Jane in a dark blue dress that Will was later to think complimented her eyes. Lady Walden and Lady Forfar swirled down the stairs and across the crowded room where the workmen made way like the Red sea parting before Moses; followed, at a more sedate pace, by the young Lady Jane whose eye was immediately caught by the sight of the green uniformed German officer and his boy sitting at a table by the bar. She just nodded her head and essayed a small curtsey, she hoped politely, as she found a way across the room to the open door of the private dining room that her mother had taken. Her last glimpse of the green hussar was him standing, staring seriously, giving her a short bow.

'That was them again, wasn't it sor?' Tom said.

Will slowly descended back into his chair a look of regret on his face for honouring these uncaring women. 'Yes, Tom. I'd hoped that they would have passed this Inn by and gone on into Town although I have to assume that they still have some way to go,' he looked distractedly away towards the door of their dining room.

'We should leave real early sor so that we are ahead of 'em and not find ourselves stuck behind them when they make their next mistake....'

'You think them somewhat unlucky then Tom?'

'They are women who use you, treat servants bad and don't care for nothin save themselves.'

'You may well be right Tom except the younger one, she seems polite and genteel.'

'Dus you fancy her sor?'

'Tom! A gentleman would never say 'fancy' about a lady.'

'But you dus dusn't you?' And the boy smiled wickedly.

Will nodded his head slowly before saying, 'Lady Alice is very pretty but not very nice. Lady Jane seems a good person.'

'You been with a lady of late, sor?' Tom said as he stuffed a considerable piece of chicken into his mouth.

Will looked at the boy and thought that they learnt a great deal a great deal too early in life in the country or at sea but he supposed the question was acceptable between two men so he answered, 'I had a petit affaire in Paris two, three months back, before Bonaparte turned up again.'

'So you need a girl real bad!' Tom snickered just like one of his horses.

The three women sat at their comfort by a long oaken table laden down with food and bottles of wine and tucked in for it had been a long and difficult day.

Lady Alice said suddenly, 'I will never travel again without my maid and at least two footmen as well as in a very reliable carriage,' she stuffed a lettuce leaf into her mouth regretting letting Lord Forfar persuade her of the economy of not taking servants with them to Belgium for neither of them had allowed for the possibility of his falling in the battle.

Lady Walden leaned back with a sigh of appreciation,

'Country victuals have a certain honesty when compared with the fancier food that we...'

'The food is close to disgusting Mama but hunger is hunger,' Lady Alice announced, 'And what do you think of the food Jane?'

Jane who had not eaten since the morning because her mother and sister had eaten all of the picnic provided by the German officer, said. 'It's a good pie and if one does not worry about the way of cooking it; a fine pie indeed,' and she pushed another morsel of tender beef between her lips as she held her slim body very upright in her chair unlike her slumped sister.

Lady Walden, who spent a lot of her energy keeping her two girls from each other asked Jane. 'You loitered in the tavern?'

'Hardly loitered, but as I passed through I saw the Prussian officer; you know, the hussar in the green uniform. He was sitting with his driver in the tavern. I nodded to him,' she smiled happily for some reason.

'Forget him!' her Mama ordered, ' He is of no importance, just an aide de camp...'

'He says that he's a Major in the Hessian Lancers and is much decorated. I wonder why he is in England? His English is very good for a German; hardly any accent at all I think.'

Alice laughed, somewhat unpleasantly, 'Don't worry about the accent sister; they are all the same in the bedchamber, rip your gown off, throw themselves on top of you and make merry.'

Jane suddenly asked, 'So the absence of Lord Forfar causes you no regrets?'

Lady Alice remembered all too clearly how much she had enjoyed their dalliances in the bedchamber and regretted their loss but she said, 'He was a stupid man and not very rich. My next husband will have to be very rich indeed....' and good in bed, she thought to herself or a lover will be necessary.

Jane looked away somewhat amused for she knew that her sister already had a replacement husband in mind. A rather odd, somewhat misogynist, and mean minded Earl. She folded her napkin carefully and laid it by her plate then thought that she would go to her room for she had spent the whole day in the company of her mother and her sister and neither had any pretensions to reading books or newspapers so that conversation was somewhat limited to complaints and the discussions on the latest fashions. Jane had the new, just begun, novel in her baggage and thought that an hour of the Jane Austen novel would be very enjoyable. Saying her 'good nights' to the other two women she turned out into the main room only to meet with the hussar again, who was just leaving his table.

Startled into speaking she said. 'Good evening sir, our paths cross quite often I think,' and then she smiled. This was unexpected both for her and for him. For her she thought the smile wasted since he was both foreign, poor, and not a candidate for marriage.

For him her smile was a stunning revelation, for the woman suddenly appeared to be quite beautiful; the serene simplicity of her regular features lighting up as if illumined from within. He swallowed hard before managing to say. 'Good evening Lady Jane...' he frowned trying to think, '...was your dinner adequate?'

She stared at him wondering what colour she would call his eyes, and then replied hesitantly. 'Why do you ask sir? If I say 'no' would you rush away to find me another?'

His face colouring he replied. 'I think my question was merely small talk, a politeness, a way of passing the time.'

Jane became aware that the boy was watching this exchange with some interest, his smiling face turning back and forth from one to the other.

'The food was good and must your boy look at me like that?' Jane said, frowning a little.

Will looked around at the Tom waiting there. 'May I introduce you to my companion?' He paused but then plunged on since he had never heard of anyone introducing a servant to a member of the nobility. 'Lady Jane, this is Master Thomas...?'

'Gilfoil sor.' A smiling Tom cocked his head on one side in question.

'Master Thomas Gilfoil of Dover and Calais. We are travelling together. I purchased a cart to carry my brother home and I also....' he hesitated before saying, '...met someone who could drive the cart and manage my horses; Mr Gilfoil here.'

Jane smiled at his obvious confusion but recognized that he was trying not to demean his servant. 'It is good to meet with you Mr Gilfoil but remember it is not polite to stare at a lady. A quick glance should suffice.'

For a moment they all stood in a silent tableau then Lady Jane said, 'You travel... Where are you going?'

'We travel to Norfolk Milady. At our present pace, Christmas looks like our arrival time.'

'Perhaps you should avoid helping ladies in distress,' Lady Jane replied, her smile returning.

Which almost stopped Will replying. 'It would certainly speed us on our way but one must help those 'in distress' if one can,' Will sounded as if he wished to continue the conversation.

'May I wish you better luck sir on the rest of your journey,' Jane said, somewhat oddly wishing that...

'You must be tired Milady; a long day.' Will gestured to her to continue her walk across the tavern and then, a moment of two later the man and the boy followed.

Not long after sunrise found Tom and Will at breakfast in the now empty tavern of the Inn. Will was occupied with writing a letter on his military writing slope and Tom was occupied with getting as much food as possible inside him. The remnants of last night's pie, a great deal of bread and butter with the contents of a jar of honey and two pots of coffee.

Will had not realized how slow their progress would be across the country and now thought that a letter to his remaining brother and sister was in order so he wrote swiftly and firmly avoiding the emotion that he felt.

Dear brother John and sister Anne,

It is with great sadness that I must report to you of the death of Lawrence on the field of battle at Waterloo. He led a great charge that broke the French line and turned possible defeat into victory, and is acclaimed a hero by the Duke.

I have brought his remains home to be interred with our dear Papa and Mama at Saxethorpe.

The journey has become more difficult than I imagined when I started. A storm drove the cross Channel ferry far to the south so that the landfall was on the south coast and by virtue of my lack of knowledge of the number of coffins returning home I found that the only way to get Lawrence home was to purchase a farm cart. I write to you from Sevenoaks but when you receive this letter we will have already crossed the Thames and be on our way north. I anticipate that the journey will take at least one week, possibly longer.

Your loving brother, William.

Carefully he folded the sheet of paper then, using a taper, he melted some dark green sealing wax onto the letter and pressed his seal ring into the hot wax as he ordered. 'Let us depart Tom. I would prefer to be in front of the ladies in the coach rather than behind them.'

It was as they loaded Will's firearms into the cart that the door of Inn opened and a lady, neatly dressed in white muslin with a dark blue travelling cloak over, appeared.

'Good morning Major,' she said quietly, even though he was dressed in his farming clothes on this fine summer morning.

Will turned in some confusion since his arms held two carbines and a pair of pistols. 'Milady. Good morning to you.' He essayed a short bow.

'You seem well-armed sir. Prepared for highwaymen and the like no doubt?'

'I'm a soldier Milady. Soldier's have weapons.' He finished handing the pistols up to Tom, then bent to pick up the four sheathed swords that lay on the cobbles, '...as you can see. You are abroad early; is your party planning an early start?'

'No sir, I think not. I awoke early and have been reading but then thought that some exercise might be beneficial with a long day in the coach ahead,' Jane stopped, wondering why she spoke to this rough clad man at all.

Tom handed the tails of the ropes that bound the cargo over to his master and watched carefully as Will tied the knots to bind the cover down.

'Do you have far to go Milady?' Will asked, even as he pulled tight the bindings.

Jane looked at this man and wondered again why she didn't just walk on. 'We travel to Saffron Walden....' she'd half turned away when she heard him say.

'That town is on our route to Norfolk, perhaps we shall meet again.' He smiled, questioning, at her back.

Jane spun around to him and stared up into his smiling face knowing somehow that they would indeed meet again if only in many years time and she said, somewhat hesitantly feeling confused. 'I have a letter to send Post and I....'

'If you are going to the Post Office perhaps you could be so kind as to send this, it's a letter for my brother....' he hunted in his deep side pocket for the sealed letter, 'I will give you two shillings to cover...'

'I would be delighted to post your letter sir and as for the cost, I believe that we owe you a good deal and that this....' she took the letter that he handed her and looked carefully at the direction.

THE RIGHT REVEREND JOHN SAXETHORPE OF ELY
& SAXETHORPE
NORFOLK.

His brother is a Bishop so this man is not foreign at all. He has just been serving in the Prussian Army for some reason or other. She turned the letter over and inspected the green wax seal, a very elaborate and ornate pattern of horses and fish sunk deep into its dark surface and she frowned.

'Milady? You look puzzled?' Will asked wondering at her hesitation.

'I... I was just being certain that you had directed it properly... and not ill.'

'It would be a kindness Milady, for my brother and sister may not yet know that our older brother is no more.'

Jane glanced over towards the heavily laden farm cart, her expression saddened knowing that the load it carried was the same as theirs. 'I'm so sorry Major, a great loss to you I think.' She looked very unhappy for him.

'There could be none greater Milady.' The tragedy was writ large upon his sad face.

CHAPTER SEVEN

The journey to Greenwich, the crossing of the Thames on a ferry and their safe arrival on the far bank at Barking proved uneventful save as part of Tom's education. The two of them now talked continuously, mostly by virtue of the many questions that Tom asked and so the journey seemed to pass much more swiftly and it had necessitated a further stop at a shop that sold writing materials so that paper, pens and ink could be purchased.

The problem of Tom's reading was solved by Will taking over the reins and Tom reading out loud from a novel that Will had purchased.

'ABOUT THIRTY YEARS AGO...' this short sentence took Tom above twenty minutes to work out and Will decided that something much more basic was needed so at their next stop he purchased a book of fairy tales written for very small children with excellent illustrations that helped tell the story.

Tom, with a little help from his new friend was able to decipher both the story and the text so that Will had the pleasure of hearing the story of Goldilocks at least ten more times in the next hour and it was only by shouting at the boy that he was able to stop him. They moved on to the alphabet since Will was convinced that Tom had just learnt the words of the fairytale off by heart and so it proved, for Tom was in immediate trouble with both the alphabet and reading the words that lay with each letter. A IS FOR APPLE took some time, B IS FOR BABY took a good deal less and C IS FOR CAT very little time indeed. Will looked at the boy, at his level of concentration and knew that the alphabet would be just the beginning of whatever it was that they had, together, started upon.

For Jane the journey from the Inn at Biggin Hill to the ferry at Greenwich, had proved uneventful; for which Jane was grateful in that it reduced the number of complaints from her sister and mother. She was unable to read since the Post road surface was uneven enough to make the small print of her book swirl before her eyes. Reduced to looking out of the window of their darkly enclosed, rather too warm, coach, she found that she spent most of the time looking out for her farmer. Stupid, she thought, to think of this almost stranger as 'her farmer' but nevertheless she watched out for every straw-hat wearing man seated on a cart or even just walking by. For Jane this was a something of a departure from her normal state of mind. At nineteen she was both of a marriageable age and expected to act like a woman. Her sister's exploits in the marriage market had kept her mother very busy but now that the Lord Forfar was gone, Jane thought that Alice and her mother would be totally involved in finding a new man for the new widow and Alice had said that the Earl would do at a push although she would have preferred someone younger. So Jane knew that the pressure on her to marry had relaxed a little, which was good, but all this talk of death, sex and marriage from her sister had undoubtedly stirred something in her that she had not been aware of before.

Another straw hat sailed into view but disappointment was her only reward. A man then; a man to marry. He must have money of course; money made the world go around and kept women like her in pretty dresses so perhaps money would be enough, for Jane liked pretty dresses but they were not a real part of her life they were just for... Another straw hat passed by with attendant disappointment.

The river crossing. Interesting, different, but the water seemed filthy and very smelly with many nasty things afloat slowly edging down to the North Sea. Ashore and only thirty five miles to go so mother had insisted on changing horses and pressing on rather than yet another night be spent in a smelly Inn on the road.

Arriving home, to their house that lay between the Howards and the castle and up the short drive to arrive at the white stuccoed and porticoed Saffron House, was indeed a pleasure for all the ladies and the sight of her Papa sent Lady Alice into state of gay abandon as she persuaded him to accept her back into the family home although he seemed more than somewhat confused about her marriage to Lord Forfar and what had happened to him.

Later Lady Jane asked her. 'Why do you not wish to return to your own house; surely...'

'Because it is small, plain and empty Jane, a bit like you. We didn't have sufficient money for the servants I wanted and now I have none. The house must be sold, the cash will come in handy for gowns and the like.'

Jane, though realizing the common sense of such an argument, was not so happy when she thought that her sister would precede her once again at all events now that she had reverted to her single but widowed state.

'Will you call yourself Lady Forfar or...?'

'Don't be stupid Jane. Of course I'm Lady Forfar; he was a baron you know. Higher ranked than Papa so that places me higher than Mama...' she plunged into the bedchamber that she had only left the previous summer so that it was as if she had only been away for a little while; on a tour perhaps.

The next day Alice needed to visit the town to talk with the vicar about the burial of her husband and his brother. With that dealt with she intended to proceed to the local haberdashers to purchase various small items of toiletry so, quite early before the sun had warmed too much the two young ladies boarded the family's small chaise, driven by a stable boy, for the short journey.

As Jane sat there looking up at the sunlit leaves that formed a tunnel over them she found her thoughts wandering to the green hussar. Where was he now? They'd not passed him but she knew that if he was in a tavern or inn then she would not have seen him but she had a return of the curious fancy that she would see him again one day and she found that all that day she would once again look at every farmer wearing a straw hat and almost see her soldier. The fact that he had the same name as the town or village that he came from meant little she knew. The other fact that his brother was a bishop seemed to indicate a family of some rank so that rather than think of him as a farmer she thought that her hussar might be a 'Sir' or a Right Honourable... and that was when she saw him. Her 'noble' farmer. He stood at the glass counter of the general store and appeared to be buying a number of books of fairy stories, a small wooden framed slate and a box of chalks such as a child might use; does that mean he is married with children.

'Good day sir,' she said quietly.

The farmer soldier, his straw hat pushed back onto his neck and held by a string, his long fair hair cascading about his face, turned abruptly to her. 'Lady Jane...' he gasped out. 'Milady, a pleasure to see you again and so soon,' he bowed really quite deeply, smiling as he did so.

'We do seem to be doomed to cross paths rather often sir,' she smiled, the dazzle of her smile, once again, wiping the plainness from her face. 'You buy books for your children Sir?'

He was about to reply when Lady Alice suddenly appeared, 'Oh!' she said recognizing the farmer who had saved them the other day but failing to associate him with the hussar. 'Thank you for your help the other day. If you come to the house Papa will recompense you I've no doubt. Come Jane, I need to visit the seamstress. I have to have a black dress made for when I am in public. None of the people around here know yet that I am a widow...' she bustled away leaving the couple to say their farewells.

'Your sister is still as abrupt and uncivil,' the man said quietly.

'She did not recognize you... properly.' Jane's voice was quiet and her face regretful.

'But you do Milady. If I were to ride up to your house would I be welcome?'

Jane's heart fluttered at the very thought of it and replied. 'My sister wishes to recompense you for your trouble it seems.'

'I wonder which of me she wishes to help, the farmer or...'

'Come after dinner sir. But wear your uniform, for my Papa has no sense of humour and would treat any man dressed as a tenant farmer... as a tenant farmer.' She smiled tentatively at the fair-haired man. 'Come at nine sir,' she turned and departed, her wide white skirt swishing away through the doorway.

Leaving the Major with words half said, 'I have no chil...dren, Milady.' As he watched the small chaise depart in a small cloud of golden dust, Will thought that she was a deal prettier than he had first noticed and wondered at his interest since marriage was, for him, a third son, just a distant possibility.

They put up at an Inn just off the Post Road so not so expensive and Will got the horses and Tom settled and fed before he dressed with a lot more care than usual.

Will had visited the town barber, for he had not shaved properly for some days, then returned to the Inn where his saddle, boots and sword belt gleamed with the polish that Tom had lavished on them. He took from the bottom of his campaign trunk the red tunic he'd worn in the Mess during the Peninsular War and was astounded, for some reason, that it still fitted him. When he turned to a faded and cracked pier glass on the wall between the windows of his bedchamber he was amazed to see his brother staring back at him. It was a shock of sorts but he was not the sort of man to let a momentary image disturb him. It was his undressed, barely combed, hair he knew, for the brothers had always looked somewhat alike and now that Lawrence was dead; the thought of his dead brother struck him anew and sadness laid its black cover over his happier thoughts.

CHAPTER EIGHT

He will, may, come tonight to collect his money, Jane thought. The thought of the handsome green clad officer made her breath come faster and she wondered at herself. A young man, of no real rank, a third son probably; he had said that it was his brother that had fallen and that the Bishop was now his elder male sibling so that would likely have left him with little money and no land so... But he was so very good to look upon and tonight she just knew that he would come so she needed to bathe and wash her hair after so many days on the road. To have to wait for her mother and her sister to bathe before her was almost intolerable but the one copper hip bath that Saffron House possessed meant that precedence would be accorded age and title. The thought of bathing in the same, dirty and mostly cold water used by the other two women was unbearable so she gave the upstairs maid two shillings to empty the tub, clean it and move it to Jane's bedchamber then refill it with hot fresh water. It had been worth the expense, Jane thought; perhaps meeting with the Major and then him smelling her unclean body and clothes was almost less tolerable than not seeing him again. She thought of the excessive cologne that her mother and sister would use and shuddered.

When the maids had finished filling her bath Jane shooed them from her dressing room and then stripped off her clothes with some great relief. She looked down at the shift that was required bathing attire and the thought of getting into her expensively acquired hot water wearing such a grubby garment. She slipped it off and slid into the warm water with a sigh of almost ecstasy. The soap that she had purchased in Bruxelles with just a drop of the Cologne seemed to make the steam of the water smell divine so she plunged her head under the water and scrubbed at her head and her hair using just a little of the soap. An hour to dry her long dark red hair, an hour of almost pleasure in that her hair, her scalp felt so very clean and smelt so fresh.

Her maid was busy with curling irons and brushes before Jane allowed herself to think on the young soldier. He would have little money and no land so what could he offer a noble young woman like herself but he was so very good to look upon and tonight she just knew that he would come if only to collect his money although she knew that she would take some part in his thinking.

At nine Will rode 'Hector', with much jingling of his accoutrements and spur rowels up to the portico entrance of Saffron House and dismounted as a groom came running. 'Were you warned that I would come? He asked of the man.

'I were told to expect a late guest sor.'

The butler whispered to him asking his name and then went to the big door of the library to announce, 'Major Saxethorpe,' and Will walked, almost marched, into the large and elaborate faux marble room that he supposed was, or had meant to be, a sort of library cum music room. Very few and rather new looking books and an assortment of paintings of no real worth attempted to fill the space on the walls; a piano forte and an oversize harp helped fill the floorspace. Six card tables were set up and a servant circulated with a silver tray laden with wine glasses. Three of the tables were full of the local gentry, in mostly out of fashion clothing, and in play, the other three tables stood empty. A tall, shambling, rather old fashioned, bewigged person wearing a blue silk knee britched suit came forward, a somewhat puzzled expression on his face.

'Sir?' he asked.

Will asked, 'Lady Forfar did not tell you that she invited me?'

The man looked relieved, a look of half understanding crossing his face, 'Of course, I think that she did mention...'

Will knew that she had not mentioned him at all or if she had he had been forgotten. She had barely recognized him in the shop and would certainly not now. The tables looked interesting though. The first two were playing some version of whist and the other, somewhat more exciting, was playing 'loo.'

'What would you prefer to play sir?' We have...' the old man looked vaguely about him as if wondering just who this uniformed man was.

'I enjoy 'loo' rather than whist but if...'

'No, no sir. I was about to make up another table which we will start after a little supper and the entertainment I think,' the older man turned away to go to the doors where he whispered to the butler.

Lady Alice fancied herself as both a player of the harp and a singer of soulful songs so it was this combination that was to dominate the supper. Her sister, Lady Jane, did service on the piano forte, that stood by the doors, accompanying her sister and it was, Will thought, competently done. Not easy, as Lady Alice constantly changed tempo, both of her singing and her harp playing. Her voice too changed pitch rather too often, sometimes hitting the highest of notes and then struggling to find some kind of lower timbre.

Will, like the other men, felt impatient and when the ladies finished their third dirge they all fell to dealing and calling out of 'trumps' and the like interspersed with concealed laughter.

Afterwards the two ladies, with disappointment writ large on Lady Alice's face, circulated around the room, talking to men of their acquaintance. When they came to Will's table he stood smartly and bowed shortly to each with his eyebrows slightly raised in question. 'Good evening Lady Alice, Lady Jane....' and he bowed again most graciously.

'Have we been introduced sir?' Lady Alice demanded.

'Rather too often I would have thought,' was his somewhat enigmatic response which left Alice staring at him since there was no memory of such a red uniformed fair haired man in her head.

'You appear to have changed Army's sir?' Lady Jane said in a low amused voice.

Will smiled at this witty woman and bowed again. 'We mercenaries do have the advantage of a number of uniforms to choose from. This one, for example, is from my days during the Peninsular Wars, when I was an aide de camp to the Duke.'

'So suddenly you are both de-ranked and have a change of nationality?' Jane said, smiling in a pursed lips way.

'Who is he?' Lady Alice demanded in a harsh whisper, as if he was not standing there.

Lady Jane smiled demurely and replied. 'He is our farmer friend. The one who rescued us when we were in dire need.'

The beautiful silver haired woman stared at the officer. 'Oh, but...yes. I see, does he have a name?' Alice asked half turning away.

Lady Jane, looking amused, almost laughing, said. 'His name is still Major William Saxethorpe of Norfolk and he's a veteran of Waterloo, for he was mentioned in Dispatches in the Times,' she smiled at the man, '...but we are stopping your game from starting. Oh yes, Alice, if I may be permitted to remind you; he came for his money.'

'Money?' Alice's pretty face was bemused, baffled.

'The inn and the food on the road the other day.'

Alice came close to her sister and whispered, 'And this is the same man?'

Jane glanced at the officer then back to her sister to quietly nod her head.

They were all country amateurs and would be cullies, Will realized, but none had the sophistication and skill to play the game at its highest level. They did, however, have a fair amount of cash about them, which he set about removing where possible. When midnight came Will had won near to twenty-five guineas which he thought was more than sufficient for a country game.

There was one very disgruntled man in the game. Young, over dressed in a light blue silk suit and a poor player who had decided that Will must be cheating in some way even though the deal passed from hand to hand and when Lady Jane came to the table and laid a small stack of six golden guineas by Will's elbow he exploded in anger.

'The women must pay you too!' He shouted out. 'You sit there, a so called veteran of Waterloo all dandified up in a red coat, a smug smile on your face, cheating somehow. How, I do not know...'

Ignoring the man and his complaints a frowning Will got to his feet saying as he did so. 'You must excuse me gentlemen. I have a long way to travel tomorrow and I think that playing cards in such an atmosphere as this, is not possible.'

'You think you can walk off with my money?' Shouted out the young blood.

Will half turned back to say. 'Curiously sir, that is the general idea of gambling games. You take a chance and if you lose you must be a sufficient gentleman to accept the loss.' Will bowed to the rest of the table and turned away again to find his host.

The crash as a chair was thrown back made Will pause and half turn to look over his shoulder. The young man was drunkenly struggling to disentangle himself whilst shouting insults. Will went over to where the host was rising, his face confused, his wig slightly askew.

Lord Walden asked in a mumbling voice, 'My dear sir, what's occurred, pray?'

Will nodded to the scene behind him saying. 'That young man does not know when to stop wagering and should receive some instruction before being allowed to play 'loo' in polite society.'

'Be wary sir!' a voice called out.

Will both heard and felt the arrival of the young man when his shoulder was gripped savagely. He reached over his shoulder and grasping the young man's wrist pulled him sharply forwards, and then, using the man's forward momentum and a casually placed boot to trip him with, sent him plummeting end over end to crash onto the 'whist' table which flattened in a great debris of cards, money and broken glass.

Will looked askance at the maelstrom of events started by the young man's fall. 'My apologies sir, for the damage to your table,' Will now looked somewhat amused, '...let me recompense you.' He reached into his pocket and withdrawing the guineas that Lady Jane had given him he handed the six coins to the now very confused nobleman.

Lady Jane came running into the room her face perplexed by the racketing noise, 'What has occurred Papa?'

'Young whatever his name is, has made a fool of himself again,' he looked angry with himself, 'I warned him to ameliorate his behaviour.'

'He is very young Papa...' but Jane looked at the soldier and tentatively smiled.

She could be, would be, a pretty woman if she allowed herself to be, to compete, perhaps, with her sister, Will thought. 'Apart from the ending it was an enjoyable evening sir.' Will turned to the girl to say, '... and the musical interlude; was interesting, Milady.'

Jane frowned a little and then said, 'You didn't like our songs sir?'

'Your accompaniment was excellent; well timed, considering the problems of the changing of pitch, rhythm and tempo.'

'You could do better sir?' Lady Jane looked faintly annoyed at him for commenting on her sister's singing even though she too believed Alice to be a poor singer.

They all watched as the dazed young man was led away by his friends, his staggering gait lending some amusement to the gathered gentry as they supped the last of their wine and prepared the stories that they would tell on reaching home for there was little excitement to be had in the country.

Finally Will was able to reply to Jane's question. 'I play the piano forte a little, the guitar a lot, it's somewhat lighter to carry, and I have been known to sing, especially when in my cups.' He looked closely, enquiringly, at the young woman to ask. 'Perhaps a duet Milady?' His look was intense, the question one that could not be mistaken.

Jane looked confused, blushing a little, and then turned abruptly to the piano, which was to hand by the doorway, she gestured abruptly in a faintly annoyed way to the stool then stepped back, then looked slightly astonished when Will sat himself down.

He started to play the 'Moonlight Sonata,' the notes falling like silvered leaves into the silent room, and she was struck by his skill, his beauty, his eyes gleaming like moonlit stones. Men, in her world, did not play musical instruments, unless they were professional musicians, although Jane had no knowledge of 'why'. It was just that it was a woman's place to play an instrument and... and he was no woman, no woman at all.

'Am I good enough for you Milady?' Will asked in a serious voice.

'You are better than good enough sir,' she gasped out in a half whisper, '... you play... superbly.'

He smiled at her gently as if puzzled by his own reaction. 'And you play well Milady. Why do you not sing? I thought I heard you when you were on the road?'

'No doubt my sister sir,' she turned for the door then hesitated, waiting for him.

Will rose to his feet somewhat reluctantly acknowledging to himself that quite suddenly he didn't want to leave this house; to leave this young woman.

A few minutes later, Jane stood by the window that overlooked the portico and watched as the red uniformed officer seemed to leap into the saddle of his black horse and turning, walked his horse away down the drive into the encroaching darkness and she felt a sudden desperate feeling of loss. Of course he was everything that no girl should want. He was poor, he was a gambler and a mercenary soldier, so that he had no future save death on a distant battlefield. Her face frowned in her sadness and she felt that it would be so tragic to see such a handsome young man... She did not allow herself to think further but turned away for the stairs and her bedchamber.

CHAPTER NINE

A splash of cold water across his face was the first thing that Will felt as dawn broke. He could only have slept for four or so hours and it felt like less. For a moment he thought that a battle was waiting then remembered where he was. The next was the face of Tom, puzzled and a little pretend annoyed, thrust into his. 'Wake up sir, you insisted on an early start, for we have a long day; you said,' Tom looked as if he wanted to smile at his master so amused was he.

Will said in a tired and sleep blurred way as he snuggled back down into the slightly damp blankets. 'Breakfast Tom. We will need some sustenance and I must...' he peered at his companion, '...we must wash. So a deal of hot water will be needed if we are to dent the mud still adhering to your anatomy.... and soap ...don't forget the soap...' his voice faded away and then he was fast asleep again.

It was gone nine, by the new clock on the Guildhall, when a chaise, driven by a liveried footman, clattered into the courtyard of the Swan Inn and stopped close to an unpainted farm cart that seemed to have some problem with a wheel or perhaps an axle.

'Major!' a female voice called out, 'I am glad to have found you before your departure. I was somewhat afraid that I might have to pursue you down the Post road.'

Will, his farmer's work clothes covered now with a goodly layer of dirty straw edged his way out from under his cart which was jacked up on a multiplicity of timbers all serving to lever the back of the cart up to allow access to the rear wheels and axle.

Lady Jane smiled at the sight of last night's elegant figure now dressed and acting as a farmer.

'Where is your fine uniform sir?'

'In my trunk with my fine manners Milady. We have suffered a somewhat unkind blow with a broken axle beam, I fear it is the great weight that we carry. It is fortunate that we purchased a spare when we...'

'So you are only slightly delayed sir?' Jane descended, helped by the footman and swirled around to stand in front of him where she smiled a suddenly confused and tremulous smile. Dear God, she thought, even as a farmer he is far too good looking for... for my own good.

Will smiled back and didn't look confused at all. He knew that he and this young woman, with whom he had some kind of rapport, would never be allowed to mix, to touch, to kiss; just to look, to admire from a distance. 'We are more than slightly delayed Milady. The axle and the wheels must need be fitted by a blacksmith and I think that the purchase of another wheel would not go amiss. So we shall stay here for another day or so...' Will had to tear his eyes away from hers as he was in danger of drowning in her huge dark blue staring eyes.

Jane managed, after a moment to say. 'My father wants to thank you for last night; for dealing with the ruffian...' Lady Jane felt out of breath suddenly.

'He thanked me last night Milady, sufficiently I think.'

'He also has... he has a task. No! Not a task but a...' she struggled to think of a word, '...a 'commission' he would like you to undertake for him,' Jane found herself staring fixedly into his eyes thinking bright, sky blue and how very handsome he was, dirty or clean.

'A commission?'

'I think; I think that it would be best if you came to the house and let him explain to you... I am not able...' Jane looked down totally unable to continue.

So it was that, after washing and a change of clothes, Major Saxethorpe rode behind the chaise containing Lady Jane wondering how it was that Fate was taking such an overwhelming hand in his life. How could it be that his path and that of the young woman seated in the carriage in front of him could cross so often. Of course the fact that they travelled the same road was one possibility but all the broken wheels and axles surely there was some kind of meaning there.

He rides behind my carriage as a good husband would. I must not turn my head to look back at him although I know that he looks splendid in his hussars uniform with his sabre and wearing his black shako with his golden hair spilling out... Stop! Jane thought, I, we would never be allowed to even think... but the tingling sensation that ran up her spine said otherwise.

Will watched the small carriage sweep away after Lady Jane had stepped down and he stopped under the canopy of the portico and gave 'Hector's' reins to a groom that came running, then he turned for the door.

'I have a deal of money; rents and other assorted valuables and the like that I would wish... I need, to take to the Bank in Cambridge,' Lord Walden's face was a little pink, as if with embarrassment, his voice hesitant and halting.

He had appeared in a plum coloured silk suit with knee britches and a newly powdered wig. A man of fifty or so, Will thought, trying to be strong but seeming not having the heart or the mind for it.

'And...?' Will asked politely.

'The roads are thick with returning soldiers, drunken soldiers mostly, all desperate for money and a coach without outriders would be...'

'...easily taken sir?'

'Yes, there are so many men with no money and some of them are still armed. They have, I'm told, brought their muskets home with them and now that they have drunk all their pay...' he left the thought hanging.

'And you would like me to accompany you sir?'

'You are a soldier sir. You know about... about protecting, people, things.'

'Money, gold? Your trust in me is very odd considering the shortness of our acquaintance?' Will stood quietly, now wearing his Hussars uniform which was somewhat cleaner after washing and pressing, before the older man and wondered if there was more to this request than that which it appeared to be.

'I would pay you... a sum, to escort my coach, my daughters, me, my Lady.'

'And your money.'

'Yes, the money,' he fell silent.

'Do the servants know of the movement of your funds from here to Cambridge?'

'No! Of course not!' The man looked surprised at the question.

But Will thought that they probably would. The nobility were notorious for forgetting that servants were in the room with them just as they were notorious for ignoring their basic human comforts.

'And how much would you pay sir?' He will have thought that young soldiers came for free perhaps.

'I thought five guineas... ten perhaps?' His eyebrows were raised in question.

'How far is Cambridge sir?'

'Only twelve miles or so...'

'Then the ten is sufficient as long as you also pay for food and drink so that I and my companion can return the same day or perhaps on the morrow.' Will thought that it would fill the endless hours while he waited for the blacksmith to complete his work. 'So will it be tomorrow?'

'I hoped for today sir.'

'Oh!' Will was puzzled that they would leave so soon but on a summers day if they left as soon as possible then they should get there before dark and hopefully before the Bank closed its doors.

A somewhat unexpected trip into Cambridge was always welcomed by the ladies of the Walden family and to-days was no exception. Jane had walked down from her room and had been surprised to find the hall bustling with servants, with a number of chests lined up. Her own small chest had been brought down earlier and she glanced about to make sure that it would be included in the coach's load. So much fuss including, she reminded herself, the employing of the Major as an outrider and guard, but could there be so much money involved. She knew that her Papa charged a certain amount for the gambling that took place one or two nights a week but surely that and the money from the farms could not justify an armed guard, surely not.

From the hall window she saw, with a shudder of excitement, two heavily armed horsemen turn into the gateway; one a boy, dressed as a man; the other, a man dressed as a... her heart almost stopped and for the first time Jane thought she knew what the word 'love' meant. To 'love' a man; not a pony or a pet dog but a man and Will Saxethorpe was surely just such a man. She knew that he could never be her husband. It was a question of rank and wealth, but that knowledge didn't stop the shiver of anticipation that gripped her at the thought that she would spend the next few hours in his company or at least near to him.

Finally, about two hours after noon, the coach was loaded and the outriders in place so the whip was cracked and they were off.

Will had caught glimpses of both Lady Alice, who looked very beautiful, and her sister, the Lady Jane, who seemed to be trying to avoid both looking at or getting too near to the him. So be it, thought Will, they are both too grand for a poor soldier.

I must not get too close to him, Jane thought, or I will say some absurd thing like... I love you Will Saxethorpe. No! don't even think those words for they would lead to a calamity surely.

The first five miles were pleasant in the extreme, Will thought. The sun shining, a cool breeze, a good surface on the road with the coach going at least six miles within the hour. The hooves making a quiet clacking sound on the hard dry surface, the sun through the leaves and the gentle warmth and it was good thinking that the Lady Jane was riding in the coach, perhaps peeking out at him on occasion.

It was as they entered the woods that clustered around the junction at the Icknield Way that Will first felt the premonition of a problem.

Back at the Inn it had taken Tom and him an hour to saddle up the two war horses, Hector and Trojan, and fit the horse-pistol holsters in place. Then the two carbines had to be loaded and tested behind the Smithy, and the two rifled muskets were strapped on, one for each horse. Will had to show Tom how it was done and then he explained how they would travel. He would ride with the coach as an outrider and he wanted Tom to maintain station back at least two hundred yards. If Tom saw a problem, like a holdup by highway men then he had to use his head to see what he could do to help but after going for two or three miles Will decided that Tom would do better and be safer as an outrider while he swept up behind. He had ordered Tom not to pull out a pistol or the carbine for fear he might get shot. He was just to mill about and then to ride off for a few yards until Will could get there. Before he mounted he tested the looseness of his sabre in its scabbard; but even drawing it in practice was enough to bring back Waterloo and the blood... the boy running and a cold shudder ran through him.

Stump Cross, at the crossroads where the road to Cambridge intersected with the old Roman Road of Icknield Way, had what looked like a very disreputable public tavern judging by the many drunken men sprawled outside in the afternoon sunlight. To Will they were obviously ex-soldiers since most were still wearing the remains of red uniforms and a straggling row of muskets were stacked against the dirty, lime-washed wall of the Inn. A pity, he thought, that men who had risked their all for England should find themselves in such a plight. He knew that drink was the downfall of most such men but the fact that they found themselves in the world alone with no work and no friends that were not Army like themselves, was so very sad. Will felt the many eyes watching as the coach rolled its way steadily through the hamlet and it was only as the horses crossed onto the Cambridge road that Will realized that some of the men watching them go were getting to their feet and that even as they passed one or two had picked up their muskets. Spurring his horse ahead he rode alongside the coach and shouted at the driver, 'Go faster driver lest we be pursued...' for at the last moment Will had seen four or five saddled horses tied up in the stable yard and he had a very unpleasant premonition.

The shouting voices, the sound of the whip cracking over the horses, made Jane aware of a change in their circumstances as the coach rocked from side to side.

The road became beech tree lined, the high canopy radiant with sunshine of the late day but Will didn't notice instead he became more and more apprehensive. His instincts, his intuition honed in many battles and skirmishes told him he was at a distinct disadvantage if there was a band of rider's behind him and he knew that such a party might well have also prepared a welcome in front of them. Stop the coach and the party would be over. The coach must keep going and that was when Will saw that the road ahead was blocked by a farm cart slewed across the track with three armed men standing in front of it.

Will pulled up his horse and shouted to Tom to come to him. He spun around to see a dust trail following but still just out of sight. 'Go into the woods Tom and give me what support that you can.' Will turning, watched as the boy plunged into the thick tree line then turned to see the oncoming riders. Four of them. Will slithered from the saddle even as he snatched his rifled musket from its sheath, a moment to check the flint and pan then he lifted the long barrel and peered down its length. The first rider came straight at him and fired a carbine in his direction even as Will steadied himself and at two hundred yards he fired. He did not wait to see the result but snatched up his next gun, a double barrelled carbine. The man falling from the lead horse upset the other three who did not appear to be natural riders. Will stood steady until they were on him and then fired straight at the first, swung away a little and aimed at the third rider who took the charge full in the chest... three down, thought Will, and where is number four? He slid his sabre from its sheath and then realized that the remaining rider had by passed the action and was, even now, arriving at the front of the coach, horse pistol in hand.

Will could faintly hear, for the noise and concussions of the musketry had deafened him, the demands of the rider, the shouted out 'Stand and deliver' or some kind of clichéd demand as the coach clattered to a standstill in a cloud of dust and that was when he saw the man stagger, dropping his pistol and then fall from his horse. Turning, Will saw Tom ride from the cover of the woods, smoke still pouring from the barrel of his musket and a pleased look on his face.

A whip like crack buzzed past Will as shot from the barricade came his way so he strode to his horse and with one powerful heave he was in the saddle and galloping at the barricade. He could hear, feel, that Tom rode at his shoulder and he delighted in the feeling, the battle feeling, the excitement, the blood lust rising. He could see one man re-loading and another carefully aiming so raising one of the horse pistols he fired and then he was upon them. He whirled his sabre about his head and lashed out at the standing man and even as he did so he felt the tear of a musket ball ripping his left shoulder and then in a second he was lashing out at the last of the men and he felt the tip of his sword rip through the man's upper arm and then he was spinning his horse looking for... but all had fallen and Tom, with carbine levelled, at the two wounded men, stood firm a few yards away.

It was as if the field of battle had come to England, for horses ran free and men lay dying in a bloody tangle of harness and smoke.

After a moment there was a sudden surge of action with Tom, still mounted on Trojan persuading the horses still yoked to the farm cart to move on and Will running back to fetch his guns and two or three minutes after the start of the attack they were on their way but this time at the best speed that the coach could make.

'Drive on! Drive on! Fast as you can driver!' Will called out to the much frightened driver of the coach.

As Will clambered back onto 'Hector' he felt blood run down his arm beneath his now even more tattered uniform and it was matched by a feeling of faintness which he fought to control. Staring back towards the Inn he caught a glimpse of yet another rider in the distance. A rider who turned his horse in a circle as he observed the field of drama then Will saw the man raise his hand, as if in farewell, and instantly knew who it was. Impossible, he thought, the man in question was still in Belgium or was he? Or was his wound and blood loss affecting him adversely, but even as the rider had turned Will saw that he wore the same green uniform that he did.

Jane had sat, next to her mother, one of her father's pistols in her hand although she had small knowledge of how to use it other than pressing the trigger, as the coach slithered to a standstill and the sound of shots, creaking harness and loud voices shouting but somehow she didn't doubt that she would be able to aim the weapon and then pull the trigger although she did doubt whether she would hit any target unless it was remarkably close. Jane noted that her father was particularly pale and held no weapon and her sister just looked very annoyed at the hold up.

'Your pistol Papa, where is it?' Jane asked.

He looked around so frightened suddenly that Jane knew that if anyone was to fire a pistol it must be her.

Her Major had given her the pistol, just as they departed, saying, 'Only to use as a last resort.' She pressed her face close to the curtain blocking the window of the coach and pulled it back in time to see the highwayman shot from his horse, his pistol flying from his hand, then Tom appearing, looking very pleased with himself. She let herself out of the coach in spite of her father's hands clutching at her and threw down the steps so that she could alight and that was when she saw the Major, sabre in hand, cutting about himself at the barricade, the sun blazing on the shining blade and that was when she saw and heard the shot that hit him just before he struck his assailant.

Jane realized that the action was over when the Major ran blindly past her to his horse and scooping up the fallen weapons he remounted but then he swayed in his saddle and nearly fell; straightened himself and galloped back towards the Inn.

As she climbed back onto the coach, her face pale, Jane thought, he goes to his doom, back to where the trouble had come from.

Will galloped, almost not knowing whence he went just that he couldn't leave his task unfinished; for there was the question of the man in green in front of him.

He had travelled only a few hundred yards when an armed, green clad horsemen emerged from the scrub lining the roadway. He held a carbine and a horse pistol loosely pointing down and had a very worried expression on his face when he called out. 'When I saw it was you sir, I warned them not to proceed; told 'em they'd be in bad trouble if they crossed swords with ye.'

Will reined to a halt in a cloud of glowing golden dust and stared, his head spinning now, at the Corporal. 'What do you do here Tully?'

'The Regiment dismissed me sor; told me that we was disbanded and you had gone, so...'

'And you have taken to highway robbery Tully?'

'Not I, sor, but my companions heard of a mighty treasure being moved for fear of returning soldiers.'

'Tully?' Will's voice was weak, his grip on the saddle insecure.

'Sor?'

'Will you ride with me again?'

'Side by side sor? You and me?' No man could have looked happier.

'Just so Tully; fall in with me, we ride to Cambridge and beyond if you're willing...'

'I'm willing sor; very willing.'

CHAPTER TEN

Mr Barclay's Bank in Cambridge was situated opposite the University and had once been a substantial mansion in that it ran to large iron gates and stone, spike topped walls, onto the street. It took some shouting by the coachman for the guards to open up but once they had done so the party was able to enter the courtyard and then they were safe. Servants came and took the chests containing the valuables watched closely at all times by Lord and Lady Walden and their eldest daughter Alice.

Jane, a worried expression on her face, went to the gate to enquire after the coach's escort only to be told, by the gateman, that they had crossed the Post road to the City of Cambridge Inn. Waiting only a moment or two Jane crossed the highway and entered the coach yard where she saw Tom unsaddling three horses and another green uniformed man attending to the arms that the battle had been fought with. Will Saxethorpe sat slumped on a bench, his sweated hair tangled about his pale face, mirrored with cold sweat, trying hard to stay conscious as he pressed hard on the wounded arm. As he saw Lady Jane coming into the yard, he stumbled to his feet and essayed a short and obviously painful bow to her as she approached.

'You are hurt sir,' it was a statement from her not a question.

'A scratch I fancy Milady,' the man stood swaying before her.

'A scratch indeed and blood drips from your fingers...' she turned to Tom and demanded, 'Why do you let him sit here boy? He needs to be indoors, lying down with a physician called to attend his wound.' She put out a hand to steady the officer and she pulled him down to slump again onto the bench.

Tom looked confused and started to answer. 'The Major said to stable the 'orses and...'

'Go into the Inn Tom and tell them that Lord Walden needs a room, now go!' Tom scurried away into the Inn.

In a few moments he brought men to carry the Major and the party retired into the Inn where he was taken to his own room and Jane supervised the corporal to cut away the blood soaked green tunic from the wound.

'That was my best uniform Milady...' the wounded man croaked, staring up at her with pain filled eyes.

'Now it is most certainly second best if wearable at all.' Jane inspected the dripping, bloody remains of the sleeve by holding it up then dropping it she turned her attention to his blood soaked shirt tearing it from the cuff to the shoulder. 'You have been shot through sir, I think,' she said firmly as she half lifted him to see his back even though he groaned in pain. Frowning, she wondered at her own calmness faced, as she was, by a bloody wound for the first time in her life.

'You are rough with me Milady.' Will's voice half whispered.

'As you have been rough with others sir. You are a soldier and should act like one. You there!' she called to a very puzzled Tully. 'Go at once to the kitchens; I will need a kettle of boiling water and if possible some clean towel or sheeting for bandaging. Go!' she snapped out and Tully jumped for the doorway and was gone in a moment.

'You give orders well Milady,' the Major groaned for now the shock was over and the pain had started.

She looked down at him and half smiled. 'One of my few talents sir. Raised to give orders; then lie back and watch as someone performed them like...'

'Like trained animals?'

She smiled her brilliant smile as she replied. 'Exactly, like trained animals but at times somewhat reluctant.'

Within ten minutes she was bathing the wound and then, in the absence of clean cloth; turning away, she pulled open her chemise and tore a piece of cloth from it to wrap around the wound.

She looks after me, Will thought through the waves of darkness that seemed fit to overwhelm him. She tears her own clothes for bandages for my wound.

He stands the pain well, Jane thought, for there must be pain indeed for where the ball had passed through, the hole, although not that large, was torn, bloody and angry looking already. She was surprised at herself for was not the sight of blood supposed to cause a high bred woman to faint instead all she felt was... love... love for the grievously wounded man.

At that moment the door burst open to reveal an excited Tom with the apothecary from the town, who carried a large leather satchel.

In a little while he had spread, what he said was an old country remedy, on the wound saying that it might, indeed it should be stitched.

'I would not agree to you stitching such a small wound sir,' Will sounded extremely tired and was fighting to stay conscious as he turned his head to almost see his own shoulder, 'Tom will pay you for your trouble...' his voice faded away and his head slumped back.

The apothecary turned to Lady Jane saying as he did so. 'If I may leave this ointment, a small potion and some laudanum, for your husband's pain. The instructions for use are written on the label.'

Lady Jane thought, 'my husband' is his mistake but by the time she had realized and had received the medication it was too late to censure the man and she thought that she liked the sound of it; married and to the Major... her Major.

Jane sat at dinner with her Papa, who was very quiet, staring unseeing down at his plate of stew, and her Mama who talked for both of them. Lady Alice, it seemed, had decided to retire early to her bedchamber in spite of the writing and sending of some letters after they had settled at the Inn.

Jane could only think of the man sleeping in a nearby room; a man who would awake to days of pain. She decided that propriety didn't matter with the sick. She would visit with him later and make sure that he didn't need another visit from physician or apothecary. Jane had no appetite and her mother's constant, heavily embroidered talk of the afternoon's adventure left her oblivious to her questions and observations; she only wanted the meal to finish, to end so that she could...

A candle flame flickered in Will's eyes; the flame weaving, curving away and then towards him, a slim blade of flaming smoke climbing up into the darkness. For a long moment Will could remember nothing of what had happened, then, quite suddenly, he recalled that Tully was here. How was Tully here? He'd left him in Antwerp or was it Ostend, shaken his hand and watched him ride away feeling desolate and now he was here, was he not? But Will couldn't be sure. For a while it seemed that he had been back in Portugal lying under nets his leg hurting like Hell itself but now he thought it wasn't his leg. The day came back in a swirling fog of dust, gunpowder, shot and cold steel but had he done the job? Yes, he thought he had. He'd got to Cambridge and somehow Tully was involved but... The candle flickered and then moved quite a way away the burning image replaced by one infinitely sweeter. My dream goes on, Will thought, I'm seeing a beautiful face... I'm seeing a... I'm seeing Lady Jane... but how could I?

'Are you well Major?' the girl's gentle voice intruded into his dream in the nicest way possible. 'You were shot through and the apothecary gave you...'

The apothecary and Lady Jane; yes, now he remembered everything. The pain was triggered by the memory it seemed but then it faded a little as he struggled to speak, to reply.

'Milady, Lady Jane... I must need thank you for your kind attentions.'

'You saved my family sir. You acted very bravely but got yourself shot.'

'The fortunes of war Milady.' The wounded man hesitated and then asked. 'How are the...?' his voice stumbled to a halt.

She looked down at him wondering what the so pale man was wanting to say.

'The men... the soldiers who attacked us... you... how do they do?' He looked so very worried.

Jane wondered how much of the afternoon he could remember.

'Three died at the scene sir and two are badly wounded. Those two will recover in time for the hangman.'

His sweating unhappy face stared up at her as he said. 'But they are British soldiers, they fought at Waterloo and on the Peninsula.'

'Highway robbery is a capital offense sir, as you must know.' Her voice was firm but a little hesitant.

'But, they fought for England and then England turned away and left them alone... alone.' His exhausted voice almost a sob.

Jane tried to be firm for him, 'England left you alone sir and you did not take to the highway to rob passers by.'

Will fell back a little and looked at this girl, soft lit in the candle light and thought how good it would be if... but no.

His voice was slurred and so tired as he asked, 'If your father could intercede on their behalf... if he...' his eyes closed and he fell asleep.

Jane thought, Papa will be the Magistrate almost for certain and he will sentence them to death and he won't intercede, that was not his way, unlike this man lying here, who took life and then tried to give it back.

The next three days were spent by Will slowly recovering. It was the blood loss that had so weakened him and only a good diet designed to build him up, beef stews, lamb chops and chicken broth were considered sufficient to the task. He was young and healthy so that he quickly regained some of his strength and finally he felt able to talk to Tully and fix some arrangement between them.

He had the man help him down to the coaching yard so that he would have things of passing interest to watch and he could sit in the sun.

'Tully?'

The small Irishman turned to him his face a mass of worried wrinkles, 'Sor?'

'Are you willing to continue in my service even though you may never have to face the shot and shell of a large army again?'

It took Tully a few moments to realize that his master was being humorous.

'It was the happiest time of my life so far sor... being with you.'

Isn't that good, Will thought, my servant likes me. 'Good, Tully. I missed you even though I had found young Tom. He's a good lad is Tom. Tully, I will expect you to instruct him where possible and I don't mean in drinking beer. Look after Tom for me won't you Tully. He's young and needs to be nurtured.' There was a long silence between the two men and then Will asked. 'When did the Walden's leave?'

'Two days ago sor; they left early with a company of sojers, militiamen, two officer's on 'orses.'

Will thought. So Lord Walden has run for home after his fright and he owes me ten guineas so when I am more recovered...

Later Tom came and sat next to him in front of the small fire that had been lit in the tavern; for Will seemed to feel the evening chill. 'How you feeling sor?'

'I feel stronger each and every day that passes Tom and I hope that you have kept up your reading practice?'

'Aye sor, that I have.' He produced his book of fairy tales from inside his jacket and opened it.

Will noticed that Tom seemed a mite cleaner and definitely didn't smell so bad so maybe Tully was keeping him up to scratch or he was getting used to the smell. 'Tom...' he asked after a moment for thought, 'Could you ask the Innkeeper how much money we have spent in his Inn.'

'Oh sor!' Tom exclaimed, '...that Lord Walden left a sum for the Innkeeper to look after your requi... your require... your needs. And he gave me some coins that he said were for you sor. Tom pulled a simple draw string leather purse from an inner pocket and handed it to his master with a tentative smile.

Will looked at the purse. 'Thank you Tom, and the Lady Jane?'

'She said, she told me to tell you, that she would see you when you came to collect your brother.'

My poor brother, thought Will, had been dead nearly two weeks and he was still not buried. Poor Lawrence, so brave, so honourable and now rotting in some common stable.

'We go tomorrow Tom. Please tell Tully and the Innkeeper. We will leave just after breakfast and ride to Saffron House then we can start for home. Start for home again....' his voice fading away, his face a frowning mask.

I think not, thought Tom. He is still far too weak, although on the mend. Well enough to travel in a carriage perhaps but he would not be fighting anyone for a good long while yet.

The weather held and every field, that the three horsemen slowly passed, had its share of men wielding scythes with women gathering the wheat into wind shivering golden stooks behind them. A world of gold and white, thought Will, as he sat 'Hector' walking slowly through the afternoon sunshine. The gold of the ripe wheat, the faded white of the men's smocks, the monotonous metronome sweep of light blazing blades making him dream of battles long gone, of men dying, of blood and death. Will knew somehow in his dazed, pain and laudanum filled mind that his days of fighting were coming to an end now; that he could never ride onto a battlefield and feel again the excitement, the lust for life... for death.

Will could feel the closeness of Tully at his right shoulder and Tom almost touching on his left and felt that he had real friends, companions for life he hoped and let himself drift off into another day dream where the face of a girl swam through the encroaching darkness; a smile and... something else.

Tully had thrust out his battle exercised arm to hold his Master upright in the saddle and at the same time he glanced across at the boy, Tom. He's a good lad, he thought, stays close and worries about the Master. Isn't like other boys with their stupid games he just thinks of this man, bit like me, Tully thought. They'd not had a lot of time for talk, just a few meals taken together, mostly in silence but then...

'You were with him in Spain then Tully? During the wars there?'

Tully had leaned back to light his pipe and puffed twice before answering. 'Was indeed young Tom, met him on the Torres Vedras; that's the defences that the Duke had built in Portugal, while Nappy was roaring around Spain. Sergeant gave me this very young boy soldier, who was an aide de camp to the Duke, messenger more like, but he needed a servant just like all the other officers then when we went a campaigning I found out that he was a very fine soldier, tough, hard and a very good fighter. Was given command of a company of the hardest men and it didn't give him one moments trouble. They all seemed to fall in love with him even when the battles grew real hard.'

Tom smiled at him from across the half unconscious body of the Major, then asked, 'How long were you together?'

'Nigh on four years, I'd say, gone in a flash it has. Even when we were charging the enemy I just knew that we'd be alright. One wound he sustained in ten battles and skirmishes, got a bayonet thrust into his leg but he didn't stop, he kept leading us in charge after charge until his leg was as red as his tunic with the blood dripping down.'

'He can still fight can he not? Did you see him? Shooting, slashing about him...' Tom's voice was excited.

'I observed you Tom; you kept your calm, acted the sojer like a real man. Reckon you saved the Major with that shot at the highwayman.'

And Tom sat the horse a little straighter, just as the Major did.

CHAPTER ELEVEN

Two nights spent wondering how he is, thought Jane. I should have stayed by his side save that then my father and mother would have... I could not, for nothing has been said, not even a real word from him and anyway my parents would reject him out of hand. Too poor and not noble enough for them but so very, very charming. Will he come? Jane had been upset that her father had remembered to pay him off so that there was no real necessity for the man to come to the house; none at all but Jane thought that when he came to get his cart she would see him, talk to him...

The next morning Jane, mooning around in her bedchamber, noticed the ostler from The Swan Inn walking up the drive and felt a shiver of anticipation run through her body. She'd left five shillings with the Innkeeper to keep her informed as to when the Major returned to his Inn and she knew that this man was the messenger. She wondered at herself, at her reaction to this... this male person. She'd been raised with one purpose in mind; that of procreation with a person yet to be selected but most certainly someone from the Quality. Hopefully a first son so that the question of wealth would be swiftly solved but Jane had read enough to know that the number of such men was few and that settling for a curate with a good living was much more the likely for her.

She finished dressing swiftly, plainly, in pale blue cotton and then hastened down to the Hall.

The two companions had laid the semi-conscious man gently onto his bed; pulled off his boots and then Tom whispered to him. 'We've arrived sor and you cannot fall as you lie on a wide bed. You must sleep, rest. We shall watch over you, guard you.'

Tully thought, my master has another servant that loves him. He is indeed that kind of man; a man who loves and is loved in return.

A little later a chaise turned into the coach yard and dropped off a young lady in a sky blue dress who, after a swift glance about the bustling yard, hurried within the Inn.

The dreams are pleasant, Will thought, with the girl coming back so very clear and it was just as if she was there with him, changing the dressing on his shoulder, wiping his pained brow and giving him a sip of... He woke fully to find that he was in her arms as she supported him, a spoon to his lips.

'Lady Jane, you are here,' he whispered.

'And have been for some time sir. You half sleep, dream and struggle with the pain in your shoulder.' Her gentle face, hair falling in a soft wave half hiding her eyes was so close. Their two faces were almost touching together and then she smiled as she realized that he was on the mend, that bad wound or no he would recover.

'I... I am feeling... feeling all the better on finding you here,' he whispered.

'I too sir,' she gasped out then stopped wondering what she meant then knowing, fully realizing that this was the man, the only man, that she could ever want, need, give herself to and without thinking she kissed his pain sweated brow.

His smiling reaction was reward enough she thought. My father would never allow her to marry an itinerant soldier. She would be cut off from the family and its money; she would be poor and she wondered if that would matter to her. A cottage in the country? Maybe that was the way that happiness lay for her, for him?

He spoke, whispered. 'I must sleep and recover myself then perhaps I should come and visit you, speak to your father...' and he slipped away into the comforting darkness where no thoughts, no decisions need be made.

'Where have you been? You are flushed of face...' Lady Walden asked of her youngest daughter.

Lady Alice said, malice dripping from her voice. 'She's been into the town; I suspect that she visits the wounded hero from Cambridge. How is he Jane?'

Jane finished taking off her hat and handed it to the downstairs maid before replying. 'It's true, I have visited with Major Saxethorpe..'

'How very improper!' Lady Walden half shouted out.

'And did you hold his hand?' Alice asked, a snide smile on her perfect lips.

'He is still unwell. His wound mends slowly; a wound I would like to remind you mother that was incurred in your service and yet you seem uncaring.' Jane's voice was calmer now and she thought that perhaps she had grown up, become more mature, in the last few days.

'He's been paid, has he not?' Lady Walden's voice was harsher now. 'He should depart and leave you alone.'

'And if I don't wish to be left alone?' The white marble hall echoed to their raised voices. The three women stared at each other, each with some degree of enmity.

'If he stays here or near here, then I shall have to send you away for I will not countenance you thinking of marriage to this...this itinerant, no good soldier.'

'About whom you know nothing.' Jane said calmly whilst thinking that she too knew almost nothing; a letter to his brother and sister, a mention in Dispatches; some idea of his status as a third son. Jane turned and hurried up the curving staircase to her bedchamber, stared after by the angry faces of her mother and sister.

In her room she threw herself onto her bed dry eyed with anger at her sister and mother's attitude thinking that it was over, soon he would be gone and she would never see him again.

On the morning of the second day Will felt well enough to dress and go down to sit in the sun. Half carried by his friends he felt safe and in a strange way, happy. He thought he hadn't seen Lady Jane since Cambridge and Will was not so sure that she had been there although Tully and Tom assured him that she had indeed been by his side. 'She come here sor, to change the bandages on your shoulder, yesterday it were, but you kept fallin into a doze.

'We left Cambridge a bit too soon, I think.

'I did say, din' I Tully?'

'You did indeed boy; said not to ride but you would insist sor.'

'I wanted... I wanted to get started with going home.'

The two servants glanced, with amused expressions on their faces, at each other for they remembered how he had muttered all the time about his Lady Jane.

The sun was warm and he felt; he felt as if recovery was on the way and perhaps if he had another dose of the medicine?

'No sor!' Tom was quick, snatching up the tall brown bottle and carrying it away across the room, almost shouting his disapproval, '...that laudanum is most dangerous. You start and you can't stop. Pretty soon you in an opium den, sucking on the pipe, always sucking.'

Laudanum, thought Will, yes; use too much and you were caught, trapped. It kept away the throbbing ache but in the end.... 'You're right Tom. It's good when unwell but not so good...'

The Innkeeper came to see him as they ate a cold pie and some potatoes with beer for their lunch. 'Your appetite has returned sir?'

'It never really left but I had some trouble finding my mouth and then more trouble with the chewing; all my strength seemed to have left me.'

'Some friends of yours came calling, at least said that they were friends.' The Innkeeper looked down the street to see if the noonday coach was coming.

'Friends sir? I have few enough friends in this world.'

'Three priests sir. Came asking if a gent answering to your description had happened past; said that you would have some form of conveyance, likely a coach or chaise.' He looked away, an amused expression on his lips.

Will looked up at the man and wondered at the rigmarole that he made of such a commonplace event. 'And you told them of me and my cart?'

'In this Inn, a gentleman's life is private especially if he chooses to pay in advance to store his cart in one of my barns?'

'Privacy is important to you then?'

'They were very aggressive and somewhat rude sir, not at all priestly,' the chubby man smiled, '...I was not inclined to give away the information about you and they were not inclined to ask nicely or to pay a little something.'

Ahh, thought Will, money speaks, as always. 'I am grateful to you Innkeeper that my privacy has not been disturbed by the ungrateful; and so...' he pulled his purse from his deep waistcoat pocket and finding a guinea he handed it to the man. 'They said nought else landlord?'

'They did say, amongst themselves, that your brother was getting most anxious.'

'Ah yes, my brother,' and Will wondered why John should send some of his acolytes to look for him. Perhaps he was worried about the unburied elder brother but knowing John, as he once had, he suspected that it would be the first time that he had ever thought such a thought.

It was as they finished their cold collation of meats and warm potatoes that a chaise rolled past driven by a footman and seated behind was a young woman, bonneted, in dark green and carrying a basket. Will recognized her instantly and half rose in his seat then subsided weakly and nodded his bow to her half seen glance.

It is him, she thought, he is better and is still here, that is good, at least now I can stop worrying about... about the man. She remembered with deep embarrassment her talk with her mother and sister two nights ago where she had broached the question of her marrying beneath her station and she still shuddered at the stream of angry vituperation, from her sister and her mother that had been poured on the very idea. Her Mama had two possible young men in mind it seemed. Both stupid and dissolute, Jane thought, and I will never give myself to them. They may take me but go willing I will not. All she could think of was the man she had just passed and she could still feel his eyes fixed upon her back as if they were living entities. She fought against turning but she could not help herself. She turned to find his eyes most certainly fixed upon her and she snapped at the footman driving the chaise, 'Take me to...' she hesitated realizing that the tale of her pursuing the soldier would soon be common knowledge, '...to the Post Office, I must...'

Will saw her turn; saw her sudden look; saw the chaise begin to turn in the wide empty road and knew that somehow she would come to him. Then he suffered a terrible feeling of emptiness when he realized that the little carriage was going to the Post Office on the other side of the wide dusty road.

The Post Office counter, was a new addition to the General Store and the staff were very pleased to see Lady Jane coming in; for the local nobility were important to have as customers. They were somewhat surprised to see the door open not long after to reveal an officer, apparently badly wounded, supported by two men who half carried him in and seated him in the only chair. His green uniform top was clean and well pressed but was sun faded and had some silver threads dangling down from the frogging on his chest; he looked as pale as a ghost with staring eyes.

Lady Jane turned from a mirror where she was trying on a broad rimmed sun hat even though the season was well advanced. 'Major. It is good to see you up and about,' she smiled tentatively.

'Yes, I am about, but I must buy some clothes for my men and perhaps a jacket for myself; my last being somewhat cut about, Milady.' His eyes were fixed on hers in the mirror, as she adjusted the hat, at the same time seeing only him.

'I'm sorry...' her breath came short and she took off the hat and unfeelingly selected another.

Two members of the staff came forward and Will said to them, 'Find something for my man here. He can no longer wear that uniform, the regiment is disbanded and the boy....' his voice almost faded away he was so distracted and weak, '...he needs... whatever he wants, for he saved my life I fancy.' His concentration was so intense on the girl in the mirror that she nearly forgot to put on the next hat her eyes locked with the man's reflection.

The two servants were led away to a kind of men's clothing portion of the store where they were helped to try on clothing of the ready made variety.

Will stared at the girl and then said, half whispered, sotto voce, 'I missed you by my side, Milady.'

Jane was frozen by his look and his words and then managed to gasp out, 'My family would be most distressed if they knew.'

'That you helped the man who saved them from highway robbery?'

'They have old fashioned views on...' she could not go on.

'Marriage?'

Jane felt her heart almost stop so great was the shock. 'Marriage sir? What mention is there of marriage?'

'I thought that all young women think on marriage, do they not?'

She stared into his eyes finally saying. 'There is a good deal of...' she seemed to shake herself back into the world of commonsense. 'We must not talk or think of such a word, in fact I must be going home.'

Will smiled at her sadly and said quietly. 'I think that I said I would come and take my leave of... your family and in particular, your father.'

'Please do not sir, he is not so well,' she whispered and half turned away to pick up another hat at which she stared sightlessly. 'We pack for our annual visit to Newmarket, for the yearling sales. We have a good number of horses for sale and then there's the racing. My Papa...'

'Likes to gamble and maybe a year of work by the stable master will be wasted,' he paused, most of the fatigue seeming to have passed, '...but I will not come if you do not wish it,' Will was unhappy to see the relief cross her face so he said. 'So I will likely see you at Newmarket, for that town is on my route to...' Will hesitated, suddenly unable to see the route clearly, for Ely Cathedral lay only ten or so miles from the racetrack and home was much further on.

Jane felt sudden relief at him not coming to the house where she knew that he would be rejected out of hand but the idea that they might, indeed almost certainly would, meet again was most delightful to her, for she knew that the meeting might be considered fortuitous. 'It would be pleasant to meet with you at Newmarket although my father, my mother and my sister might not think so.'

It is as well that my mother and father are not alive to monitor my romantic associations, Will thought, but he knew that his very religious sister Anne and his brother the Bishop would do all that they could to make sure that he married a rich widow at the very least or if he was lucky an heiress in her own right.

'Look sor!' Tully stood before him totally changed. No more uniform but a simple tweed jacket and waistcoat with corduroy trousers and riding boots. Tom stood by him looking very pleased with his selection of clothing for his new friend.

'Perfect Tully. You look very smart and not at all like a soldier.'

'Only ting sor, we don't look like how a servant should look either.'

'That's right Tully, you look... you look like a gentleman's companions, friends.'

Lady Jane surged to her feet and swept away between the three men and only Will heard her whispered, 'Goodbye, sir'

It was two more days and nights before Will felt able to ride without pain. As for the shooting of muskets and the wielding of a sabre he trusted that he would meet with no one of a belligerent nature before or indeed after arriving home.

His little party prepared to leave with the cart's axles well greased and its cargo tied down, all the boxes and chests stowed and a goodly supply of straw and oats filling all the spaces left. Will noted that Tully and Tom had left a man sized space heavily lined with a thick bed of straw with all the guns loaded and carefully held in place so that the man in the cart would have good position for defending and Will knew that the space had been left for him to rest in.

He had spent the last two days wondering if he should go to Saffron House and say farewell to the Lord of the Manor and his family and decided against it when, as they took the Post road that led to Newmarket, he quite suddenly changed his mind. He was wearing his newly repaired, washed and pressed uniform with a black sling to support his arm and sitting gingerly on 'Hector's' back, feeling somewhat better in himself and thought that presenting himself in good condition might help his cause. Bidding his worried companions wait at the gate he walked his horse up the tree-lined drive. Dismounting, sliding with some difficulty off his horse under the portico, he handed the reins to a waiting groom and went slowly up the steps to the door.

The baronet was seated in his study staring at a desk covering jumble of the books of the estate accounts when Major Saxethorpe was announced and he wandered out into the Hallway to greet his visitor whom he not seen since the journey to Cambridge.

He stared, glassy eyed, at the soldier standing at the foot of the staircase, wondering who he was, wondering. 'Good morning sir?' He said in a faltering voice.

'It is Major Saxethorpe.' Will frowned, worried by the man's odd memory loss.

'Ah a Major; you have hurt your arm?'

'The gunshot; the other day?' Will thought that the man's mind wandered somewhat.

The older man scratched at his lopsided wig struggling to think then said, 'Ah yes... a gunshot, the other day?'

'In your service, the highwaymen?'

'Oh yes, of course, the highwaymen,' Lord Walden turned and walked slowly away.

'I improve by the day sir.' Will called after him then looked around the somewhat over large, over furnished, marble ornamented space hoping to catch a glimpse of the youngest daughter thinking that the aristocracy are all mad. 'You go to the Yearling sales at Newmarket?' A remark half shouted across the hall at the retreating back of the old man with his rolling, shambling walk.

The door of the Drawing Room opened quite suddenly as if his voice had called the house to life and out came Lady Alice, a little flustered as if she had expected a more important person. She wore a brilliant green gown with no trace of mourning about her and she stopped when she saw the young officer, looking quite dashing, booted, spurred and caped, his fur shako tucked under his right arm, his left in a black sling.

'Major,' she cried out, '...allow me to thank you for your heroism on the road,' she swirled up to him, her hair a brilliant silver white with a fine smile in place on her face.

'It was my... pleasure, to guard someone like yourself Milady.'

'I thought the whole thing most exciting; yes, and you are recovered from your wound?'

'A little sore still but undoubtedly on the mend.' Will looked around, realizing now that it was unlikely that he would be given even a cup of tea.

They spoke a few sentences more out of politeness then silence fell on the two of them and Will realized that this was his cue to leave so, with one last glance around, he bowed and made his excuses.

Going back into the Drawing Room Alice went and sat by her sister to say, 'Your Major was just here....' she observed the way that her sister's head came sharply up and colour appeared instantly on her cheeks.

'My Major?'

'Saxe something, our hero from the road... him, the poor one on the farm cart.' Alice noted that Jane's breath now came short and she was having difficulty not moving. 'He's off to Newmarket four days early but his cart is very slow he says.' Alice went and sat at her harp playing a run or two as emphasis for each line that she said. 'Or he may go to Ely, to the Cathedral for some reason.'

To bury his beloved brother and for his other brother, Jane thought.

'...or he may go home. Does he have parents I wonder, he lives somewhere near the coast, perhaps they fish or something'

Jane sat there for a while longer, wishing that he hadn't come to the house, wishing that he'd stayed, wishing... Then she got to her feet and went to the piano forte where she played the opening bars of the 'Moonlight Sonata' hoping that he might hear and just as he rode away, he did, with a smiling glance back at the house.

She knows, Will thought, she feels as do I.

CHAPTER TWELVE

The yard in front of the tavern at Stump Cross, on the Icknield Way, was empty as the cart slowly rumbled past. A smocked and straw hatted Will noted the absence of soldiery, drunken or otherwise and assumed that the militia had been in attendance and driven them all away. Sitting next to Tom as he drove, he was reassured knowing that Tully sat in the belly of the cart, a musket to hand, ready for trouble.

Will had studied the route but was still undecided as to whether to head for home or for Ely Cathedral and then there was the Walden family who would head to Newmarket in the next few days. He couldn't be sure that his brother would be at home in Saxethorpe, much more likely would he be at the centre of his Diocese unless, and that was when he remembered the three priests who had been looking for him and at almost that exact moment he saw three dark shapes caught in silhouette against the dust from a large coach just leaving the Toll Gate. There was, he knew, no chance of avoiding them and no question of outrunning them so...

'Just ignore the priests Tom. Tully, let me do the talking.'

Tom said. 'Them'll just know that you is a gent sor from the way you speak like. How about you act like you a farmer and let me do all the talking; never mistake me for a gent.'

Will looked at the boy, with his sun browned face and his hair awry blowing in the wind and knew that once again he was right; so he nodded and tilted his straw hat over his face and leaned back a little to snooze; just saying. 'Keep your head down Tully unless I ask you to appear; for we have three men a side do we not.'

They slowly got closer and Will, watching slit eyed from under his straw hat, hoped that the cart would pass muster. Closer still and the three black figures gathered together then moved down to the tollgate.

'Hoi! Driver!' One dark figure shouted out in the unmistakeable accent of East London.

Tom reining in, called out, 'Dus I pays you the toll sor? Master give me a shillin for to hurry up to Newmark't; so if you could open up the gate...' Tom held out his shilling and smiled tentatively at the three tall black clad men who somehow could not have looked less priestly with their unshaven chins and mean expressions.

'Where be you agoin'?' The leader of them asked in a strong Cockney accent.

'I just told you, din' I? Newmark't yearlin sales. Master wants to buy himself a horse....' Tom knew that he'd said the wrong thing with three fine war horses following the cart but he carried on bravely, '...them's his brother's' he waved vaguely back' '...and he wants...'

'Three fine horses and him asleep even though we talk?'

Tom gestured at Will saying with a sneer in his voice. 'Him's not the Master; him's a thatcher that I'm givin a ride to. Master's Lord Walden and he wants us to set up for... In a few days time he'll be coming. He's a magistrate and Justice of the Peace and he'll be needin his horse's for gettin about the fair grounds.'

Two of the men had walked around the cart and realized that they couldn't peer in for the cover was tied real tight save for a few loops at the front...

'We're looking for a cart or carriage. A heavy loaded cart and two men. Have you seen....'

'It be gettin on for the early harvest of the spring wheat sor, every road has its share of carts laden down with the wheat and straw. Where's the gate keeper?'

Will thought that Tom played the part far better that he would ever be able to do but at the same time he wondered to himself and at the suspicion that seemed to have formed in his mind. Why would his brother seek him? Did these priests want to harm him and if so why? Will knew that his sister Anne, who had raised him after their mother's death in giving birth to him, loved and cherished him. Not so John, but the Holy Boy of Saxethorpe as he was known then, had always treated him properly apart from the odd remark or secretive pinch. Yes, that was true, John did not love him. John loved God that was for sure and John loved John and had cut his own path through life. Being... acting saintly from the first time he attended services but the loss of his mother may well have changed him and he had made some remarks that seemed to indicate that he thought it Will's fault.

'If you see a cart like yours tell them that a reward awaits them at this Toll gate; if they be the one, the one we want.'

The burly gate-keeper coming down from his cottage looked at the priests with a suspicious eye and took Tom's proffered shilling. Tom looked down at the dark clerical figures and felt danger coming from them so he said, 'Most certainly sor. I'll be sure to tell everyone I meet. How much is the reward then?'

'Two guineas boy, just for helping the Church...' but the priest's voice was drowned out by the opening of the gate, the crack of Tom's whip, the rumble of wheels and the clatter of metal shod hooves.

After a few minutes, Will whispered, 'Thank thee Tom. That was well done indeed.'

'They din't believe me though sor.....' his statement was flat but certain, '...they just couldn't say nuthin with the gatekeeper there and they couldn't search the cart noither. So they just let us go but them'll follow as soon as they have a conveyance.'

Will looked back, a worried frown on his face, before he said, 'Take the next side lane that you see Tom. We must seek cover.'

Tully popped up from under the canvas cover and breathed deeply, 'It's a mite stuffy under there sor.'

Will thought to himself, my brother sends men who are not what they seem. They look like priests but do not act it. Unshaven with dirty and horny hands, they look like and almost certainly are villains wearing the black robes of the clergy. Where would they get such clothes? Ely Cathedral; almost for certain.

'They are up to no good Tom, Tully. For some reason they seek us, to harm us I think; so we'll go to Newmarket instead of Ely and we'll see what occurs.' Will pulled his straw hat down over his face to shield it from the sun, which was now high in the sky and feeling very hot.

At the next lane entrance Tom slowly turned the farm cart onto the rough surface and then up the shallow hill that rose in front of them.

After a while Will heard Tom say, 'Dullingham is the next village along by here...'

He heard, as if from a great distance, Tully say, 'See the markers on the trees Tom? Diddycoys, the Romany must be hereabouts.'

Will was waking reluctantly but he was suddenly wide awake for gypsies meant trouble to law abiding folk. 'Where Tully?' His head came up, his face worried.

'All about us Master, the marks lead down along here. Must be the horse sales; the Romany love a horse sale; a chance to steal and deal.'

'I always thought that you had a touch of the gypsy Tully?' Will peered about him, looking forward then turning to look back.

'Born and bred sir. Lived in a caravan until I was old enough for the army then...'

'Then we met on the Torres Vedras.'

'And a very comfortable billet that were sir.'

'So you're a diddycoy then Tully?' How could I not know that, Will thought. 'Think that you could talk us through their camp when it comes, maybe hide us for a while?'

'Most certainly I could talk the lingo and baffle them with me smooth ways.' Tully's dark, saturnine, big nosed face lit up with the delight of it.

Will felt so very tired suddenly so he said, 'Tully, hop up here and let me take your place. You can wear this smock and the straw hat and I can go back to sleep. If we meet the Romany you decide what to say. If we meet those priests you tell them what Tom said; we are off to the races and the Master's doing a bit of horse selling.'

It was an hour later that Tom heard horses behind him, horses being whipped, horses or their owners in something of a hurry. The sunlit lane was narrow, the hedgerows pressing in trying to hide the track so that there was, for the moment, nowhere to pass. He turned rising up in his seat and jogged the dozing Tully to wakefulness for behind them was a black painted coach and four, the driver and passengers on top all garbed in black robes. A coach of Death thought Tom, not of Hope but...

'What is it lad?' Tully asked.

Tom gestured over his shoulder to where four black horses snorted and sweated into the warmth of the afternoon.

'Major, stay down in the cart for we have company, God fearing company.' Tully called down.

From inside the cart Will muttered. 'Turn off if you can Tom, let them pass if they will.'

A clearing appeared ahead, smoke drifting across the lane and suddenly they emerged into a large Romany encampment with many bright painted caravans formed up into a circle, strings of horses and a good number of brawny young men who slowly stood and moved forward towards the lane. Tom urged his horses to the right leaving the lane free for the coach to pass and it did; it had to for the Romany are not noted for their religious inclination.

Will was later to think that the reappearance of Tully and the fact that he had been born to the Romany was God's way of saving them for he talked his way into the camp with a mixture of the truth and a fabricated romance of battles and bodies and of pursuit by religious fanatics.

Tom settled his horses and the cart just off to one side upwind of the camp and then they made a fire and prepared their evening meal.

At the doorway of the nearest caravan appeared two gaily dressed young women who idly watched the three men. The sight of the making of a fire, the producing of three rabbits, a cooking pot, two loaves of bread, onions, a slab of farmhouse cheese, potatoes. The skinning of the rabbits, the chopping of onions, the rough peeling of potatoes, the boiling of the water in the pot all seemed of unending interest to the two young women. A boy, a Romany and a man with his arm in a sling. Who was he and why did the others do all the work they asked themselves.

Will's horses, securely fixed on lines, grazed the long grass on the edge of the clearing, looked very fine and would be worth a deal of money at the horse fair the days following so one of the girls whispered to her sister then wandered off to talk to others of her family.

As the sky darkened; sitting around the blaze, the rabbit stew bubbling merrily, Will, feeling the pangs of hunger, watched the life of the camp then, feeling the fatigue of day sweeping over him leant back but was brought to wakefulness by an urgent whisper from Tully.

'Those girlies you been watching master. They be goin around the camp talkin, pointin to us.'

'So?' Will thought that the girls looked pretty and wild, like the girls in Spain.

'The horses sor; they'll take the horses if they can.'

To be left with the cart and no horses; the thought was unbearable.

'So, what do we do?' Will asked.

'We double the lines on the horses and we get the carbines from the cart and watch. Tom and I will share the duty, you'd best rest...' and so the short summer night slowly passed. The fire was kept going, always a man or boy walking about holding a gun and looking serious.

Will lay on the straw in the cart, the horse-pistols to hand and worried about it for a few seconds then fell asleep, firmly asleep.

Close to dawn, when Tom was on watch, the horses started to snicker and then one of them neighed. Tom immediately shouted, 'Tully!' then running forward a few paces until he was clear of the camp he fired his gun into the air. In an instant, it seemed, the camp came alive with the gypsy horses, unused to gunfire, rearing up and neighing wildly. Tully ran forward, his carbine aimed into the darkness, Will reared up in the cart a pistol in each hand and resisted firing after the shadows running from beneath him for he knew that they must be gypsies from the same camp that they were in. The horses, battle trained, did not rear as ordinary horses would but they did snort, paw the ground and neigh frantically then Tully was amongst them, calming them, his long knife glittering in the remains of the firelight, to check the leashes, the double lines.

'All well sor, but oi'll be staying awake until dawn, shouldn't be too long now.'

'Thanks Tully, unfortunate that... The Romany will be upset.'

'They steal from each other all the time sor... You have to watch what you've got... In the mornin you and me'll go see the leader... maybe you could slip him a little silver... they like that.'

CHAPTER THIRTEEN

The day after the Major had departed Jane fell into a deep sadness knowing that the chance of them meeting again was remote even if they were both headed for the great Horse Fair and Races at Newmarket. It was such a very large affair with the nobility and the gentry kept well separated from the rough hoi polloi but there was a chance and since God had thrown them together perhaps he would do so again. Jane was not of a religious inclination but she did find herself praying to the All Mighty in the hope that... Stupid, she thought, he and his cart will be lost in the huge swirling mass of humanity and the horses and then she remembered that one of the pastimes that her Major seemed to enjoy was cards; gambling and the place for that was the Stewards Club, where the Walden's stayed each season, where a smartly uniformed man might gain easy entry and Jane could see, in her minds eye, a red uniformed officer stamping, spurs jingling, into the gaming rooms.

The sales didn't start until the Thursday, one day on, so Will decided that now that they had become almost part of the diddycoys he would wait for one day to give his arm some rest and exercise and maybe do something about his clothes. His German uniform was really destroyed now. The green woolen jacket torn to ribbons in places, the silver frogging hanging in tatters and he knew that he could no longer wear it in any circumstance so he threw the jacket onto the fire.

There was a scream and a young girl threw herself at the fire to rescue the smouldering jacket.

Will was astounded, amazed at her antics but Tully said, 'The Romany waste nothing sor. She'll make something pretty out of that, you'll see.' He smiled at the girl who was about ten or eleven, '...here, Missy,' giving her a couple of pennies, '...see what can you turn for the Major here, a jacket would be good, a bandanna for his head, a scarf for his arm maybe.'

In five minutes half the women from the caravans had gathered around him to find something that would fit, that would make him look like one of them.

An hour or two later, the green jacket had black cotton sleeves, the silver frogging had gone and was replaced with dark red and green ribbons that gave it almost a festive look, his own black pants were still useable if a little stained but when they sewed for him a red, black and green bandanna to bind tightly around his head concealing his long fair hair Will knew that he had found his disguise. He looked and felt just like a diddycoy, a Romany. With his long knife tucked into his belt he knew he was one of them and they cheered him so much like them was he now so he climbed back into the cart and rummaged around to find his guitar case.

Everyone watched with interest as he opened the box to reveal the old Spanish instrument that he'd won in a card game in Spain. Such was the time spent waiting for something to happen in his years there that he had got one of the Spanish Militia to teach him some simple tunes, something of the country and after two years of practice, sitting alone and playing nearly every day he had attained some degree of skill and confidence that only his damaged shoulder might impede him. He sat before the fire and tuned the strings and he could feel the evening coming on and the Romany gathering around him so he started with a gentle love song which he sang in Spanish then he segued into a flamenco dance with its crashing crescendo's. The fire lit clearing, the flames casting deep shadows and quite naturally a dancing girl and then her beau came forward and within a few minutes the clearing spun with dancer's shadows. Feet pounding the dust, hands clapping the ancient rhythms, skirts swirling, raised hands clicking fingers keeping the tempo, soulful ululations spilling from the women's throats. This was their music, a part of them mislaid over time but just waiting to emerge and now it did as Will played into the night. A night where cider and beer jugs passed from hand to hand and for a little while, happiness returned to the Romany.

Tom came to Will as he took a drink of the cider during a short break from playing and asked. 'Would you be teachin a 'companion' to play such an instrument sor?'

Will looked at the shadowy faced boy whose tangled brown hair seemed to flame red in the fire-light and nodded slowly. 'It takes a deal of time Tom. Only practice will affect a skill in the art of music making but for you, a carrier with his own cart and horses, the guitar would while away the hours on the road most pleasantly. So yes, you can learn...' And, Will thought, one day, if the boy keeps up his studies, I will have to buy him his own instrument.

The brown and gold Walden family coach, overheated by the last of the evening sun, moved as fast as the four grey horses could shift it. At twenty two miles it was a comfortable days journey on a Post road, except that Lord Walden's nervousness about highwaymen meant that speed seemed to be of the essence, that as well as the arming of the footmen and driver.

Jane suspected that her father carried rather too much money about him and that his main intent at Newmarket was to spend it. She did not, could not understand the desire by some, mostly men but certainly some women, to gamble away their wealth. Her father could barely constrain himself when near the gambling tables and having created his own small den for the playing of whist and 'loo' was not above throwing away a whole night's takings in foolish wagers. Her sister too, appeared to be infected with the same desire. The idea that you could win money for no effort was one that came easily to the wealthy since that was what they had done for generations but now a year's earnings could be won or lost in a few moments and she had seen the sick look on her father's face as he lost and almost the same look when he won, very curious indeed. The Major too seemed infected with the same disease except that he played most carefully only risking when winning seemed possible. Jane hated these excursions to race-tracks although the Yearling Sales always held her interest. She had made a point of learning as much as possible from her father's horse trainer although failure was the main characteristic of her Papa's ventures, in horses, in cards, in the newly popular roulette. He just couldn't win and Jane suspected that he would run out of money very, very soon and then what would the women do?

Inside, the coach was warm, too warm, hot really. Jane felt perspiration run down her spine from the nape of her neck and kept her eyes firmly on the passing scenery. Her father sat opposite her next to her mother but they didn't speak to each other. Lord Walden sat staring at the small, heavy chest on his lap. The top was a panelled and engraved metal plaque showing birds that seemed to be singing to each other and it was a favourite of Jane's since it normally sat on a table in the Drawing Room and had bon bon's, glacéed almonds, in it. She suspected that now it contained all the money they had in the world; a lot of cash but not enough for Lord Walden whose sweat dripped with some insistence onto the shiny metal.

Lady Walden had not been happy since getting home from Belgium. Her husband; something had happened to her husband. The suave, assured man had gone somewhere and a frightened and puzzled creature had taken his place. He seemed to be only half aware of where he was and what was happening around him and the journey to Cambridge to pay off the bank loan had in some way pushed him further into his own dark world for now he had few debts but little money.

What would she do? He was dying, of course, but what of was not so obvious. It didn't seem to be something you could catch but it was something bad for it came from within. She knew that he'd borrowed money against the estate...a mortgage...over a certain time and he had managed to pay back the money but now they had so little and everything depended on the Yearling Sales. They had some very good young horses and they should fetch a good price but now another problem had arisen. Lord Walden had announced; not just told her, announced; that he would win back the difference, it was just a question of being scientific in the way that you placed wagers, and then they would be safe again but Lady Walden knew that he would lose and that Saffron House would have to be sold and their comfortable lives would be over.

Sir Rupert Marlbeck was favourite, Alice thought. Sir Charles was a poor second at best. It was a question of money and breeding. Rupert was a first son and his father, the Earl, was old and unwell, the estate unencumbered by debt, mortgage or the pretensions of younger brothers, just an assortment of sisters and cousins. Charlie had prospects but they were, at best, second rate since he was a second son. His married elder brother had a pregnant young wife who should pod fairly soon. If it was a boy then Charlie, charming though he was, was gone; fallen at the first fence, outstripped in the first furlong let alone the last.

Lord Walden sat, the motion of the carriage rocking him from side to side and the rhythm of the rocking seemed to sing inside him. I must win; always double the last losing wager; that was the answer. I know that it doesn't always work but this time it must, it must, it must... it must.

He sits there muttering to himself, Jane thought. She'd heard, indeed she'd known, when she was younger, about madmen and women, those creatures who went through what remained of their lives muttering to themselves and sometime shouting out some remark, some comment, some very odd order. Grandpapa had been like that, she thought, and one day they had taken him away to an asylum. Papa had never been very nice to her because she had not turned out to be the boy that he wanted, that he needed; but he had never beaten her or locked her in her room. So I must live, she thought, from day to day and the image of a dashing young Major came to her and she half smiled for she knew that her sister would not want him or try to take him away; he of little breeding and no money.

Jane decided that she was much too warm so she had the coach stopped and then climbed on top with the two grooms and she wondered for a moment what would they be thinking, the gentility imposing itself on their space. It was so very pleasant, so cool and she thought that perhaps the grooms, both of whom she had known for most of her life would not begrudge her these short moments of pleasure.

The traffic, carriages, carts and sometimes a mass of horses being driven to the Fair gave real interest but since nearly every man wore a straw hat her hobby of checking each face soon lost its charm. God would have to push the man into my arms, she thought, for it was certain that her family would resist any other effort.

In the morning light the gypsy column of wagon's, caravans and carts churned up a deal of dust so that the rising sun made a golden haze that accompanied them, for they had many horses, pony's and donkeys in the column. At last they came down the hill onto the flatlands where the famed Newmarket races would be held and after some miles they mingled with the immense crowd that was swirling through the sunlit dust and the smoke of cooking fires.

Tully turned to his master to ask, 'Why do we come here sor, your priests will be here for sure? Surely we could dodge them by leaving soon.'

Will wondered why as well and thought that probably he hoped that he would see Lady Jane even though knowing that his presence would not be welcomed by her family especially, Will smiled to himself, as he was now a gypsy to all thoughts, intents and purposes. The brilliant colours of the ribbons that now adorned his cart cheered him for some reason. They blew, red, blue, green and especially red in the wind caught by the sun so that the funeral cart was made to seem a happy place for a dead man to lie and not the grim black of funerals and the sadness of families.

When they had settled, in a place that the gypsy family knew well, a traditional place, Will, Tom and Tully also made camp since they looked not so different to the others so after they had paid their dues they set about seeing the grounds for themselves. Tom didn't want to leave his horses so it was Will and Tully that set off to walk the fairgrounds, see the acts of the tumblers and fire eaters and to buy some food from one of the many vendors and never had Will felt so free. He was home from foreign lands and amongst his own people even if most of these were thieves and vagabonds but he felt at home.

He felt a sudden pang of conscience at the thought of his beloved brother. It seemed an age since he had devoted himself to thinking on the man and when he did the thought that the hero was suffered to be confined in an old farm cart instead of the fine family vault at Saxethorpe Church, would momentarily worry away at him. The vision of his so handsome brother contrasted so unfortunately with his current diddycoy appearance. His mood changed yet again as he and Tully wandered through the swirl of the crowds, of the smoke of cooking fires, of farmers and their families, local gentry with their overdressed wives and daughters. Slowly Will stopped looking for the fine dresses and clothes of the nobility thinking that they must be on the grounds of the Royal

Newmarket Stewards Club and that was when he saw, across the Show Ring, the Lady's Walden. The mother was wearing a dark red gown somewhat unsuited to the warm summers day, Will thought. She did sport a white lace parasol as did her eldest daughter Lady Alice all garbed in white lace and silk and very pretty she looked.

At first Lady Jane, in a floral, light muslin dress, was almost invisible behind the other two women but her wide summer straw hat decorated with pink roses caught his eye and quite suddenly there she was just the other side of the Ring, now half filled with yearlings stirring the dust into wind blown spirals of golden light, who were being sold by the lot amongst a great deal of price shouting from the auctioneer.

So pleased was Will when he saw her and so excited his mood that suddenly he leapt up on the high, five bar, red painted rails of the Ring, and whipping off his multi ribboned bandanna, he bowed to the young woman. The wind caught at his long fair hair blowing it out like the mane of a palomino; he was poised, grasping the top rail and he bowed again.

The flare of the sun in his golden hair caught her attention and she smiled and laughed at him as he 'halloed' through the noise of thundering hooves, the neighing, the snorting of very frisky young horses and then she curtseyed to him.

She sees me, Will thought, maybe she loves me as I do her. At that moment, came an agonizing moment of pain, of darkness, of fear. Something very hard and very heavy struck Will's left shoulder sending a shaft of the purest pain through him at the same time he felt a hand grasp his jacket and pull him violently backwards. In a moment, a numbed, barely conscious Will hit the ground knocking what little wind he had, clean from him. Hands pulled at him, darkness swept over him, the sound of shouting, a bellowing of angry voices, a roaring of savage cries, the howling of a mob; a tearing at him, hands lifting him, carrying him and then the blackness came.

Jane stared across the Ring to where her Major had been quite suddenly pulled from his perch by what looked like three black robed priests, dumping him on the ground but only a moment later she saw a sudden surge run through the crowd, the flash of steel as knives caught the sun, a mass of rough dressed but colourful men had leapt on the priests and Will disappeared under the turmoil.

As the swirling crowd seemed to return to normal, a few heads turned, some fingers pointed, some shouting of distant remarks could almost be heard in the turmoil and Jane wondered what had happened and was suddenly very worried for her Major but now everything was as before like the ripples in a lake after a stone is thrown in and then calm returns.

'Jane!' her mother spoke sharply, '...we are returning to the Club to have lunch... come now.'

Her mother had seen nothing, Jane thought, and Alice was immune to anything other than her own immediate concerns. Jane didn't know what she should do about the fracas in the crowd but she did have the odd feeling that her Major would be well that somehow he would survive, that he would keep turning up like a bad penny or perhaps that was not the right expression.

CHAPTER FOURTEEN

Well, in that she was wrong, for Will Saxethorpe was far from well. The blow to his wounded arm had numbed his whole left side and he knew from the blood flowing steadily down under his shirt that his wound had re-opened. Supported by Tully they staggered through the crowd back to the gypsy camp. 'What happened Tully?' Will gasped out, pain roaring now through his body.

'It were them priests sor; they attacked you when you climbed up the ringside and pulled off your cap; once they saw your hair...'

It was indeed my fault, Will thought. His excitement at seeing Lady Jane for, it appeared to him, that love can be most unfortunate. 'And then Tully?'

'One of 'em hit you real hard with a cudgel and the others pulled you down...'

'But how did you manage on your own?'

'It twern't me sor, it were the Romany. They saw you being attacked and then they cut up the priests. Last I saw, the black hearted villains were running for their lives...' he paused to help Will who was getting slower and slower as he left a steady trail of blood dripping from his sleeve. Tully pushed his Master's arm back into the sling knowing that getting it a little higher would slow the flood of blood. Slowly now they made it back to the camp and Tom ran to help.

Will was to wake some hours later lying under the cart, his shirt stripped from his shoulder and a new layer of some kind of gypsy ointment smeared on his wound. Tully had paid off the old woman with a small coin and prayed that the remedy would do more good than harm.

'Tully...' he gasped faintly, '...what's happened?'

'You were nearly kidnapped sor by those black-hearted priests although why...'

'And I'm back with the cart?'

'It happened nearly a day and night past sor; your shoulder is going to be mighty painful.'

I lost a day and a night, Will thought, they did indeed set me back and the aching pain claimed him again.

The voices around him went on and someone sat him up to feed him some kind of soup, which went warm and grateful into his stomach. Then another fear hit him. 'My stake Tully?'

'Is safe sor....' he dangled the well-filled leather purse before his master. 'First thing I looked for but they were not after robbing you, they wanted to take you. They had that big black coach close by and must have hoped that no one would stop them.'

Will didn't, couldn't, reach for his purse he felt so very tired, beaten, exhausted.

It was several hours later that the idle mention of a big, and very rich, card game at the Royal Newmarket Club was sufficient to rouse the interest of Major William Saxethorpe.

'Tom, I think I might venture a few hands later tonight.' Will said in a somewhat tired but thoughtful voice from his bed under the cart.

Tom sat, cross legged, with the guitar correctly positioned across his lap as he essayed careful, gentle brushes with his right fingers, placing his left to make the most basic of chords and, somewhat distracted he answered. 'Dressed like a diddycoy sor? D'you think that they'll let you in to sit with them Lords and the like?' Tom sounded highly amused at the thought, '...them ribbons make you look very cheery though...' and he struck again one of the chords that Will had taught him.

At least, Will thought, I'll not have to listen to the endless repetition of the same three chords, 'Tully, d'you think that you could saddle Hector for me, while I dress?'

In spite of the remonstrations from his companions, an hour later, freshly shaved and dressed but pale of face, a Horse Major of the Household Cavalry left the encampment watched with some amusement by all the gypsies for Tully had sold them the story of Will the 'cully,' a confidence man, a card sharp, for they all aspired to such a title.

In the candle and lamp lit darkness of a summer's evening, the grand saloon of the Royal Club bustled with most brilliant of crowds for this was one of the premier events of the racing calendar. Officer's aplenty caught the eye and their ladies swirled by in a brilliant kaleidoscope of silken colours with the flash and glitter of jewellery, most real but some not.

Lady Jane, after being introduced to a new Earl and a Knight of the Realm by a slightly annoyed sister who felt that Jane should be prepared to take over whichever man looked like falling at the first fence. But Lady Jane had made her excuses and moved away to take a small gilt chair by the wall to await whatever life and fate would push her way.

As she sat, mostly unnoticed, Lady Jane wondered if the Major was still somewhere in Newmarket, since he had not turned up the previous night, and if he was well after the melee he had been in. He'd been dressed as a gypsy for some reason not known to her but she had begun to think of him as a man of many disguises. She remembered the man climbing the rails of the Ring and then sweeping off his gaily ribboned bandanna to... to reveal himself as the Major, her Major with his flaming golden hair. She smiled through her worries knowing that that might be the last she saw of him although something told her; told her what she wondered; that he was gone or that she would see him again?

Lady Jane thought that being a wallflower for the whole of another evening was not conducive to pleasure so after an hour, where she was comprehensively ignored by the passing crowd, she was about to make her escape when there was a flicker of a red tunic, the flare of golden hair, a clatter of spurs and she knew that her hero had arrived at last. Her eyes followed him as he walked slowly looking most unwell, face pale, his bad left shoulder hunched forward, his arm in a black sling. He had walked slowly through the crowd peering about him and she noted that he had not seen her and for some reason she did not want to call out to him. Being seated in such a crowded room it was unlikely that he would notice her especially as she was sure that he had come here for one reason only.... to wager, to gamble on the turn of cards.

A large salon bathed in cigar smoke, a room with many tables filled with eager gamblers, a roulette wheel at the centre of the room surrounded by a bejewelled necklace of women each with hand's full of gambling chips and gold sovereigns and through the excited mob a slow wandering young officer of the cavalry. Finally, near the quieter back wall of the salon, he found the table he wanted.

A pale and sweating Lord Walden was being fleeced, Will thought, by three young bucks as he caught the flicker of a badly palmed card in one man's hand.

Acting just a little drunk, a slight trip over his spurs and an apologetic smile he asked, 'May I join you gentlemen? I have funds but the roulette table is so very crowded...'

One of the bucks just nodded and smiled thinking that a drunken officer was always a good mark and so Will settled a little rowdily at the table and smiled around hoping that Lord Walden would recognise him. But he did not; he just stared down at his cards and the stack of chips and coins on the table before him.

Soon after Will's entrance to the 'loo' game his steely will and phenomenal memory for the cards soon had the cullies on the run. It was unfortunate that Lord Walden was too drunk and to overexcited to even notice his presence. It was not long before the stakes had risen, Lord Walden believing that he should double and redouble and when, after several pain filled hours, the Jack of Spades, the 'Pam', the top trump, fell naturally into Will's hand he was able to sweep the table clean of money and chips.

There was a stirring as the young men, considerably poorer, rose as one, and the Major thought that now was an appropriate moment to leave also, 'Good evening, Lord Walden, 'gentlemen,' (which he said somewhat sarcastically) perhaps another hand or two later?'

But silence greeted him. Lord Walden stared down at the now empty table as if unable to believe what had happened.

Lady Jane had stood, far away and part concealed behind the decorative ferns and palms that lined the room, for the whole three and a half hours watching the fall of the cards and had been astonished that her father had not noticed whom he played against.

'Major,' she spoke very quietly through the hubbub, as he slowly passed her.

He turned and smiled gently at the sight of the serious young woman. 'Lady Jane. How pleasant...' he bowed stiffly, his eyes locked onto hers.

'You have stripped my father of his...' she hesitated, getting angry now; knowing that she was being extremely rude.

'He did not even acknowledge my presence in the game although we have met several times.'

'It is the drink sir,' her look was severe, '...he cannot see very well and when he is in his cups with cards in his hands.'

'He should not play madam,' the Major, his heavy money filled shako clutched against his chest as he stepped closer to her. 'If you wish it, I will return his money.'

Suddenly she was wondering at this gambler, this man; he would return her father's losses? So she said acerbically. 'And he would loose it at the next table.'

'Yes, he would, but this way I may be able to return his stake to you. For the journey home and...'

For a brief moment hope surged in her breast thinking that this man would give her father back his money even though he too was a gambler and then she realized that he meant something else. 'Why would you do that sir?'

He stared at her and she felt her knees go weak for she knew, she absolutely knew.

'If I have sufficient money, cash; and your father has none then I may be able...'

'You wish to buy me sir?' Her face was now taut, hard with anger.

Will looked at her very steadily, his brow beaded with sweat and, in spite of swaying with the pain in his shoulder, as he tried to ascertain how she felt about such an outlandish idea. 'I would rather not put it like that but your father only seems to care for money.' Fatigue swept over him as he spoke and it seemed that he lost control of his thoughts and his voice. 'So what price do you think he would set on your head?'

Jane spun around, her dress a bouquet of dark green silk and flaming orange roses, petals flying, to run from the room.

Will knew that he'd made a terrible mistake but now was determined to carry on with the embryonic plan that had unexpectedly appeared in his mind in the last few minutes. Buy Lady Jane? He thought not but if he could show the family that he had some wealth?

Jane moped; walking from room to room, not something she usually did, around their suite until her sister, returning late, asked. 'What ails you sister? A face as long as a fiddle must mean some disappointment or other?' But she didn't sound as if she cared, it was just something to say.

Jane stood, letting her dressing gown slip to the floor, and climbed into the small four-poster bed to contemplate a long dark night. Alice prattled on about some Earl or other and how a Duke had tried to talk to her but Jane saw only the pale sweating face of the obviously still very unwell Major. How could he say such things to her? She tried to remember his exact words and then she realized that she had interrupted his flow of speech and that she had pre-empted his remarks, that she had placed her interpretation upon him. He had robbed her father, who even now sat in the living room staring at the wall. Robbed, culled her father, stolen most of his money and then had suggested... Buy me, she thought, would he buy me if he could? She remembered the calculating look in his eye, the same look that he had when he played cards. Was she just part of some game that he played? Was...? Darkness seemed to sweep over her, her dream man disappearing into the gloom of her thoughts, her man, her Major...a thief... a cully.

A poor night's sleep, rolled in a blanket under the cart, the dull ache from his shoulder combined with the stupidity of what he'd said forcing Will to change his plans. 'Tom, Tully I need to return to the club this evening, I have some unfinished business there.'
'A poor evening at the tables sor?' Tully asked, his face worried.
'Rather the opposite. I took a deal of money but it was who I took it from that's my problem.'
'Best to run then sor. If you be a cully, as I've told these Romany, then it's best to go before they find out that you have funds.' Tom looked and sounded apprehensive.
'What we'll do. I hope it will work... is, we shall prepare to leave and then you'll come to the Royal Newmarket Club at ten tonight, say, and we will proceed from there, camping on the

road,' Will sounded more certain than he felt for he knew that in his excitement of the previous night he had upset Lady Jane most grievously.

Early that same evening the Major, his arm in a tight new sling, limped into the hall of the great house that formed the Royal Club and asked a servant, 'The family of Lord Walden, are they down?'

The dark grey clad footman looked at this dilettante of a fair haired, un-wigged officer and thought him worthy of a crown at the very least. 'I could find out for you... sir.' But he did not move just looked Will in the eye.

'So, if I, by chance, were to have a shilling about me?' Will knew a good deal about bargaining now, thanks to Tom's tuition.

'A half crown perhaps sir,' the servant asked in a worried tone.

'I have only two shillings for such information. It is, I believe, a take it or leave it situation,' the hard voiced Will watched as the servant scurried away into the back portion of the hallway. Five minutes later he returned with the information that the family would be returning at four for the afternoon tea after the Yearling sales in the Main Ring.

So it was that a Major of Horse sat quietly at a table in the card room playing whist for low stakes with three old ladies. A clashing at the main doors signalled the arrival of someone of importance and moments later the figure of Lord Walden made a staggering appearance at the entrance to the card room.

'It is Lord Walden...' one of the old ladies said as she fanned out her cards.

'He is unwell,' another dowager said, '...he has lost his senses, knows not what he does... they say.'

Will watched carefully, thinking the same. He is indeed unwell and should be put to bed for he had stood swaying, face sweating, in the doorway and then stumbled away when he realized that the serious gaming had yet to start. Will laid down his cards and smiled apologetically as he left to follow the man. Walking as fast as he might Will caught up with the baron as he staggered up the last few steps.

'Perhaps I might help you sir?' Will offered the man his arm but the more than somewhat drunk man swayed past him without a glance or a word of thanks. 'Lord Walden, it's Major Saxethorpe.'

The reply was a low curse and the turn of a heavy shoulder, 'Go thief, robber...'

For a moment Will thought that the old man recognised him from the previous evening and was angry but then realized that he had not looked at him.

'Go away, you'll get no money from me. Go, or I shall call the Steward.'

So he knows where he is, Will thought, as he stood to one side and allowed the old man to stagger down the corridor to where it ended. He stood staring at a set of fine, tall, double doors but seemed to realize that they weren't his rooms and turned back, his face befuddled. A passing servant whispered something to him and took him to a door further back, knocked and then opened it.

Jane sat in her dressing gown, her face and slim body still damp from the bath that she'd taken; for the Show Grounds and The Ring had been very dusty. She sat alone and considered her and the family's future. She took up a silver backed brush and started the one hundred sweeping strokes that turned her hair to a dark glossy sheet of almost dark red light.

A steward from the main ring had come with the money from the sale of the yearlings, some five hundred and seventy guineas in gold. Her Papa took the money, signed a receipt and plunged the heavy leather purse deep into an inside pocket all the time looking at her, her mother and Alice with a hunted and deeply suspicious view as if... He intended, he said, that he would go to the saloon and double his stake then we can go home tomorrow wealthy again. But he will lose it all, Jane thought, and that will be the end of us for he is most certainly unwell and we will be poor and ruined.

The image, in Jane's mind, of the Major making his most inappropriate suggestion rankled indeed. Prove his worth by giving them back their own money? Was that a way a proper gentleman acted? Jane suspected that the gentlemen that she knew would just keep the money but he'd offered to return the lost money had he not? To her, not her father. Jane had been surprised at her reaction and thought that thinking ill of the Major for the whole length of the game had disturbed her mind. She had no idea what else there was that she could do. She'd spoken to her sister but Alice's only worry was that her father would be unable to afford a properly elaborate wedding and something to settle on her. Jane's mother had become a twittering mass of nerves whenever Jane tried to speak of the problem so all was unresolved. By morning, Jane suspected all would be revealed. Her father would be insolvent, bankrupt and their estate would have to be sold. Then a life of living as the unwelcome guest of relatives, no money for clothes, a forced marriage to the first man who had any money at all, children and an early death. Or the Major's unkind offer. Buy me would he, I think not; but an excited shudder ran down her spine at the thought.

The Major was doing quite well in a medium stake game of 'loo' when Lord Walden, clad in pink silk and dusty white wig, staggered into the gaming room. Will watched the man's progress from table to table; his intense stare at the state of play, ignoring the looks on the faces of the other gamblers, the looks of pity and disgust.

The plan fell, fully formed now, into Will's mind so he stood, with some degree of pain, and made his way to where Lord Walden was looking around with confusion writ large upon his face.

'My Lord...' Will stood before the man, a questioning look on his face,'...how are you today?'

The tall pink clad man peered around this interloper as if he wasn't there and he didn't reply.

'A game of cards then sir?'

'Cards?' his lordship asked, his attention caught by this red clad soldier with his arm in a sling. He looked right into Will's eyes but there was no sign of recognition there.

'A table of 'loo' perhaps?' Will asked.

'Yes indeed, 'loo,' my favourite game I think...' his forehead wrinkled in confused thought.

A coin or two for the footmen and a table was swiftly set up. Moments later three strangers asked if they could join and Will nodded his assent.

Later he was to think that it was like a long bout of 'deja vu' so similar was it to the previous night's game. Milord Walden had no idea of what he did and Will had his work cut out getting rid of the other players for his plan was to strip this invalid of all his ready cash and so it went, in the way of serious card games, on for several intense hours so that the clock struck midnight before a resolution seemed in sight, for Will had had several scares but as the clock struck twelve he laid down his hand to clear the table.

Lord Walden stared unbelieving at the emptiness of the green baize topped table before him as if his predicament had finally come home to him and he swallowed, in one gulp, the large glass of cognac that stood at his elbow. 'We will continue sir.'

Will looked at this unhappy man sadly and then said, 'You've no funds Milord,' a blank statement of fact.

The glazed eyes of the man hunted across the now emptying room for someone or.... 'Footman!' he snapped, '...fetch the Steward at once.'

Ah, now the problem starts, Will thought.

Later the Major was to think that it was one of the best or possibly worst nights of his life. The Baron Walden persuaded the Steward to write an IOU for the value of his estate. Four thousand pounds. A somewhat undervalued estimation in Will's opinion but since winning would not be a problem.

A crowd gathered since the story of the unwell Baron being fleeced by the Army officer had spread throughout the Royal Club. The Stewards had tried very hard to prevent the card game proceeding but the Baron had insisted most vociferously.

CHAPTER FIFTEEN

It was a warm, soft, moonlit night as the creaking cart rolled steadily along the Post Road to Norwich, a journey of some fifty miles not that Will planned to go the whole way knowing a cross country route that would be somewhat shorter and safer.

He laid, his pain preventing sleep, in his straw lined space next to his brother and thought about what had happened. He was now rich but his reputation was in tatters not that they knew him well but he fancied that he would not be welcome back at the Royal Newmarket Club. The game, everyone agreed, was perfectly straight but such was the difference in skill levels that it seemed unfair so he had been warned off but not before he had cleaned out the Baron. He had reclaimed the IOU for four thousand in cash but had kept the Deed of Debt against the property known as Saffron House Estate.

He'd had Tom turn off the Post Road as soon as possible, even though it was still quite dark, for fear of meeting with the priests again for Will could tell that they meant him real harm maybe even death and yet he couldn't understand why. He knew that his brother disliked him or he most certainly had five years ago but to kill him? What possible prize could be in the offing?

They had slowly crossed the flat country to the east of Newmarket the horses walking steadily but slowly into the rising sun. At a place called Icklington they came across a small roadside inn which seemed, from its general appearance, to be a well set up sort of place and Will decided that they would rest and have a fine breakfast.

His shoulder was still very sore but after three hours sleep and a large meal he felt able to go on. 'Let's see if we can make it to the other side of Thetford then?'

Tom's sleepy eyed face looked at him across the breakfast table. 'The horses sor. They get tired too. Awake all day and walking more than half the night. They need to be rested and I feel a mite battered myself.'

Will had never heard Tom complain before and when he glanced at Tully he realised that they had been awake the whole night while he lay down struggling to sleep in the bed of the cart. 'You're right Tom, I am being selfish, so when breakfast is finished you may both go back to your beds. I have some difficult letters to write...so....'

After they had retired, much to the amusement of the landlord, Will went into the small town where they had an apothecary from whom he was able to purchase a quantity of laudanum for the easing of his pain.

Back at the inn he set about the writing of his letters. The difficult ones.

William Saxethorpe, Major.

Dearest Lady Jane,
I must apologise deeply and most sincerely for the unhappiness which I have inadvertently caused both you and your family but I hope, with this missive, to explain my intentions.

On my first night at the Club I saw that your father was being fleeced by a group of 'cully's' and decided that aside from causing a large fracas it would be easier if I in turn 'fleeced' them. This I did even though both you and your father were upset by my actions. When I spoke to you afterwards you leapt to conclusions about my intent and my reaction was most unfortunate.

The second evening; when I arrived at the Newmarket Club I found your father trying to get into one of the high stake games. The gentlemen of the club were polite enough to prevent him playing but I realized that he was determined to play so I provided him with the opportunity. My intention was to take all his money from him and then return it to you but it became apparent, when the Baron won a few hands, that he would just go to another table or take a chance with roulette so I reverted to my original plan. However my fatigue was such and the hour so late that the idea of giving his money back to you was impossible for me to contemplate.

By the way, your father wagered his entire fortune on the last hand, suffice it to say, he lost. It is therefore my duty to inform you that you and your family are now destitute but your only debt is to me.

I return home now but I will come to visit Saffron House in the near future; say one month. In the mean time I will arrange for funds to be placed in your hands so that you might continue to live there. I suggest that your mother and sister make efforts to find alternative accommodation. You and your father are welcome to stay at the house until my plans are complete.

Yours William Saxethorpe.

Will carefully folded the paper, used the candle to melt some dark green wax into a satisfactory blob then pressed his seal ring down into the hardening wax. He stared at the letter as he wrote the directions thinking how cold it sounded, how hard his voice was. What had happened to the nascent love that he'd felt for this woman? Had her harshly incorrect words produced such antipathy in him or was she still the woman he loved and he knew, was certain, that the reason was money. The Baron had thrown away his money and it was Will's misfortune to know how much pain would be caused by his ruination. If only he didn't know how lovely Lady Jane was, how loving she had been whilst her mother and sister were so very grasping. He felt that he should mount his horse and... but no, he had a now urgent task to perform, he must bury his brother. The other letter then.

Will pulled another fine sheet from his writing case and started another difficult letter; this to the Household Cavalry,

Colonel of the Horse Guards,

Sir, You will know of the demise of Colonel, Lord Lawrence Saxethorpe at the great battle just passed at Waterloo 18th June 1815. I regret the amount of time that has passed but a good number of problems have occurred during the passage and journey back to Saxethorpe, St Mary's where the family tomb is and where he will be interred. The date will be about the 17th July 1815. If any of his fellow officers should wish to pay their respects to their former commander then they should repair to Saxethorpe for the above date.

Yours Sincerely, Major of Horse William Saxethorpe.

Will sealed the letter and marked it for Express delivery.

Since he was now convinced that his brother John was responsible for the attacks upon him he decided that he must be forthright and make all the decisions that were right and proper. First, the burial and the service. This would be held at Saxethorpe in the family chapel and Lawrence would be laid to rest by the side of his father and mother in the family tomb. He would then pay his respects to his brother, kiss his sister and then leave, but to go where? He thought his plan childish since it was so unlikely to go smoothly and he knew that he would have to have Bishop John officiate and that he could not possibly just walk away from the sister who had raised him and whom he loved so much so he pulled another piece of paper toward him and started to write.

Lady Anne of Saxethorpe.

Dearest Annie,
I write with some dismay at the delays of my journey. There is much to say but it cannot be expressed in a letter. My grief at Lawrence's death, the hardship of the journey including being set upon by what looked like renegade priests. The disaster of a broken cart, many other delays and other unfortunate occurrences including being attacked by Army veterans. We should be home in a few days assuming that the largely restored cart does not break again. Looking forward to seeing you, all my love and affection, Yours Will.

I shall send them Express at the next Post Office that we come across, thought Will, and immediately started to plan from where he should send the letters and decided that it would be safer if he rode 'Hector' some way off their actual route in order to confuse his pursuers, for pursuers they most certainly were and sending the letter would give them some knowledge of where he was and the route he was taking.

Returning home Lady Jane sat in her seat in the Walden coach, she suspected for the last time. The story, except it was no fairytale, of the previous evening when she had refused to leave her room lay on her mind as if made of lead. Her imagined lover had turned out to be a common card sharp, a 'cully' of the worst kind. He had stripped her father of both his money and his dignity and she found herself staring at the poor man as he rolled with the carriage's motion, his eye's staring, his mouth drooling; a caricature of a lunatic. He had been robbed blind at the card table, the other guests informed her, by a handsome young Army officer who had stripped him of his money and apparently redeemed some IOU of her father's, although she did not fully understand this. The Major's one redeeming feature was that he had paid their account at the Club so that they could leave but Jane had no idea what they would do when they returned home, for it seemed that their estate had been ventured on the card table as well as all their ready cash. They would be poor now and Mama and Alice did not seem to realize it even though they shared the same information.

Poor Papa, this visit had destroyed him. He had been unwell before they came but this was of a different order, now he was most definitely a very sick old man.

The man, the Major of her dreams, had done this thing. Turned her poor father from a proper man to close to a madman, a lunatic unable to grasp even the simplest of occurrences. What would they do? What could they do? Jane glanced at her so pretty sister now dozing; the customary venomous look now relaxed in her sleep. Jane wondered what made her sister so very unpleasant to her. She'd asked her once but the stream of vituperation and invective had been most hard to bear so she had stepped back into her accustomed secondary role. Now her father's health and the lack of money would prove, she thought, insurmountable. Only the opportunity to become a Governess lay before her but who would look after Papa; Alice's marriage plans were well advanced it seemed so she could be discounted and as for Mama. Jane could not see her mother looking after her father for she was a woman without any homemaking skills. Unless she threw herself on the charity of her family she would end up on the streets and her father? Slowly the pain of her thoughts numbed her mind and she fell into a doze.

For two days the rumble and grating clatter of the steel shod wheels on the cart formed the background for the lessons that Tom had now begun to regret. His master never seemed to allow him any time to lie back and think about his new cart and horses and if he wasn't reading then he would be practicing the guitar. The advantage of 'practice' as encouraged by his Master was that he could now pick out a simple tune and strum away in the right key for the singing of his sea shanties.

Will thought, I don't know if Tom's reading practice is more stupefying than his guitar practice but I do know that I shall go mad very, very soon. After so long a period, arriving at a real town would be something of a delight so that the milestones pointing to Norwich came as a great relief. Knowing that only five miles, then four, then three and when he saw the square tower of Norwich Castle he could almost feel the good food and the warm bed that would be waiting somewhere in the city. Down East hill and beyond lay the great cathedral with the City drawn up tight around her grey stones and that's where the Blue Boar was as well as Will could remember from his somewhat misspent youth. When he saw the ancient building Will decided that it would be the very first place the renegade priests would check so he asked Tom to proceed over Bishop's Bridge to the King's Arms, a somewhat newer establishment where they were made very welcome and where the landlord was delighted to receive a gold guinea in exchange for a guarantee of privacy.

Once established in a suite of rooms at the end of a long corridor with the horses nicely stabled and the cart locked into a back area Will was able to relax and plan for an evening of diversions. He didn't know what it should be called but he suspected that young women and a lot of wine would be involved. The warm auburn hair and angry face of his erstwhile friend did interpose themselves momentarily into his mind but a quick shake of his head and a large glass of wine soon chased away this image.

The Drawing Room at Saffron House was sunlit at teatime and the three Walden ladies were taking tea in the approved manner.

Lady Walden and her eldest daughter wore day dresses of the highest fashion. The mother in a dress of brown silk, Alice in her favourite gold dress that had rather too much gold lace sewn to it.

'I shall write to my sister,' this single sentence was sufficient for Jane to realize that her Mama did indeed realize the seriousness of their position and was planning some kind of retreat.

'And what of Papa?' Jane's short sentence was enough to discountenance her mother.

'What of him? He can stay here,' her voice was sharp but at the same time disinterested.

'And who is to look after him,' Jane asked, a worried frown on her brow.

'You, who else,' Alice's harsh sardonic voice interjected.

'Me? Alone here?'

'You'll have Papa for company.' Alice said in a now ironically complacent tone.

'What about money, for food, for servants? Jane now sounded worried and had begun to wish that she'd taken up the Major's first offer. Perhaps not his second but most certainly the first suggestion for the absence of ready cash had already proved somewhat difficult.

Her mother said, doubtfully, 'I... I will try to raise a loan from my sister, against my jewels, and will send you some money.'

'If... if she gives you money? What if she does not?' Jane's voice was sarcastic now.

Her mother looked away and she said in a tremulous voice so unlike her own, 'I don't know.'

'Alice, you could ask your new fiancée for a loan, could you not?' Jane's tone was very sarcastic now.

Even Jane was surprised at the look on Alice's pale, confused face, for she had not mentioned to her new husband to be the fact that there would be no marriage settlement, that she would come with nothing save the money from the sale of her

135

marriage home, which she suspected was under some kind of lien or mortgage from the Bank, that and her rather beautiful body.

'I think not. I barely know the man. I only...'

Jane thought, my sister, hesitant, embarrassed; not possible. The problem of what to do had not gone away nor was it likely to. Papa lay, tied to his bed, upstairs. The doctor had said that if he wasn't tied down he would just wander away and it occurred to Jane that that might be the solution to their problem and she wondered how the complete lack of interest shown to her by her parents had produced this callous streak in her. Curiously she didn't seem to care about the problem in the correct family way. Of course she loved her Mama and Papa in theory but they had never shown the slightest sign of affection for her and now was the time when such affection would be at its most important. Her anger at the Major had increased as the family's poor position had become more and more apparent. She knew that she was being unintelligent about him. If it hadn't been him it would have been another 'cully,' or card sharp at the Newmarket Club and then she had rejected the Major's 'offer'; so, it was, in part, her fault as well. Jane had to thank God that her mother and sister had not been party to that particular conversation.

There was a polite knock at the door and the last of the footmen entered carrying a folded and sealed note which he handed to Lady Jane, since it was indeed addressed to her.

She suffered a sudden frisson of excitement a shudder running the length of her spine as she stared down at the seal, horses and fish, so very odd.

Lady Jane Walden,

Lady Jane, outside Saffron House, my travelling companion Tully, whom I am sure you will recognize, will be standing by his horse waiting to converse with you. He has express orders not to leave Saffron Walden until he has done so. May I suggest that you talk with him as soon as possible. You will find that it is to your advantage.

Sincerely Major W. Saxethorpe.

Post Script... Do not tell your mother or your sister of this communication.

Jane sat there for a moment trying to take the note in. What did it mean? Did... She realized quite swiftly that sitting there with her mother and sister staring at her was not the thing to do. The thing to do was to go outside and find the emissary from the Major so she rose swiftly and with a short, '...Excuse me.' she left the room.

Waiting under the impressive but poorly built portico was the short, corduroy dressed, ratty faced, figure of Tully, the Major's so called 'companion', looking quite exhausted.

'Tully?' the blue gingham clad girl bore down on the Irishman, anger growing for some reason in her mind.

'Lady Jane. Good afternoon. You received my Master's note then?'

'Of course I did, you just sent it in, did you not?' Jane felt ready to explode with anxiety and anger.

Tully frowned, a somewhat unpleasant thing to observe, and ignoring her sarcasm said, 'I have a verbal message for you also.'

'Well, get on with your 'message' then,' she snapped out, her anxiety almost overwhelming her.

'The Major asked me to tell you...'

She said desperately, 'Please Tully, just give me the message.'

'He has two thoughts he wants to impress on you.' He waited for her to say something but she stared at him in silence. 'Firstly, the matter of secrecy. If you break silence on this matter he will never contact you again.'

Jane felt suddenly bereft even if she did not know what she would be promising to do but the thought of the absolute loss of the Major was unbearable; so she just nodded.

'I have a purse for you, and you alone. It contains one hundred guineas in gold and bank notes and it is for the maintenance of yourself and your father. Absolutely none is to be given to your mother or Lady Alice. The insults the Major suffered are sufficient for him to feel in need of some kind of reprisal. He has written to your Steward, Mr Bailey, of whom you once spoke well, with instructions as to the staffing of Saffron House and the

Estate. This is only of interest to the Major but he did ask that I mention, in case you have not fully grasped your situation, is that the Major is now the owner of Saffron House Estate and takes full responsibility for the running thereof.' She stared at him, '...So you see Lady Jane that the Major has your comfort and safety as his main concern but I must tell you, remind you of the pledge of secrecy which goes with the gold.' Tully held out a heavy leather purse so that it was before her eyes but not near enough for her to seize.

Her eyes flickered between the purse and Tully whilst she tried to work out what it all meant but she could see nothing rude or arrogant in the message only the fact that a servant delivered it was so very odd. The money would save her father and quiet her mind on the subject of debt.

'Do you promise?' Tully asked quietly.

'I do. Thank the Major for me please.' She stopped as the gold heavy purse dropped into her waiting hands. 'And that's all he said?'

'He did mention, in passing, that he would come to inspect his new house when his present business was finished.'

'Business?' Jane asked, still dazed.

'The burial Milady. You must remember his brother; the coffin in the cart. He's had to take him home and then he will return here but he did say he would prefer it if your mother and sister had left by then. He anticipates a time of about one month, perhaps a little more...'

'A month.' Jane whispered, he doesn't come for a month so will I be able to eke out the hundred guineas on household staffing and expenses?

'I shall go and see Mr Bailey now Milady and then return to Norwich, excuse me,' he bowed and after a few minutes walking his horse away he disappeared under the brick archway to the stable yard leaving the pale young woman staring after him.

Lady Jane went straight to her room and concealed the gold in her own special hiding place which she had found when her sister insisted on reading her diary out loud to Mama and Papa, much to their amusement. A loose floorboard in her closet beneath her neatly placed shoes and when Jane was sure that no one would look she ventured back down stairs to the Drawing Room.

'What did that servant want?' Alice's voice was demanding.

In an instant Jane could see what she had not seen, really seen before; that her sister and mother were arrogant, demanding women so she decided, almost for the first time in her life to 'lie'. 'It was a message from a creditor, the butcher, about the money that we owe.'

Her so pretty Mama, a disgusted look on her face said, ' I hope you sent him about his business Jane!'

'He left Mama...' but she thought that her mother should have been more sympathetic to local tradesmen who had a living to earn not just expect the nobility to live off their hard work.

So a small lie was enough for the moment but Jane wondered how she could conceal her source of funds for very long but she could, at the very least, satisfy the shopkeepers.

Why did he do it? She thought. He feels guilty? He knows that he's hurt us and... No, that was wrong; he had a plan and I rejected it and him. He doesn't care about us but he does care about me, I think, otherwise why would he send a man a hundred miles on horseback. He worries about me, maybe, but he's still a bad, bad man who robbed my father. He might as well have knocked him down and stolen his purse... he didn't, but... Jane decided she would have to go and talk to the Estate Steward, Mr Bailey.

'Mr Bailey,' she stood pink faced before the corduroy and tweed dressed Steward whose wind and sun burnt face seemed to glow in the darkness of the potting shed office, the worry of this encounter writ large upon him as he pulled off his wool shooting cap.

'Milady?'

'I... I received a note from...' Jane didn't know how well the Steward would know the Major if he knew of him at all.

'The Major?' He said, nodding politely.

'Yes, the Major... Major Saxethorpe. He said that he was writing to you and I wondered...'

The man frowned deeply his embarrassment showing. 'The new owner of Saffron House Estate has given me both proof of ownership and instructions as to the running of the Estate. He sounds very knowledgeable as to the workings of a large...'

Jane didn't wish to know about the 'new' arrangements she wanted... what did she want? 'Did he say anything about... about us...'

'You mean your family Milady?' Bailey had something of a soft spot for Lady Jane whom he had known since she was a small child.

'Yes, Mr Bailey. Did he mention what we are to do?'

'Yes. His instructions are quite firm on that point,' Jane stared at the man, 'He thought that you might well come and talk to me and that I was to tell you what...'

'Why did he not tell me direct?'

'He thought, he writes, that Lady Walden or your sister might see what he had written and this he did not want made public. Apparently he wrote a letter to you but did not send it.'

Jane stared hard at the man as she realized more and more how their lives had changed. 'And what are his 'instructions'?' She asked very hesitantly.

'He does not give instructions Milady, he merely asks, suggests, that your mother and sister be allowed; encouraged, to go but that you and your father be allowed to stay. He has set aside a sum of money plus the income from the estate for the maintenance of yourself and your father. With a nurse from the town perhaps, certainly someone to watch over him at night.'

Jane's mouth opened as if she was going to interrupt but the Steward overrode her unspoken comment.

'The staff of the big house is to be cut to the very minimum and the male workers to be given tasks on the estate to complete the list of...'

'There is a list?'

'Apparently he saw, on his last visit, a number of rather obvious maintenance problems about the house, the Home Farm and the gardens which he would like remedied.'

'He acts the Master.' her face pink cheeked and worried.

The big Steward, a somewhat concerned frown on his face said, 'Indeed Milady, he is the Master.'

CHAPTER SIXTEEN

Will, bleary eyed after the last night's celebration, peered through the oriel window out at the street scene below the Inn. The bridge over the river Tas was crowded with country people coming to Market Day, driving sheep, cattle and even a few pigs so that a scene of utter, noisy, smoky confusion seemed to reign outside the Inn.

Thank heaven, he thought, as he pulled himself back into the quiet of the large bedchamber, that I am within and not without. Now, breakfast, he thought, and went to ring for a servant wondering at the same time about where Tom was, for his small bed was empty.

The upstairs maids brought hot water, coffee and a breakfast of fresh, still warm bread, good cheese, ham and pickles. His queries after the whereabouts of his companion brought the information that the boy was in the stables feeding the horses. It was, as Will stirred his coffee into a sugary blackness, that he thought of the canals, the river Bure that emptied into the Broads. He had been raised not so far away so all was soon obvious to him. He munched the bread and cheese and could see that going by canal and river up to Saxethorpe would be a good way of avoiding the renegade priests, if that's what they were. Surely they would not think that a man with a cart would come by water? Even if they did, an attack would be much more difficult.

Will sat eating bread and drinking half cold coffee while he thought through the plan, his headache easing. It was slow, that was its main fault, so perhaps he should ride ahead, it was, after all, only two hours or so. He could see his sister and perhaps his brother, the Bishop, although he was not so keen to find out the problem that must lie between them.

A somewhat grubby Tom knocked on the door and then entered. 'Horses be fed sor,' he took off his cap and dropped it, in a small cloud of hay droppings, onto his unmade bed, '...how d'you feel this mornin?'

'Moderate Tom, only moderate. I may have taken a glass too many last night.' Will smiled at his friend.

'More of a bottle too many sor. It's a wonder your head is still upon your shoulders.' He came over and picked a piece of the cheese from the round on the table.

'Are you hungry Tom, if you are...'

'I had my breakfast below sor; and very fine it was.'

'Good, good,' Will thought what a find this boy was, 'I have been giving some thought as to a plan for the next day or so...'

Riding a road, that had once been so familiar, dappled sunlight pouring down through the beech trees in full leaf Will felt almost young again. Even his shoulder no longer throbbed with that dull pain of the last few days and he could gently flex his left arm without the sharp jabs of agonizing pain. He had cut down his doses of laudanum and this morning he was doing without even though he felt some kind of compulsion but his thoughts easily drove away these irrelevant desires. His horse pistols thumped softly against the saddle leathers and his fighting sword fell pleasantly by his side and he thought, in spite of the lack of practice that he could manage any encounter with the priests with their cudgels and the like. It was good to have 'Hector' between his legs again after so many miles in the cart and the horse seemed to be enjoying the journey after trotting behind the cart for so long.

He had left a message for Tully with the Innkeeper and he hoped that his man had been successful on his mission south. How had Lady Jane reacted he wondered and he knew that his ineptness of writing and manner might well be responsible for yet another misunderstanding.

An over warm attic room of sloping ceilings and small dusty, cobwebbed windows. Lady Walden had ordered her husband up here so that she could avoid thinking on him. Out of sight and out of mind was the way she thought. Jane sat by her Papa's narrow bedside as he dozed and wondered at this strange Major and farmer that Fate had thrown her way. His skill with cards, and his fighting ability were both strange talents for a passing stranger or perhaps they were not. His ill thought out words, his anger at her attitude, not that it was not somewhat justified, had all provoked her and then the purse, the letters to her and the Steward...how strange it all was.

Her father groaned and tried to pull himself free from his straps as slowly his eyes filled with a cunning look.

'Let me be... let me go.' He moaned out.

'Papa, the doctor says...'

The invalid stared up at her, 'Who are you? What d'you want with me?'

'It's Jane, Papa.'

'Jane?'

'Yes... your daughter.'

The hunted look was on his face when he squeaked out, 'I have no daughter Jane... my daughter's not called...' he stared wildly around the small room, ' ...her name's...' his voice slurring his eye's closing with some finality.

The doctor is right, Jane thought, dementia. Perhaps it went from father to son since Grandpapa had gone completely mad in a few months when Jane was a little girl. She remembered how lovely the man had been and then, quite suddenly, they had tied him to the bed, a madman, just as his son was now. How very sad, perhaps it would be for the best if she had no children and Alice the same.

The door opened and her mother entered. A quick glance at the sleeping invalid and then she crossed to a closet built into a corner from which she took a long silken coat, held it against her body to admire in a cheval glass standing there then said. 'What d'you think Jane, is this still in the fashion? I don't want to be embarrassed at Aunt Electra's house, one should try to keep up even if one has no money.'

Jane opened her mouth to reply but her mother required no answer, just turned and left the room.

So Mama and Alice are planning to move out, Jane thought, something of a pity that they did not see fit to consult with me. So I am to be Papa's nurse. They will be able to say that they saw that he was alright before they left and indeed they had. Jane would stay and they would go.

She wondered at what had become of her so settled life in so short a time. Cannon shot at Waterloo had brought home her so... so beautiful, but so avaricious sister. Almost the same cannon had set her mercenary Major onto his path home; a fated path that had crossed with hers so often, so calamitously. Her father finally going mad, how was she to be able to weave this tragic circumstance into her story with the Major. He tries to save her family, admittedly by a circuitous route, but nevertheless the purse filled with gold coin and five pound notes would save her and her father or was it intended to buy her gratitude. There would be only one way in which she could repay this debt; she would have to marry this... this man, and repay him over her whole lifetime and she wondered how she felt about that? The trickle of excitement that ran up her spine when she thought of him told her that her day dreams of only a few days ago was probably going to come true and she wished... wanted...

Jane sat on in the attic in an old, somewhat broken rocking chair; her back straight, her hands neatly folded in her lap, as required by their last Governess. She'd been a firm but pleasant young woman of noble birth fallen on hard times; very well educated, Jane's musical expertise and good French could be traced back to Anne Hardwick. Jane's letters to this woman had failed to elicit a reply of late; she had vanished, hopefully into marriage but more likely a workhouse and an early death. Jane shook her head, such thoughts of another's past was wasted, she had more than enough troubles of her own and the thought that Anne Hardwick's path was a quite likely one for her, if she was foolish enough to refuse this man, William Saxethorpe.

Morris, the curate of Saxethorpe village church, was relatively old for a curate, thirty nine years of age and a Cambridge graduate with no money of his own. Charles Morris was a brilliant scholar whose inclination to religion was an attempt to find something to do in a world at war with the French and Americans. The Army, Politics, the Law all had been found wanting by him since he only wanted to study, read and conduct such experiments of a scientific nature that came as a result of all his research. The running and maintenance of a medium sized church, the services, the caring for the poor and all the other duties of assisting the absent vicar had proved both satisfactory and easy so that he had plenty of time for his other activities of which biology was his favourite which was why he was by the river bank when the heavily armed horseman happened by.

The curate, a tall thin man with somewhat receding brown hair was sweating in the traditional ecclesiastical black clothes with a disarranged white stock at his throat as he crouched on the bank taking samples from the river into green glass, screw topped jars and he was a little startled at being hailed by a uniformed officer mounted on a large black, white blaze fore headed horse and seemingly armed to the teeth.

'Ho there sir!' the soldier called out.

'Ho there yourself sir,' the reply came in a prompt if slightly annoyed voice from the curate.

'I look for the Vicar of Saxethorpe. I have been to the vicarage and a woman there, said look on the riverbank. I look, and there you are.'

'So I am, but I am not the vicar.' Morris shrugged his shoulders in a broad gesture. '... if you wish to speak with him then you have a long wait since he has been in Norwich Town this two months past,' the curate finished his filling of jars and started to write, with a stub of pencil, on the labels affixed to the sides. 'It's important to write down the time of day, the date and the location of the sample otherwise the experiment is without meaning...'

'But you are an ecclesiastical gentleman are you not?' Will asked.

'I am the curate of St. Mary's but I have...' he hesitated to start to write upon another jar.

'I have a burial to discuss sir.'

The curate looked up realizing that time was of the essence so asking, 'And the unfortunate...?'

'He was indeed unfortunate but the ending must have come very swiftly.'

'God can be kind...' Charles Morris said, starting to stand, '...sometimes,' he added sotto voce. ' And the name is?'

'It is Lord Lawrence Saxethorpe, Baron Saxethorpe, somewhat tardily returned from Waterloo. The battle that is.'

The curate looked up at the soldier wondering where the coffin was; 'Lord Saxethorpe? We are expecting him; the mason's started work some two weeks ago on the two stone coffins.'

'Hector' at this point decided to curve around in a tight circle as nervous as the curate, who, a curious expression on his face and his arms full of glass bottles struggled up the sloping river-bank.

'Two coffins sir?' Asked the pale-faced soldier.

The curate looked up at the soldier noting the threadbare worn quality of his uniform then said. 'That was what was ordered. I received a letter from the Bishop in Ely and he specifically asked for two stone coffins to be prepared in the family vault.'

Will thought, two dead brothers? Perhaps Holy John was doing God's work for him attempting the filling of the second coffin; but why would he do that? Will wondered. 'Perhaps, if you can spare the time, we might repair to the 'Fox' and partake of some liquid refreshment and perhaps luncheon as I have been on the road for some hours?'

'Perhaps, after introduction, since it is so warm, a glass of beer would be very welcome. My name is Charles Morris, late of Cambridge and currently the curate of St. Mary's. And you are?'

The soldier dismounted with some difficulty since his left shoulder was still bound with his arm in a black sling; so he slithered to the ground uttering a slight groan of pain that the motion caused him. 'The name is Major William Saxethorpe, of Saxethorpe Hall I suppose. I have been on campaign for the last seven years or so ending with the fracas at Waterloo.' The Major thrust out his right hand to the stick like curate, thinking that the open look on the man's face promised some degree of friendship in the future.

The curate took the soldier's hand thinking, seeing in his minds eye the fresh cut letters on the second of the stone sarcophagi, 'Major of Horse, William Saxethorpe, who fell, saving his country at Waterloo' and found himself smiling as he thought to himself and then said, 'Not often I get to shake hands with a ghost, Major.'

'There has been some kind of mistake, a misunderstanding perhaps.'

The curate looked puzzled and glanced down at the four glass jars he was holding before saying. 'The Bishop of Ely came here himself to make the arrangement and he seemed very certain that both his brothers had fallen,' the two men started to walk back towards the small town, with the Major leading his horse.

Will looked and sounded somewhat annoyed. 'Well, he is mistaken, for I am here.'

Charles Morris turned to the soldier to ask. 'Without wishing to doubt your word sir, is there perhaps, some way in which you can identify yourself?'

Will stopped walking for a moment then remembered that all his personal papers were, even now, in his baggage that was being carried upstream with the coffin. 'No. I have no papers about my person but I will have them to hand when the coffin gets here.'

Charles thought to himself that this is a trustworthy man, he could feel it. The uniform, the horse, the pistols, the well worn sword and the wounds that he suffered from all tended to indicate that his story was true. So he allowed himself to be led into the Inn where they sat down to luncheon with a deal of beer and wine.

Will found himself telling the tall plain man the whole story from the battlefield to the contest with Lady Jane.

The curate now looked with some sympathy on the soldier; a man who had lost so much and gained so little and also the mystery of the two coffins puzzled him greatly. Of course, this man's brother was so well known in the little town, Holy John of Saxethorpe who had risen through the Church at meteoric pace and all based on his piety and visions. Now it seemed that there might be another side to this man, this prince of the church, this Bishop. He orders two coffins, the curate still had the ordering letter filed in the study of the vicarage and knew that he could not have made a mistake.

After luncheon the two men, strengthened by their consumption of a further bottle of claret ventured to the largest tomb in the churchyard, a tomb that had been the final resting place for the Saxethorpes for over a thousand years. A Saxon noble family that had survived the Norman invasion by their skill as soldiers, holding onto their lands mostly by political cunning but also by their prowess in battle. A Saxethorpe had served the King or sometimes the Queen or Republic but by virtue of the distance from London they had crouched on their remote estates and had outlasted them all but today's crisis threatened all their history for it smelt, to the curate, of something far worse than political advantage, it smelt of the corruption, of evil.

The tomb was a substantial stone edifice, mostly plain with just some Ionic columns topped with urns on each corner but it had been dug deep for the ancestor who had built it believed in the future of his family and knew that he must provide for a substantial number of occupants. The entrance stood open and the approaching men could hear the rap and chip of hammers that cut the letters into each stone coffin and then they were walking down the steps and stood looking at the two open sarcophagi, stared at, in the sudden silence, by the two masons who were working there.

One of them, an old bearded man, gasped and looked down at the lettering then back up to look at the soldier again... 'I could swear sor... that you are... are you not?

'It seems that the Church has been misinformed mason. I did not die at Waterloo; my brother did, but not I. Do not bother to change the letters, they will do as well in a few years time when I reach the end of my allotted span.' Will could not have looked sadder but then he turned to his new friend to say, 'Charles. If you would be kind enough to prepare to receive my brother, a lying in perhaps in the church? Not too long, just a day or so. A chance perhaps for the local gentry, the tenant farmer's might like to offer their final respects to Lawrence.'

Before he left the dank space Will stopped for a moment by the double tombstone that half filled the centre of the crypt. His mother and his father's final resting place; together forever. Will's head bent in unaccustomed prayer for a moment before he turned back to the Curate.

They made their way up the steps into the churchyard feeling the human relief to be away from the haunts of the dead.

Will stood at the top of the steps, the sun catching at his so fair hair, a light easterly breeze from the sea making waves in the sundried grasses of the graveyard. 'I shall visit with my sister at the Hall; maybe she can resolve this mystery and in the morning, perhaps I will accompany my brother John to the church, if he is at home.'

At the church gate Will mounted his horse with some help from the churchman, saying as he did so. 'The boatmen said that they thought tomorrow at ten if they kept going late. They'll tie up just below the church and perhaps you could organize pallbearers and the like so that in two days...'

'And the Bishop?' Charles Morris could see that there must be something of a problem to come.

'If he is not at home then I shall send him a letter by Express. He can come or not; the decision will be his.'

CHAPTER SEVENTEEN

The date for her mother's and sister's preparations to quit Saffron House had arrived. A large and very elaborate, over decorated Coach with four matching black horses, two liveried footmen and a further two coach men as drivers had arrived just after sunrise. There was a considerable rushing about, a deal of shouting from Alice, mostly complaints about the absence of her Earl; the one she was to marry very soon and then; a silence fell on Saffron House.

Jane noticed it when she reached the end of 'Sense and Sensibility' the latest novel from the pen of Miss Jane Austen and it was as she closed the finely leather bound cover of the novel that she sensed the absolute silence. The shouting had stopped, the complaints had ended; the sound of horses being fed, being watered had faded away into the wood creaking of the old house.

Jane looked over at the tortured face of her once beloved Papa now seemingly locked into some kind of very unhappy dream and knew that his wife and first daughter had truly abandoned him to his sad fate. Her mother and sister not coming up all the stairs to say good bye to her was one thing but to ignore the fate of the man who had looked after them for so very long a time. Tears sprang into her eyes as she thought what a very sad and unhappy family he had created, where the only cement between them had been the constant supply of money to pay for dresses so that he had had to resort to lower and lower ways of making money just to satisfy them. There had been a time when local Society had been enough for him but of late the need to go to a Spa at Leamington or to have to give a ball to compete with the very rich families that lived about here. Gowns and more gowns until he came across the only way to increase his income. Gambling, more and more and now he was gone as was his wife and eldest daughter.

At Saxethorpe Manor the gatehouse stood as it had since Will was a lad. A small stone built edifice with a thatched roof and he was delighted when he saw that his elder brother had seen fit to keep the estate in good order in spite of being a full time soldier. As he rode his horse through the open gates Will really felt the weight of being finally, after all these years away, back at home and he spurred 'Hector' into a canter to shorten the time to ride across the park to his sister's house. The sweep of the long avenue of limes stretched far down towards Saxethorpe Hall so that it was not even in sight on this side of the Estate. The Dower House was close to the main house with the small road that led into Saxethorpe from Cley by the Sea running past only a mile or so away.

As he grew closer Will started to feel that not all was well as he started to pass a near continuous line of stone laden carts that rolled steadily from the side entrance of the Estate. It worried him, for his brother had never spoken of further building at the Hall. Perhaps some major repairs... perhaps.

As Will rode through the ornamental gates to the gardens surrounding the Hall he was astounded to see a toiling mass of workers that laboured around the eastern end of the substantial Elizabethan house that sat on its hillock by the bubbling head water stream of the River Bure. What was his brother building? What on earth? Then the revelation struck him that his brother, his so God fearing brother, was desirous of building a chapel and a large one at that. Dedicated to who, Will wondered, and then decided on St John, of course. His brother was using his new fortune to impress the Church. Throwing money to his God. Buying his way into Heaven perhaps and that was when Will noticed how run down the gardens about the house were, how overgrown. His brother, dead only a few weeks but John must have started construction long before he knew of his brother's death... strange, unless Lawrence had consented to the construction.

Will sat his black horse, the strong easterly wind blowing the black mane and his fair hair, staring at the building site. Then, in the distance, he saw two coaches coming down the drive from the west entrance, the black vehicles reminded Will of his ecclesiastical friends especially as each was pulled by four black horses. They pulled up some two, three hundred yards away, in a cloud of fine white dust, and Will observed with interest as men scurried to their sides; the doors were opened, the steps pulled down and from the first vehicle a richly clad, in purple robes, man descended whose balding tonsured head gleamed in the setting sun. My brother, Will thought, come to inspect his new church and perhaps to go to a funeral or two. A kind of cold livid rage seemed to fill Will's heart but he knew that he must try to be polite to his brother so, even as the small group of priests moved onto the stone floor of the foundation, Will spurred 'Hector' forward.

The nave, paved with finished stone, the columns almost finished, reared up in Gothic style for in time they would support a wooden roof. The party, all darkly clad, moved forward to where the altar would one day stand and such was their chatter that none heard the thunder of steel shod hooves approaching.

Then with a loud clatter of horse shoes and a scattering of workmen the war horse bearing its red uniformed, golden haired soldier cantered down the aisle and for a long frightening moment Bishop John thought that his elder brother had returned from the valley of death.

'Hector' curvetted in his excitement, snorting, whickering and stamping at the stone floor while Will stared down at the cowering group, contempt writ large on his face. 'Brother John!' he called out, 'I have returned from the wars. Have you no welcome for me?' For he could see the ashen face of his brother half hiding behind the substantial foundation stones of one of the columns.

A pulling together of feelings, thoughts and robes the Bishop John of Ely stepped forth, black rage surging up in his heart but struggling to get his voice under control. 'William, you have returned and are welcome.'

Will thought that this would be a good time to ask difficult questions. 'You see I am alive and well brother. The curious order for two sarcophagi to be carved for the family tomb might need some explaining?' Will slid from his horse and now he marched, heels smashing into the stone floor, spurs ringing out, rowels spinning, ablaze in the sunlight, forward, ignoring the ecclesiastics gathered around his brother.

The Bishop stood there, a cold voice coming from a cold heart. 'A misunderstanding, brother. It is with joy that I welcome you back to life and Saxethorpe Hall.'

The tone of the man's voice belied his words of 'joy' but Will expected nothing else. He was a man now and battle hardened so that this Bishop was no threat to him as he had been when he was younger. The fact was that it was John who had driven Will away into the Army but it was the understanding Lawrence who had bought his commission in the Household Cavalry.

'This...' Will looked around at the stone skeleton of the Chapel and wondered why. 'Why this John?'

'It is in celebration of God.' They had moved slowly away from the whispering group of clerics until they stood by the stone mullioned frame of a large stained glass rose window that hung from a web of ropes awaiting the support of brick and stone.

'And you would kill for your God?' Will asked as he looked down on the rotund figure so unlike his own.

'I must do what I must do for God.'

'You must kill your brother?'

'You are to be a sacrifice to God. A necessary ending of a useless life.'

'So you admit that you...?'

'Why not, since it was God that told me to kill you.' The pale eyes of the priest managed to look snake like.

'One of your visions then?'

'I have always followed my voices and they have never let me down.' The Bishop's face was cruel in its intensity.

'Well, they failed you this time.' Will said with easy contempt.

The purple dressed man, gold crucifix swinging on his chest, looked up a little angrily at his taller brother and then said. 'They never fail; you will die and before Lawrence's funeral, it is certain and the word comes from God.'

Will felt an icy chill run up his spine hearing the so sure tone of his brother's voice and knew that he could not stay near his brother for the only defence that he could see would be for him to kill his brother first but then he would be apprehended and hung so that his brother's prophecy would have come about.

Will said, 'The funeral will be on or about the 18th July, you will not be officiating but you may...' Will could not bring him self to say it.

'I will be there as will you William except that I will stand before my God and you will be lying in your coffin.' John crossed himself.

The soldier turned away and using the base of a column as a mounting block he remounted his horse, looked down for a moment at the priest then turned his horse toward the Dower House.

Is this possible? My brother, a High Church priest, a Bishop, threatens my life and makes no bones about it; he has decided, or his God perhaps has decided, that I am to die. The French couldn't do it but brother John is more determined it would seem. I wonder what my sister; his sister, has to say on the subject and how does he plan to kill me, more villains in clerical black perhaps, each armed with a cudgel?

The Dower House stood as it had stood in Will's youth, a hundred and fifty yards or so from the Hall. Will had been, more or less, raised there and he knew every inch of the place, its gardens and out buildings. For some reason his father had tried very hard to keep him and John apart. Holy John was a Holy Terror his father used to say and one like that was enough. The constant preaching, the constant condemnation of anyone and everyone that John disapproved of; the main target being Will, so much younger, so much weaker.

The door to the Drawing Room opened onto a fire burning in the grate and a fortyish year old white wigged woman, dressed in black, sat, reading the Bible as the maid led the young officer into the room.

The maid, all of a flutter gasped out. 'Milady, you may have trouble believing it but Will is come home.' The maid, Aggie, almost jumping around in her excitement pulled at the shoulder of the woman in mourning dress and the cool gray, but red rimmed, eyes of the woman looked up ashen faced then total relief showed there for a long moment before love swept her away and she stood her arms opened wide.

'Will!' she cried out overwhelmed and tears started to pour down her face, 'John told me that you'd died at Waterloo.'

Will stood there smiling with delight. 'Well, John was wrong about me but not about Lawrence.' Will moved to the lady and hugged her, kissed her, 'Feel solid enough for you do I Annie?'

The woman was now incoherent with sobbing but Will knew that she was more than glad to see him. 'He would put me in a nunnery if he could Will....' she choked out, '...he's always been a religious maniac but now I feel that he has been driven mad by his God.' Tears rolled down her face and Will mopped at them, a little clumsily, with his handkerchief, kissing her cheeks and holding on tight to her.

Will said, 'I saw him at his... his edifice.'

'It's his own chapel, dedicated to Saint John. I fear that he thinks himself an apostle of the Lord. He never stops preaching at me...' she gestured with the closed Bible, '...but the worst thing is he never stops talking to God.'

'Where does he stay? The Hall?'

'Yes, and very luxurious he's made it. No expense has been spared. You wouldn't like it, nearly everything is silken and in purple, of course, and the number of crucifixes is immense.'

'Well, dearest Annie, I am indeed glad to be here at the Dower House although he has not made me welcome at the Manor; rather the opposite. May I stay here tonight?'

'Tonight? You may stay here forever.' She couldn't stop herself touching him, cuddling him in her arms, crushing him to her.

After they had taken tea William told his sister everything that he knew and he reiterated the savage threats that his so religious brother had made. They sat in the silence of the Drawing Room, noticeably minus the religious influence of Brother John, and thought on the problem, then Anne asked Will what he would do.

'I will give John every chance. If he attempts to carry out his threats then I will regard us at open warfare, something at which I am rather good.'

The evening post stage, that arrived at eight of the clock in July, clattered into the yard of the Golden Hind Inn in a cloud of dust, and a scurry of small potboys and ostlers. The only passenger for Saxethorpe was a tall, thin, dark clad man wearing a tall black silk hat and a severe expression.

A little later, in a great crashing and jangling, four, war horse mounted Household Cavalry officer's rode into the yard and amid a deal of shouting and ordering to the eight servants and guards that rode with them, they entered the tavern in the red of their tunics and the glitter and flash of the high polish of their riding boots.

It was later, after an early supper with his sister that Will decided that perhaps he would ride into Saxethorpe and see if Tom or any military mourners had arrived at the Golden Hind.

Apologising to his sister and telling her that he would come and fetch her for the lying in, Will rode away.

As he cantered through the evening light Will found that the threat from his brother became more and more extraordinary. He himself had acted out of character, the sight of the chapel angering him so but the threats from his brother were absurd if John had not taken himself so seriously. To threaten to murder your own brother under orders from God; surely this was a sign of madness. Will had told Anne what John had said and she'd answered that it was something of a miracle that he hadn't physically attacked Will such was his mental state. Will kept thinking of the past few days and wondered how far Tom had got with the cart. He should, surely, have arrived here by now but had he not that could mean that something had happened to the cart. An axle, a wheel or something else to slow him down but a black painted coach and four devilishly black horses is what had happened.

Tom, lolloping through the late afternoon, his cart now an easy pull with the lead coffin gone had wended his way quietly, clip, clopping along. The guitar lay cradled across his knees as he practiced his now five chords and sang along with his sea shanties; not that they always fitted but mostly they did, so that he didn't notice a horseman behind the cart. When two priest like figures stepped from the undergrowth and held up their hunting shotguns he had carefully put the guitar into the back of the cart and then turned, with a smile, to the men. They'd ignored him and set about pulling the cover from the back and started to root around looking for....

'Hay! the damned cart is full of hay..' a tall clerically clad man snarled.

'It's a hay cart, for the carrying of hay...' Tom managed a baffled sort of look which considering that they had torn his carefully baled hay to pieces as they looked for the coffin. 'Farmer Brown is going to be very unhappy.'

'Where's the coffin boy?' the other man asked or rather shouted.

'This is Farmer Brown's hay cart; if he has a coffin cart I've never seen her,' Tom said in what he hoped were placatory tones, fortunately the men had missed the guitar which even Tom might have had difficulty explaining away.

'We're fucked!' the rider shouted down, '...where the hell is that coffin?'

Tom looked at the arguing men and wondered what they would have done with the lead coffin even if they'd found it and he also wondered what they would do to him. At this moment an open carriage appeared coming from Norwich with two gentlemen seated inside and two outriders. They stopped to look at the scene before them and even as they did so the men in black disappeared into the undergrowth.

'Highwaymen!' Tom shouted out, '...they were after my hay...'

When Will got to the Golden Hind he found a somewhat smug young man seated before a substantial supper of beef pie and small beer, the ancient beamed room barely half full of farm workers and the like. Pipe smoke swirled around them and although it was early the closeness to the end of the week and pay day made for a jolly atmosphere. Tom spotted his Master as he came in and stood, still chewing on a piece of the somewhat tough beef.

'Tom! You got here in fine style and on time which is more than I expected...' Will was pulling off his riding cloak and seating himself. 'A bottle of your best claret Innkeeper...' he shouted out above the hubbub of the tavern's crowd, which turned a few heads, then he settled himself down beside his companion.

Tom, his mouth still half full said, 'I met with them clerical gents sor and they were most upset by the absence of the coffin and your baggage in the cart.'

'You did?' Will looked astonished for some reason. He had thought that he was the target for his brother but now it seemed that.... No, he had no idea what was happening he just knew that he must get his brother into the church and under guard as soon as the boat arrived. 'Well I'm glad that no harm came to you Tom, when did the boat captain think that he would make Saxethorpe?'

'Early tomorrow; perhaps by ten of the clock, was what he said.'

'We'll meet with him after breakfast then. We'll need the cart to carry the coffin again Tom but this business must be concluded swiftly.'

Will settled himself in the spacious chair set before the unlit fire just as, with a tremendous military racket the four Guards officers clattered down the stairs. Seeing their ranks Will was forced to leap to his feet.

'Colonel Sir, Major William Saxethorpe at your service.'

Lord Provely, the somewhat overweight man who had presumably taken the place of Lawrence Saxethorpe waved indolently saying as he did so. 'Condolences Saxethorpe, Lawrence was a fine man, fine officer too. The Duke ordered me...us to come; couldn't manage it himself, Affairs of state...' the farm workers made a quiet circle for these London toffs to occupy. 'We've taken a private dining room...' his eyes flickered over Tom who had carried on munching on his pie. 'Where you're welcome to join us...'

Will did join them as he was expected to but made his excuses after explaining something of the problems associated with the funeral. He left the dining room where the travel weary soldiers, all of whom had been at Waterloo, were getting somewhat merry.

As Will re-entered the tavern his eye was caught by the sight of a gaunt black clad figure sitting now quite close to where Tom was holding court with three young men so Will decided to see if his new friend the curate was still up and about.

Evensong was a service to which both Will, the curate and the general populace seemed somewhat unconcerned about for the church was empty save for the choir of young boys and what was probably their older brothers and some fathers. Will went to sit in the Saxethorpe family pew and enjoyed the music a good deal more than he had as a young lad. After several hymns, a sung psalm and a very pleasantly elaborate exit of all the members of the choir leaving only Will and the Curate in the body of the church.

The Curate advanced on Will his serious expression of humility still in place until he smiled at the sight of his new friend.

'It is by courtesy of your brother that the choir and indeed myself are so very well fitted out. The visiting Bishop comes here when he is at Saxethorpe and expects to be entertained both in the religious and the secular way. Keeps me on my toes.'

Will stood wearily, his red uniform, which blazed with the gold epaulets of his rank and smiled in return thinking that religion would not be so bad if all its representatives were like Charles Morris. 'A fine show indeed and very musical I think, much improved since the last time I came for a service.'

'Once again, your brother John I think. He works hard in the service of the Church.'

'I have a story to tell you Charles. A sad story indeed.'

It was more than an hour later that Will finished confessing his unhappiness with his religious brother's life and ambitions.

'You are sure that he threatened you?'

'He spoke without contradiction, he said I would die before the funeral so that I could be buried along with Lawrence.'

A silence fell over them, a stone echoing silence that seemed full of threats then Charles asked, 'Why would the men sent after you want to waylay the coffin of your brother?'

'In that I think is the answer to all. The Bishop wants my brother's body but for what reason?'

'Is there anything in the coffin with him?' Charles sounded a little diffident about asking such a question.

The sad faced soldier said quietly. 'He was... I had him... They cleaned him up and pumped some kind of preservative, I don't know its name... into him. He's wearing the uniform that he died in, and his sabre... the only other thing in the coffin is his 'If I should fall letter,' it was in his breast pocket covered in blood, shot through I think.'

'Did you read it...the letter?'

'No, it's usually addressed to the next of kin...'

'Was it addressed to the Bishop?'

Will tried to remember but couldn't. ' I was too upset, I couldn't see for tears... my poor brother.'

Charles wondered if it was the letter that was the problem. The body was the body and nothing, save God, could alter that but the letter?

'When we have the coffin tomorrow I suggest that we have it opened and take out the letter and any other documents that....'

'There's only the letter, that I'm sure of.'

Charles looked narrowly at his new friend then asked, 'You searched through his pockets?'

'No!' Will sounded shocked and a little angry wondering if Charles thought him some kind of grave robber. 'I took him to an undertaker in Bruxelles which was where they found the... the last letter.'

'Which you didn't read?'

Will found himself staring into the curate's eye's wondering if that had been his mistake all along.

CHAPTER EIGHTEEN

A room locked and barred made Will feel safer, for he now had concluded, like his sister, that their brother was mad as a hatter. Will laid in the big bed and went through it all step by step and he couldn't find any reason why his brother should want him dead. Then, his thoughts straying towards Lady Jane Walden he fell pleasantly asleep.

A dull morning with a siren wind from the east woke him. It was only six but Will roused the Innkeeper to arrange breakfast. Will and Tom checked all the guns and then Tom drove the cart down to the town quay with Will following on 'Hector'. They came down the ramp from the stone cobbled roadway to the narrow dock arriving just as the church clock struck nine times.

The curve of the river, the tumbling water on the weir, the low light as the sun tried to break through, and there at the quay was the riverboat neatly moored and dangling from the boom, now rigged as a crane, was the lead coffin. Already on the quay was the military baggage of the two brothers and all surrounded by four men in clerical black.

Will snatched a horse pistol from his saddle even as Tom slid the rifled musket from its sheath as they rumbled down the jetty. Even as they closed on the bad men Tully appeared on deck, amongst the crew, with a carbine pointing at the priests. 'Haloo sor!' he called out merrily, '…they've arranged a noice welcome for ye.'

As Will got nearer the priests backed away even though each one clutched at a knife or a cudgel.'

Will shouted at the men, 'If you wish to see the coffin and pay your respects, my dead brother will be in the Parish Church of St. Mary's within the hour. Tell the Bishop that if he wishes to come and see his brother he will be welcome but you gentlemen will not. Give me any excuse and I will shoot one of you and then draw my sword; vain threats I know but true ones for this is the body of my brother that you threaten.'

Anger burnt hot and bright in Will's breast as he watched the men slink away. He set Tom to replacing the rifled musket and gave him the other carbine then went on board to see his man.

'Tully, I am glad to see you, and you managed to catch up with the boat?'

'Met them on the Aylsham lock as you suggested, and just as well, sor, for those thieves were awaiting us here only showing themselves when we had nearly finished unloading. I asked the captain to hold the coffin until you came with the cart otherwise it to would have been on the dock.'

'You've done well, as ever Tully.' Will frowned, trying hard to concentrate but nevertheless wanting to know what had occurred in Saffron Walden, '...and my message to the Lady Jane Walden?'

'She has both sor, the message and the purse.'

'And how did she take? What did she say... do?'

'She looked pensive, puzzled, but she thanked me and said that she understood the instructions you put on her. I told her I was to talk with Mr Bailey and later, just before I departed; I saw her go to Mr Bailey so...' he shrugged his shoulders and smiled tiredly.

'You must be fatigued Tully?'

'I slept on the boat sor, all the way up here; very pleasant indeed.'

'Good man Tully. Now we must get the coffin onto the cart and then to the church. Tell the captain to be most careful of my brother,' Will, who eye's constantly scanned the shore for sight of the black clad men added, '...I have employed the local gravedigger and his assistants to help with the burial.' Will stopped, feeling overwhelmed by what was happening to him. A dead brother, a young woman, his two companions, so good, so kind to him and his still living brother who was, could only be totally evil, whose 'voice's' had driven him mad. Shaking his head he went forward to help tie down the coffin with the ropes and knots that Tom had trained him in the use of.

Charles Morris, now garbed in his curates cassock, stood amongst the four Guardsmen, now in their full ceremonial finery of gleaming breastplate and helmet, high riding boots, spurs, sabre on hip; the whole group a blaze of red and silver in the gloom of the old church. When Will marched into the church beside his sister, her black dress a foil for her younger brothers finery. His worn regimentals seemed shabby compared with the other officers but his bearing and his valour in battle stood him in good stead with his fellow officers his heels crashing on the stones of the ancient floor, his spurs jingling in the silence. They were followed by Will's two companions both armed to the teeth. Behind them came the still sealed coffin carried on the shoulders of six burly farmers who staggered under the weight of it.

As the pallbearers lowered the great coffin onto the catafalque, Lady Anne Saxethorpe was shown to her place in the family pew by Charles Morris.

Curate Morris wondered at how little he had known of this family that was so important in the town. The fact that the Lord was a soldier on active service with the Duke was one factor in the emptiness, generally, of the pew but the fact that Lady Anne, reputed to be very religious locally, rarely came except for the few high days. When the Bishop came that was another story for he would bring both her and all the servants from the Manor so that the church would be packed out. Charles had always rather assumed that Lady Anne was an elderly lady but seeing her on this sad day he noticed that she seemed much younger that he had thought for it was as if she dressed to look far older than she was... odd.

It was only a little later that Will decided to abandon the idea of a long lying in; all he wanted was to get his brother safely into the family vault.

The word was passed around the district so that the next day all was ready for the Service, the church full of the gentry and farmers with their families; the four Household Cavalry officers, one at each corner of the coffin, the fifth, William Saxethorpe, standing before coffin and altar, swords reversed point down, plumed helmets gleaming in the half light. Only Lady Anne sat in the Saxethorpe pew when Charles Morris started the Funeral Service as the choir ended the Requiem.

Of the Bishop there was no sign nor any sign of the black clad ecclesiastical men so awaited. Tully and Tom, both heavily armed, along with four of the tenant farmers waited but nothing happened as the service went at it's sombre pace. The pallbearers came forward to carry the coffin out to the tomb and the Service was over. Lifting, with some real difficulty the men staggered towards the great door of the church that led direct onto the Churchyard but even as the big double doors creaked open a shouting and howling mob of ragged figures rushed at the cortege. Each waved a steel shod cudgel and the scream of imprecations seemed to fill the air.

As the heavy coffin led the way it was the first to fall as the unarmed and unprotected farmers ran for their lives but behind came the chief mourners the first of which was Major Will Saxethorpe closely followed by the four Guardsmen and within a moment swords met cudgels, blades met flesh, for these soldiers were the very cream of the military, with Waterloo not far behind them so blades drew blood even as heavy cudgels crashed at honourable defence. The melee was fierce and short only the crash of musket shots, the spatter of ball torn flesh, the bark of carbines and horse pistols fired at point blank range and the leading four miscreants were down and out, the rest running for their lives.

As swiftly as it had started; it was over. Barely had the musket smoke dispersed across the sunlit churchyard, the exhausted, panting officers each seemingly with a gore covered blade, stood about the cracked and splintered coffin. Their fellow officer, a hero, had been insulted and suborned by these villains and they all stood ready to fight again but of the enemy there was nought to be seen.

Two black clad figures, Charles Morris, his arm protecting Lady Anne, pushed through the crowd of astounded and amazed parishioners and hurried to Will's side, 'William! What has occurred?' Charles voice burst from his lips.

Will, his breath coming short, gasped out. 'A visitation from God I suspect Charles...' he paused to look about him, 'I did not expect such an attack. I'm not sure just what I was to expect but such a savage melee...'

He turned to his fellow officers to thank them but his eye was caught by the sight of his 'companions' carrying their discharged weapons on the edge of the crowd. 'My thanks to you, friends' he shouted out, '... all of you who fought here today....' Portentous stuff, '...fought here today' indeed, he thought. He turned back and then the sight of the dropped and shattered coffin caught his eye.

'My God, what?'

Charles, seeing the broken and split lead, said. 'It's the weight of it Will, the lead lining, the farmers dropped it and it's split open.'

The mourners stood, with mouths open, to stare at the broken sides of the coffin with the still uniformed body half exposed; the ashen face turned to the sky; the still blood stained sword in his right hand. On the corpse's chest, clasped in the man's pale left hand, was the bloodied letter, torn by shot but with the seal still extant. The red uniformed officers had gathered around, knowing, feeling that this was how they would have been if the chances had run against them.

The Curate, his face a mixture of sadness and curiosity, stepped forward and pulled the letter from the dead man's final clutch and turning handed it to Will saying, 'Yours Will, I believe, your brother's final words.'

It was at this moment that, from the church's gateway, a large party of ecclesiastics came, chanting a psalm, censors swaying, aromatic smoke filling the air, preceded by a large elaborate black and gold crucifix being carried before the purple clad person of the Bishop of Ely, as they made their way, slowly and dramatically towards the crowd around the coffin.

Will thrust the letter into his tunic and, his stained sabre still held loosely in his hand, and turned to face his brother.

Charles Morris was later to remember the scene as the most dramatic he had ever witnessed. The tight group of red and silver armoured soldiers gathered about their fallen comrade and the advancing black, menacing mass of religious men. Finally the two parties stood face to face; the psalm fading into silence from the lips of the priests.

Will said in a ringing tone, a slight smile on his face. 'A warm welcome indeed brother, and here you see the outcome...' he waved his left hand at the bodies scattered between the two parties, '...three dead I believe and three needing the help of a surgeon and all the fault of your overweening pride I believe.'

The Bishop didn't deign to glance at the fallen he just said with some menace, 'I know nothing of your troubles with...' he looked briefly around at the battle scene. 'I have arrived to see my brother into his tomb and bless his journey to his God.'

'Well, your merry men have given him a great send off, one such as he would have appreciated; plenty of gunfire and swordplay over his body.' Will stood aside so that the Bishop could see the broken coffin with the exposed body.

Bishop John took a somewhat startled step forward to stare down at his erstwhile relative, his eyes hunting for something and the realization that all his plans had been for nought with the body so close to its final resting place.

The curate stepped forward. 'I feel that recriminations should be saved until after the burial, so if the pall bearers may finish their task.' The six men came from amongst the onlookers with looks of embarrassment and muttered apologies at their dropping of the coffin. The Curate bent to remove the lid and the upper part of the shattered shell and set the broken pieces aside before gesturing to the farmers to pick up the base of the coffin with its occupant still just in place and the cortege reformed for the last fifty yards of its journey.

The tomb was large but not sufficient to hold pall bearers, the Curate, the Bishop and the chief mourners so a very pale Lady Anne, the Bishop, William, the Colonel of the Guards and the two undertakers gathered in the small space as the body was lifted from its deal boards and placed carefully, reverently into the stone sarcophagus.

As the Service was read, Anne, tears streaming down her face, stepped forward and kissed the brow of the dead man before stepping back but none save William took her place.

'Dust to dust, ashes to ashes...' all passed for Will in a black despair of sounds and sights. From Anne's kiss to Bishop John's kneeling beside the stone sarcophagus his purple gloved and ringed hand stretched out to savagely grip on the stone edge where soon a slab of granite would seal Lawrence in forever.

The Bishop and his entourage had departed, the coaches rumbling away towards Saxethorpe Hall leaving William and Anne together with the Guard's officer's to repair to the Golden Hind to celebrate the Wake.

The whole village followed them in and Will took some delight in ordering food and drink for all, and being much cheered therefore, before going into the private Dining Room to be with the other officers, Lady Anne, Curate Morris and one other person who stood quietly near to the unlit fire, a tall man, dark of dress and visage, sombre in aspect and manner.

After some time and a great deal of excited discussion as to the mornings events William, having glanced a number of times at this curious intruder, walked over to introduce himself. 'I am William Saxethorpe sir, and you are?'

The man, looking down a little from his tall, thin height and pursing his lips, answered. 'I am Mr Crindal of Crindal Laythorn, Attorneys at Law.'

'What do you here Mr Crindal?' Will asked, unsmiling.

'I am here to ensure that Lawrence Saxethorpe, Baron and Knight of the Realm is, in fact, deceased.' He paused somewhat portentously then carried on in his deep, dark voice, '... and after this morning's fracas I think that I could testify to the certainty of his passing,' he paused again, '...an extraordinary 'performance' My Lord. Are all country funerals so exciting and diverting?'

'Well, I wouldn't say that many country funerals are quite so 'diverting' as you put it.'

'But the mass of clericals and ex-soldiers that appeared to attack you and the mourners? Is this some kind of, what do the Italians call it? A vendetta, that's it... a vendetta. Well, my Lord?'

'You mistake me Mr Crindal. I am not the Lord in these parts.'

The man looked both surprised and acerbic since not making mistakes was one of his most closely guarded desires in his business life. 'You are William Saxethorpe, brother to Lord Saxethorpe, are you not?'

'Yes, but...'

'Then according to the normal rites of passage you are the next in line to inherit the titles and the estates. The will...'

'My older brother, the Bishop of Ely, is the new Lord of...'

'I fear not,' the tall, frowning lawyer interrupted, '...you are the next in line. Your 'brother,' the Bishop of Ely, was 'adopted', but not legally, by the late Lord Saxethorpe. A boy and a girl, I think, waifs left by the wayside. The laws of inheritance are very firm on the point, a child born of the noble parents has first right over the adopted child, it is only correct I think.'

Will stared at this dark figure a baffled expression on his face wondering how he could not have known of this oddity of inheritance. His brother had never mentioned it, not the once. Why would that be? Did he assume that Will knew? Suddenly he remembered the last letter and reached into his inner pocket to withdraw the blood covered letter.

Across the room Charles Morris had been watching the encounter between Will and the sombre man and when he saw Will extract the letter from his pocket he excused himself from the company and walked over to join his new friend. 'You plan to read the letter then Will?'

Before the soldier could reply the lawyer said dryly. 'His Lordship should perhaps be given the privacy that...'

Charles Morris was quick of intellect and was able in an instant to reconstruct all that had followed before. 'His Lordship?'

'Lord Saxethorpe, yes, sir. I am here to read the last Will and Testament of the late Lord Lawrence Saxethorpe to the beneficiaries.'

Will looked from one man to the other his thoughts muddled by the events of the day but knowing that now... 'That must be why brother John acted as he did.'

'It must be indeed Will, your brother knows that he has no right to the title and the estates, whilst you live, and does not wish to relinquish them,' Charles Morris sounded so very certain for he thought the problem solved.

'But how did John think that he could get away with this... this crime?'

Everyone in the room was now staring at the three men, the silence as total as was possible.

'I think that was why he needed to bury both my brother and myself side by side. Only then could he inherit.' Will was deeply shocked almost more so than when he had not understood the demands that had fallen on Holy John

'Lady Anne...' Will started to say.

'Is no 'Lady' I'm afraid,' the lawyer interrupted.

Will turned to the gently smiling woman who had largely raised him, 'Did you hear all Annie?'

She shrugged her shoulders. 'I heard enough I think Will. You are to be the Lord Saxethorpe,' she paused to look down at the floor then up to smile again at the young man, '...and my brother must retreat to Ely,' she slowed again, frowned, then added, 'I shall go with him of course.'

Will stared at this much beloved woman who had raised him, horror writ large upon his face. 'You will not Annie. You will stay where you are for as long as you live and a pension will...'

The lawyer interrupted him to say. 'That is a part of the Will, Milord, the pensions to be paid etcetera. I think it best if the reading could be postponed until everyone concerned is summoned; that includes your 'adopted' brother John, the Bishop.'

Will, now thoroughly confused, stared about himself. 'Yes, very well. I shall send a message to the Bishop and...'

'You must read the letter Will,' the curate, somewhat anxiously, said, '...it may well contain some continuance of the explanation.'

Will looked at his new friend then down at the bloodied letter and then broke the seal to unfold the creased paper to read,

To my beloved Will,

We both know that you will never be reading this unless I have fallen. In it I must explain what father explained to me; the reasons why you have never known that you are heir to the family estates and not our brother John. It was to protect the feelings of John and Anne that Father made me swear to secrecy and I have obeyed him for so long after his and mother's deaths. He felt that John and Anne deserved to keep their pride and not have their forebears exposed as the road travellers that they were. Your arrival so late in Mother's life seemed to father to make the lives of John and Anne even more important. He was proud of John's achievements and of the wonderful care and love that Annie gave to you even though she herself was so young. Father never made the marriage arrangements for her that would have been natural for he feared that she and all her friends would find out her secret. If you feel inclined to keep the secret yourself I leave up to you but remember that when you succeed to the title the people in the county will wonder why your apparently older brother has not inherited but that, as I say, I leave up to you.

You realize that Holy John is no friend of mine or come to that yours but Annie must be protected and loved at all times and to this you must swear.

And so I take my leave of you and wish you God Speed through life. I'm sure that in leaving my estates and its good people in your hands they will be looked after by you in my stead.

God bless you Will, and Goodbye

Yours forever, Lawrence of Saxethorpe.

Will handed the letter to the curate wishing that he had read the letter in Belgium when he had first held it but regrets about the past were a waste for he knew now what path his life would take and thought that the sooner he started on his new life the better.

Charles said, nodding. 'A good farewell letter with the explanation laid out before you. What more proof is needed?'

Will said, his face worried, 'I suppose that I must now go to the Hall and beard brother John if he is still there.'

Charles replied. 'He will have left I think, but it is curious how he knew that Lawrence's final letter would reveal all.'

'He came up with an alternative plan or God did. Kill me and all his problems would be over except that he must not appear to be involved...'

'The churchyard melee?'

'He must have lost control, he panicked and ordered my death. He needed the coffin just in case so if it existed he could obtain the letter and then he would be safe...'

'Well, the secret is out now Milord, you should be safe.'

'Except that he is a religious fanatic; sorry Charles, but he is. He believes that God speaks to him direct from Heaven and that everything that he does is sanctioned. He's always believed that.' Will paused to think on these strange events then added. 'Mr Crindal, if, by chance, I should die would my brother still inherit?'

The dark man nodded slowly saying. 'If you have not provided an heir for the estates and title, then yes he could inherit although it might be contested.' He looked somehow pleased with the idea of litigation.

Will stood, somehow alone, in the middle of the small crowded room, knowing that the pursuit for his life would continue endlessly unless. 'Mr Crindal, could I leave my estates to another, maybe not the title but the estates?'

The tall man nodded saying. 'It might be possible but it would be much better if...'

'And if I adopt someone legally, a boy, a young man, could he inherit?'

'It might make for an interesting case in law but I think the answer must be yes.'

Will thought, you may be even luckier that you think young Tom.

A dramatic, a seemingly heaven sanctioned sunset soared in red and gold far into the evening sky as the mourning cortege, mounted on war horses and armed to the teeth entered the park and trotted down the long tree lined drive. William riding in the group of officers led the way followed by Tully, Tom and three mounted farmer's, all armed. The two miles passed quickly beneath the steel shod hooves clattering, casting sparks into the dust cloud that followed them.

At the great house, a window shutter banged in the evening breeze that came from the sea, a blue line on the horizon. A forgotten door swung lazily caught by the same puff of air and Will realized that his erstwhile brother had gone, retreated to his cathedral ship floating at Ely, his dream over, blown away.

The party tramped through the house where nearly every room was draped with purple cloth and every wall had its own crucifix. Will pulled, his face angry, at the drapes to find that the walls were untouched, they had just been cheaply covered in purple cloth. The house was empty, no servants, not one person, no life and Will once again thought that John was an agent of death, not a celebrant of life.

They marched around to the half finished chapel and Will stared up at the Gothic arches caught against the sky and wondered at the cost to the estate then, catching a glimpse of a workman just coming from an out building he called out. 'Ho there, sir.'

The heavily built man wearing rough, lime whitened clothes stopped, then walked over to the officer. 'Sor?'

'And you are?

'Roger Thompson, Master Builder.'

'I would like it if you terminated your work; stopped building, this chapel will never be finished; rather, that it will be pulled down.'

The frowning workman looked around the site before asking. 'Are you the owner of this place sor?'

'It seems that I am. I am Lord Saxethorpe.'

'Then the Bishop...?'

'He's gone I think,' Will said somewhat hesitantly.

'The whole party did leave in some haste but no one said anything,' the Master builder added as if he wished to know more.

Will looked at this ruddy-faced man, his mortar whitened clothes, his rough hands and knew him to be honest so he asked. 'The account for this... this building? The two men stared at each other.

'There is no... or very little money owing. The diocese of Ely is a prompt payer so...'

'So no money is owing and the Church itself is the...' Will asked hesitantly but he could see that with his brother still alive there could be no question of the Estate paying, for his brother was, had been, at best, a hesitant communicant and believer. So the Estate would be solvent, that was to his advantage, so many things could be achieved now that he knew. Only the Steward might know. 'The estate Steward?' Will asked.

'Mr Colman was sent somewhere by the Bishop. I know not where.'

Life at Saxethorpe did, over the next two weeks, start to return to normal. In the Hall, the domestic servants were restored to their posts and pulled down all the purple drapes, which Will gave to them, so that the cottages and village houses were to have luxurious purple curtains and furniture coverings for many years to come. The gardeners were re-called to start the restoration of the gardens about the Manor House.

Lady Anne had returned, more than somewhat puzzled, to the Dower House where Will was to sleep in his childhood room.

She knew now that brother John was gone from her life and she felt a deep gratitude to God and Will for bringing it about. Aggie brought her tea and she explained briefly what had happened at the Inn with especial reference to her losing her title which, she well knew, had never meant anything to her. The Master, Lawrence's father had insisted when she was eighteen, that in future she would always be known as Lady Anne of Saxethorpe. She had protested, standing in the Great Hall holding the hand of little Will, that she had no right. But Lord Peter had over ridden her protests saying that the title would help to protect her and Will. He'd scooped up the little boy and kissed him on the forehead, saying, '...one day Will, one day.'

For Anne it had been the oddest of days, starting with her conversation with the curate who had been somewhat worried about her. Then had come the Service, with poor Lawrence there before her. A box was all that she could see but she knew that her Lawrence was sealed inside, once so loving and now so dead. Then the extraordinary attack, the unnecessary deaths of those poor men, ex-soldiers all and then that most shocking of all possible sights, Lawrence's poor dead body, ashen, blood drained, lying before her. The mausoleum, the open coffin and then finding that she was kissing his dead brow. A last kiss, Anne thought, a very last kiss.

The consolation offered her by the curate, a warm, kindly man had helped a little and she had had to resist the temptation to tear off the wig which had made her life a purgatory; an itchy and hot purgatory. Then the revelation of Will's rank; all had led to a feeling, well concealed, of joy in her heart.

CHAPTER NINETEEN

Will sat before a small fire, his battered and blood spotted red tunic thrown away now. It had, it seemed to him, to have been unlucky in some way, foolish of course to think such a thing but he wanted now to start his life afresh where he could and he glanced across to where Annie sat seemingly rifling through the Holy Bible and frowning when she found some reference or other.

Will frowned on seeing her concentration and found that he had to ask. 'What do you do, Annie?'

She didn't even glance up so concentrated was she on the Scriptures but she did say, 'Charles, told me how wrong so many of my thoughts were. My reading of the Bible seems to him to be at fault. John told me...'

'And Charles has a better, gentler interpretation?'

'He most certainly has. He says that John, no, I shall not say what he says...'

Will smiled gently at her. 'I would trust the word of our curate far above the words of John. Charles is a very good man and intelligent. His view of his faith is open to discussion but he adheres I think, to the idea that Jesus said we should love each other and I think that that is what Charles does.'

Anne looked across at him then gently closed the Bible knowing that she would place a lot less emphasis on its writings in the future; she smiled at Will. 'A busy day for you Will, my new Lord Saxethorpe.'

Will looked at her with love shining in his eyes. 'You will be safe with me Annie, you and Aggie, until the end of your days.'

The next day Will had his two companions given pleasant rooms in the Stable Block; in Tom's case directly over the stables where his horses were now comfortably installed.

Will, his spirit somewhat heartened, set everyone to work and did more that his fair share of the hard manual labour that restoring Saxethorpe Hall to its former dusty glory entailed, only the continuing absence of his Steward was there to annoy him. Finding a competent man seemed a priority but at the end of the second week the annoying vision of a dark red haired girl became impossible for him to ignore.

Will had asked a tailor from Norwich to attend the Estate so that measurements might be taken and cloth chosen. His brother's clothes did fit him well and he knew that, with time, he would be able to wear any and all without compunction but not for now.

New clothes; suits, jackets, britches and boots would set him up and stop reminding him of his sad loss.

On the Monday of the second week, just after the tailor and his two assistants had arrived at the Hall, Will was passing through the Stable Yard when he spied his companions sitting in the sun taking the air, Tom reading what appeared, at a distance, to be a novel, Tully smoking a pipe and Will thought that they needed some occupation more profitable to his endeavours.

'Tom! Tully!' he shouted sharply.

The two of them looked up startled.

'I have need of you in the Hall, now.'

The two of them looked at each other then back to their Master before hurrying to follow him.

Tom whispered to his companion. 'Him becoming a Lord has surely changed him.'

'He's just very busy Tom. I've known him this seven years or more and he has never shown any side... or pride. He was just like his brother.'

In the great, much beamed bedchamber that was once his brother's the three men and the tailors were gathered, surrounded by many bolts of cloth, bundles of undergarments and all the impedimenta of fashionable dress.

'More clothes sor?' expostulated Tom, '...I have no need of more. You have already provided me with a suit and two jackets of tweed plus...'

Will managed to look disgruntled at having his orders contested. 'The tailor is here now and you will be outfitted in the best, that is my order. To be my companions on my travels you must look the part.'

The clothing was to be ready in five days so Will planned to start his return to Saffron Walden as soon after the final fittings as possible.

On the Saturday following Will and his companions set off for Norwich to finalize the Will with Mr Crindall and then for sure to turn 'Hector', 'Trojan' and Tully's horse 'Liebling' south to Saffron House.

To Will the problems of dealing with his brother and the affairs of re-organizing the estate had somehow hardened him; cooled his passion, frozen his emotions and what he had hoped to be a short diversion became two days of concentrated meetings with Mr Crindal. The question of the succession was one that mazed him the most for the idea of Tom being his heir if he should die before an heir had been born to him was one that Mr Crindal liked for it had the smell of litigation about it so that the legalities must be most carefully constructed and precedents found and bound up in the Will and then a somewhat simpler Will, for the reversion, was needed for Tom.

There was a great deal of document signing to be done then it was off to the tailors to try on their new apparel. As they rode through the town Will wondered at what he had done. He knew that he could not tell his protégée what he had done except that he would broach the subject when he felt the time was right.

Newly dressed all three of them looked like gentlemen of wealth and position even Tully, with his big nosed Romany looks. Tom, growing like a weed with his good diet, stood as the very epitome of what the son of noble house should look like. A well fitted dark green jacket and tan britches worn with shining new riding boots; as he and Will stood together staring into the large tailor's mirror both knew that something important had happened. That Tom could no longer just be the driver of an old farm cart for he looked what he was, the heir to a large fortune.

'I'm glad that you had your hair cut Tom. You look the proper gentleman now.'

'But I am not sir, I am acting a part like some player in the theatre.'

Will looked into the eyes of the boy reflected in the glass of the mirror and said. 'From now on Tom, you must fit yourself to the role as an actor would and I think that I must enrol you in a school.'

'A school sir. I would'st rather die; learning Latin and the like...' the horror of losing his freedom was spread across Tom's features.

'Maybe a tutor then Tom; to give you the civilities, the manners.'

Will saw Tully looking a little sad and disregarded so he said, 'Tully, you will always be my man. I don't think that you are cut out to be a gentleman, that's perhaps a step to far, but you will never go hungry and then there's the question of marriage.'

'Marriage sor?'

'You might meet a lady one day that meets with your approval and you could bring her to Saxethorpe, perhaps a cottage, something of that order.' So Will's companions were well satisfied as they mounted up to leave Norwich.

It was early afternoon on the second day when a saddle weary Lord Saxethorpe slid from 'Trojan' under the portico of his new dwelling, Saffron House. Will was just about to ask Tully and Tom to walk the horses around to the Stable Yard but spying a boy carrying a feed net, he shouted out, 'Hallo, groom!'

The boy turned to him, a puzzled expression on his face, 'Sor?'

'Could you take these three, give them a rub down, then feed and water them well.'

The boy turned as if looking for someone and then replied. 'I would sor, but who are you and...'

A woman's voice came clearly. 'Do what the Master asks of you Jim, and do it well.' There she stood, wearing a blue and white check muslin dress and white apron, Lady Jane Walden, her face as serious as her voice had been. The groom grabbed the reins from Will and led the horses away towards the stables leaving the four to stare at each other then the men all bowed and Lady Jane curtseyed.

Will, wanting to be alone said, his eyes never leaving Jane Walden for a moment half turned to his companions and said. 'Go with the groom please and see to the horses. When they are rested a little you should ride into the town and take rooms at that

Inn where we were before...' the two 'companions' nodded, knowing that their Master had a difficult time ahead of him.

Lady Jane had not moved, concentrating her every thought on this man trying to separate the daydream from the reality of him. So tall, so broad of shoulder, well dressed enough but travel stained for she knew that he had ridden for at least two days to come so far but he did not seem fatigued rather that he seemed tense, anxious, even so she thought to ease the tension in the atmosphere so she said. 'You are at least five days early sir, and who are these gentlemen that you do not introduce me to?' Jane's voice seemed sadder than it should have been.

Will smiled a little at her reaction to his two companions. 'There was no need for introductions surely Lady Jane, for do you not know my 'companions', Tom and Tully.'

This man loves to disguise himself, Jane thought, and now has taken to disguising his servants both of whom appeared very well dressed indeed. 'Tom? Your driver? Tully, your Army servant?'

'In a previous life Milady they were those things but now we ride together, talk together, eat together, drink together, companions and friends.'

A silence fell between them until Will picked up her first remark, her first question. 'Did I give you a date on which I would return?' Will's voice was serious even as some blocked off corner of his mind reacted to the sight of this beautiful young woman. Her hair was uncurled and uncombed, flying in the light breeze, her cheeks a little flushed and she bit at her lip in her worry and confusion.

'You said a month and it is five days before. I might have been a little more prepared for your inspection.'

Will blurted out, somewhat sharply. 'I did not come here to inspect you Milady.'

The girl smiled at his mistake. 'I was not referring to myself sir, but the Saffron Estate.'

'Yes... yes of course... that's what I meant.' Now it was Will who appeared confused, embarrassed.

Jane thought to ease the situation so she said. 'It is close to tea-time sir. Mr Bailey and I have become accustomed to taking tea at three in the Steward's office so if you would care to join us?'

Wills half baffled look said more that he could have said. 'How are you Milady, and how is Lord Walden?'

She wished, momentarily, that he had separated these two questions so that her response might be more reasoned so she replied. 'I am well sir, my father is not.'

An abrupt answer, Will thought, to an abrupt question. I must learn to be more circumspect otherwise I will lose her again. 'Your father has not improved then in the past month?' The two of them walked slowly towards the brick archway that led to the long row of stable and workshop doors that lined two sides of the wide Stable Yard.

'According to his physician, and I must thank you for bearing the cost sir, he will never improve. He will live for some time longer but not improve in his health of mind.' Jane looked away, the ongoing nature of her father's breakdown still filling her mind.

They had stopped and she stood before him with her head bowed.

'And there is nothing to be done?' Will asked quietly.

'The physician recommends that my father be taken to a hospital. There is one not far...' the tears now rolled without stopping down her face streaking her complexion with gleaming lines.

'I will cover the costs of the hospital Milady.' Will sounded sad indeed.

'Thank you sir,' said with a sob in her voice. 'He no longer recognizes me sir. I have gone...' Jane thought, I have lost my father and I have no one to share my grief with save this man.

'And Lady Walden?' The note of cool dislike sounded in Will's voice.

'She has not yet returned from her, my Aunt's house.' Jane's voice sounded flat and empty for she knew that her mother would not return whilst her husband lay strapped to his narrow bed.

Will opened the door that they stood before and they both entered the small office. The Tithe table was heaped with papers and ledgers and Mr Bailey was writing carefully in the rent book. He glanced up and then stood smartly, a somewhat worried expression on his face. 'You have returned sir, a little early I'm afraid; the re-organization that you suggested is very nearly in place but last weeks rain did interrupt...'

'It's of no matter Mr Bailey.' Will thrust out his hand to his Steward, 'Perhaps you can take me through what has been achieved.'

The clatter of the pump, the rush and gurgle of water, the crash of the kettle hitting the small iron range. The delicate tinkle of porcelain cups and saucers made a domestic background to the men's talk, the rustle of papers and the unrolling of plan sheets. At some point Will glanced up to see Lady Jane clinging two handed onto a great time and smoke blackened kettle as she directed the boiling water into a large silver teapot, seeming to wrap herself in the fragrant steam that arose.

Will's only thought was that he had never seen such a beautiful sight.

Jane's glance up as she pushed the lid onto the teapot became more baffled as she intercepted his look. 'The tea must draw sir, then...'

'I was once a soldier madam. I know how tea is made.' His voice was, to his annoyance, a little harsh and admonitory.

She looked at him, slightly amused now, for his strong words were backed up by a slight blush. 'You are no longer a soldier sir, no longer a Major of Horse?'

'I... I am... not... although they continue to keep me on half pay. I know not for how long.' Will realized that his thoughts of her was beginning to interrupt his business conversation and only the lull created by her pouring the tea allowed him to recover himself somewhat.

Mr Bailey observing their reactions to each other thought that there was more than a passing relationship in their attitude but thought it wiser to allow the silence between them to develop unaided.

Finally, as he sipped the tea, Will was able to ask. 'How d'you look after your father?'

She stared at him and glanced briefly at the Steward who was trying to efface himself. 'I... we, have a Day Nurse and two Night nurses. They are the largest expense on the house.'

'Why two nurses at night?' I must say something, Will thought. It must be quite horrible for her, for anyone in the same position.

'My father becomes very restive at night for some reason and I cannot manage him on my own...' she sounded a little desperate thinking that he found fault with her.

The Steward chimed in to say. 'It's true sir. I wrote to you of the problem. You didn't reply so I took it upon myself to employ extra help. He does become very... agitated.'

'Only at night sir, he becomes....' she could not go on for her tears had returned.

Somehow Will found that he had stood and gone to her, taken the cup and saucer from her and folded her into his arms. He was later to marvel at his response for he had decided, as he rode, that he would find a more amenable woman to marry, perhaps someone from his own county but all that thinking was now gone because his love had returned with some force. 'You are not to worry Jane. I will attend to matters and will speak with the physician as soon as possible.'

Later Mr Bailey had a one horse curricle brought up so that Will and Lady Jane could set off to tour the estate, for Will had yet to see it all. In a curious turn of events it was Lady Jane that took the reins and whip and drove the horse forward.

A lane that followed an almost circular path around the periphery of the estate had been constructed some long time in the past and it was this hedge-lined passage that they travelled along. Some time later, a time where Will could only think what a wonderful woman she was as he gazed at her intent profile.

'This is the side entrance to the Home Farm...' Jane announced in a diffident voice as they came to an open five-barred gate. 'The farm is largely arable but has a walled garden and greenhouses... for...'

She is lovely, Will thought, unbelievably lovely. Intelligent and humble, not that he knew if the two words belonged together but Mr Bailey had been happy enough for Lady Jane to take him, to drive him, on the tour of inspection. He barely heard as she reeled off the figures for the production of grain last year and the expected figures for this. The cattle, the small milking herd, the vegetable gardens, the chickens, the geese, ducks and on and on. The tenant farms. She seemed to know every detail of what they produced and how good they were as farmers. Will found that it was better, much better, to remain all but silent and let her tell the story that she seemed to know so well but finally, after more than two hours, they rolled back into the Stable Yard where Will handed Lady Jane down saying. 'That leaves the House Milady. Perhaps tomorrow would be better, than to go on now. Besides I must go to the Inn and join my companions.'

She looked at him in astonishment, her face suddenly pink in her anxiety. 'A room at the Inn sir? But you have a choice of six here in the House.' Jane felt almost hurt as if he rejected her, her face blushing a little now.

'Would I not compromise you Milady. An unmarried man, an unmarried woman, un-chaperoned in an otherwise empty house?'

She looked as puzzled as if she had not thought on it, which, in fact, she had not. 'I doubt sir, that I need to fear for my reputation. The house is hardly empty with nurses, maids and the like. I come from a ruined family sir, with a mad father; there is little that letting you stay in your own... house might engender,' she ended a little breathless and pale now.

Will looked around the now empty yard, for the groom had led the curricle and horse inside, and realized that he needed to say what he had to say before. 'Perhaps, since you put it like that, that I might stay but only on one condition.'

Jane stared up at him and then slowly nodded, 'You had best tell me of this condition sir.'

'That we talk. That I tell you of the events that have occurred and that you once again listen, politely I hope, to my request for your hand in marriage.' Will realized at once that his gaucheness had exceeded his caution and that now he was where he was a month previous.

'You... you have an unusual way of putting things sir,' her expression gaunt, '...but I will listen to you, especially as I am in your power.'

'In my power Madam?' Will said abruptly. 'You are not, and I suspect never will be, in my power. We may even be married but you will never be in my power.' He tried to smile, flustered though he was.

'Like you sir, I, perhaps phrased my thoughts badly,' she paused to allow him to speak but he was silent. The late sunlight beat at them, a summer breeze tried to cool the anxiousness of their feelings.

'Please Lady Jane, please let us start again from the beginning.' Will saw the young groom appearing at the entrance to the stables and he waved at him. 'Hallo,' Will called out, '...could you saddle up 'Hector' for me and bring him here. I must be off.'

'So now you are leaving, sir. We appear to have many important things unresolved, left unsaid.'

'I have decided that staying in the same house as you might unhinge me which would be unfortunate indeed. I will stay at the Inn in Saffron Walden and in the morning we shall come. If you could arrange for the physician to be here and perhaps some lunch... no. I realize that you have no 'cook' we will...'

Jane looked at him levelly and she thought him lovely in his confusion so she said. 'I have been the 'cook' for some time now and can prepare whatever you wish. Luncheon would be simple...' she stopped then added, '...but why not take the time now to see the House, the changes that you asked for are mostly done and perhaps we could talk.'

'No. I fear that my fatigue might make me say the wrong things again. I am... was, a simple soldier and have had little practice in the arts of conversation and politeness, the civilities, as it were.' His head bowed in his frustration.

A calm faced slightly smiling Lady Jane looked at him for a long moment before saying. 'Sir, I believe that our differences are somewhere behind us. This month, on my own, I have found some purpose in life and found that I enjoy my own company as long as I have some reason for living. I believe that we could talk and make allowances for any faults that might occur. I should enjoy hearing of what has befallen you, of Tom and Tully, and I must assume that you succeeded in interring your poor dead brother?'

A silence fell between them until Will said. 'The question of the rightness of me staying with you at Saffron House is resolved by my sleeping at the Inn. Tomorrow we must have out our differences and I must make my declaration to you in a formal and proper way,' Will paused, his face very serious now. 'When I do make such a declaration you will not laugh at me, will you my Lady?'

'No Major. Mr Saxethorpe, no, I will not. The question of rank...'

'You're right Lady Jane, the question of rank is not important, not now.'

Behind them the groom led 'Hector' from the stable and over to them and Will turned to the horse and offering his left foot allowed himself to be half lifted into the saddle.

'Your shoulder sir? Have you fully recovered?' She looked a little anxious as she had noted the grimace of pain that crossed his face as he hauled himself into the saddle.

He looked down at her and thought her the most beautiful creature he had ever seen. 'There was some further injury at Newmarket but now I think, finally, I am on the road to recovery, so good evening Lady Jane; tomorrow at ten of the clock.' He turned away in a clattering of hooves, and trotted his big horse towards the archway.

At the archway Will turned his horse and looked back, smiling at the beautiful picture laid before him, then raised his hand in farewell and he was gone in a clatter of hooves, leaving, for a moment, his silhouette, caught against the cloud of dust that they'd raised, by the setting sun.

Lady Jane walked slowly back to the House her mind in a turmoil. Once again he had asked her to marry him in the most offhand kind of way. A matter for discussion indeed. The man was truly gauche but lovely in so many ways. The question of rank would still hover over their relationship married or not. She still had to ask her father's or rather her mother's permission to marry but felt somehow that Will had resolved that problem for himself and obviously didn't care about her status but like all things in life it would have to be discussed. Jane thought that she would write to her mother and sister after tomorrow when the Major, no not the Major, when the Master had gone. Quite suddenly she realized that he had not said how long he was staying and if he went... then where to?

The night was a torment for Will Saxethorpe as he went over the short doomed conversation that he'd had yesterday and his ignominious retreat at the end. How could he string together words so very badly? He was an idiot that was what he was and although the exhaustion of the day and a bottle of quite good claret caused him to fall asleep, his sub conscious kept working at the problem so that he awoke with his mind buzzing with the same arguments as the previous night.

For some reason, but she suspected herself of vanity, Jane had dressed in the sheerest of white muslins, as if for a ball, or so it seemed to Will as he slid, somewhat clumsily, off 'Hector,' avoiding putting any weight on his left arm.

She stood, elegantly relaxed, a smilingly quizzical expression on her face, under the shadow of the portico waiting for him. In her hand she held a thick, heavily sealed envelope which as he walked up the wide stone steps, she said, frowning a little, as she held it out to him. 'Good morning, Milord, did you sleep well at the Inn?'

Will, once again flustered by her windswept beauty, barely registered what she said but just answered. 'Yes it was fine... as usual and what is this?

'It came not five minutes past, an Express from Norwich.'

Will stared at her, barely sparing a glance for the heavy envelope in his hand. 'Is coffee possible? I was anxious, so I missed...'

'Come in Milord. I had just prepared coffee when the dispatch rider knocked.'

They walked through the open double doors that led into the hallway and Will was impressed with the cleaning out of impedimenta, that he had requested, leaving this impressive room rather austere but something more was bothering him although for the moment he could not put his finger on it.

They sat in the Drawing Room, all white with sunlight streaming though the eastern windows, facing each other seated on two small silk covered settles, a low table set between them. The pouring ceremony was conducted in silence until each had a fine, porcelain, coffee filled cup in hand. There was much sipping in silence with Jane's questioning look being ignored by his downturned frowning face.

'Well now!' He said firmly, looking up.

'Milord?' She smiled at him, gently since he seemed unmanned if she really smiled.

'Let us go straight to the heart of the matter...'

'Let's.' Her smile was getting bigger by the moment.

'Why are you smiling so?' Will's face was now a mass of confusion.

'You have not opened your Express and sit there like an ogre up a beanstalk.'

'I know what is in the letter so therefore there is no need,' he picked up the envelope and studied the direction on it and then he realized what had happened, 'Ah... you, you read?'

'Yes. Someone, an attorney by the return address, thinks that you are a Baron and Knight of the Realm.' Her smiling look of enquiry seemed to fill the room.

'Well, yes, that is why the question of rank need not come up,' and Will sounded quite pleased with this part of the conversation.

'So that only leaves whether or not I wish to marry you?' Jane thought that this matter should be resolved as soon as...

'Yes, that is the crux of the matter. Do you? Will you?' He asked with a somewhat eager look.

'Lord Saxethorpe, I feel that the full ceremony is required before I can decide.'

Jane noted that he barely noticed his title being used just acted as ever. Before she could stop him he had plummeted to his knees and taken her only free hand. She had only a moment, to put down her coffee cup, before he was kissing the back of her hand.

'Marry me Lady Jane Walden... otherwise...'

'Otherwise sir?' she half whispered.

'I shall be forced to abduct you, take you away to my castle and have my wicked way with you.'

She stared at him a light smile on her face. 'On balance the second offer sounds more amusing but a bit less certain as to the outcome so my answer...is, yes. I loved you when you were a penniless Major and now you have an Estate and a title to go with it. Did it cost you much or did you win it at the tables?'

Will frowned, 'How very rude you are. Win it at the tables indeed?' and he started to laugh.

After several hours of the telling and re-telling of his adventures the young couple, arm in arm, walked slowly back into the House each surprised with the ease that they seemed to settle their differences now.

'If I had not succeeded to my brother's titles would you have agreed to marry me?'

She looked at him, a quizzical smile on her face, her head tilted to one side then said. 'Probably, almost certainly... only my mother's...'

'Your mother dislikes me I think.'

Jane shrugged casually as she said. 'Well, now that you have a splendid title...' she left the line hanging.

'But you will still ask her?'

Jane smiled and bit her bottom lip before saying. 'Yes, it is only polite but I shall put it in a most advantageous way; title, wealth, this large house and by the way... marriage.'

He looked at her and nodded slowly. 'I dislike returning to our reality but we have some very difficult decisions to make.'

'If you refer to my father's health; then that decision has already been made.' Her face had become downcast but there was a firmness of purpose in her voice. 'I have discussed the problem with Mr Bailey and he informed me that if the savings on his nursing could be changed into the fees charged by the hospital there would be a shortfall of some thirty guineas a year,' her words fell into the dead silence of the house. She knew that this man needed to know more of her intentions so she continued, 'I must find some paid work. I know now that I am capable of performing some task or other, perhaps I could work for you?'

'But you have agreed to be my wife?' Will sounded serious knowing that some kind of problem was coming.

'Yes. But I will have to earn my keep even as your wife. I will... I must work at something. I have incurred some substantial debts, to you mostly, and somehow I must repay them.'

Will's face was serious now. 'You are beginning to sound foolish Milady. The woman who marries me will want for nothing. The money you speak of was, in one sense, yours, foolishly thrown away by your father. It is fortunate that I was there to pick it up but at no time did I consider his money to be mine and come to that...' he stopped to look around the Hall where their conversation had brought them. 'You remember the letter, the somewhat thick letter that came today?'

She looked up at him now, so very serious, so very beautiful her wind tossed hair framing a light frown. 'Yes, of course.'

'It is a gift to you. It does not depend on you agreeing to marry me, it is for you alone and forever, for it is truly yours.' He reached into his side pocket and pulled out the long thick envelope which he handed to Jane.

'Should I open it Will?' She asked, a pensive and puzzled look on her face.

He realized that for the first time she had called him by his given name and knew now that they would be happy for as long as they were allowed to be, 'Yes... why not... I want you to, I think... yes, open it.'

Jane carefully undid the red tape that still bound the seal and realized then that he had not touched it. A gift for her he'd said; not a marriage gift then, just something that one person gives to the person that he loves. She unfolded the heavy parchment and even as she did so she knew exactly what it was. A Deed; the Deed to Saffron House Estate, a gift indeed.

There was a long silence between them until she said. 'We are to marry, yes.' It was not a question now. 'Yet you have given me my freedom with this Deed. Are you not afraid that I might...?'

'Of course I'm afraid, but I hoped that my love for you...' he couldn't finish.

'... and my love for you would be enough,' she added.

'Is it?'

'Is this a test of my love Will? Should I tear it up?'

'It's not a test Jane it's a gift given in love.'

Over the years to come they both remembered that it was at the foot of the great staircase in the hallway of Saffron House that they kissed properly for the first time.

With the gift of the Deed their relationship did change. In retrospect it was much for the better for something in Jane relaxed and she became the woman that she knew she could be. She carried on her work at the House, she arranged, herself, for the terrible task of transferring her father to the hospital at Thaxstead, and signed the legal agreement so that one day very soon the House would belong to her alone.

Driving the curricle she arrived at the Inn and strode into the tavern amongst all the men ignoring the flicked glances of the standing and nodding farmers and their men who knew well who she was.

Will and Mr Bailey were sitting with Tom and Tully at a table near the barrels each with a pint of ale their heads close together as they talked. Jane walked to the table angry for some reason but suddenly she knew why. For so much of her life she'd been excluded from all the important conversations, the important decisions and now she saw that nothing had changed. She knew instinctively that they talked of the Saffron House Estate and they were not including her. 'Good morning Milord, gentlemen...' her voice cool. She was startled by the alacrity shown by the men as they leapt to their feet and even more startled by the bows presented to her so that she was forced to curtsey in reply.

'Lady Jane, a very good morning to you.' Will's voice seemed to fill her every sense, the murmurs from the others unheard by her, her eyes locked onto his.

She said. 'You talk of important matters? I interrupt you?'

'Yes, my Lady, we talk of important matters; combining the estates together to better...'

'And you did not think to include me in this discussion?' Her tone and facial expression were of a sudden, angry.

Will suddenly smiled, 'A preparatory talk only my Lady. We would, of course, discuss with you how you would like the two estates to be joined.'

'Two estates, joined sir?'

'Yes, your three thousand acres and my twenty two thousand...'

She looked at him open mouthed, truly astounded, 'Twenty two thousand...?'

'We, my family, has been around for a rather long time, buying the odd field here, the odd harbour there...'

'Harbour sir?'

'Norfolk is a long way by road from London so a harbour and two coasters for the taking of grain and...'

'And, Saffron House is...'

'It is called economy of scale Milady... the bigger the better.'

'But...?'

'Saffron House Estate is still yours my Lady as will be Saxethorpe.'

Jane became aware of the looks that Will's two companions were passing back and forth, she frowned at them, 'What are you two looking at?'

'A fair bootiful sight Milady....' answered Tom cheekily.

'If you are to be a gentleman Tom, then you must learn to be circumspect in what you say and do.'

'A little like me then,' said Will with a little smile, '...we shall learn together Tom, maybe with the right teaching you and I may well end up as gentlemen.'

Will rode with Lady Jane going back to the House which gave him the chance to admire again her skill with the horse, the whip snaking gently down the horse's side; the reins urging the horse on. For a while there was no conversation between them until Jane broke the silence, 'You still plan for Tom to be turned into a gentleman then?'

'He is as smart as a whip Milady and a very fast learner. He has already moved on to novels and the like in his reading and it is only six weeks since we met, his mathematics... I should say his mental arithmetic is first rate, better by far than mine.'

'And when you have finished with him?

'I have a tutor in mind...' Will became a little hesitant, '...and you should know that he's an orphan. I do not plan to throw him out even if his remarks can be a little acid.'

She smiled to herself thinking that this man was kinder than any she had known.

Will's face had become serious so he turned to her desiring to broach the next subject as if it was separate. 'I must tell you...'

Lady Jane turned her head to look at him as she heard his voice become much more serious. 'Yes?'

'Because my brother still threatens my life. I must make sure that the succession to the Estate is secure.'

Jane nodded, thinking that the need for heirs was what drove marriage in the nobility and come to that, divorce, so she nodded.

'I have decided to adopt Tom, if he'll have me for a father.'

'Adopt?' her voice amazed. This thought had never occurred to Jane for she saw that her own role in this marriage was now under some kind of threat.

'Until... until I... we, have produced a male heir then the Will would be altered back.'

'So Tom, if by accident you were to die?'

Yes Milady, which brings us back to the Deed for Saffron House Estate. You would be safe here and perhaps as happy as I could make you from beyond the grave.'

Jane, straining every muscle, reined in the horse to stop dead, in a great squealing of brake and rattling of harness, just one hundred yards from the gates of the House and turned swiftly to Will. 'You must not say such things, Will; we are not even married and you talk of death.' Her voice was choked and her eyes filled with tears.

'My brother, the Bishop, still has the threat hanging over me and...'

'It's a nonsense sir! He is not your brother! He threatens your life and you can do nothing it seems.'

Will smiled at his irate bride to be and thought her wonderful to look upon so he said, to placate her. 'I take all these steps to ensure that our children will succeed and Tom will live a happy and secure life with or without titles.'

She sat there breathing a little heavily staring straight ahead, then said or rather announced. 'Then we must need to start on the marriage immediately. No time must be lost?' She turned to Will her face flushed with excitement and passion.

'My Lady, I did not tell you this to...'

'You have faults my Lord but I still wish to marry you. You have given me so much and I have only... myself to give and this I do willingly.' And they kissed deeply, passionately.

Two farm workers walking past, scythes on their shoulders, glanced at each other and smiled.

The inspection of the house, which had involved the removal of the two defective, poorly built wings, the making good, the painting, the re-gilding of some parts of the library and the removal of the more vulgar furniture that Will had suggested a month before was complete and the house looked the better for it restored as it was to its original early Georgian proportions. The couple wandered from room to room holding hands, smiling at each other and sometimes kissing until Jane asked. 'When do we go to Norfolk... to Saxethorpe?'

'I was, I was thinking that I could ride north tomorrow. You must write to your mother. We must decide on a date then I shall send a carriage for you.'

Jane, her face determined said. 'You will not sir. I will ride with you to Saxethorpe and I will arrange anything I need.'

'But Jane...'

'No, my lord. I will not let you out of my sight until we are married and perhaps not even then.'

They had arrived at the double doors of the main east facing bed chamber and Jane threw them open so that Will could see...

'Heaven's Jane; it's changed and for the better.' He sounded pleased, for the room and bed were made up, all polished with a small fire guttering even now but all looking warm and cosy.

'This will be our bedchamber sir, when....' What will he be thinking Jane thought to herself. Will he be dreaming of the conquest to come or is it just a place to sleep for him.

'It was a little ill-advised Lady Jane to present an unmarried and quite young man with such a sight but I think that I... we... can wait until we settle at Saxethorpe Hall. Where, if I remember correctly there is a quite splendid bed chamber constructed I believe for a member of Royalty sometime in the past but this room will, I think, see something of us over the years...' they kissed again and again until Jane broke away.

'Luncheon sir, it must be prepared. I have a lamb stew and dumplings, a little heavy for this time of year but the lamb had to be slaughtered and I thought...'

Will thought, I have indeed found my life partner, if it please God to give me a life.

CHAPTER TWENTY

Luncheon was over. The meal, some claret from the cellar and coffee until all were replete even Tom and Tully. Will decided to take a turn about the gardens with Tom so he set Tully to preparing for their departure on the morrow. They would take a carriage, two in hand, which Tom would drive and Tully would be the outrider with the other horses following on behind the carriage.

Will led Tom on a walk of the slightly ragged gardens of the House and after some time said. 'Tom, in your mind, do you think that your task with me is drawing to a close?'

Tom looked around at his Master wondering what was to come. 'I have been working on the old cart sir.'

Will stopped him to ask 'Is that all you desire Tom; from life that is?'

Tom looked up at him, clean and fresh faced now, hair trimmed, his clothes well looked after and Will thought him a perfect young man.

'I feel that I have been very lucky indeed to have met with you sir.'

'Your voice, your manner of speech has changed a little, young man.'

The boy frowned, 'I spend most of the day with you sir, so I suppose that my manner of speech has become somewhat like yours.'

'Indeed Tom, you are becoming a gentleman, if that's what I am.'

Tom had stopped walking and was now serious faced knowing that something was about to be said 'I will not be happy to leave your service sir. I am as happy as I have ever been and a lot happier that when I was on the cross channel packets. The horses were good though...' he nodded and smiled.

Will turned the boy to face him then asked, 'What would you say Tom, to being adopted by me?'

Tom stared up at him then asked 'What's 'adopted' mean, exactly sir?'

'You would become, legally at least, my son.' Best to leave it plain and unadorned, Will thought. Tom is fast enough to see the ramifications of the act.

'Just legally sir?' Tom seemed worried, anxious even.

'No Tom. You would be my son.' Will's face was very serious now.

'But you are about to marry sir.'

'I am Tom and I hope to have a whole herd of 'sons' just like you. But I do need an heir at this moment. Someone I can trust. Trust to look after Lady Jane and the Estates.'

'You still fear for your life sir?' His voice anxious, manifestly worried for his Master.

'I do indeed Tom. My 'brother', the Bishop, has sworn an oath to kill me or to arrange for someone to kill me and then he would or could inherit Saxethorpe.'

Tom thought of the Bishop; of the great Manor house at Saxethorpe of all the land and this man was asking him to... 'Do you believe that I am capable of such a task sir?' He asked, frowning now.

'I do Tom. You would have guardians in the form of Charles Morris, the curate, and the lawyer, Mr Crindal, who would help you, educate you, look after you.'

'School sir?' Tom frowned at the thought.

'Certainly Thomas, you must need be educated but I think that you would find Charles Morris to be sympathetic kind man and a good teacher.'

Tom stared at this man and for a stranger the two dressed so much alike might well have seemed to be father and son or perhaps brothers and so Tom asked the question that would decide his fate. 'Would you love me as a father would, sir?'

Will stared at the boy who seemed to have grown more mature in the last few moments and then asked. 'Would you love me as a son should?'

After a long moments silence for thought, that was most certainly necessary, Tom said, 'I already do love you sir, for you have saved my life and given me some reason to live.'

Will smiled at his friend. 'And I love you Tom and you have also saved my life.' Will held out his hand for Tom to shake and with a momentary hesitation to stare at the proffered hand, Tom did.

Jane was later to think that as the two of them reappeared in the Dining Room it seemed to her that Tom had grown taller, more serious and that Will and he looked somewhat like a father with his son.

The journey to Norwich was accomplished in much the spirit of investigation, of a finding out about who Lady Jane really was and the search for the soul of Will, his childhood, his feelings and all the parties, including Tom and Tully, felt a kind of contentment with their lot.

Will and Jane sat, holding hands, side by side for a good deal of the journey. There were long silences as the summer's golden fields rolled slowly past and they formulated their thoughts so as to give the least possible offence.

'How d'you know that you love me?' Jane asked, watching his face closely.

He turned to her as he tried to think of the right words. 'I think it is because my thoughts turn to you whenever they are not seriously involved with some kind of estate business.' That must be alright Will thought, no mistakes there.

'So... on a busy day you may hardly think of me at all?' Jane shrugged her shoulders.

He stared at her puzzled by her determination to fault him. 'No, of course not, but no one can think on one thing alone, it might drive you mad.'

'So I might drive you mad if you thought of me too much?' Her look cheeky, a giggle not too far away.

The word 'mad' was completely wrong Will thought and he struggled to find some way of pleasing her. 'I think of kissing you, of holding you, of loving you.'

'Having your way with me is your idea of love then?' Her words were provocative indeed but amusement still showed on her face.

'No! of course not.'

'So you are not so interested in me...' she had to stop because he had started to kiss her.

Later he said, 'So, and how d'you know that you love me? No lawyers answers please.'

She turned to look at him and then said. 'I think of you constantly and when I see you I shiver and shudder with the thought that you might kiss me, hold me...' she smiled up at him as he leaned anxiously forward, '...of course, I don't see you that often so sometimes I completely forget who you are and then I remember that you are my Major, my gambler, my fate.'

So he kissed her again, and again.

It was Tom's turn to sit in the carriage which he did with a certain amount of aplomb mounting the step, closing the small door firmly, and seating himself in a small folding seat opposite to Lady Jane. He clutched the guitar which with a high spirited pair of horses pulling the carriage he had had no time to practice upon. He looked at Lady Jane questioningly and then, when she did not speak, was forced to ask. 'Would you mind Milady if I were to practice, essay a few scales; the Master says that practice makes perfect.' He smiled at her knowing perfectly well that the man driving, Lord Saxethorpe, both hated hearing his scales and being excluded from any conversation that might occur.

'Of course you can practice Tom and perhaps you might show me the way of handling the instrument, the... what do you call it? The fingering?' Jane felt, rather than saw the quick glance that Will cast over his shoulder at the two of them huddled over his guitar and with the first notes drifting on the wind he whipped up the two horses into a faster trot.

Later, not much more than half an hour later, Tom decided that the horses needed to rest, be watered and have their oat bags for a while. Both Jane and Will were delighted that the boy was so circumspect especially since it meant that he would stop strumming the guitar.

It was a further ten miles on that they came to be near Thetford where the famous Golden Boar coaching Inn sat by the Post Road as it had this past three hundred and fifty years.

At dinner in the tavern, for the blue muslin clad Lady Jane had turned down Lord Saxethorpe's offer of a private dining room, that the conversation between Will and Jane turned to the wedding.

'You must invite such of your friends from Walden that you wish to see you marry...' Will said.

After a long frowning moment for thought Jane said, 'In our penury they were adverse to helping us... only you...'

'But is that not the way of the gentry?'

'It is, but I do not need their shallow friendship especially since Saffron Walden will be only my second home.' She looked at him levelly as if asking him to refute this argument.

'You have no childhood friends? A best friend, someone to share life's most splendid moments?'

'No. And if I had my sister would have taken them from me or pushed them away. It is sad that I have no friends but perhaps with time and the move to Norfolk...' she left the line and thought hanging.

Will thought how alike they were. All his friends had been actively discouraged by brother John and the Army, it did not pay to make great friends of fellow officers since there had always been a battle or skirmish just around the corner, a battle that very often had few survivors. So Jane had no friends; a pity, so they must make friends amongst their neighbours or perhaps be their own best friends. Yes, that was the way of it, Jane would be, was... his best friend.

'Have you written to your mother as yet?'

She looked at him saying as she did so 'Yes, of course. I have asked her and Alice to the wedding. I made the direction for the letter to be Saxethorpe Hall, I hope that that was not presumptuous of me?'

'It will be your home Jane...' Will said quietly, '...but did you not ask for a speedy reply?'

'Since we have no date for the wedding but that there is some degree of urgency, I put the 1st of September as a probable date.'

'Three weeks from now? How did you phrase it, the invitation, exactly... for the words 'some degree of urgency' would seem to infer...'

'You have a wicked mind sir.' She smiled up at him.

'Your mother...'

197

'We will marry, Mother's permission or no. If she is there then all to the good if not....' she shrugged her shoulders.

'And Lady Alice?'

'She did not reply to my last two letters so I have no idea of her situation and intentions,' she sounded as if she did not care overmuch.

'Family is important my Lady.' Will thought that his own was, in some ways, a poor example of love and friendship.

'We both have difficult families. Families beset with difficulties; my father... your brother... difficult.'

Tom and Tully had edged away a little and remained silent but tried not to hear too much. The noise in the tavern, the pipe smoke, the rattle of the metal plates, the clash of the pewter mugs, cries and singing as a night of merriment stretched before the locals and they cared little for the gentry who came into their place.

'So, it would seem that you would prefer a simple marriage?'

'I want to marry you sir, so as little as possible should be placed in the way of that taking place. The simpler the better I think. Such family as we can manage, a few friends...' Jane glanced at Tom and Tully, '...and for me that would be sufficient,' she looked at him with determination shining in her eyes.

'I thought, that since it is the only wedding that we are likely to have that we should...'

'An elaborate feast is what you have in mind sir with all your tenants and perhaps your brother and sister?'

Will stared at her, confused again. He had always thought that women wanted a large, splendid and elaborate ceremony and a huge feast, but it would seem that Jane was in something of a hurry. 'Perhaps we should wait until we are a little further along, until you receive a reply from your mother?'

'As I have just said sir, nothing she could say would affect me, my decision... so...'

Will took her hand and gently kissed it smiling up at her the while.

Norwich in the rain, fortunately a gentle damping of the dust and, hopefully, a filling of the kernels of the wheat which stood tall in every field that they passed. Will was now beginning to think like a farmer instead of just a land owner; he worried when the wind blew or if dark clouds started to pile up in the sky but he worried mostly for his tenants who faced a severe downturn in the price of wheat now that the war had ended. He did have a plan of sorts but he wished to talk of it with the curate Charles Morris. His harbour lay at the core of the plan; the sight of his two sailing barges laid up on the mud for more than half the year depressed him for some reason and he knew that tradition was his worst enemy. There were so many ways of doing things that would set in the cement of time that it would take a brave man to smash it up but for some reason, Will thought that he was the man for the job but he would need reassurance; so Charles Morris.

So this is Norwich, thought Jane as she walked, staring at the cathedral in its shallow valley sliding down to the water, for everywhere there seemed to be water; lakes, ponds and rivers. It would take some getting used to after the gentle countryside around Saffron Walden but she knew all too well that marrying, especially in the nobility, was a contract for the woman; she would end up living wherever her Master called home and Jane supposed that she should be grateful; he was after all the most considerate and kindest of potential husbands. He had set her free; she still could not understand how she was supposed to feel about that. Was she her own mistress or was she so indebted to him that she was still subservient in all matters of consequence.

Norwich, had shops, warehouses, places of entertainment, a theatre and it was but an hour or two from his house, his home. So this place, that felt so alien to her now, would one day become her home as well and most certainly home to her children. She felt a surge of... of what? Excitement? The kind engendered by her married sister's talk of love making but the end result would be, God willing, a child. That was Will's plan was it not. He wanted, needed, an heir and she was the... she could not properly think of herself in the same way as the cows on her Home Farm, the sheep and the ram, the sows and the boar, but, stripped of its human emotion, it was exactly the same. He would act the bull, the boar and she would be the sow, the cow. How did she feel about that? She knew that lacking female friends, especially married ones, had left her with little emotional response to the idea of being a kind of breeding animal but she knew now that that was what she was. Now she had a kind of freedom, for he had given her the right to decide, had he not. She could just refuse him but she knew that she wouldn't; she wanted him, that was the truth of it. The child bearing as and when it came must be faced as all of life's problems had to be faced.

Jane found herself facing an impressively ugly, very large square building on a low hill and thought that it must be a castle; Norwich castle then. Someone must be the Lord there and she supposed that in the fullness of time she would meet that person. She turned slowly to take in the town, which now lay a little below her and she could see that the waters of the county surely met here for the faint sunshine glittered off the surrounding countryside all around her. So the decision was made then. She had said to Will that she would marry him but ever since he had given her the Deed to Saffron House her willpower had weakened a little. It would be so easy to return to her former life, to restore her mother and even her sister. A life of easy luxury would lie before her as if her father had been restored to them and she knew, felt that that was almost exactly what she didn't want. She had never been really happy. Content perhaps in the cosy life of a youngest daughter only the threat of a forced marriage casting a shadow of sorts upon that life but now she had the man of her choice and by strange circumstance he was exactly the man that she might have created for herself. Odd, very odd. A baron, good looking and rich, yes, her decision was, most certainly, the right one.

The evening meal was taken in the public dining room at Jane's insistence, a decision that she was later to regret.

Will was known to the Innkeeper now so that the food and service was of the best that was available in a country town like Norwich. The table was set a little apart from the ordinary people but was laid with good linen and cutlery. Jane, dressed in her green satin and muslin dress a scarf about her neck, her back to the room, was seated opposite to Will with the two men, for Tom looked and acted the man, between them and the hoi poloi and thus was the scene set for an evening of high drama that would make the Saxethorpe family famous in the town for many years to come.

A tall, well built gentleman, by his manner of dress, came in and looked around the crowded room. Seeming to see what it was that he wanted to see he made his way to a table for four and made himself comfortable, removing his high hat to reveal long rakish black hair, his right hand raised, and, fingers clicking, attracted the attention of the Innkeeper. Wine glasses, two bottles of claret and three mugs of beer were brought to him and he seemed inwardly amused that the Lord Saxethorpe and his party had not noticed him.

The Inn door was pushed open and two somewhat rougher men appeared who made their way, without havering, to the table of the gentleman. They did not greet him in any way but just sat and picked up the jugs of beer which they promptly finished off almost in one swallow. The gentleman barely acknowledged their arrival concentrating his attention on the Saxethorpe party. He could see that they dined well and drank sufficient of the claret to make them very comfortable with their circumstances. He too drank deeply of the claret himself and found it drinkable but not much better than that.

At some point Tom, who was seated facing into the now crowded tavern, noticed the looks on the faces of the three men and felt that perhaps a surreptitious word to his Master would not go amiss. 'Milord, sir. Sorry to interrupt you but...'

Will in the midst of a slightly drunken spate of conversation with Lady Jane felt some degree of annoyance at Tom's words. 'Yes Tom, you have some problem with the food, the wine?'

'I think that you may have a problem sir,' Tom pointedly did not look towards the three men, '...but the table... don't look sir!' He whispered urgently, '...the table with three men that sits about four tables away. They stare at you a great deal sir and I feel that they might mean mischief against you.' Tom smiled at his master.

Will, quite suddenly sober, nodded, falling into the boy's play acting so that he was able to lean back and glance about the room. 'Yes Tom. I see what you mean. Tully.'

The man looked away from his mug of beer a half smile on his face.

Will half whispered speaking confidentially. 'Perhaps you and Tom could go to your room and prepare the guns. Tom has pointed out that we have unwanted company or the danger of it.'

Tully, well used to the stratagems of his master stood and gestured for Tom to follow saying loudly as he did so. 'Very well master, we'll attend to that for you. Come Tom, work to do.'

'What's happening Will?' Jane asked, for she could detect that the change of mood that had settled on the party.

'We are being carefully watched by some men at a nearby table. No! Don't look around.'

'But what does it mean Will?' Jane's voice was worried now as she stared into his eyes.

'I don't know Jane, although some connection with my brother could not be excluded.' He paused and looked closely into the young woman's eyes. 'I think that we may find out very soon for one of them is coming this way.'

Making his way through the crowd, George Banham, ex-Captain of the Norfolk Yeomanry pushed his way forward until he stood behind Lady Jane, then said brusquely to Will. 'When you've finished with this whore sir, I would be grateful if you could pass her on to me.'

Will, temples now suddenly white with barely concealed rage, slowly climbed to his feet and replied icily. 'And to whom have I the... the 'honour', of speaking?'

Jane, breathless at the insult, climbed to her feet and turned blushing, to face this man.

'George Banham, late of the....' he hesitated to finish the boast for he thought that it was possible that this man facing him had been a soldier.

'It is being 'late' Mr Banham, as in the 'late' Mr Banham when you insult my companion so. You must be very certain of your facts to say such a thing. Are you so certain?' Will's words were full of menace.

The sneer, for which George Banham had become locally famous, now appeared on his curling lips. 'If you find fault with my expression then you know what to do sir.'

'Very brave. You sound very brave for one, an ex-soldier, who stands alone but perhaps you are not alone. A coward with rough friends then.'

'You insult me sir.' The man looked suitably affronted in a play acting kind of way.

'What would my brother have you do Mr Banham?'

The whole tavern was now silent listening to this curious argument and now they wondered who the brother might be.

'I don't know your brother sir.'

'Do you know me then sir? Or perhaps you have made a mistake in your cups?'

'You're Lord Saxetho...' Banham realized that he should not have admitted that he knew the baron's name.

'I see sir. You have instructions, perhaps from the Bishop of Ely to come here, insult my wife to be and pick a fight with a certain Lord Saxethorpe. Then kill him in the resulting duel. That, of course, leaves open only the possibility that it might be you that is killed. Duelling is illegal sir and I for one would not contemplate it. If you decide to attempt to kill me or any of my party then I think that self defence would be my answer.'

Will now realized that the other two men had got up to stand, shoulder to shoulder, close behind Banham and he saw the flicker of steel in the hand of one of them and realized that they hoped to make a rough house in which Will could be knifed, killed.

George Banham decided, ill advisedly as it turned out, to draw his sword on the unarmed Will Saxethorpe but suddenly, from one side an unsheathed epeé sword, spinning in a silver arc of light, clattered down onto the table's white linen surface shattering glasses as it fell. Every eye in the Inn saw it fall even if they did not know from whence it came so Will had more than sufficient time to pick it up. 'Now sir. Innkeeper!' He shouted. 'We are being molested by these men, known robbers I would think, perhaps the Constable should be called.' Then Will had to parry the first thrust from George Banham.

In a moment a very angry and vengeful Tully had stepped between Lady Jane and the three belligerent men and as he was holding the two horse pistols, the whole crowd seemed to step back.

Banham lunged again at Will who had little trouble avoiding the thrust but the table, which lay between the two men, made swordplay difficult, so Will, his sword flashing in the candlelight, drove back the ex-soldier until he could round the table and stand in the clear space which had formed naturally about the men. In what was later to seem a well rehearsed movement George Banham fell back so that Will had his back to the two companions of the duellist. There was a blaze of brilliant swordplay, from both men with thrusts and parries and then there was a flicker of steel as a knife was thrust forward but the appalling, eardrum shattering, CRASH! of a musket fired at close range stopped the knife finding its target. The man with the knife was thrown violently backwards a burst of blood pouring from his chest, the long knife falling from his numbed fingers. A loud collective 'Oooh' came from the lips of the many witnesses and the second man tried to escape but was held by the burly farm workers, who disarmed him easily.

In the interim the swordplay between the two men continued with George Banham trying desperately to parry the many cuts and thrusts that fell upon him.

Will thought, how dare this disgusting man insult my wife to be in such a way or come to that any woman. He will pay, and he will pay with pain, blood and in full. The anger he felt increased by far his strength and skill, his blade becoming a blur of silver light as he carved both the air and the body and clothes of his opponent. Blood drops flew in a wet red corona spattering the excited watching faces. Sword torn fragments of cloth danced in the air and Will felt the blood lust surge up and....

'Stop! Stop it at once Will!' Jane's voice sang in his head and he knew that he must, he must stop. The rattling clatter of George Banham's sword hitting the stone flagged floor; the dull thud of his bloodied knees crashing to the hard ground and for him the knowledge that never again would he risk turning his hand against an unknown stranger.

The tavern's door crashed open and the Town Constable and his deputies surged in, truncheons at the ready. Many voices rose to greet them with the tale of what had happened. The body was carried away amidst a babble of accusations. A much bloodied but not over wounded George Banham was arrested and Will placed some guineas and silver onto the table so that the Innkeeper could arrange for the cleaning, the removal of blood and then he knew he had to face his much angered wife to be.

In a private room now, a small fire had been lit, a four branch candelabra filled the dark beamed room with light and Will faced Jane with an apology on his lips.

'You have no need to apologise Will for it was a fault not of your making, but...'

'It is the 'but' of which I am afraid Milady,' Will's voice and his manner were now so subdued.

'I will tell you Will, so that it need never be spoken of again. I will say it so that you never have to, but you must remember this moment. You are not a soldier now and killing is certainly the most heinous of crimes.'

Will's mouth opened in silent protest, his face full of demurral.

Lady Jane, her face pale in her anger said. 'You have, in Tom, created a dangerous young animal. You should have observed his face Will. In saving your life, as he most surely did, he also found that there was a kind of thrill, an excitement, the...' Jane had few words for what she'd seen on Tom's face and the very same look on the visage of Will but blood lust was the common expression and most certainly it was the right one so she said it to this most repentant man. '...blood lust Will. You were going to kill that stupid man weren't you?' Her breath came a little short.

Will sat now, collapsing into a chair, knowing that she was right. He had turned his 'companion' into a... He knew no words for what he'd inadvertently done. His own reaction to the assassin had been equally stupid. He'd thought his 'battle' days were over but now he knew that it was only a very thin veneer of civilisation that covered the savage that was Will Saxethorpe.

'Lady Jane, I must apologise for everything that happened, especially my own... savage... behaviour,' he paused to think on, '...as for Tom, I believe that you are right. He is young and I should never have enrolled him, no, never allowed him.'

'Will, he's killed at least three men now.' She sounded so worried, '...as have you. He see's himself as your protector and that he has some kind of right to 'kill' whoever threatens you.'

Looking very contrite Will said 'Yes, Jane. You are right.' The realization taking him by surprise for he had just not thought of what arming a boy might do. 'What have I done? Allowed to happen. It is entirely my fault and I shall take whatever steps I can to remedy the situation.'

'You cannot bring those men back to life Will.' Her voice had a cold finality about it.

Will thought, the fear surging through him that he could lose her with this one final battle. Or maybe it would not be the last battle with his brother. John and God made formidable opponents together and he would be unlikely to give up on one of God's commands. 'I would promise Jane if I thought that through my life there would never be another challenge like tonight's but I cannot, for Brother John would say that he and his prophecies have never been wrong.'

Set faced, Jane stood before him. 'You are probably, almost certainly, a good man, Will Saxethorpe, and I would never fault a man for defending what is his but it is Tom that I fear for. You have, I think, killed many men in all your battles but Tom is not a soldier nor do I think that you want him to be one so we must take whatever steps are necessary to prevent him ever again being in a position where taking a life is thrust upon him.'

Will thought, my brother wishes to ruin my life and is a fair way to doing just that. He rose and turning went to the door, 'I will speak with Tom...'

'You must be gentle Will, for he knows not what he does.' Jane's voice was steady and firm. 'You must try to help him, to educate him out of this. If necessary send him away from you so that he no longer feels the need to protect you.' Will, his face tremendously saddened, just nodded and turned to leave.

In the small bedchamber a happy and excited Tully and Tom were re-loading the weapons when there was a firm knock at the door. They were both astonished to see a grim faced Master standing before them.

'I must need to speak with you Tom.' Will closed the door behind him saying as he did so. 'Stay Tully, you must both hear this from me.'

He paced up and down the small panelled room as he tried to muster his thoughts. 'Firstly I must thank you both for once again saving my life but I do have some later thoughts which I must pass on to you both but especially you Tom.' He paused and sank into an old leather wingback chair for he now felt totally exhausted and he recognised the symptom for what it was. The 'blood lust' always had this fatigue as its corollary. The savage speed of his fighting, the aggression, the terrifying strength that allowed him to batter his opponent into submission had to be paid for but he recognized now the livid excitement on Tom's face and knew that ungoverned, he would kill again.

'Tom...' the eager faced boy turned to him.

The oaken, linen fold panelled Great Hall in the castle was crowded, the air murmured with excitement, tobacco smoke swirling up to the heraldic painted roof beams, for the matter was serious, with a mass of onlookers some of whom had been at the Inn last evening. Six rows of chairs had been assembled opposite a low dais with a heavy carved oak table upon it that served as the bar that witnesses would be called to before the Lord Lieutenant of the County and High Sheriff Lord Hazleton, Justice of the Peace and Magistrate, an imposing and heavily wigged figure, dark of feature but with the light of sharp intelligence in his eyes. He wore the heavy official robes of his office and his entrance onto the stage was dramatic to a fault.

It was his task to make the decision on whether or not a man had been murdered or did it fall under the heading of 'self defence'. Out of the one hundred and six witnesses, ten had been called to testify. One by one they stood and rendered up their version of the evening events.

Will, Lady Jane Walden, Mr Crindal, Tully and Tom sat, wearing their best in the front row of chairs a turbulent mass of excited people all around them.

Mr Crindal stood on occasion and made sure, with well directed questions that the stories adhered to one line. All confirmed the innocence of the boy Tom and his master Lord Saxethorpe and as such was the legal decision handed down. Self-defence was the verdict at this preliminary hearing.

Later, in the Lord Lieutenant's study, the High Sheriff and Will Saxethorpe were to meet for the first time. Will explained his story, the circumstances, the coming marriage and the story of his brother, the disinherited Bishop. The short wiry haired and wigless somewhat gray-faced Lord Hazleton listened closely to the argument put forward succinctly by Mr Crindal.

'It seems that you have aroused the ire of a most important man; your own brother, even if adopted. But this is difficult to prove and even when questioned George Banham has proved recalcitrant but the trial is not for some time and in the meantime I will question him again pointing out the disadvantage of continued stubbornness. Well, we will see. The trial, Lord Saxethorpe, will be just before Christmas; we must hope that you will be able to attend, for you will be the most important of the witnesses for the prosecution.'

The rain had gone, fading away to the west leaving skies of a misty blue flecked with traces of white cloud chasing across Jane's view and her mind for the party was now of sombre mien. Tom sat on the driver's seat, his shoulders rigid in his agony, Tully rode his horse, the creak and slap of the pistol holsters seeming loud, as an outrider before the carriage. Will and Lady Jane sat silently apart each concerned with their own thoughts.

The road from Norwich to Saxethorpe ran alongside the waterway so that the sparkle of sun on water cheered them a little. Long avenues of beech, horse chestnut and limes lined the road making for a shady, pleasant drive of some two hours before the first glimpse of Saxethorpe church could be seen, the tall grey tower sailing above the green leafed surrounding beeches.

Lady Jane and Will had not exchanged a word other than the politeness' of a shared carriage. They were later to think of this journey as the second test of their relationship.

Jane thought that sitting in a carriage, even now crammed with loaded weapons could not be conducive or right. She appreciated his position but somehow felt that he had encouraged the poor boy. She looked up at Tom's rigid back, his white neck and wondered if Will's warnings would have any effect. There was the problem that if Tom were ever to be holding a gun facing a truly bad man then he might once again make the wrong decision. He might kill some poor man who was in the wrong place at the wrong time, an innocent of sorts, and Jane wondered if Tom would be able to deal with that or would he raise some kind of mental barrier that would cover the feelings of guilt that he was beginning, courtesy of his mentor, to feel now.

The carriage rattled its iron-shod way up the cobbled road into the little town making its way to the Inn, for a letter sent Express the previous evening to the curate suggested a meeting that was both necessary and urgent.

Jane thought the little town charming and pleasingly quiet. Even the Inn, although she placed no objections this time to a private dining room where they were to talk with Charles Morris and take a late luncheon or early dinner. She noted that Tom and Tully were both absent; Tom to care for the horses and Tully to carefully watch the other clients. So it was that it was just Will and herself that met with the curate.

The tallish curate, receding hair fluffed around his face with an intensely curious expression as if life's mysteries were just there for him to unlock, all he would need was the key; but as he rose to his feet after first carefully putting down his wine glass, his bow was just right, his smile not deprecating and Jane felt that she too could become friends with this clergyman.

'So, you are well sir?' Charles voice was lightly amused.

Jane looked a little puzzled by his opening conversational gambit. 'And you Milady? The evening just past had it's exciting moments did it not?'

Will replied. 'So news travels fast Charles.'

'At least two Express riders came into town late last night, each with very purple stories to tell. The Inn was positively buzzing with tales of daring-do.' His smile was warm. 'But it is very good to meet with you Milady, I have heard much of you from his Lordship,' he nodded towards Will, '...and all of a most complimentary nature.'

Lady Jane's polite smile slipped somewhat as she said. 'Thank you sir, it would be true to say that last evening was exciting but not perhaps, for the right reasons.'

The story was re-told in order to separate fact from fiction but the conversation ended when Will asked if Charles would undertake to educate the boy Thomas.

'He must be taught the difference between right and wrong Mr Morris,' Lady Jane's voice was most urgent, '...something that a clergyman is perhaps well equipped to do.'

Charles Morris looked a little baffled for he knew something of Tom and of the world from which he had come. 'Tom is learning by example.' He glanced over at Will, then continued, '...his Master, his mentor sets him a fine example of how a man should act. Tom does so and then finds that both his Master and his Lady disapprove. Difficult for him and, I think, not a fault of his own making.' He stopped to think then added, 'I will undertake his education, for he is a very bright boy and I will try to cool his ardour for his Lordship. He does, I'm sure, know the difference between right and wrong it is just that he sees the world in black and white. The good must be loved and respected, the evil killed. Perhaps with time I can modify such a simple viewpoint of the world,' he smiled at his two new friends and nodded with satisfaction.

Because of the lateness of the hour Will decided to stay at the Inn and took several rooms to accommodate the whole party. A message was sent to Lady Anne to expect them early on the morrow.

CHAPTER TWENTY-ONE

The sun shone on the carriage as they trundled through the gates of the Estate. The long tree lined avenue stretched away into a soft heat haze and Jane was impressed. She did not want to be but she found that a drive of nearly two miles tended to have that effect on her and indeed nearly everyone which was, after all, the intention of the designer. Then the great Tudor manor house appeared, rearing up heavy, black oak beamed from the mist. Large windowed, tiled and bricked gables, the gleam of clean glass, the topiary of the gardens near the house, so neat again, so solid, so old and Jane felt that she was coming home. A very odd feeling but knowing that this man had been raised here was almost enough for her. For a moment, as they approached the house she wondered whether her mother had replied to her letter.

'The Dower House, where Lady Anne lives, where I lived when I was younger...' Will gestured towards a much smaller house in the Georgian style sitting in a walled garden off to one side.

Jane looked at him puzzled, then asked. 'You did not live in the manor house?'

'My father judged it best to keep John and myself apart although John was a good many years older than I. John had, apparently, decided that since my mother had died giving birth to me that I was some kind of fair game, an enemy.' Will paused to shake his head, '...of course, I was not told the story of John and Anne so I was used to the idea and had no knowledge other than his dislike of me.'

'But your Anne?' Jane asked confused, '...she was condemned to be your nurse maid, never to marry?'

'So it would seem and I did not ask my father I just accepted things the way they were. Mostly John would be away at some monastery or later the Seminary at Cambridge and Anne was my mother since I knew no other.'

'A sad story sir.' Jane did indeed think so and understood a little more of this man she was to marry. Raised almost alone, no siblings, sent away to school and a life of hunting, shooting and soldiery. The Army at sixteen, taught to kill so young, no wonder he was a brilliant duellist and she had a momentary shudder at the thought that this man, that she was to put her care and her body into the hands of was a fighting machine, a killer.

Their relationship had become a little more friendly since meeting with the curate but Jane knew that the problem of Will and Tom would become difficult at times since they were both so very alike. Tom seemed to have grown in the few weeks that she had known him and it was not just the clothing. His recently dented confidence was still a factor and Jane knew that she would have to act as surrogate mother to the boy and she looked forward with some interest to the process.

The house grew as they became closer and Jane realized that it was a very large house indeed and she wondered what size of family the Saxethorpe's had been in the distant past in order to justify such a large dwelling. Many cousins, aunts, uncles, nieces and nephews and, she supposed, sheer pride on the part of the Lord of this Manor.

A little away from the house, and part concealed behind high red brick walls stood the small but near perfect stone fronted and red brick Georgian house that could not have been much more than thirty or forty years old, Jane thought, and wondered both at its proximity to the main house but the walls and the sheer beauty of it, every detail perfect, the iron work of the gates superb but seeming strong. Through the lattice of the gates she could see a positive rainbow of rose colours that seemed to be trying to burst out onto the plain facade of the Tudor dwelling that overshadowed it.

The carriage slowed and stopped opposite the Dower House and Will said, 'Tully, see if you can find my Steward would you, we'll be here in the Dower House. Ask him to come....'

Tom, very correctly, handed down Lady Jane and for a moment she hesitated before circling the carriage to take Will's arm and together they walked up to the black painted front door. Black velvet mourning drapes still surrounded the doorway and Jane ventured only. 'What a very pretty house Will, it is perfect in so many ways.'

'It's where I was raised Jane,' at that moment the door opened and a tiny, somewhat wrinkled maid person stood there looking faintly annoyed.

'Aggie!' Will stepped forward and scooped up the diminutive figure who giggled and laughed at her Master.

'Put me down at once sir. That's not the way for a Lord to act and I suppose that you'll be wanting tea. I made some of your favourite biscuits.'

'Thanks be to God that you are still doing the cooking Aggie for no one makes a biscuit quite like you; and where's Lady Anne?' He carefully put down the little person although she was not so very old.

'She heard you coming so she has gone to....' the maid stopped and smiled up at Lady Jane.

Will said, broadly smiling, 'Jane, this is Aggie, my sister's one and only maid.'

'Aggie? Is that short for something? Jane said smiling broadly at this spritely woman.

'Agnes of course, but Will started to call me 'Aggie' so long ago that now everyone in Norfolk calls me that and what should I call you, Milady.'

Will interrupted to say. 'For the moment Aggie, she will be known as Lady Jane Walden but hopefully, for only a short time.'

'Lady Jane then, come in Milady, Lady Anne will, no doubt, be down shortly.'

A perfect design of hallway centred on a fireplace that seemed just right with stairs flanking and curving around the chimney-breast so that with the light from the tall windows on the front of the house all was lit in a soft, warm haze of light. Even as Jane and Will entered, they heard the slither and slide of silk as a tallish, black dressed and white bewigged woman came gracefully down the stairs on the left. A wonderful figure, graceful and elegant, only the blackness of her dress pulling her down, Jane thought.

'Will!' her voice was warm and so happy. 'You are home again, I was so afraid that you might slip away and you look well.'

'Annie! It's wonderful to be home and to see you looking so fine...' for a moment they just stood and looked at each other and then she pulled the young man into her arms. 'I have heard such stories Will, I was so afraid.'

'I'm home Annie, and I bring you a wonderful present. A friend I hope, a companion.'

Lady Anne turned, her face close to her brother's to smile at this new woman, this wife to be.

Jane thought, they are brother and sister so and then, but they are not brother and sister are they? 'Lady Anne...' Jane curtseyed deeply, 'I am Jane Walden.'

'So you are, Jane. May I call you Jane?' and Anne smiled a dazzling smile.

Strange, Jane thought, a smile, so familiar but she had raised Will from a baby so... 'Of course Milady.'

'And you shall call me Anne, Jane. Come, it is time for tea and since Aggie has been slaving over it for some hours, the kitchen running red hot with more buns, cakes and biscuits than you can imagine.' She took Jane's arm and led her to a tall doorway to one side of the fireplace and into a small but comfortable looking Drawing Room where a table had been laid and so started the next part of their story.

After tea, Tom had been fetched to partake of the food and a plate, prepared for Tully, was taken out by Aggie, there was a little small talk but Tom ate in silence and Will was restive so Jane said. 'Perhaps Will, you and Tom should do the tour of inspection that you planned for; perhaps you will come across your Steward en-route. Lady Anne and I will find more that enough to talk about I am sure...' and Anne smiled her agreement.

So, it was into the sudden silence of a near empty house that the two women faced each other.

Lady Anne's certainty had almost escaped her she felt. Will had brought home a somewhat plain, regular featured young woman with a very good figure beautifully dressed in a light muslin white dress but not the raving beauty that his highly overwrought descriptions had brought her to expect. But the intelligence that shone from these wide set eyes, the wind blown hair that seemed not to worry her, the serenity of her slightly puzzled expression.... 'We must get to know each other Lady Jane.'

Jane did not miss the change to some degree of formality and wondered if she should follow suit but decided not to. 'Anne? If we are to be friends, and please God that is what we will be, then there must be no barriers between us. Do you not agree?'

A silence fell between them almost as if gates were in danger of closing.

Lady Anne decided that she would like to try to be a friend with this woman, this stranger. It would, she knew, take some considerable time but with... 'I do agree, if we are to live closely. Well, nearby...'

Jane looked at this so pretty woman and once again thought she saw something of Will in her expression, her look, but then realized that this was impossible since there were two bloodlines. That was not possible Jane thought, it was impossible that... and then she realized that it was not impossible, not impossible at all. 'This house...' Jane found that she had to hesitate before adding, '...is so very beautiful and so unlike the other, the Manor. I fear that I shall envy you, the comfort of it.' She looked around the so pretty room with its oyster pink silk walls, honey coloured wood panelling and cream and gilded furniture.

'Have you been into the Manor yet?' Anne asked, the slight smile wreathing her mouth that made her look even more like Will.

'No.' Jane smiled her happiest smile which made Anne smile in reply and she could see now this girl's beauty. 'I am beginning to feel that Will is too busy...'

'Will is always busy with the Estate, he has such plans.'

'As long as I am not excluded from them I shall not mind.'

The silence returned with each woman looking at the other trying not to say anything offensive at the same time wanting, needing, to find out.

Jane said, 'What if I tell you of my very short and rather boring life; boring that is until I met Will.'

Anne, noting that she would have to reciprocate, nodded.

Jane wondered at the youthful look of her sister in law to be. The whitened wig made this woman look somewhat older but she did indeed look quite young. 'You never married?'

'I thought you were to tell me of your life?' Anne asked.

Jane frowned. 'Born, grew up on an Estate at Saffron Walden, learnt the usual things from a succession of governess' then I met Will. Oh yes, I have a mother and a very beautiful sister. And a mad father, my life to date.' She looked suddenly so very sad and knew that she must write that night to her Steward for news of her father.

So sad, Anne thought and now she must trot out the usual lies that made her feel so very tired. 'It seems that I was taken from the hedgerow when I was very young. Has not Will told you this history?'

'He has, but was somewhat vague as to the details.'

'So I must repeat it all yet again?'

Jane looked at this pretty woman and thought that yes she must for it already was in a fair way to being a family secret and that she did not like. Her father had become mad but she'd made no secret of it for Jane knew that if she did then one day it would come flying out to hurt her. 'I think Anne, if it is too soon then we may delay but if there are secrets...?'

'Secrets Jane?' Anne now looked sad and put down.

Jane looked down at her hands and then suddenly up as if to confront the other woman. 'I feel, I don't know, but I feel that something already lies between us and I cannot imagine a lifetime that must be spent in edging around the sensitivities of one or the other of us.' Jane now looked positively anxious.

After a long moment Lady Anne said quietly. 'What are you thinking Jane? I have said nothing that is not common knowledge and you have been here at Saxethorpe barely an hour or two.'

Jane looked deeply into the other woman's eyes thinking, the truth Jane, tell this woman exactly what you are thinking. 'Tell me then Anne, tell me why you and Will look so very alike. You are not brother and sister but you do look...'

'I raised Will,' Anne interrupted suddenly, '...perhaps facial expressions?' Her face coloured a little.

'No! It is more than that Anne. When I first met you in the hallway I instantly thought that you were mother and son who looked so very alike and then I remembered that you are not blood relatives or are you?'

How could it have become like this so very swiftly, Anne thought. Years of careful preservation of the truth and this young woman had seen through it in an instant.

'There are secrets Jane,' she said very quietly, '... and Will does not know of them, nor should he, I think.' She looked down at her clenched hands then slowly up again to stare, tight lipped, at this woman who was set to smash a lifetime's work. No, a lifetimes lies.

'So you are his mother?' Jane asked simply.

Anne thought of lying but knew that she could not keep it up for an hour, with this young woman, let alone a lifetime. 'Yes. I was very young... and...'

'How old were you?' Jane's face was a maze of worry lines now.

'Just fifteen when I had the baby, Will.'

'But how?'

'... was the secret kept? Well, my lord had decided to build me a house, this house, a Dower House. It took just eight months to finish.'

Jane looked astounded, amazed. 'Good Heavens above, but what of...?'

'Lady Saxethorpe, Willa, who had cared for me for twelve, thirteen years? She was a willing conspirator I think. It's not uncommon for the old ways out here in the country, to still carry on...'

'But you were, was it the Master who?'

Anne smiled. 'Yes, otherwise Will should not inherit should he?'

'But....'

'It doesn't matter Jane, only brother John would care and I think that you and I should keep him separate from this particular truth.'

The door burst open to reveal Will with Tom just behind. 'Come on Jane, you've your new house to see.'

Jane and Anne just smiled at each other content to keep the old secret hidden.

The Great Hall of an ancient Tudor house is a very impressive place, thought Jane, walls of linen fold panelling with huge tapestries hanging in dusty magnificence above the dado, great crucked beams for the long roof, a raised dais for the Master's table and a really very large fire hearth with roasting spits and a large assortment of ovens for the baking of bread, the cooking of pies and the like. A huge stone sculptured mantel stood above the hearth, a shield of stone surrounded by ancient arms, arranged in a giant fan shape, pikes, swords, muskets and barbed objects that Jane did not know the use of save that they were for the taking of human life and all covered in an ages thick layer of dust.

Tom stared up in awe at the bedraggled triumph that hung above him and Jane supposed that all men, well the young anyway would be excited by such a display. Will led her around showing her where she would sit for the high days and holydays. 'At my right hand Milady will be your rightful place.'

The smaller halls, dining rooms, kitchens and places where it might be possible to keep warm in the Norfolk winters and then up the great heraldic emblazoned carved wooden staircase to enter onto a long north facing gallery lined with grime and time blackened paintings. Then bedchamber after bedchamber, most dusty and cobwebbed with frowsty hangings and curtains, mouse droppings on the floor and the flutter of bat wings in the eaves and Jane thought that she would have work enough and to spare, reworking this house to make it liveable.

And then, Will flung open a hugely heavy, oaken, much studded door, with pride in evidence on his face. 'And this Milady, is to be our bedchamber.'

Huge, gigantic, vast and completely unliveable as was evident from the layers of dust, skeins of cobwebs, silken drapes and hangings dripping with time torn threads, the tapestried walls dim and dark with age and all overlaid with the smell of centuries of disuse.

'Will...' her voice was firm, '...there is little possibility of this room being ours for I think, you would be unable to find me in all these dark, damp and dismal corners.'

'Oh!' Will said disappointed. 'You don't like it? It's not big enough, it's...'

'I will require a very clean, smallish room that does not dwarf me, one that is light and has close access to a room for bathing and dressing.' She smiled at him and then added, 'I will take a day or so to walk around the house with a builder, a decorator too and I will decide which part of this pile we can live in. We need a space not too much bigger than the Dower House and I'm not suggesting for one moment Will that Anne should change with us. A few rooms then, cleaned, redecorated, new drapes. It will take some time but we are not in such a hurry I trust.' Jane looked up at him, at his disappointment and thought that this man has had no home since he left the Dower House to join the Army. Seven years of war and encampments but now she would make a home for him.

Will said. 'But we need rooms now; for the wedding, for your mother perhaps and for you; separate apartments of course.'

'What we need Will, is a large work force, men for the painting, women and girls, laundry women, repairers and the like and perhaps we may be able to do it by the first, if not then we shall delay.'

Jane swirled around, her skirts spinning out about her, a happy smile on her face and Will thought he had never seen her this happy, this excited.

Then, next day, when Jane had given up on her mother replying to her letters an Express letter came from her Steward at the Saffron House Estate.

My Lady Jane Walden,

I received a visit from your mother, Lady Walden. She tried very hard to open up the house claiming that she had the right to do so. I pointed out that you were now the owner of the Estate, which she found very difficult to understand or believe. I advised her that she should take rooms at the Inn and this she finally did. A day later your sister arrived in some state and I sent her to the Inn to join her mother. I only send this to advise you that they are travelling to Saxethorpe even now.

May I wish you much happiness on your coming marriage and I hope to see you soon. The work that you requested is even now being carried out and should be finished by mid-October after the harvest is in. Yours Sincerely J. Bailey, Steward.

Lady Walden, seated, still huffing and puffing in her rage at the Steward and by proxy at her own daughter, could not imagine how the tale that he told could be true. She knew of no man who would willingly give an entire large Estate to anyone let alone a woman to whom he was neither married nor properly affianced. According to the Steward, the orders to exclude her from her own house, she knew that in thinking that she was in effect lying to herself but it was the house that she had married into and therefore... No, it was not possible that Jane had specifically ordered that neither she nor Alice should be allowed to enter Saffron House. The house was locked and the furniture sheeted the Steward said. There were no servants of any kind and no money had been left to pay for them; his orders were very clear, Lady Walden and the Countess Warlbeck would stay at the Inn or not as they decided. So here she was, as her sister's poor carriage turned into the Coaching Yard, but Lady Walden knew that she could probably obtain some credit at this Inn and she found herself thinking of the chicken pie that the Inn was well known for.

It was on the morrow that Lady Alice arrived in her very splendid coach and four with its two liveried footmen and two coachmen. The equipage swept into the busy yard scattering ostlers and pot-boys in all directions. Lady Alice, in high fury, positively leapt from the coach and stormed into the Inn where she demanded that she be taken, at once, to Lady Walden's suite of rooms.

Her look of contempt around the Inn's best rooms was of a very high order, Lady Walden thought. She'd charged into the room positively snarling at anyone who came near her and only the sight of her mother, seated at a heavily laden table of pie, vegetables, a large sugary dessert and a bottle of mostly drunk claret, stopped her moaning and then turning she ordered, 'Go, go all of you. Leave us... Mother! What are you doing here?'

Lady Walden smiled, this was mostly due to the mellowing effect of the wine and the pie but also because she was away from her own sister who had kept her in some penury. 'Hallo Alice, good journey?'

'I asked you what...?'

'Bailey wouldn't let me into the house and...'

'You should have ordered him to.'

'He had specific orders from Jane. We were not to be allowed in because there are no servants, no food and no comforts of any kind...' she took a large sip from her glass.

'You should have...'

'And you did not try? I found him unswerving in his loyalty to the new owner of Saffron Estate.'

'D'you mean the stupid Jane?'

Lady Walden frowned with the effort of concentrating and found that she got some pleasure from seeing her eldest daughter bested. 'The not so stupid Jane I think. She recognized the Major for what he was; a younger son taking home his dead brother and then inheriting what sounds like a substantial estate...'

Alice flounced over to a settle and seated herself in a flurry of pink silks.

Lady Walden said. 'Shall I order another bottle and perhaps another pie?'

Alice sat there brimming with malice and then remembered that she was hungry and then thought that she could bill Jane for the Inn and the supper which gave her some small pleasure.

Jane sat at tea with Lady Anne being served by Aggie. Jane was garbed in her working attire of poplin checked dress and a pretty, lace edged apron which she deemed both adequate and a setting out of how she would dress in the future.

Lady Anne, black dressed, with a small white lace collar and wearing her best white, curled and waved wig sat in a comfortable leather wing back chair and looked carefully at her new 'friend' and knew that it would be some time before she really knew this young woman. She appeared both intelligent, kind and very observant but that did not mean that at some future time she might not develop another side to her personality.

The doors to the garden were open but Lady Anne had become accustomed to taking tea indoors which she knew was to avoid the prying eyes of the staff from the Manor. The less they saw the less they could talk of for Anne knew that if the knowledge of her relationship with Will were known then the scandal would resound around the county. Already the furore over the disinheriting of John and herself still echoed about the countryside but fortunately all the ire had been born by Holy John, whom she had never liked for he was not a likable person. She thanked her God that John had been away at the Seminary when Will had been born...

Jane sipped her tea and wondered how to continue the conversation of the previous day without causing upset so she asked her next question. 'There is, or rather was, according to

Will, a great degree of resemblance between him and his older brother...?'

'We are to continue with more questions?' A now very pale-faced Lady Anne asked somewhat anxiously.

Jane thought, I must not hurt her but surely I should know before entering this family with all that meant. 'Will is of the same stature, as his borrowing of his brother's clothes indicates.'

'They have ended up the same size... yes...' Anne sounded more and more hesitant.

'Why is that a problem Anne?'

'It's not, Lawrence was... a very nice man.' Anne had to fight to hold back the tears.

'But he spent little time here?'

'He was a professional soldier, becoming the Colonel of the best Regiment in the land; the Household Cavalry. He had no time so the Steward and I or John perhaps made decisions if Lawrence was abroad....' she bit at her lips looking ruffled and upset, almost tearful.

Milady Anne is very emotional about Lawrence almost too much so, Jane thought.

A thought entered Jane's mind so she asked, 'I have never seen a likeness of Lord Saxethorpe, your... or of Lawrence.'

'There are none, Lord Peter ordered...' Anne hesitated until Jane wondered again for she had asked Will once about his brother and he'd said that he had been like a father to him. Was that possible or was the web of lies...?

Aggie poured more tea for them and offered Jane a buttered toasted tea-cake which she took and found delicious. Jane realized that the room was delicately perfumed from some flowering bush on the terrace. 'The perfume...?'

'Mock Orange.' Annie said, 'I always keep that door open when it's blooming.'

She seeks to divert me, Jane thought but now she had the oddest of thoughts. ' So you were fourteen Anne?'

'Must you go on Jane, it is not so important now. Lady Willa was dying and I was of child bearing age.'

'But you say, no, suggest, that it was Lord Saxethorpe who, although he was a very kind man you say. He rescued you and

John from the hedgerows and yet you... How old was he, Lord Saxethorpe, at this time...?'

'Fifty or so.' Anne snapped out.

'And Lady Willa knew?'

'I said so, did I not.'

There was a long silence covered only by the sipping of tea and the eating of tea cake. Lady Anne's face was scarlet with embarrassment which seemed odd to Jane considering what she had told, no, inferred, only yesterday. But, as Jane pushed a last delicious fragment of the bun into her mouth, she wondered how old was Lawrence and where was he when Anne was a very pretty fourteen year old.

'How old was Lawrence when you were fourteen Anne?'

Lady Anne just stared at her, the colour of her cheeks seeming to fade into her normal paleness and that was when she decided that she would be friends with this young woman but only if she told all; all the truth. Somehow she relaxed enough to put down her tea cup and then she stood and reaching up pulled the long pins from her wig, removed it and shook out her hair, a blaze of silken fair hair lightly streaked with an almost matching grey short hair that would fit under a wig but soon would be no longer needed. 'I was very pretty I think, nubile is the word and I was very much in love with Lawrence. I knew of course, that we weren't related. I knew that I was adopted and John knew it too. Lawrence was sixteen and was devastating in his looks. Tall, fair of hair, a real man, he knew that one day he would inherit but his father seemed well and strong. We were, apart from Holy John, a kind of happy family, at least that's what everyone thought, but I was an ill educated, young, very young girl.'

Jane looked at this so pretty woman knowing now what was to come.

'I knew where to look for company; the village school in Saxethorpe, I had three good friends who could visit but there were no boys and everywhere I looked there was the most handsome of men. He rode like a dream, he hunted, fished, shot superbly. A man amongst men and I fell in love with him so that when... He had drunk a little more than he was used to; he touched me and I fell into his arms. A dream coming true for me, if not for him. Being a country girl I knew a good deal about what happens between a man and a woman but I had not realized how wonderful physical love could be so it was not just one night, one tumble in a hay rick but a summer, easily the best summer of my life, a summer of love. Everyday, all day sometimes and all the time I knew that a baby was almost inevitable and when I missed, and I had started only a year or so previous, I knew that we would be in terrible trouble but running alongside our wild lovemaking was the fact that Lawrence had had a commission bought for him by his father. Subaltern to the Household and Lord Wellesley. Lawrence was so excited, so delighted with the idea of the Army, me as well but really just the Army, so I waited until he had gone and then went to Lady Willa who was already unwell. She had been so kind to me, a waif from the hedgerow, because she knew that having given birth to Lawrence there could never be another child hence Lord Peter's finding of stray children. She was wonderful, sympathetic and kind, for I was so afraid that I would be turned out onto the byways and die there. We three had many talks and a decision was made for me. I would have the child but everyone would be told that it was Lady Willa's even though she was somewhat too old and that's how it happened, perfectly. Lord Peter had started construction of the Dower House for he planned to retire in a few years and get Lawrence to return.' Anne seemed to run out of words so tense was she.

Jane wondered, 'Did, did you tell Lawrence that he was Will's father?'

'Lord Peter decided not to. Lawrence was so happy in the Army and he had campaigns to fight and he rose in rank so fine a soldier was he. In the end, when Lady Willa died, Lord Peter embellished the story but when, ten years later, as he was dying, he told his son and Lawrence came to see me. He swore undying fidelity to me, I was still only twenty four, and he took me to bed again but this time I knew about life and birth and I was reluctant to give birth again as indeed Lawrence was reluctant to marry me. It was indeed a very difficult situation for us both and I did not care for the complications that marriage would bring....' she paused to sit in a comfortable chair by the window to enjoy the evening air and turned to smile up at this young woman. 'It could not be, Lawrence was truly married to the Army. He was very loving when he came home and I think was largely faithful although he had no need to be. He already had an heir for the estate although I think he regretted in some way taking Will with him to Spain but he so enjoyed being with him as indeed I had enjoyed my sixteen years with my son but I'd created a lie that I had to live with and only Aggie to share my pain...' and she did indeed look so very sad.

Jane looked at her with great sympathy. 'But now Will is back home. You must be happy with that now?'

'Yes, of course, but it was Lawrence dying. Somehow I had hoped that one day he would come back to me but I was just a little chip of a girl to him, one that had grown, one who had raised his son but still only a girl found in a hedgerow not his true love I think; but yes, it is wonderful that Will has come home and I suppose that if Lawrence had not died in that battle then neither of them would have come back and probably Will would have died in some other pointless battle.'

Jane smiled warmly at this woman, her future mother in law even if they could not admit to it. 'I'm so happy that Will has come home to you Anne, even if...'

'In a somewhat sad life, in many ways it has become the happiest of times. You will marry Will, have babies and perhaps the Saxethorpe's can become a normal happy family again.'

Jane crouched down by the seated woman, slipped her arms around her and gently kissed her cheek. 'And I hope that you will become a mother to me too for Will has extensive family plans that seem to include me and do not fear, I shall never tell.'

'Tell what?' Will's strong, happy voice came from the inner hallway.

Jane stood and smiled at this man as he bustled in lifting the lid of the tea pot as he passed, so happy in his farmer's clothing, his face tanned, his hair awry, then she said, 'Lady Anne was telling me how very naughty you were as a boy and the very wicked things you got up to.'

'Not so wicked I think.' He smiled again, so happy to be home with those he loved.

225

CHAPTER TWENTY-TWO

Jane knew that her mother and sister would be upon them at any time soon so she set the servants to preparing their rooms but could soon see that the ill decorated, paper and silk wall coverings were peeling and drab so she sent a footman to Saxethorpe to engage rooms at the Inn for the two women.

Tom sat in the Curate's study on a hard backed chair and stared over his teacher's head at the window that showed a sea of sunlit leaves that swayed above a thousand years of graves.

'You are not listening Tom,' the curate said as he laid down the Latin Primer and the look on his face was sympathetic for he knew of the lure of the outside world on a young mind. 'Perhaps Tom we should take our work outside, I could tell you the names of plants, insects and animals in Latin; that way we could combine two pleasures into one?'

Tom looked back down to his Primer and thought that anything would be better than this so he stood and smiled tentatively.

The coach was varnished in brown with a great deal of gold ornamentation, the coat of arms on the doors of particular note. Inside Lady Walden and her eldest daughter sat silently for they had been talking repetitively for the last six hours. Lady Alice was dressed in spectacular style, a wide gown, in the latest style, with much gold lace over a silk of blue. Their faces were set, each offering some degree of enmity to the other for both considered the other a rival.

'So, the stupid farmer, the Major, turns out to be a baron of some rank,' this delivered with anger again by Alice, as if there was some fault on the part of the Major for not telling them of his possible accession to the nobility.

'But it will be very pleasant for Jane when she marries him. A deal of money I imagine...'

'Did she not say what his income is?'

'No. She would regard such knowledge as vulgar in the extreme.'

'It is the only kind of interesting information to have about a man.' The bitter faced woman said, who was already regretting the speed with which she had plunged into her own marriage.

Silence was the main ingredient of remainder of their journey. Their own thoughts sufficient to occupy them. The shock Lady Walden had suffered at being unable to go into her own home. Of course, it was no longer her home but the fact that Jane was now the new owner and the wretched girl had not advised her, not written. Then there were the changes; both wings pulled down; the house now as it was when first she had married; how very odd that was. But the Steward rudely ignoring her order to unlock the house and call for servants, how extraordinary. She had had to go to the Inn and stay in their disgusting and smelly surroundings until Alice had come. But this coach was very pleasant compared with her sister's poor conveyance.

'Where is this stupid place? Alice's voice almost cracked in its acrimony.

'It is a little beyond Norwich I believe, Jane's last letter gave little information more than that but it is quite large although she was not specific as she too had not actually seen it herself.' Lady Walden was worried and wondered why the Major had not revealed to them his true background.

'What's his stupid title then?' Alice snapped at her mother.

Lady Walden wondered why such a thing should be of interest to Alice since her husband was an Earl and commanded a large income. 'Lord Saxethorpe, I believe, he is also a Knight.'

'Very common, positively ordinary.' Alice almost snarled so very angry was she.

'How is your husband, you mention him but little...'

'That's because there is little to mention. He is a dull fellow. Does not read, only shoots or fishes; dislikes music, the theatre, plays, the opera and dislikes gambling, especially horses and cards. He wants only two things...' she paused to place an implacable frown on her forehead for now she had come to the crux of her complaints,'...an heir and then another heir so that he has someone to leave his money to.' She was pale with anger and Lady Walden realized that her first daughter had made another poor choice.

'And why is Jane the owner of Saffron Estate pray?' Alice ground out.

'According to Mr Bailey the Major gave her the Deeds to the Estate before he asked her to marry him.'

'Clever, that. She says, thank you sir, and yes I will marry you and he gets the Estate back and all in five minutes.' Her voice still bitter but this time in anger at her sister.

'Mr Bailey said that the Deed did not depend on her marrying the Major. Even if she had said no she would still be the owner but it does mean...'

'I know, I know, you will have somewhere to go under sufferance from your youngest daughter instead of back to your sister's.'

Lady Walden smiled, realizing the truth of that statement. Now she and her pride were safe when Jane married her Major. Lady Walden could go home and resume her life. Then she thought, worried about money. Would Jane make her an allowance? How embarrassing that she should have to ask her daughter for money but she knew that Jane was a kind woman who would not stint her mother although the tone of her last letter had been very firm on the question of money. There would be little apparently until the debt to Saxethorpe Estate was paid off and many changes to the running of the house and the farms. Some time would pass before...

'Jane has always been generous has she not?' Lady Walden asked plaintively.

'She has had little to be generous with but now...' Alice answered, '...well, we will see, will we not.'

That evening Jane and Will were invited to supper at the Dower House together with the curate Charles Morris. Lady Anne had also invited Mr Crindal, who had returned to Saxethorpe, to have the adoption papers signed and so the scene was set yet again.

A country meal had been ordered and was to the liking of the company in general. Some good claret had come up from the well-stocked cellar of the Hall so that generally all was very pleasant.

Charles Morris sat at Will's left hand and opposite to Lady Jane only a flower decoration, consisting largely of yellow and white roses, and a six branch candelabra stood between them. Lady Anne sat at the head of the table, dressed, as ever, in black but tonight she had a bright green silk scarf about her neck covering her bosom in a most modest way. Mr Crindal sat next to Lady Jane his sombre expression and his dark clothing setting off her royal blue gown, her shoulders bare, her hair brushed into some semblance of order, shining with health.

Will talked largely to Lady Jane and Charles Morris. The talk was largely of the Estate and what plans Will had for it. At times, as Charles would expound on a point; Lady Anne would watch him closely with a somewhat puzzled expression on her face as if wondering what a poor curate was doing at her dining table.

Mr Crindal held Jane's attention with his talk of the progress of the case against George Banham and the added details of the adoption of Tom and so the meal proceeded until the men stood to allow the ladies the opportunity to seat themselves by the small fire that had been lit.

'Mr Morris...' Lady Anne smiled up at the man who was juggling with coffee cup and saucer, '...I have been reading the new Testament with the change of emphasis that you suggested and comparing the Gospels and find...' she stopped speaking finding that she had almost nothing to say except to engage the curate in conversation of some kind so enjoyable did she find his speaking and thinking.

'You find...?' Charles smiled down at this so pretty lady who was not wearing her customary wig, her golden hair combed out into pretty waves, thinking her much younger than she had appeared on the previous occasions that they had met.

She smiled, her cheeks becoming somewhat pink, 'I find I have run out of words to say on the subject of the Bible. My range of conversation is somewhat limited and perhaps you might undertake to instruct me on something other than Holy Scriptures.'

'But I am a cleric... a curate. It is all I am good for surely?'

'I am told that you are also a... I'm sorry that I do not have a word for what you do; the study of the flora and fauna?'

'Biology. I am something of an amateur biologist.'

She smiled her dazzling smile, so like Will's, and said. 'Then you shall instruct me in the basics of biology,' she suddenly looked a little dismayed at her presumption, 'I do not ask too much I trust?'

Quite suddenly Charles Morris knew that he was being presented with a most unexpected chance; one that he had never even considered. 'No, of course not, you may ask for anything that you wish.' He looked so steadily at her that, pink cheeked, she sought some change of subject.

'You will perform the marriage service yourself Charles?'

For a moment he was confused, the conversation and his thoughts overlapping in a most odd way. Marriage. He had never even considered it for his family had been largely destitute by providing for his education and no money meant no marriage.

'I will...' Charles stared down at this pretty woman, '...I will, of course, perform the service; the marriage, it would give me the greatest of pleasure.' Somehow both he and Lady Anne, in just those few moments knew that he spoke of two things and that time alone would resolve the conundrum that faced them.

Across the fireplace Lady Jane, seated in a small silk covered armchair had observed the interplay between the cleric and his parishioner and wondered at all the changes that such a union might well bring about.

Aggie poured more coffee for all and threw the occasional worried glance at her mistress. The curate and the Lady now seemed oblivious of all the others as if they were alone in the room until even Will noticed.

'You two are as thick as thieves Annie?'

She looked up pale and replied. 'We discuss...' she looked at Charles as if seeking permission to tell an untruth, '...the religious connotations of marriage. The ceremony that is.'

Lady Jane smiled for she saw in Lady Anne the same confusion that she felt when near to Will.

Will too had a sudden premonition then shook the foolish idea from his head.

The coach had entered Saxethorpe at sunset and stopped at the Inn.

'Driver!' Alice shouted out, '...go and ask where the Estate is situated?'

The two women sat in silence until the coachman reappeared. A polite knock at the lower panel of the door and Alice dropped the window to stare, set faced down at the man. 'Well?'

'It be a coupla miles on M'am; the main gate that is....'

'So?'

'The Innkeeper says that the gates'll be closed and locked by now.'

Alice heaved a sigh of disgust, 'So the gatekeeper will have to open them.'

'Apparently they don't have a gateman Milady. If you want to get in you have to go to the east entrance, that be seven odd miles on; it'll likely be dark.'

'Can you not open a gate coachman?'

'If it not be locked, barred or bolted Milady.'

'Dear God they cannot even afford a gateman...' Alice whined petulantly.

'The Innkeeper says that rooms here have been reserved for you Milady.'

'And why should we stay here pray?'

The man, looking somewhat abashed, said. 'Perhaps because they were a locking the gates.'

Alice, white faced and furious shouted down. 'Let us go now! This instant, to the main gates.'

In the light of a fast fading sunset the coach arrived at the wide open main gates of the Estate and a gatekeeper came out even as they thundered through.

Alice snarled, 'See! Everything here is stupid and backward, they say the gates will be closed and they are not.'

Lady Walden turned from looking through the crinkled back window to say. 'Well they are now. The gateman has just closed them.'

'How far!' Alice shouted up at the driver.

'The big house be two miles or so and the Dower House is nearby...'

Alice frowned, thinking that a drive of two miles was a good length indeed.

Lady Walden said a little querulously. 'Two miles... that's quite long isn't it? At Saffron House it's only two hundred yards or so.' Lady Walden could see that the estate might well be quite large.

'Driver!' Lady Alice shouted up.

'Milady?' the driver called back down.

'Did they say how big the Estate was?' Even as she asked Alice knew that the reply would not please her.

'Did mention that it be near fifteen miles to the other side milady with a gate at each point of the compass.'

'Fifteen miles across,' gasped Lady Walden.

'Perhaps it is long and narrow,' Alice snapped back but thinking that she should perhaps have paid more attention to the Major even when dressed as a farmer.

''Bout twenty two thousand acres Milady, the innkeeper said, all arable, well mostly anyways; long coastline, two sea villages as well as Saxethorpe, 'parently been on Saxethorpe land this last hour or so.'

Shut up you stupid man Alice thought, how could Jane of all people find such a man.

Lady Anne was very pleased with the curate of Saxethorpe who seemed, unlike her brother, to be more of a secular cast of mind so that every aspect of the conversation did not always turn to the Almighty. They had talked now for something approaching an hour when they heard the dull thunder of hooves, the creaking of leather and wood, the calls of the coachman

Will looked up from his dessert and turned to Jane murmuring, 'A large coach and four Milady, perhaps your mother and sister?'

Jane surged up from her chair and started for the hallway.

Lady Anne, looking surprised, asked. 'Should not Aggie?'

'She's busy...' said Jane as she disappeared, in a swirl of blue silk, into the hallway.

Mr Crindal smiled and remarked. 'The French would appreciate Lady Jane, very egalitarian her answering the doorbell.'

A ringing of the bell was heard again followed by the creak of a large door being pulled open.

A footman dressed in a very ornamental livery of gold and blue stood there waiting as the door opened to him. 'We are looking for Saxethorpe Hall but no lamps burn in that....' he turned to look at the huge dark silhouette of the Manor House, '...so...?'

Lady Jane, her bare shouldered blue gown settling around her; her well-brushed hair gathered into a chignon stood there and said. 'You've come to the right place. Please tell Lady Walden and my sister...' but the footman was already hurrying back to the coach.

It was only two or three minutes before Lady Walden and Alice were striding up the wide pathway to the Georgian house where the open door cast a long, warm, beam of candle and lamplight.

Lady Jane advanced a pace and said, caught in semi silhouette by the bright lit hallway, 'Mama, how lovely to see you...' she peered past her mother to see her sister, '...and Alice too.'

The three women met under the porch and the usual kisses were exchanged although Jane could sense the two women were in high dudgeon about something.

For a few moments, whilst cloaks and bonnets were removed, Jane had a moment of two with her mother. 'You did not advise me of your arrival, if it had not been for a letter from Mr Bailey.'

'Alice was anxious to proceed.'

Jane turned to her sister a light smile of interrogation on her lips. 'You were anxious Alice. About what pray?'

Alice looked away, for a brief moment, from a candle lit mirror on the wall where she was adjusting the wave in her hair to say. 'About your choice of husband of course.'

'You find him dubious or unpleasant?' Jane asked as if barely interested in the answer.

'He seems never the same person; a soldier, a farmer, a savage...fighter...' a glimmer came into her eyes as she said the last.

'I think that the changes of garb came as a matter of necessity rather than choice; but it is of no matter since I have agreed to marry the man, whatever.' Jane smiled a somewhat grim smile for she knew that the first shots in a long battle had just been fired.

The two older women turned to Jane on her last remark and stared at her in silence.

'Come and meet Lady Anne Saxethorpe; my sister to be and Will who, of course, you have already been introduced to, several times.' Jane turned to the large doors of the Drawing Room pushing them open to reveal the comfortable, candle and lamp lit room.

Will stood by the lit fire with Lady Anne seated to his right. Mr Crindal stood by his chair and the Curate was scrambling to his feet as the doors opened.

Jane walked in saying. 'Lord Saxethorpe, I'm sure that you remember my mother, Lady Walden, and my sister...Lady?'

'Countess Warbeck, sister.' Alice said, delivered in a vicious tone of voice.

Jane said back to her a gentle smile on her face. 'Ahh, Countess, so you will precede me, but then you always have.'

Will, dressed in a dark green suit of silk, a jacket and waistcoat with a white silk shirt and stock, bowed and said, 'Lady Walden. Your Grace, welcome to the Dower House at Saxethorpe Hall. It is the home of Lady Anne Saxethorpe. I, we do not live here; but come and meet my sister Anne.'

It was some time later when all the introductions had been made and coffee had been served that the ladies, with hidden yawns, were beginning to feel the effects of their long journey. 'Where are we to stay Jane?' Lady Walden asked in a half whisper.

'Yes...where?' Alice added.

Jane with a barely concealed smile said. 'I reserved you rooms at the Inn in Saxethorpe. None of the rooms in the big house are suitable as yet and this house is much too small for guests to stay. Mr Crindal here, our lawyer, and Mr Morris are returning to Saxethorpe shortly and will be able to guide you.'

'We know where the Inn is but...surely there is room?' Lady Walden's eye's flickered in the direction of the big house.

Lord Saxethorpe's voice came from the shadows. 'Lady Jane has already said that nothing there is up to your standard so the next best place...'

Countess Alice, her face smiling now, seemed to acquiesce as she said. 'Yes Mother, let us leave these good people until the morrow when we all will be less tired.' She stood to smile her very warmest smile; at Will. For Lady Anne there was barely the thinnest of courtesy smiles and curtsies and Jane was comprehensively ignored as the party swept out of the room led by Mr Crindal and Mr Morris.

They heard the front door bang closed and Jane said. 'Well Anne, my sister, improved rank or no, is still the rudest person in England,' she smiled at Lady Anne and added, '...my apologies for her boorish behaviour.'

Will returned from the hallway saying as he did so. 'Your sister has changed Jane. Remembered who I am for a start.'

'She reacts well to men Will. Well, rich men anyway, and you seemed to enjoy her compliments.' Jane said in aside.

Which drew a confused look from Will who realized that Jane and her sister were frequently at odds or at least in contention. He knew that Alice had tried very hard to keep Jane back but now; with their estates so very far apart the likelihood of a chance meeting was remote for the charms of the London Season left Will cold and he felt that Jane shared his point of view.

Later the couple, arm in arm, walked to the gate, with Will carrying a lantern, for it was a very dark night, and at the gateway he diffidently raised her hand to his lips and kissed it, then seeing the questioning look on her face, he kissed her lips and smiled saying. 'Not so long now, my love, when we need not part in darkness...'

Jane thought him a lovely boy for that was how he seemed to her. If she could control, prevent his instinctive heroism she thought that they might be very happy together. 'So Will, do you name the day?'

He smiled, slightly embarrassed and then said, 'Charles has been reading the Banns this month past.'

She looked up at him, smiled a tiny smile and said. 'But I have not accepted you much more than two weeks surely?'

'I tried to be confident so, not wishing to delay.'

'Mmmm, I shall have to think of some way of taking my revenge on you for your presumption.' She might have said more but his lips cut off her retort in the most delightful way for she could feel the warmth of his body pressed so very tightly to hers.

Jane retired to her bedchamber, the one that had once been the childhood accommodation of Will although no traces of him remained. She washed and prepared for bed but waited as if knowing...

A light knock at the door followed by one even lighter. 'Enter,' said Jane.

The door opened to reveal the night dress and shawl clad figure of Lady Anne who entered quietly, a worried expression on her face.

'Anne?' Jane asked.

'It is your sister that has made me worried Jane. She asks so many questions. You are sure that you never?'

'I have not seen her for nearly six weeks and now, well, you heard our conversation. It is just that she is of a vicious character and seeks always to do harm, to me usually. I wish now that I had not invited her since she did not invite me to her wedding.'

'She didn't invite you?'

'She expected me to look after our father not run around the country going to weddings; even hers. No doubt she had spun a web of lies that could be refuted by me. It would be to do with money, my father, the Estate and all lies, but now that's in the past.'

Anne thought that Jane brought 'baggage' with her not unlike herself so the nuptials would be fraught with danger of one sort or the other.

As Anne turned to leave Jane said quietly. 'Anne, please be quiet in your spirits, do not fear my sister and mother. No matter what is said or done you will remain here, a beloved and honoured person. There is no mistake that has happened in the past that can alter that. While I remain, so will you and Aggie just the way you are. So good night, and sleep well sister.' The two women kissed and Anne left.

CHAPTER TWENTY-THREE

Dark clouds rolled in from the North Sea on a stiff easterly breeze and Will thought it necessary to leave his lantern on a large round table in the centre of the entrance hall for fear that he might take a tumble trying the stairs in the darkness. His single candle-stick did little to relieve the deep gloom of his bedchamber but he had never felt the necessity for candles to burn unprotected. His fear of fire was far greater than any fear of intruders so he blew out the candle as soon as he was comfortable in his brother's bed.

It was some hours later at the darkest part of the summer night that a rattle, a creak, a groan of wood and steel being wrenched apart could be heard; if by chance you were awake. Will was a heavy sleeper so, content as he was with his life, all designs, such as marriage, adoption and the making of complex Wills being done it meant he could sleep without worry save the everyday concerns of a farmer.

A rough, battered face caught in the light of the single candle, near to burnt out in the lantern, as the man opened the lanterns door and, lips pursed, blew out the one light in the whole huge Tudor edifice. The darkness, which seemed to descend like a black cloak over the two men crouched by the table surprised even them.

'Why'd you do that, stupid thing? Numbskull! Idiot!' whispered the smaller of the two, '...how are we to find the right room now?'

' 'E said, top the stairs, door opposite, can't miss 'er...'e said like.'

'Well, you tell me where the stairs are and then finding the door might not be so difficult?'

'Them's over there... aren't they?'

'I don't know where you are let alone where the stairs be.'

' 'Ave you a flint and steel? We cud light a candle then...'

'Why I brought you with me I cannot imagine... follow me...'

'Where are you?'

'Look! Hold onto my coat... Where are you idiot?'

It was when the more foolish of the two men fell on the stairs that Will stirred in his bed. The thump, the moan, the whimper sounded clear in the absolute silence of the very old house and Will came awake in an instant. Will had been born, if not in this house then very close by and the layout of the ancient structure was part of his very makeup so he rolled from under the eiderdown onto the floor and listened, staring the while at the ghostly outline of the starlit window. Mutterings, grunts and whispers came almost heard, then another thud as someone backed into the door. Will thought, as he did with most things, that some form of armament might not come amiss so he crawled to where he knew the fireplace was, knowing too that a selection of heavy metal instruments would be racked up there.

"Ere's an andle...' a rough voice whispered as quietly as possible.

'Then turn the fucker, let's get this 'ere done,' the small man thought that unless events improved rapidly then he would be off and away, if he could remember the way in this almost total darkness.

Will fondled the various pokers, shovels and the like and found himself rejecting the more lethal of them on the grounds that Lady Jane would be most upset if he were to kill someone in what one day might well be their bedchamber.

'I 'eard sommat...' a whisper came from the velvet blackness.

'It were me, idiot...' too sharp a whisper the small man thought.

Will laid there staring into the darkness then he caught a flicker of movement as someone crept across the open window, hands outstretched, feeling his way and for a moment Will could see the shape of a heavy built man so, without thinking of the consequences he struck, with all his strength, the shin of the leading figure, with the long, heavy, iron poker.

The scream that came from such a large man was quite exceptional thought Will, and would have done credit to an upstairs maid so high pitched was it. The querying bellow that came from the second man had the effect of locating him quite precisely so that when Will took, what amounted to a shot in the dark, he was fairly precise in his direction if not the force of the blow. There was a blinding flash as a pistol was discharged and

Will was interested in how long the flame from the barrel appeared to be in this absolute darkness. It did, of course, completely blind the three men but only Will crouching on the floor had the momentary advantage of knowing exactly where the two men were, so flash blinded though he was, his next two heavy blows were completely accurate since they were followed by two very heavy thuds as the two men fell unconscious to the wooden floor.

Will laid still for a bit since he wasn't at all sure whether it was two or more intruders that he had to deal with but a silence only broken by the heavy stentorian breathing from the injured men then in the distance Will heard the shouts of what sounded like Tom and Tully coming. So he carefully got to his feet and circled the unconscious men to open the door to the upper hallway where he saw the light of approaching candles and oil lamps crossing the hall.

'Up here lads.' Will called down. 'We've had visitors, late night visitors.' Will was curiously happy to hear the thunder of heavy boots pounding up the oak staircase.

It was somewhat unfortunate, from Will's point of view, that both the men had broken limbs so that what with the expense of the physician, Dr Carlson, plus his man for the mixing of the plaster of Paris and Tully sent to Norwich to bring the Constable that Will found that his breakfast time seriously broken into. When he had managed to persuade Tom that it was hardly necessary to bind the two men, considering their injuries, as they would be most unlikely to run away.

He finally made his way to the Dower House at seven of the clock only to find that Lady Jane and his sister were both up and about.

'We have heard Will. More heroics in the night then.' Lady Jane was quite sharp with him as she now assumed that he was completely indestructible and at least the two men were both alive if in great pain.

'Milady, I did try not to hurt them too much but it was very dark. A bit hard to judge the strength of one's...'

'You didn't kill them that's the main thing. What were they doing in your bedchamber?'

'Well, they tell me...'

'They told you? Without coercion?'

'Well Tom did twist...'

'Please don't tell me what Tom did. How was he in your room?'

'He heard a scream and the gun fire then came running.' Will took two slices of the toast that Aggie had just made for him.

Jane sat there, her forehead creased in her concentration before she asked, 'And what did the man... the men say?'

Will smiled at her concern then said. 'You realize that I have been searching for my Steward for some days past?' He awaited her reply then when she just sat silent he added, '...seems he had to go to Ely to see brother John. Apparently the Bishop may well have promised the Steward a farm of his own if he undertook a certain, task.' Will took an enormous bite of the marmalade coated toast and munched happily.

'They came with guns then?' Jane now looked worried.

'Yes, they both had pistols but I got them, the men, not the pistols that is...'

'So your Steward?'

'He was put in by my brother... our brother.' Lady Anne spoke for the first time. 'At the time I did wonder why someone so, so rude and uncouth should be honoured with such a post.'

Will said, after pouring most of a cup of coffee down his throat, 'Well, now I need a new and very good Steward.' He smiled at Lady Jane who was still not in a good humour. 'I don't suppose that I could have Mr Bailey?'

'No Will, you cannot have my Steward, find one of your own... Make Tully your Steward...' she added as an afterthought for she was discountenanced for some reason or other.

'I would love to have a man I really trusted, like Tully, but he has no knowledge of running such a large estate and farming in general so I must need speak to... I don't know who I would ask but...'

'Ask Charles Morris or better still Mr Crindal. He must know all of the great Estates hereabouts.'

Good advice, Will thought. Thank Heaven that she is not stupid, that someone so very bright will stand at my side through the coming years and Will smiled at her as he said, 'I've decided that we should advance our nuptials at some speed. I shall ride to see Charles this morning. How would Saturday be for you, my love?'

Anne smiled at her son's incautious proposal but thought it charming.

'That is only three days my Lord.' The girl looked up at him, her face flushing pink.

'We have few to invite that we have not already invited. Only the time and day were omitted; Tom could ride to all the farms.'

Jane looked at him, worry made manifest on her face. 'You will need Tully by your side sir, armed. You may not have thought through the whole plot. Your last Steward, Mr Colman, is still missing and may, having heard of last night's debacle, try again.'

Will had thought on it but decided that he could manage but Jane interrupted his train of thought.

'If Tully is to ride to Norwich then I shall accompany you to Saxethorpe. I shall be ready when you have finished your breakfast.' Jane leapt to her feet and sped from the room. Will, as many married men will tell you, found that it was easier to agree with his lady than to fight every battle afresh each day so he took another two pieces of the toast and looked for something sustaining to put on them.

Jane had, in some strange conjunction of feelings that had occurred some weeks before, had had made, by the best dressmaker in Saffron Walden, a riding costume. Not the silken affairs fancied by the gentry but a dress with divided skirt tailored somewhat in the male fashion to be worn with proper riding boots, a leather jerkin and a wide brimmed hat. She had not known then that she would be riding in earnest but saw it as a useful costume for the riding about the Estate and the gathering in of the yearlings. As she swiftly dressed, caring not for fashion and looks she somehow achieved a kind of careless beauty that she was not aware of. As she tramped down the stairs Will, waiting, he suspected, for some little time was astounded by this almost man but gloriously beautiful woman in her dark green costume, leather jerkin and broad hat. He bowed and she smiled which, he thought, completed the picture.

Their first ride across the Estate, undertaken as it was in the early morning sunlight, was the most beautiful occurrence, Will thought, in company with a superb horsewoman. Her side saddle on Trojan and him on Hector, they cantered, then galloped and arrived in Saxethorpe seemingly in a matter of moments.

Jane looked over at him taking in the way he sat his horse, a true cavalryman, his clothes rough but in his easy manner looking so very happy.

Why did I not know how well she rides, Will thought. We could ride forever and with God's help we shall, although Will was not sure whether God was on his side or Holy John's.

They arrived before Morning prayers so went to the Golden Hind to talk with Mr Crindal.

The serious man sat at his breakfast as he awaited the arrival of the Post Coach that would come at thirty minutes past nine. He listened with considerable interest to the latest episode of Will's story and then attended to the problem of the question of the Steward and told them that he would put the word about as soon as he reached his offices in Norwich but he held up little hope for acquiring the services of a very good Steward since most Estates spent considerable time bringing on, training, their Steward. It was the task of a lifetimes work and such men would be unlikely to leave their present employment.

Meantime, Jane asked after her mother and sister and was informed that they were still abed but that breakfast had been ordered.

'My nearest and dearest are still asleep Will so....'

A cup of coffee later, Jane and Will repaired to the vicarage to talk with Charles. As they passed, leading their horses, townspeople bowed and curtsied their respect and excited comments seemed to follow them.

They met with Charles, just as the Service finished, with him hurrying back to his home at the vicarage in a whirl of white cassock and flying hair; for he thought himself late for the tuition of young Thomas. Surprised at the presence of both Lord Saxethorpe and his bride to be waiting outside, he faltered a little then said. 'Good morning to you both,' all said in a scurry of bows and nods.

'We received another visitation last evening Charles, well, dawn is more like.' Will said in what he hoped was a casual tone of voice.

'Two rough men, now seriously injured of course, having met with the Master here.' Jane added, in a somewhat sarcastic voice.

So they went into the Vicarage where the couple told the Curate of their latest adventures and the reasons why Tom would not, that day, attend on the Curate.

Jane asked. 'How is Tom taking to schooling Charles?'

The man smiled and answered. 'In the schoolroom he is a mouse but get him outside and he is lion, animated and curious. I taught him Latin in short sentences about the plants, the river and the animals. He learnt as much in one hour as I managed in one month at Cambridge. A fine student, it is just a question of finding the way to teach him...' Charles seemed to run out of words as he noted that Will Saxethorpe was looking at him with some degree of curiosity.

'Why are you only a Curate, Charles?' Will asked.

Charles had to say, 'I have no influence or family money and since I require only a simple place with simple people to care for and food and shelter, of course. I have no wife or children so a curacy offered at two hundred a year.'

Will, who had made a point of searching the Estate's records had discovered that it was he who paid the Vicar some five hundred pounds per annum and thought it odd that he had never met the man. 'The Vicar?'

'Has...' Charles voice became somewhat hesitant, '...has not yet returned. He has other concerns in Norwich it would seem.'

Indeed, thought Will, so following up the conversation he asked. 'We have yet to decide on a suitable remuneration for the instructing of Tom and the guardianship of him too.'

Charles shook his head, saying, 'I have time and enough to instruct the boy and as for the guardianship, please God that I am never called upon.'

'I will regulate this when I am over my present trials and tribulations,' Will said in an abstracted voice.

Jane meantime had taken to wandering around the Curate's study looking at the many glass jars, the glass fronted cases of butterflies, each insect pinned and most carefully labelled, then she smiled and said. 'You are a most meticulous man Charles and very curious too.'

The curate walked over to her to say 'There is a whole world out there about which we know nearly nothing, but many men are curious now. God was credited with all and so that must be but even I am fascinated by such things as these....' he lifted a glass fronted box in which two black beetles were pinned on a white card. 'See, apparently identical but examined under my new microscope...' he pointed at the instrument set on a large worktable under the light from a good sized window, '...there are several distinct differences and they are not just the sexual ones for these are both female. At least I think they are.'

Jane stared at the man for a long moment then said. 'You shall come to dinner again Charles. You are looking a little thin I fancy. Tomorrow night, yes?' Jane turned away and then looked back to add, 'To discuss the wedding Charles.' A statement of a kind or perhaps a question that needed answering. 'Our wedding will be on Saturday, three days hence if that is convenient to you and your flock.' Her words fell into the silence of the two men so she said to Will. 'I shall go now to the Inn to see if my Mother and sister are... well.'

'Ummm Lady Jane?' Charles called out to her disappearing back. 'I am supposed to 'instruct' you both,' he managed to look a little embarrassed, '...in the meaning of marriage.'

Lady Jane caught at the door, turned back with a cheeky smile to retort. 'And who Charles, is to 'instruct' you, when you marry?' And she was gone, her laughter echoing down the long, stone floored corridor of the vicarage.

Jane tramped up the wide wooden stairs of the Inn to her mother's suite of rooms, her riding booted feet thundering on the loose old treads. A knock, then another and the door was pulled open by an irate Alice who, all disarrayed, hair uncurled, wearing only a shift and an angry expression, said, after looking Jane up and down. 'What on earth are you wearing? Farmer's clothing no doubt.'

Jane stepped into the room, which was in a fine state of disarray, to see her mother, with a glass of claret in her hand although the hour was so early. 'I see that you are not ready to visit with me at the Manor so perhaps you will come when you are ready.'

'Morning Jane...nice wine. What about taking luncheon later?' Her mother seemed already the worse for drink and Jane had a premonition that she would find her relatives unpleasant to have nearby.

'I have much to do today; the wedding is now set for three days hence. Saturday at eleven.' Jane paused to take in the fact that her sister was pouring herself a glass of the claret. 'If you are late you will miss the ceremony. If you miss my wedding you may as well just go home. Good day to you.' Jane turned and was gone leaving her mother and sister open mouthed.

'How dare she!' Alice half screamed.

Lady Walden looked abashed and somewhat frightened at the change in her youngest daughter and would have hastened after her had she been dressed.

Jane walked, or strode rather, back to the Vicarage where she banged on the knocker to tell Will that she had returned. She pulled tight 'Trojan's' girth and led him to a mounting block that stood outside the building.

As Will opened the door he saw his fiancée mounting her horse, her face set in anger and he hurried to join her. 'Your mother and sister, they are well?'

'I am on the brink of no longer having a mother and sister since all they can think on is themselves....' she turned 'Trojan' in a flurry of skirts, mane and her own hair, her hat falling back onto her shoulders as she drove in her heels and cantered away past the church.

It became a kind of race with, in the end, the two horses at full stretch, galloping down either side of the driveway, down towards the Manor House. Will managed to get there first but only by a neck or so. He dismounted and took Jane's reins as she slithered from her horse her face now flushed by the wind but still angry.

'You have some added problems with your mother and sister?' Will asked.

'They will not stay here. You must send to the Inn that the bill be presented to my sister. They treat us, they treat you as if you are some kind of charity and pay for all.' She turned to look up at her husband to be with a look of pure fury, '...and I will not have it.' Jane stormed away into the Manor knowing that only work would be sufficient now to modify her feelings.

I am marrying a woman of surprisingly firm opinions, thought Will. Her mother and sister abandoned her to look after her father and now she has had sufficient of their rude and uncivil behaviour, good. Will led the two steaming horses to the stable yard and handed them over to a groom.

Two days of unremitting effort was required of the newly organized staff of the house. The Great Hall was washed down and the floor scrubbed. The huge tapestry hangings were removed to reveal a filthy spider's heaven of cobwebs and dirt. A scaffold was erected and four men first scrubbed the upper walls and then lime washed them. The hangings were set aside to have the dust beaten from them and then some kind of cleaning and repairing would have to be done but this could be a winter task. A small sitting room with a decent fire was cleaned and painted up. A bedchamber, the one once used by Lawrence, was thoroughly cleaned, the tapestries removed for cleaning, a coat of lime wash, the panelling and furniture polished with bee's wax, the carpet beaten and then washed before replacing. The kitchens cleaned out, ceiling painted and all the preparation tables thoroughly scrubbed with decent fires lit to prepare for the wedding breakfast and Jane barely spoke a civil word to anyone; in fact she barely spoke at all much to the dismay of her staff, just worked as hard as they did... harder.

The villains had been collected by the Constable of Norwich in an old cart so that the bouncing and jarring of the journey alone must have constituted part of the punishment. Then Tully was pressed into service riding hither and thither over the Estate delivering messages with Tom and his cart serving to carry food and drink from some distance for Will discovered that even if Jane did not wish it he wanted his wedding to be truly memorable.

Mr Morris came to dinner. Riding in the rough but serviceable carriage that Jane sent to fetch him he arrived on time, for some reason looking slightly embarrassed at the fuss and bother that fetching him seemed to him to entail.

Welcomed by Lady Anne, wearing, for the first time in many years, a light muslin summer dress in pale blue, under the orders of Jane which, for some reason, she found difficult to disobey, the two middle aged people were, for the first few moments, somewhat tongue tied.

Lady Anne said, thinking better to talk of the weather than nothing at all. 'A beautiful day sir.'

Charles, in a moment of unaccustomed gallantry and truthfulness replied. 'Not as beautiful as you are Milady,' then blushed, something he had not done for at least twenty years.

She turned away smiling and suddenly happy thinking that perhaps Jane knew more of men than she did, to lead him into her Drawing Room where wine waited.

The filling of glasses helped to fill the silence that fell between them then Lady Anne said 'We have been busy with the preparations for the wedding sir.'

'I too...' Charles smiled, grateful that the impasse had been broken, '...although I spent only five minutes revising the order of Service at Lady Jane's request.'

Now seated, each with a glass of claret, facing each other another moment of silence fell as Anne tried to imagine what influence Jane might have over the Curate. 'Lady Jane asked for some... changes?'

'Yes, I thought them appropriate to the circumstances of their forth coming marriage. It was to do with obedience and the sharing.' Charles found himself staring at the pretty, blazingly fair haired, wigless woman sitting opposite, almost unrecognizable as the woman who had sometimes attended the Services since he had arrived at Saxethorpe.

'I'm sorry Milady but I am distracted, since you seem to have become altered in your appearance in some way?'

She smiled warmly at him saying, 'I suppose that that's a question Mr Morris. Yes, Lady Jane said that we have had enough of mourning and since the wearing of black clothing seems only to be a surface demonstration of our unhappiness it would be best put away and something more suitable, for the celebration of a wedding, should be worn instead. Lady Jane kindly lent me this dress and then she insisted that I abandon the 'wig' so Aggie dressed my hair and very cool and comfortable it feels.'

The black dressed curate leaned forward a little to say. 'As I said in the hall; it is a change for the better; you are most beautiful. Sorry Milady I must apologise for the lack of civility, for my gaucheness, I am unused to being alone with a... Please excuse me.' he stood, suddenly embarrassed.

She looked up at him serious but not angry. 'I am not upset by what you perceive as your lack of civility.' She smiled up at him as he stood dithering before her, a man neither coming nor going. 'In fact it is so many years since I received a compliment that I can only enjoy the feeling,' she stood to face him. 'You cannot leave until I give you permission Mr Morris, may I call you Charles? I don't want you to leave. You were invited to dinner with us and that is what you shall do. You'll sit next to me and we can talk. Perhaps if we talk for long enough you will find that your senses and civility will return and we can be as we were before...' her face was pink now as she felt so flustered.

After a long moment Charles said slowly. 'I'm not sure that I want to be as we were before...'

She looked away, a little smile on her lips.

Charles, still red faced and confused said, '...and I'm not sure that sitting near you would be for the best.'

She looked at him for a long moment then said. ' Well, I shall enjoy your company as I have in the past and I think our friendship can increase in the future.' Now Lady Anne realized that she too had exceeded the bounds of civility and so both were saved when Lady Jane swirled, in her dark blue ball gown into the room and quite suddenly stopped. 'Oh, please excuse me...' she gasped out as if coming across a compromising situation.

Charles Morris managed to look even more embarrassed and took two paces back as if to efface himself.

Will strolled into the room beautifully dressed in his latest dark green suit, his new boots gleaming with all the spit and polish that Tully had worked into them. 'Good evening everyone, Lady Jane.' He took her hand and kissed her fingers which he noticed, with a slight frown, were rough with the cleaning and scrubbing.

'My Lord...' she looked him up and down, '...you look splendid in, another new suit?'

'It is indeed new, straight from the box and...' he paused, hesitating, for he had just noticed Lady Anne in her new garb, 'Lady Anne, Annie... you've, you've changed so. I don't think that I have ever seen you other than in black?'

'Jane thought I needed a change. Too long in a wig and black dress.'

'Well, you do indeed look very pretty.' Will showed all the signs of confusion. 'Does she not Charles, look very pretty?'

'Lady Anne does indeed,' the curate's voice quieter, calmer now as if some decision had been reached.

Will turned back to Jane to ask. 'Your mother and sister, are we to have...?'

'They did not have the courtesy to reply to my, our invitation, so let us assume that they will not come.'

Dinner was consumed in a curious way, the occupants of the table being concerned only with their ostensible partners. Jane talked mostly to Will, both being concerned with her reaction to her mother and sister with a side conversation, conducted sotto voce, about the changes to Lady Anne. She and the curate appeared to be completely captivated with each other's company talking almost exclusively about the life of a curate in Saxethorpe, his duties, but mostly about his hobbies and preoccupation with science. As the meal ended the sound of a large carriage was heard outside and as it was nearly dark they all looked at each other with some surprise.

A banging at the door and Aggie hurried to open up, revealing two tipsy women, laughing and cackling. Jane hurried forward to speak with them.

'Why are you here Mama?' No voice could have been colder. 'You are very late if you expect food and drink...' her expression was very severe.

'We've had dinner daughter we're just out for a drive about.' She laughed, so in a drunken state was she.

'You cannot come in here in this state Mama. You...' she hesitated, '...and Alice will return to the Inn.'

Alice smiled maliciously and said or rather snarled out. 'We are coming in dear sister.'

There was a long moment where Jane stared at her elder sister and thought through the problem, then she said. 'You are not coming in Alice.' Jane's voice was level, clear and very final, '...and if you fail to leave now I shall write to Earl Marlbeck telling him of your behaviour.' She smiled coldly thinking that she had learnt something from her sister over the years if only the advantages of blackmail, '...and if necessary I am prepared to 'embroider' the truth, in much the same way that you would, dear sister.'

Alice stood there trying to understand that here, in this place, she was in the thrall of her younger sister, who stood there, head cocked on one side in question, and that she had little choice in the matter so she turned and stormed away into the darkness.

'Go with her Mama and try to be sober for the church service.' Jane, without smiling, closed the door in her mother's face.

Will observing from across the hallway thought that this woman was showing a backbone of steel in her dealings with life and her vicious relatives. She turned sharply and saw him watching her and then, to his surprise, she suddenly burst into tears. Will hurried to her and took her in his arms and heard her whisper. 'You had best be kind to me Sir for I no longer have anyone in the world.'

Will gently stroked her hair and whispered back. 'You have me and I will love you until the end and perhaps beyond.'

CHAPTER TWENTY-FOUR

Lady Anne met the curate as he stepped into her hallway and for some reason inexplicable to her she said, completely out of context. 'Will you always be a curate sir?' A puzzled frown on her face.

Charles had to think hard on this. 'Well, I had become resigned to that being the case but William did mention a possible preferment at Saxethorpe...' he too looked puzzled.

'To replace the missing vicar you mean?'

'Yes, it seems that he is...' he shook his head, '...It does not matter Lady Anne.' He looked saddened now.

'Why does it not matter Charles?' Anne sensed some odd change in herself.

'I am too poor... far too poor.' He half laughed at the thought of marriage.

'For what? For what are you too poor?' A slight edge of desperation had crept into Anne's voice.

'We are not able to talk, you and I. I am too poor to marry and therefore we can never...'

'I think we can Charles; talk that is, for William, or rather Lawrence has settled a thousand pounds a year upon me which is an enormous sum for one of small needs.'

Charles now looked, if possible, even more anxious. 'It makes it even more impossible Milady.'

'You will call me Anne,' her voice was so certain now, '...and if the pension is a problem then I shall refuse it.'

The tall, thin, dark clothed man stared at the beautiful woman with true astonishment on his face. 'I could never ask that of you.'

A strong voice came from behind them. 'You won't have to Charles. I say what happens here.' They both turned to see the stern figure of Lord Saxethorpe standing in the shadows holding the hand of a slim young woman. 'You will be the next vicar of Saxethorpe and you will have six hundred a year and Anne will have her pension but you will have to marry her, of course.'

And Jane started to laugh, so happy was she for them both.

A somewhat tense early breakfast had been taken at the Dower House with the sleepless Charles staring red eyed at the beautiful woman sitting at the table end thinking, William wants me to marry her and I want to marry her. Was it possible? A very few days had passed since meeting Will and his life had been changed forever it seemed to him.

Jane sat before a cup of steaming coffee and wondered at her feelings. At the ecstatic excitement that threatened to overwhelm her and make her dance around the room she looked up as the door of the Dining Room opened and Will's head appeared around the door.

'The carriage is here for you Charles...' he smiled widely, glancing at his wife to be and his sister before adding, 'No making of mistakes during the Service. Annie will be bringing Jane along to the Church, and remember what I said Reverend.'

Charles looked up at Lady Anne and smiled tentatively.

Her smile back to him could only be described as... loving.

Will strode back to the Manor House but was stopped by Tully and Tom appearing from the Stable Yard leading three horses.

'Morning Tully, morning Tom. Any sign of the wicked Steward?'

Tully pulled at his cap before addressing the Master. 'We know he be the culprit sor. It were he that must have arranged...'

Will smiled at his two friends before saying, 'Tom, you are let off your schooling until after the wedding is well over.'

Tom frowned a little before saying. 'Oh good, sir. Mind you, I quite enjoyed...'

'You are not meant to enjoy lessons Tom, you're meant to suffer, be bored, at least I always was. Anyway you are going to be too busy with other matters.' Will hesitated to pull tight his horse's girth then added, 'It'll be your job to give away the bride.'

Tom looked truly astounded. 'How can I do that sir? I'm only thirteen.'

Will frowned at him before saying. 'After the service Lady Jane will be your mother and I trust that you will love and respect her.'

'Of course sir, but what has that to do with my 'giving her away'.'

'Someone has to do it and you are her closest relative, geographically speaking, anyway she thinks the idea charming, as do I.'

Tully burst into laughter at the thought and sight of the totally gobsmacked boy.

'And you Tully....'

Tully suddenly stopped laughing.

Will leaned in close to say. 'You Tully, are to be my groomsman...'

Tully started to smile then realized what his Master meant. 'But sor?'

'Tully?' Will's tone was questioning.

The Irishman looked worried at the change in direction by his Master, wondering what he had done amiss. 'Sor?'

'I also have need of an Estate Steward...' Will's mien was serious now, '...and I've a mind to make you into one.'

'Me, sor?' Tully was truly confused.

'Yes, you Tully. I need someone that I can trust that will obey my orders and you are that man.' Will sounded certain although...

'I know little of farming sor. I could learn but...'

'You will learn Tully, for you and I will perform the task together and we will learn together.' Will smiled and thrust out his hand to seal the deal.

Tom looked from man to man delight on his face. 'Congratulations Tully, you'll need to ask for a mighty amount of the 'salary' no doubt.'

Will looked at the boy laughing, saying, 'And you remember both your place and the fact that you'll be spending your inheritance.'

The boy looked up at him and said, a roguish smile on his face, 'I think to spend your son's inheritance sir.'

'My son's?'

Tom nodded his head in a serious and knowing way before saying 'It be a well known fact, in the country, that is, that strong women produce strong boys and there can be few stronger women than Lady Jane.'

Jane from the front doorway could only smile at the laughter coming from the three men wondering what could amuse them so.

The morning of Saturday, dawned cool with clear pale blue skies so that all augured well for a wedding. Everything was ready, as ready as it could be that is. The Great Hall was a wonder, washed and polished with great vases of flowers everywhere. The kitchens were so busy that a low thundering noise seemed to come from that area along with a deal of steam, smoke and delicious smells.

At ten, the groom and his groomsman, Tully, set off for the church on horseback. Unusually for them, they were not armed save for the dress swords that they both wore, swords that Tully had ground the usually blunt edges to a razor sharpness. At five minutes past the hour of ten the best open carriage, driven by Tom, gaily bedecked with flowers, especially roses, pulled up at the gateway to the Dower House.

Inside, Jane stood in the hall, dressed in cream silk, with yellow roses in her bouquet and sewn to her gown. Lady Anne complemented her colours with a flowing bright green gown in silk, her hair set and curled in a most becoming modern style.

Jane looked at the other woman and asked seriously 'Will I do for him Anne? Am I good enough?'

Anne turned from the mirror to smile at her soon to be daughter and gently smiled before saying. 'You are beautiful Jane, young, intelligent and Will loves you. He can ask for naught more and neither can you.' Taking Jane's arm she led her through the open doors and down the path to the carriage.

Tom thought he had never seen a more beautiful sight than these two women and he handed them into his carriage with great care.

In his small room in the vicarage the curate, Charles Morris, had bathed, shaved and then dressed as well as he was able. He knew why he did it but it was as if he had no control over what he said and did. So even as he walked over to the church stopping momentarily to make sure that the groom had arrived he knew that today was momentous in more ways than one.

At the Inn, an untouched beer to hand, the somewhat nervous groom thought that his bride must nearly be at the church so he asked his groomsman. 'What is it o'clock Tully?'

'We must start walking in two minutes sir or earlier if you are feeling anxious.'

'Yes. Yes, Tully, let us go. Tom may be driving too fast or...' as the groom stood there was a loud cheer from the unusually full tavern for both the Baron and Tully were popular but even as the cheers were still ringing in the air, there appeared, at the head of the Inn's stairs a most beautiful woman; a smiling woman with almost silver hair wearing the most wonderful gown made of white silk who walked, elegantly, lightly, down the stairs to take the arm of the groom.

'Your Grace. Your presence in unexpected.' Will gasped out.

'My sister marries and I am not to be there? Of course we are expected.' She looked back up the stairs as her mother, wearing her dark green silk, came, somewhat nervously, down.

The church was abuzz, completely full of the local gentry and their ladies and children, all of Will's tenant farmers and their families plus the town folk and all wearing their very best clothes for everyone had been invited. Hearing the great kerfuffle at the wide open doors, everyone stood and a hush descended but the sight of the groom with a very beautiful woman in white on his arm astounded all including the Curate, who stood waiting at the vestry door. Charles, knowing of the possibility of a row before the altar, rushed forward and with much bowing and scraping managed, to Will's relief, to steer the two women into the Saxethorpe pew just in time for the organ to burst into life and the choir into song and the congregation almost cheered when Lady Jane appeared on the arm of the very well dressed Tom with Lady Anne carrying the train of the simple cream silk dress the veiled Lady Jane was wearing.

Jane threw a glance at the family pew and instantly knew that all out war had been declared. Her sister, still standing although all others sat, seemed to be saying that she wanted everyone to look at her and not her sister in which, to a certain extent, she succeeded.

Lady Anne also could see the problem and she with Aggie at her side went to the pew and pushing open the door forced Alice to give way.

'What is that servant doing in here...?' gasped Alice.

'She sits here with me every Sunday and will continue to do so madam.' Lady Anne said firmly.

Lady Jane had arrived at the altar rail and Will with Tully stood to be by her side. She looked at him, a question in her eyes.

The wedding service started and even Alice could not bring herself to interrupt or create a ruction even when Charles asked if anyone had any reason for the marriage not to take place.

'You may kiss the bride.' the curate eventually said and Will did so with alacrity but even as he did so his bride whispered, 'From whence did they come?'

'It was so unexpected... I...'

Lady Jane Saxethorpe turned from her husband and took the six paces to get to the family pew where she confronted her smirking sister.

'Alice, Mama. If you ever wish to see me or the Saffron Estate again you will leave now. If you do not then I will take every step at my command to ban you, to stop you both and you may rot in hell before I would ever help you. Mama you will have to chose. Goodbye.' She turned in a golden flare of skirts and veil. Smiling happily she seized Will's arm and marched him up the aisle through a sea of smiling faces.

The wedding breakfast was to remain in the memory of all there for a good long time. There was a number of reasons for this; first that the feast was exceptional with seemingly unlimited food, wine and beer with a huge cut glass bowl of punch for the ladies; secondly for the apparently outstanding happiness of the newly married couple and thirdly for the grand music and dancing that followed the food.

Jane, who had expected to be worried and made anxious by the presence of her mother and sister found instead that a huge sense of relief had swirled over her, of a task long contemplated, never attempted but now finished. A sister, who had disliked her forever, was now gone. Jane knew that with a few kind words her mother could be restored to her and then her life would be complete. So she danced away the evening with her new husband and he...

Will could feel that Jane was almost a new woman. He had loved her desperately but now felt even more enamoured of this vivacious, loving woman in his arms and, if truth be known, was almost unable to wait until the carriages started to arrive to take away the happy and exhausted guests. The many farm carts, all decorated with branches and flowers had departed so that children might be abed and that, as midnight approached, Jane signalled the end by asking the musicians to cease playing.

Even as the great front door closed, on the most tardy of their guests, Jane quite suddenly realized that the time when she and her new husband would be alone was almost upon her. Never one to shirk her responsibilities or put off the inevitable but now with ripples of excitement coursing up her spine she turned to her loved one to ask. 'And now sir?'

Will looked at this flushed, excited woman and thought again that she had grown more beautiful day by day as he had known her and now she asked the final and best of questions. 'Now Madam?'

'Yes Will, now.'

So, without further ado and conversation he took her hand and led her across the Hallway to the great carved staircase. They had started to mount the creaking stairs when Jane asked anxiously. 'The candles? The lamps Will?' For many were still lit.

Will smiled down at her saying as he did so. 'It was the last task that I laid upon my groomsman Tully and your adopted son Tom that they come here and douse every naked flame leaving only safe lights....'

'Faithful friends those two....' she smiled up at him in what she hoped was a sensuous way

'The best.' Will thought that if she kept smiling at him like that then he was in a fair way to being undone.

He pushed open the door to the State bedchamber and was astonished to find it both un-cleaned and untidy. 'What! What is this?'

'You said I could choose which ever bedchamber I wished.' Jane looked up at him almost serious now. 'I told you that this room is both too large, too dark and far too dirty so...' and she took his hand again and led him down the nearly dark corridor to a doorway that he could barely remember entering and when Jane pushed open the door he was astounded to see a bedchamber painted out in white with gold leaf decorations, a fire throwing a warm light over the whole room and the bed dressed in white and gold silks with the rest a sea of white flowers.

Jane half whispered. 'Not dark at all, as you can well see my love. If this is to be my classroom, the room where I must learn about love, then it is best if I, and you, am able to see.'

She led him into this lovely room and closed the door then turned to him as he stood, almost affrighted, in the middle of the room. Jane walked to him, pulled his head down to kiss him most thoroughly then drawing breath she said. 'First I must take off this dress, perhaps you might help me.' And so the night began.

Sunlight streamed through the eastern window throwing a brilliant halo of light around the body of the young girl leaning on the sill, the simple shift she was wearing glowing translucently.

She turned as she heard the snuffling breath of her husband in his sleep. How lovely he had been, how kind, how gentle. Firstly she had made him undress her something that had made them both laugh at his inept, rough fingered struggles.

'There are two bows at the top that must be undone, else I shall remain dressed...' Jane peered over her right shoulder at the pink faced young man who had yet to find the right end to pull. 'I had assumed that a man of the world, like yourself would be familiar with the undressing of a young woman?

Will, suddenly looking pleased with himself as he pulled out the long silk cord which wove down his bride's back said. 'I should say madam that in my experience, which is not that great, that the young ladies in question were generally only very lightly clothed.' He disappeared as he unthreaded the cord from the eyelets the sight of the bare skin revealed, giving him some trouble.

Jane heard Will's heavy breathing from behind her so she said. 'But you do know the how and the wherefore of love making, do you not sir?' Jane felt the back of the dress slip away and she eased the front away from her breasts so that the cream silk dress slid down to pool at her feet. A simple silk shift still covered her so she turned to her husband as he stood, now very pink faced. 'You do not answer me sir?'

'You are so very beautiful Jane.' Standing before him like that, almost naked, very open to him looking up at him with love in her eyes.

'You intend to remain clothed sir?' She reached up and tugged his stock loose from around his neck. He just stood there as she unbuttoned his waistcoat.

She undresses me, is that right? Will asked himself but it was almost the most exciting thing that had ever happened to him.

'My sister says that all men are rough with their women, savage even; do you intend to be a savage with me sir?' She pulled open his shirt and was stopped for a moment by the sight of his fair chest hair so she wound a tendril around her finger and then leant forward to kiss his skin.

'I will not be rough with you Milady.' Will stood almost but not quite embarrassed as Jane undid his trousers.

'The boots may prove a problem sir. You should have had Tully pull them off for you; now I shall have to be your servant, your valet.' She gently pushed him down onto the bed so that his feet were off the ground.

She is the most beautiful creature on earth, Will thought as he half laid back staring at his new wife's back and bottom as she straddled his leg to tug off first one boot then the other which she sent spinning across the room. Then she turned to him her chest heaving with emotion, 'If you will not....'

Will reached for her shoulders and pulled her close to him, smiled gently down at her then lifted the shift from her body. Her naked skin seemed to glow like gold in the candlelight and for a moment he held her at arms length to look at her then he pulled her close to kiss her. 'We must go to bed Milady for tomorrow is another busy day...'

'A busy day sir? Do we not have a busy night first? She reached for him and pulled his underclothes down and away leaving him completely naked.

'A busy night indeed...' Will gently pulled her onto the big bed and took her in his arms.

He had taught her, somewhat diffidently, the arts that he had learnt in the brothels of Spain, Portugal and France and she had understood his words and better his actions for the lessons he had learnt had been about pleasing the lady. Eventually she had become so excited herself that she had forced him... no, not forced but rather made herself join with him in love-making. If a child comes from this, was Jane's thought as the most overwhelming delight convulsed her body then I think that we will have to have many children.

In the early morning light Jane ran over to the bed and stabbed a finger into her loved one's tummy, which convulsed and his eyes opened.
How did I manage this, Will thought, she is so very lovely and... She smiled cheekily at him. 'What?' he smiled, '...again? Are you not a little sore?'
'I am very sore sir but in a short while coffee will be brought in and then we will have to wait until... anyway we will have to wait and I am not sure if we have made a baby or not.' She stared at him a challenging smile on her face.
'If we have not made a baby Milady I shall be very surprised but I do find that one more 'go' might be possible before coffee.'
And that's what they did...had one more go.

At breakfast, Will said, with a somewhat self satisfied air that the High Sheriff of the County and Lord Lieutenant Lord Hazleton would be coming in three days as he progressed around the County to attend the Assizes. He would be staying the night and, 'It would be wonderful Milady if he could stay in the State bedchamber.'
'Three days is not very long sir.' Lady Jane looked straight at her Lord for there had been much talk between them about how long it would take to make a baby.
'Well, my Lady, he is coming and only the State bedchamber is good enough so....' he smiled at his wife, a smile of love.
So it was three days of the most intense housekeeping that Jane had ever witnessed. Ten craftsmen and ten cleaners and

seamstresses worked long into the nights to complete her plan but in the end everything was done, close to perfection.

CHAPTER TWENTY FIVE

By an odd twist of fate it was three days later that the rumble of large coach's wheels were heard in the courtyard of Saxethorpe Hall, the grinding of many metal rims and steel shod hooves echoing off the old brick walls. Will was in the Estate office, the books spread out before him, when he heard and somehow knew. Jane was in the State bedchamber ordering the housemaids to finish their task; she heard and she knew. Lady Anne, busy in the kitchens of the Hall, heard and she knew as well.

Two coach's, black painted with a silver crucifix and coat of arms on each door. Eight black horses each with funereal black feathers nodding above each gleaming head and four black liveried coachmen and grooms sat atop each coach. They had slowed and settled on the cobbled yard when Jane reached a window to look down. They have come straight from Hell she thought.

My almost brother is the stuff of nightmares, Will thought, as he stepped from his office into the sunlit Tudor courtyard.

Tully took Tom by the shoulder and pointed silently at the guns racked up in the stables, for he knew when a battle was about to begin.

Lady Anne came up the steps from the kitchens and thought as well that her 'brother' had come straight from Hell or was headed there.

Down from the coach's stepped seven priests garbed in black with silver embroidered cassocks over. The last to alight was the purple clad figure of the Bishop and there was a long moment whilst his black and silver cope and mitre were placed with due ceremony about him so that as he turned towards the House, Lord and Lady Saxethorpe with Lady Anne stood waiting with fifty or more domestic staff at every window and door with every eye watching, knowing that something, no one knew what but that something was happening and no Bishop could have wished for a more interested congregation and as the priests and footmen arranged themselves into a column; the last act took place as a large silver crucifix was raised behind the prelate. As all seemed ready it was time for something to be said but all the civilities were forgotten.

'You have come brother,' a blank statement from the lips of the Lord Saxethorpe, '...but with no apparent reason, for you come without invitation.'

'God told me to come Will.' The priest looked self satisfied and very certain.

'And what is God's purpose in your coming here?' Will, his face now as pale as a sheet of paper asked.

'I come to consecrate his Holy Chapel; the Holy Chapel of Saint John.'

'There is no chapel of Saint John or any other...'

'Hush Will, I saw it with my own eyes as we passed just now.'

Will wished that he had had the chapel demolished as was his final intent. 'It is unfinished John you cannot consecrate an unfinished...'

'But you can Will, and then you will not be able to demolish my chapel.' The Bishop's voice was light and mellifluous.

'I thought it was God's chapel?' Will asked bluntly.

Jane looked up at her Lord and Master and thought him strong in his sarcasm.

'It is my offering to the Lord and cannot be touched after this day.' The shallow smiling Bishop turned towards the entrance to the courtyard and started to walk slowly away followed by the procession of black and silver clad priests. After a few steps he started to chant the Fifty Ninth Psalm. 'Deliver me from mine enemies O my God... defend me from them that rise up against me...' and the dirge was picked up by the whole procession who slowly followed the crucifix as it wended its way out through the arched gateway.

A carriage and pair was turning towards the entrance but was forced to stop by the presence of the column of clergymen and moments later the door opened and the figure of the Lord Lieutenant stood there, finely dressed in pale grey silk but wigless. He was astounded to see such a strange spectacle before him and one where he, the most important man in the County was ignored.

Will saw him arrive and hurried towards him. 'My Lord. My apologies, you come at an inopportune moment for you see you have been pre-empted by my erstwhile brother. He has decided to consecrate his unfinished chapel to prevent me demolishing it.'

'It appears that your troubles continue Lord Saxethorpe,' the grey haired man stared towards chapel where the procession was, even now, disappearing amongst the stone Gothic arches. 'Pray, what will you do?'

'Truly sir I have no idea of what I can do; I deal with a madman,' he hesitated for a moment then said. 'Please excuse me.' Will turned to hurry after the crowd that followed his brother.

Later, the Lord Lieutenant was to think that it was as if God himself was setting the scene as in a great drama. The roofless unfinished chapel, its stone arches rearing up against the sunlit afternoon sky, the mullioned windows each with a splendid stained glass scene standing, supported and protected by a maze of cut timbers. Hanging above the nave and altar was the great rose window. The story of the Redeemer was told in glowing reds, gold, brilliant blues and below, the procession, led by the Bishop approached the altar followed by the crowd of servants led by Jane, Lady Saxethorpe.

The Bishop turned to face his congregation a pleased smile on his face. He waited while an acolyte placed a carved eagle lectern before him and another set a mighty gold and silver bound Bible on it then he stepped forward and started to intone the XXXV psalm, 'Plead my cause, O Lord, with them that strive with me; fight against them that fight against me. Take hold of shield and buckler and stand up for mine help...'

'Stop!' the sharp, powerful voice of Lady Jane cut through the air. 'Stop in the name of God!'

The Bishop was indeed startled enough to stop and stare down at this small woman wearing a cotton work dress with a lacy apron over and knew somehow who it was. 'Lady Saxethorpe?'

'The same sir, you must and will stop for you have no rights here.' Jane looked pale faced but very determined and she seemed braced for all that might occur.

'Madam, the crucifix is upon the altar and I am in my rightful place. I will continue the Service and no one on this Earth shall stop me.'

Will had made his way to his wife's side and stood there admiring her strength allowing her to...

'I shall stop you Sir if you do not desist, for this place is now my home and no cleric will tell me otherwise...' Suddenly she reached forward seized the great Bible and pulled it forward on the lectern.

With a bellow of the purest rage Bishop John tried to stop her, and in the struggle the huge book slipped over the polished wooden edge to thud, to crash to the stone floor. The bishop's face, set now in a mask of the purest evil as he pulled a pistol from beneath his robes and pointed it at the woman. 'Unclean whore, you shall be sent direct to Hell for touching the Holy Book, you shall die and now...'

The Lord Lieutenant thought that the Bishop had gone much too far and more so when...

The Bishop pulled back the hammer of his pistol.

Will, stunned by such a sight, stood aghast.

A scream of, 'No!' came from the lips of Lady Jane.

As the pistol fired a white faced Tom raised his musket but at the last of the split seconds that he was allowed he heard the cry from his adoptive mother and knew that she would be very upset if he killed the Bishop so he raised the long, rifled barrel gun and saw the perfect target, a huge wooden block and tackle dangling over the altar so he aimed and fired in an instant.

The small lead ball from the Bishop's pistol hit Lady Saxethorpe fairly in the left shoulder spinning her around in a thin veil of blood drops as she dropped to the flag stoned floor.

The wooden block and tackle, taut with the heavy ropes that supported the great Rose window, was not designed to withstand the impact of a musket ball fired from only a few yards below, and burst into a cloud of splinters, metal bolts and the cogs and wheels, which gave it its strength, disintegrated. At once, the sisal ropes that webbed the stone surrounded window, unwound and leapt away like so many spinning snakes.

The Bishop, smoking pistol still in hand had spread wide his arms in imitation of Jesus' last agony, a look of triumph on his pasty face.

Will had dropped to his knees and gathered his new wife into his arms.

Lady Anne was ripping at her camisole to make a bandage for she saw all the blood....

The Lord Lieutenant, who was standing, half deafened by the gun shot so close from young Tom, reached down and pulled the long rifle from the boy's numbed hands and turning dropped the weapon behind a large pile of stone blocks...

The Rose Window, spinning on its axis, the sunlight striking multicoloured patterns from the stained glass, descended swiftly now.

Will looked up from his unconscious wife to his brother with murder in his heart but God had other plans.

The large and very heavy stone and glass window plunged towards the outstretched armed figure of the Bishop.

Maybe God does exist the Lord Lieutenant was to think later as he watched, helpless to intervene as the great mass of stone and glass crashed onto the purple clad cleric crushing the Bishop into a bloody mess so that he could not be seen only that it was the remains of the window and the stained glass weeping face of Jesus that seemed to bleed endlessly across the stone floor.

EPILOGUE

A possible sad ending for our hero of the battle of Waterloo except that God was kind yet again and Lady Jane, although shocked and wounded deeply, would recover well especially as her new husband made it his life's work to nurse her.

'Tully! Ride fast, fetch the physician, a surgeon and make it swift!' and he did.

'Tom! Fetch a sheep-fold to carry your mother upon...' and he did.

'My Lord,' Will had come to the Lord Lieutenant of the County to apologise. 'I do not know where to start. Such a strange occurrence, so very odd. The Bishop coming, the rose window falling as if a message from God.'

'Well, Saxethorpe,' the older man said with a sympathetic and yet knowing smile. 'I saw everything so it must be described as an accident or perhaps divine providence.'

'But the block and tackle collapsing at that exact moment?'

'Yes, yes, very odd and providential.' He nodded and smiled.

Tully was later to ask Tom where the long rifle was and Tom, somewhat puzzled, said he would fetch it later. Tom had thought for a very long time about the exact sequence of events at that bizarre moment and decided that it must have been the work of God for he could not have explained it himself only knew that he had not to upset his new mother.

Lady Anne applied herself to the nursing of Lady Jane and with the help of the apothecary and physician from Saxethorpe and the well nigh continuous presence of her son Will, managed to keep infection from the young woman who soon awoke and whose first question was about her husband, her second about her adopted son, Tom, and her third and most important about the baby she thought that she must be carrying. Well, in that she was correct for the missing of her normal monthly pains two weeks or so later, meant, to her, that she was indeed carrying and since her husband gave every appearance of loving her, she laid back into her down filled pillows, smiled with some relief, kissed her husband and fell asleep.

The story ended, as all fairy tales should, with a wedding, this between Charles Morris, the new vicar of Saxethorpe, and Lady Anne and her retirement to the vicarage in the town so that Lord and Lady Saxethorpe, Will and Jane could go and live comfortably in the Dower House with their new baby boy. For all fairy tales must have a perfect ending. Tom went to school every day to his tutor, the newly married vicar, and would end up by going to Cambridge. Tully became the Steward of the vast Saxethorpe Estate, more knowledgeable every year and in spite of the hard times faced by most of the country ordered a very prosperous business.

And so the story ends, Lady Jane to have several more sons and daughters, Will to be as happy as a man can be.

Made in the USA
Lexington, KY
16 May 2018